MASTERPLOTS II

JUVENILE
AND
YOUNG ADULT
FICTION
SERIES

MASTERPLOTS II

JUVENILE
AND
YOUNG ADULT
FICTION
SERIES

4

Sev-Z

Indexes

Edited by

FRANK N. MAGILL

SALEM PRESS

Pasadena, California   Englewood Cliffs, New Jersey

Library of Congress Cataloging-in-Publication Data
Masterplots II: Juvenile and young adult fiction series/
edited by Frank N. Magill
   p. cm.
   Includes bibliographical references and index.
     1. Children's literature—Stories, plots, etc. 2.
Young adult literature—Stories, plots, etc. I. Magill,
Frank Northen, 1907-
Z1037.A1M377 1991   91-4509
ISBN 0-89356-579-2 (set)   CIP
ISBN 0-89356-583-0 (volume 4)

LIST OF TITLES IN VOLUME 4

SEVENTEENTH SUMMER

Author: Maureen Daly (1921-   )
Type of plot: Psychological realism
Time of plot: World War II
Locale: Fond du Lac and Lake Winnebago, Wisconsin
Principal themes: Love and romance, coming-of-age, family, nature, and education
First published: 1942
Recommended ages: 13-15

*A young girl grows toward womanhood during the summer of her seventeenth
year. In June, Angie Morrow begins dating Jack Duluth; in July, at the family dinner
table, she must recognize that he has a flaw; in August, Jack and his family prepare
to move to Oklahoma, and Angie leaves for college—but with his class ring and
wonderful memories.*

Principal characters:
> ANGELINE "ANGIE" MORROW, a girl from a close family, who has
> just been graduated from high school and is preparing to go
> away to college
> JACK DULUTH, a gentlemanly caller who works in his family's
> bakery and dates Angie after breaking up with Jane Rady
> MARGARET, Angie's oldest sister, who is engaged to Art
> LORRAINE, the sister who goes to college in Chicago
> KITTY, Angie's youngest sister, who needs occasional babysitting
> MRS. MORROW, the girls' mother, a housewife
> MR. MORROW, the father, a salesman
> SWEDE, Jack's best friend who likes to sail
> MARGIE and
> FITZ, teens who sometimes double date with Angie and Jack
> MARTIN KEEFE, a two-timer who dates Lorraine
> TONY, an older boy with a fast reputation

The Story

This story of Angie, who grows up in a Midwestern town just between the Depression and World War II, sounds a quintessential note in American young adult fiction. Like its predecessor from the nineteenth century, *Little Women* (1868-1869) by Louisa May Alcott, *Seventeenth Summer* is a classic. A twentieth century account of another family of four sisters, it is a warm story; if the reader becomes the fifth sister, the book typically turns into a story of wish fulfillment. Angie is no Jo March (that is, a tomboy), but she is the writer in Maureen Daly's book, and she has Jo's dedication to education and her naïveté around boys. Almost dazzled by being asked for a date by a popular athlete, Angie slowly begins growing into her future.

On their first date, Jack and Angie walk out to the lake where Jack and Swede Vincent keep a boat, and Jack lights a pipe while he thinks about life. When Angie thinks back to the specialness of her first date, she recalls the sheer happiness of living. Jack does smoke and drink, and before long, Angie is going to parties where there is drinking. In writing about these behaviors, Daly (perhaps unwittingly) helped prepare the way not only for a subsequent writer for teenagers, S. E. Hinton (*The Outsiders*, 1967), but also for the disappearance of almost all young adult print taboos, beginning late in the 1960's.

Angie discovers that agony soon follows ecstasy: At Pete's (the local gathering place for young adults), Jack dances with his former steady, Jane Rady, even though he had brought Angie. A crisis of confidence comes over Angie, who imagines that all other girls simply know how to act around boys. Still, her mind drifts back to the wonder of that first starry night with Jack.

The sexual revolution has not taken away the magic of first kisses, and Angie enjoys both anticipating and remembering hers. Her sexuality is coupled with a healthy eroticism. In love with life, she yearns to learn and explore; consequently, she experiences the pain of growing: ". . . I could not help wishing that there wasn't so much sadness in growing up." She has ambition, more than Jack, who favors physical work although he says that his ultimate ambition is to be a pilot.

No doubt one of the reasons that young readers have kept this book in print is that they can identify with Angie, who expresses the hopes of many a young girl. She challenges Jack to "start now to work on ourselves so we would be, maybe, great people when we grow up." Whatever the year, that is a liberated young lady speaking.

Angie and Jack end August at cross purposes: He wants physical love, whereas she can wait. At the last party of the summer, he leads her away from the circle by the fireside into the dark, where the luxuriance is Keatsian. He proposes.

The next day is cold, like autumn. No longer is Angie able to keep the swiftness of the passing of time out of her awareness, a sign of her waning youth. On the way to college, with Jack's class ring, a ring she first noticed him wear one June night in church, she also knows that nothing will ever quite match the wonder of summer at seventeen.

Themes and Meanings

One of Daly's particularly evocative touches is her yoking of Angie's psychological development with the ripening of nature over a summer season. Angie is at home in the garden and out in the countryside and fields; her personal maturation is matched by the maturing of the blossoms of spring; when the story ends, harvest is at hand and autumn is in the wind. She is a young but rapidly maturing Persephone; several more years must pass, though, before she will pause alone to admire the beautiful flower with a hundred blossoms.

Daly has an ease with metaphoric language, as in this line: "Growing up is like taking down the sides of your house and letting strangers walk in." She also writes significant openings: "I don't know just why I'm telling you all this. Maybe you'll think I'm being silly. But I'm not, really, because this is *important*."

According to Dwight L. Burton, "The fact that the book is written in the first person adds impact through giving the reader the impression that he is peeping into a high school girl's secret diary." Recent research has identified the diary to be a transitional object for the teenager, much like the blanket and teddy bear for the toddler; hence, Daly's book aligns itself with a genre deeply rooted in the feminine psyche. An even younger adolescent wrote Anne Frank's *Het Achterhuis* (1947; *The Diary of a Young Girl*, 1952); both Maureen Daly's novel and Anne Frank's record have special significance simply because of the age at which each author created her text. When combined with the symbolic use of flowers, gardens, fields, and pastures, the milieu of Daly's "diary" lets critics and readers alike recognize, along with Burton, that *Seventeenth Summer* "perhaps captures better than any other novel the spirit of adolescence."

What is the most neglected relationship in young adult literature? Alleen P. Nilsen and Kenneth L. Donelson say that it is probably the mother-daughter relationship. In *Seventeenth Summer*, the parents facilitate the separation process for their daughter's successful transition to adulthood, being neither too close nor too distant, allowing sufficient freedom for the learning of responsibility. Mrs. Morrow is a study in successful mothering, a mother able to be firm when firmness is due and one able to let Angie have her head when grow she must. Both parents are supportive. Significantly, the mother is not threatened by her daughter's emerging sexuality, nor is the father threatened by his daughter's desire for education. This book presents a functional family, as opposed to a dysfunctional family (as in Bette Greene's *Summer of My German Soldier*, 1973). Daly's dedication is noteworthy; it reads, "To My Mother."

Context

Daly's astonishing achievement is that she began the book at age seventeen and finished it at twenty. Although modern young adult literature emerged in the 1960's, Daly actually began the modern period of young adult writing in the early 1940's. Some forty years later, as a grandmother, she wrote *Acts of Love* (1986), the story of her daughter's seventeenth summer, when Megan fell in love with a cowboy. From a farm in Pennsylvania, the family in this book moves to California when a highway construction project cuts through their land. Dallas Dobson heads west too.

Critics early recognized the classic stature of *Seventeenth Summer*, and as years passed, May Hill Arbuthnot noted in 1969 that "if the title . . . were changed to *Fifteenth Summer*, the entertaining story would seem as contemporary as the day it was published." As the decades go by, the appropriate beginning reading age lowers, because the onset of menarche has been dropping approximately one year per generation since 1850.

As late as the mid-1980's Nilsen and Donelson could write, "Many girls who read *Seventeenth Summer* come away with the feeling that they are reading a slightly old-fashioned, but contemporary, novel." Such a statement remains true: The book seems to have the luck of the Irish. Adolescence may not be universal (although puberty is), but when a story told by a young girl who is moving through the passage from childhood to adulthood not only mirrors this experience for generations of women but also does so in an artistic way with appropriate leitmotifs, then that story is likely to be a text that lives in time and over time. That is why *Seventeenth Summer* is a classic.

Nancy Vogel

THE SHADOW GUESTS

Author: Joan Aiken (1924-   )
Type of plot: Fantasy
Time of plot: The late twentieth century
Locale: Courtoys Mill, twenty miles from Oxford, England
Principal themes: Family, science, and the supernatural
First published: 1980
Recommended ages: 13-15

Cosmo Curtoys learns of an ancestral family curse, and the knowledge leads him to strange experiences and personal insights.

> *Principal characters:*
> COSMO CURTOYS, a young boy who leaves Australia to live with his cousin
> EUNICE DOOM, Cosmo's cousin, who is a professor of mathematics
> MR. MARVELL, the man who runs the experimental farm and uses the farm buildings at Mill Place
> MRS. TYDINGS, the housekeeper at the Mill House, who lives in a little cottage across the lawn
> MR. GABBITAS, the white-haired headmaster at the Morningquest boarding school

The Story

   The Shadow Guests is a work of fiction that involves realism, the historical past, and the supernatural, combining a story of adventure with extraordinary happenings. The fictional setting is the old Courtoys' Mill Place, which is located near Oxford, England. The mill house is surrounded by big trees, a river, a wooden footbridge, a real island, and other mill buildings. On the other side of the island is a weir: water hurling down in a smother of foam. The peaceful estate is lovely, but it has a mysterious air.

   The plot covers a sequence of events in Cosmo Curtoys' life. After his mother and brother disappear in Australia, Cosmo's father sends him to England to live with his cousin, Eunice Doom, an attractive mathematics professor at Oxford. She lives in the old family home at Courtoys' Mill. When Cosmo arrives at the mill house, he finds he enjoys the farm that has belonged to his ancestors. Cosmo does not enjoy the boarding school in Oxford he must attend. At Morningquest, he has to deal with Mr. Gabbitas and cruel teasing by classmates. Cosmo looks forward to weekends when he can return to the Mill House and help Mr. Marvell, the grounds keeper.

   Soon after Cosmo's arrival, Eunice tells him of the ancient family curse: It states that every firstborn son in the family line will die in battle at an early age, and the boy's mother will die of grief. After learning of the family curse, Cosmo discovers that the Courtoys' Mill House and grounds are haunted by strange apparitions and poltergeists.

In a series of fantastic occurences, Cosmo meets three ghosts of the family past: The first is Con, a Roman slave who is practicing to fight in the games at Corinium; the second is Sim, a pathetic youth training to fight in a medieval crusade; the third is the ugly and unlikable Osmond from Medmenham. Cosmo fights Osmond in a sword battle but knows that he cannot win. Osmond's mother appears as an evil witch and blinds Cosmo with her black cloak. He falls through the floor into the icy weir water, and he struggles to keep from drowning.

Cosmo later awakens in his own bed and learns that he has been near death from pneumonia. His father, Richard, is sitting by his bedside. He tells Cosmo that he was saved from the rushing water by Lob, the family St. Bernard. Richard also tells Cosmo that his mother and brother were found dead on a little slope of hill in Australia. Cosmo now knows that his mother and brother walked into the desert in order to break the age-old pattern of the family curse. He also knows that the curse hangs over him.

Themes and Meanings

The Shadow Guests has three major themes: the family, science, and the supernatural. The story examines the history of the Curtoys' lineage. Cosmo Curtoys discovers that his ancestral line carries a deadly curse; it has affected every generation since the Roman occupation of Britain. As a younger son, Cosmo is not doomed by the curse. His own mother and brother, however, mysteriously disappear and are later found dead.

Science holds a central place in the story. Cousin Eunice is a brilliant professor of mathematics. She talks about the worlds of space, matter, and time. Eunice states that there may be more than three dimensions, some things can be in two places at once, and the definition of time can be wrong. She believes in curses and compares curse vibrations to those of radiation; both are powerful forces that can change entire landscapes and generations. The discussions between Eunice and Cosmo explore the concepts of Albert Einstein's theory of relativity, parapsychology, cosmology, and the Pythagorean number system.

The theme of the supernatural is also one that serves to unify the novel. Bizarre events happen at Mill Place, such as the coach-and-six that always passes by the yard gate when the moon is full. One night, a strange white object falls out of Cosmo's jacket sleeve. On the farm estate, he experiences hallucinations and hears strange voices. A heavy wardrobe falls on top of Cosmo and almost crushes him to death. One afternoon after tea, his entire bed comes clattering down the steep house stairs.

The three themes in *The Shadow Guests* provide a common thread that combines the layers of the past, the present, and the supernatural (or future). *The Shadow Guests* presents a mythic pattern of romantic adventure, magical experience, and fantasy. The reader is also reminded that truth is not simple: There are many unexplained phenomena and possibilities that affect the entire universe—wonders that were, are, and will be.

Context

Aiken's *The Shadow of Guests* is a work of fantasy. As in *The Moon's Revenge* (1987) and *The Teeth of the Gale* (1988), the work presents a hero who is involved in strange and intriguing adventures. In Aiken's novels, dynamic characters allow readers to experience historical events, romantic quests, gothic settings, period language, and improbable events. Like Cosmo Curtoys, many young people face family disappearance or death. Unlike Cosmo, however, they are not involved with haunted estates or shadow ghosts from the past.

A versatile and prolific writer, Joan Aiken has written in many forms. She has published plays, poems, short stories, and novels. Like her father, Conrad Aiken, she demonstrates a remarkable range of writing skills and techniques. She has written in many genres, such as historical fiction, fantasy, folklore, and realism. Aiken was born and reared in England, and many of her stories are set in England and its countryside. Her novel *The Wolves of Willoughby Chase* (1963) depicts an old English country home. Resembling Courtoys' Place in *The Shadow Guests*, a unique English estate is also the setting for *Midnight Is a Place* (1974) and *Return to Harken House* (1990). *The Stolen Lake* (1981) is about twelve-year-old Dido Twite's return to England.

All of Joan Aiken's works are meant to enchant and transport. Her novels, however, are not always based on accurate and exact happenings, as she often rearranges history to suit her stories. Unlikely episodes and action-filled plots are her trademarks. In her works, Aiken illustrates that life is not always easy. The world is filled with evil and hardship, but virtue and strength can prevail in the end. There is always hope and promise for future endeavors.

Dixie Mae Turner

SHADOW OF A BULL

Author: Maia Wojciechowska (1927-   )
Type of plot: Moral tale
Time of plot: The 1960's
Locale: Arcangel, Andalusia, Spain
Principal themes: Animals, coming-of-age, and family
First published: 1964; illustrated
Recommended ages: 10-15

The people of Arcangel expect Manolo to be a great bullfighter like his dead matador father, Juan Olivar. Because he does not want to fight and kill bulls, Manolo believes that he is a coward, but Manolo discovers that it takes as much courage to determine for himself what he will do with his life as it does to fight a bull.

> *Principal characters:*
> MANOLO OLIVAR, the ten-year-old son of a famous matador, who tries to live up to his father's reputation for bravery
> SEÑORA OLIVAR, Manolo's mother, who hates bullfighting but accepts Manolo's destiny as a bullfighter
> SIX MEN OF ARCANGEL, admirers of Manolo's father; they take the responsibility of training Manolo in bullfighting
> COUNT DE LA CASA, a patron and friend of Juan Olivar and of Manolo, a breeder of bulls for the bullring
> JAIME GARCIA, Manolo's best friend
> JUAN GARCIA, Jaime's fourteen-year-old brother, who secretly practices with the bulls in the pasture; he desperately wants to be a bullfighter
> THE DOCTOR, who has treated many gorings in bullfighters; he sparks admiration from Manolo because of his skill in saving lives
> ALFONSO CASTILLO, now crippled, a wise and understanding bullfight critic who was a friend of Manolo's father

The Story

Manolo has lived in the shadow of a bull all of his life because his father was a famous bullfighter, killed by a bull at the age of twenty-two. The people in the small town of Arcangel expect Manolo to become a famous matador like his father. When Manolo reaches the age of ten, six of the townsmen begin Manolo's education in bullfighting. He is expected to fight his first bull at the age of twelve as his father did. Although Manolo's mother does not want Manolo to become a bullfighter, she sees it as his destiny and will not interfere. Manolo, however, does not want to fight or to kill bulls; his empathy for them when they are dying is too strong. Manolo sees this as a lack of courage and is determined to fulfill the expectations of the towns-people so that his father's memory will not be dishonored. He believes that he has lost control over his life.

Count de la Casa, a breeder of bulls, decides that Manolo will fight his first bull at the age of eleven instead of at twelve. Jaime's brother Juan secretly takes Manolo to the bull pastures at night to train with the cape and muleta for the *tienta*, or testing of the bulls, so that Manolo will not disappoint his father's friends. Lacking both influential friends and money, Juan is unlikely to get a chance to perform at the *tienta*. Juan, however, practices regularly, because his only goal in life is to become a matador. One night, Juan and Manolo break into a bullring to practice caping with one of the bulls. Juan is tossed by the bull but is saved from a goring by Manolo. Afterward, however, Manolo feels sick, a reaction to his fear; he perceives himself as cowardly. He admires Juan's bravery and skill and determines that Juan will be given a chance at the *tienta*.

Two days after the incident, a young matador is gored by the same bull that the boys had been caping. The town doctor, on his way to attend the matador, insists that Manolo accompany him. Unlike the other townspeople, the doctor does not glorify bullfighting, seeing it as a tragedy. Manolo admires the doctor's skill and perceives his work as a noble thing. He decides that if he did not have to be a bullfighter, he would like to become a doctor.

With the doctor's help, Manolo obtains permission for Juan to attend the *tienta*. The night before the *tienta*, Manolo's mother reveals that Juan Olivar was a great bullfighter because he loved what he was doing. He would never do anything he did not want to do. She states: "What he did was for himself, most of all for himself."

At the *tienta*, Manolo meets Alfonso Castillo, a famous bullfight critic. Castillo is disgusted with the pressure put on Manolo to be like his father. He tells Manolo that real courage is doing things in spite of fear rather than having no fear. He encourages Manolo to be true to himself, to allow no one to make his decisions for him. As a result of Castillo's encouragement, Manolo reaches a decision. After successfully caping his bull, he asks for permission for Juan Garcia to finish the bullfight for him. As Manolo enters the stands, the doctor offers to help Manolo become a physician.

Themes and Meanings

Symbolically defeating death lies at the heart of this novel. In the setting of Spain, death is defeated vicariously by the townspeople of Arcangel every time their hero, Juan Olivar, defeats the bull in the bullring. When Juan Olivar is killed by a bull, the people of Arcangel put all their faith and hopes in his young son, Manolo, to rescue them from death and to give them an identity.

Courage is the central theme of the book. One must have courage to defeat death. In the beginning, Manolo sees courage as a physical act, as the willingness to face death without fear. In the end, he perceives courage as a moral act. Shortly before the *tienta*, Manolo finds out from his mother that Juan Olivar, the great hero, was also afraid of the bulls but that he never showed it. Manolo then performs a great act of courage. After caping his bull, he turns the bull over to Juan Garcia for the final kill, despite what the men of the village might think. Manolo finds another way to defeat death by becoming an apprentice to a physician in the village and following his own dream.

Context

Shadow of a Bull is Wojciechowska's second and best-known children's book, winning the Newbery Medal in 1965. The realistic bullfighting background results from her learning bullfighting in Mexico and from her love of Andalusia, the setting of the book. The problem of overcoming fears is a problem familiar to Wojciechowska. Her father, a pilot, insisted that she parachute from an airplane several times when she was only ten years old. That event began a lifetime of confrontation with fear and of enjoying the battle. *The Life and Death of a Brave Bull* (1972) also has bravery, of both man and bull, as its theme. Another work, *The Hollywood Kid: A Novel* (1966), has a very different setting but repeats the theme of self-determination, when the central character must choose between leaving home on a journey of self-discovery and staying with his recently widowed mother. The problem is similar to Manolo's choice between loyalty to his father's memory and following his own dream of becoming a doctor.

Shadow of a Bull is a perceptive novel in a realistic setting revealing the conflict of an adolescent boy wanting to lead a very different life from the one that society expects from him. The author carefully explains the symbolism of the bullfight for the young reader so that Manolo's decision to defeat death by becoming a physician makes for a sensible alternative to becoming a matador. This book reflects two basic human struggles—overcoming fear and gaining self-determination—in terms that an adolescent can understand.

Sue R. Mohrmann

SHANE

Author: Jack Schaefer (1907-   )
Type of plot: Historical fiction
Time of plot: 1889
Locale: The open range, the Starrett homestead, and Grafton's saloon, Wyoming
Principal themes: Coming-of-age, friendship, gender roles, and family
First published: 1949
Recommended ages: 15-18

When a rider with a mysterious past becomes a hired hand for the Starretts, home-steaders on the open rangeland of Wyoming, he is able to save the family he comes to love from the driving ambition of a ruthless cattleman and his hired gunman, but he is unable to free himself from the pattern of frontier violence.

Principal characters:
> JOE STARRETT, a homesteader, whose determination to build a
> place for his family makes him a natural leader among the
> other homesteaders
> MARIAN STARRETT, Joe's wife, who matches him in her vision of
> the kind of home their place can become
> BOB STARRETT, their young son, who retells the story of the
> coming of Shane and of growing up in Wyoming
> SHANE, a stranger running from his past who befriends the
> Starretts in their conflict with the rancher Fletcher
> LUKE FLETCHER, a rancher whose resistance to change leads him
> to violence

The Story

When young Bob Starrett sees the distant figure of a horseman riding into their valley, he is drawn to it out of idle curiosity, but on closer inspection he senses that he has never seen anyone like the approaching rider. The stranger's carefully patched clothing suggests an unfamiliar elegance, and his easy, fluid movements suggest a suppressed vitality, an energy waiting to be released. For Bob and the Starrett family, the rider's chance drifting into their valley is to change the course of their lives.

The rider, who is only passing through, stops to water his horse at the Starrett homestead. He admires the permanence of the place, the shingled roof, the tight fences and solid buildings. When Bob's father, Joe Starrett, invites the stranger to dinner, they engage in a mutual appraisal, "a long moment [of] measuring each other in an unspoken fraternity of adult knowledge," that forms a bond of friendship between Joe Starrett and the man who introduces himself only as Shane.

For a brief interlude, Shane becomes a part of the Starrett family. He sheds his town clothes and his gun and dons the clothing of the farmer. Joe Starrett delights in showing Shane his place and his dreams, and Shane finds temporary peace in sharing the Starrett dream and the Starrett work. In a scene that foreshadows the coming conflict, Joe and Shane undertake to remove a stump, a remnant of a giant old oak that died long before the Starretts came into the valley. The stump has been a sore spot on the Starrett homestead, and Joe has been working on it off and on, but to no avail. When Shane and Joe tackle it together, the combination of Joe's strength and Shane's energy and precision with an ax becomes a force equal to the task.

The rancher Luke Fletcher, whose land surrounds the Starrett homestead and whose cattle fill the valley, remains an unspoken menace. His way of life depends on open range. Too many homesteaders spell the end of the open rangeland and an end to the cattle barons like Fletcher. Fletcher cannot see that he must change or break. He is sure that he can buy out or drive out the homesteaders and keep things the way they are. Because Joe Starrett is the strongest among the homesteaders and the natural leader, Fletcher targets the Starrett place. He knows that if Joe Starrett can be broken, the rest will leave of their own accord. Unwittingly, Shane stands at the center of the conflict: Break Starrett's man, break Starrett; break Starrett and break the homesteaders.

Fletcher attempts to draw Shane into a situation in which he can be outdone. After Shane whips one of his cowhands in a fistfight and he and Joe take on and defeat Fletcher's foreman and four of his hands, Fletcher ups the ante by hiring a gunfighter, Stark Wilson. Wilson provokes and kills one of the homesteaders in an uneven gunfight that Shane bitterly brands as murder. Shane's bitterness comes from an inner knowledge. Unlike Fletcher, Shane has been here before. His condemnation of Wilson appears to be a comment on his past and a clarification of why he does not wear a gun.

When Joe Starrett refuses to be bought out, Fletcher maneuvers him into a situation in which he must face a confrontation or appear to be cowardly. Starrett knows that he cannot survive a showdown with Wilson, but he also knows that he will lose what he values most in life if he turns away. Marian, who has come to love both men, asks Shane to stay to save Joe. When Shane agrees, he knows that the time has come for him to acknowledge his inner identity.

Shane has to pistol-whip Joe in order to keep him from facing Wilson and Fletcher. He tells Marian that he is going to Grafton's saloon, not only for her but also for Joe and young Bob, so that the Starretts will have a place and young Bob can grow up to be "straight inside as a man should." When Shane faces Wilson and Fletcher, he is dressed as he was when young Bob first saw him, and Bob knows that he is looking at the real Shane. When Shane rides away from Grafton's, both Wilson and Fletcher are dead. Fletcher's time is finished, and so is the time of the gunfighter. Shane has been badly wounded in the gunfight, but he seeks no help and forbids anyone to follow him. He reassures Bob that things will be right now and rides into the night on the same road that brought him into the valley.

Themes and Meanings

Young Bob Starrett is the first to glimpse Shane riding into the Wyoming valley where the Starrett family has settled, and he is the last person to speak with Shane when he rides out of the valley that has changed with his passing. Because the reader sees Shane through the retrospective narration of Bob Starrett, Shane is imbued with the stuff of legend, and his actions are epic. Beyond the naïve hero-worship of the young narrator, however, the reader sees that Shane shares human frailty; moreover, Shane recognizes that his moral development is incomplete. His internal struggle to realize his humanity and to understand and accept his lot in life provides the story with internal tension.

In Bob Starrett's eyes Shane is godlike, yet Bob's admiration for him does not diminish his regard for his father. Joe Starrett has the qualities that provide young Bob with a model for growing up. He is brave in the face of danger, gentle with the defenseless, and modest in accepting the leadership thrust upon him by the other homesteaders. Above all, he has a steady strength that stems from his vision of his family and from the life they are building. Joe is complete in a way that Shane is not, for he has taken another direction in life.

Yet Joe Starrett alone is no match for Fletcher, the men he can hire, and the gunfighter that his money can buy. Joe Starrett's life is simple and straightforward. His very mortality defines his courage. Shane's past is wrapped in mystery and shrouded in sorrow. He is Olympian in his power and wrath, estranged from the commonplace and isolated by the very qualities which make him a heroic figure.

Shane's gift to Bob Starrett is twofold. He provides Bob with a vision of human potential that is both admirable and frightening. Shane's invincibility is a part of his natural being, but it is also the result of what he has been. In Shane's past there lurks the suggestion of the hired gunfighter. Shane's sojourn with the Starrett family is a kind of rebirth, an awakening of his better instincts. Shane sheds his cynicism when he takes up his gun in a just cause. In killing Wilson, he kills a part of himself and becomes worthy of Bob Starrett's love and admiration.

Although the rancher, Luke Fletcher, dies in a gunfight with Shane, his death is really the result of his unwillingness to bend with the forces of change. His actions stem from his determination to preserve a way of life that has seen its day. All across the American frontier, the great ranches were giving way to the homesteader. The land they took from the Sioux, Cheyenne, and Comanche was being taken from them by the Starretts and thousands of others like them. Those who survived adapted to the inevitability of change. Those who resisted were eventually swept away by drought, hard winters, lawyers, and men like Shane.

Context

From its first publication in 1949, *Shane* has been immensely popular. *Shane* was Jack Schaefer's first novel, and it propelled him into immediate success. Since its publication in 1949, it has gone through seventy editions and has been translated into more than thirty languages. Its enduring popularity might be ascribed to Schaefer's treatment of theme and to a sense of authenticity that permeates the novel. In *Shane*, as in Schaefer's other works, he treats the struggle of the individual to know himself and his place in the larger context of the human condition. Shane's external struggle may be the stuff of the action-packed Western, but it is secondary to his internal struggle to know and accept himself as he is, not as he might have been. Schaefer's works express the belief in the worth of the individual and affirm that one is not a powerless entity shaped and ruled by social and psychological forces beyond one's control. In *Shane*, Schaefer establishes the thematic context for the greater part of his work. His characters' major victories are won within; the physical confrontations are manifestations of an unflinching integrity and an insistence on being true to oneself.

As a former newspaperman, Schaefer was insistent on getting it right. There is an authenticity of time and place that sets *Shane* apart from the run-of-the-mill Western, for *Shane* not only tells a good story; it also tells the truth about a time of transition on the American frontier.

It is not surprising that *Shane* is set in 1889 somewhere on the rangeland of Wyoming. In *The Frontier in American History* (1920), Frederick Jackson Turner set 1890 as the date which marked the closing of the American frontier. Moreover, the last great struggle between cattlemen and homesteaders took place in Wyoming during the so-called Johnson County War of 1891. The large ranchers attempted to defend their rights to open range by insisting that they were the targets of continual rustling, a charge that had some substance. Under the guise of protecting their herds and putting an end to rustling, the cattle barons imported hired gunfighters who began a program of assassination and terror in order to drive out the small ranchers and farmers. It is not recorded whether a paladin rose among the victims to bring about frontier justice, but it was just such a vision that brought Schaefer to create *Shane*.

Schaefer's heroes share a common trait. Like Shane, they are willing to face the truth about themselves and they have the courage to accept the consequences of self-realization. These characters have flaws and quirks of behavior that take them into harm's way, but they speak to the reader more eloquently with the passage of time for they represent the values from a time so ephemeral that the idea of the western frontier has more substance than does the reality. It is this vivid portrayal and universality that makes the work appropriate for young readers and popular among them.

David Sundstrand

THE SHINING

Author: Stephen King (1947-   )
Type of plot: Thriller
Time of plot: The 1970's
Locale: The Overlook Hotel, in the mountains of Colorado
Principal themes: Emotions, family, and the supernatural
First published: 1977
Recommended ages: 15-18

Demonic forces at the Overlook Hotel destroy its winter caretaker, Jack Torrance. The supernatural abilities of his young son, Danny, allow him to fight off the evil forces that control the building.

> *Principal characters:*
> JACK TORRANCE, the winter caretaker of the Overlook, a writer
>   and temporarily recovered alcoholic
> WENDY TORRANCE, the wife of Jack and mother of Danny
> DANNY TORRANCE, Jack and Wendy's son, who has the "shine,"
>   or second sight and telepathy
> DICK HALLORAN, the elderly summer cook at the Overlook, who
>   also has the "shine"
> TONY, Danny's imaginary friend

The Story

   The Shining investigates the behavior of Jack Torrance, a man with an addictive personality who is also prone to acts of violence. Jack has been fired from his Vermont teaching job for beating a student. Now, with his drinking problem under control and his marriage seemingly on the way to recovery, he has a chance to resume his stalled writing career with the offer of a winter caretaker's position at the remote Overlook Hotel high in the Colorado Mountains. Unbeknown to him, this hotel has been the scene of many bizarre and violent events, including the first caretaker's murder of his family many years before.

   What starts out as a second honeymoon for Jack and Wendy ends up as a bloodbath. The house exerts some form of seductive control over the addictive personality of Jack Torrance. It begins in the boiler room, where among the boxes of old records and journals that had belonged to the first, deranged caretaker, he unearths records of previous unsavory events associated with the hotel. Jack begins to revert to his violent behavior.

   Warned by an imaginary playmate, Tony, Danny Torrance is aware of his father's mental decline and has visions of a word he cannot fathom, "REDRUM" ("murder" spelled backwards). He senses that the Overlook is not a healthy place and experiences supernatural manifestations that show him prior acts of violence. At one point, Danny is assaulted by the long-dead, bloated, rotting corpse of a woman who had been murdered in her bath.

Wendy, realizing that her husband is insane but knowing nothing of the power that the Overlook exerts over him, barricades herself in their quarters. In a psychotic rage, Jack shatters the door with an ax, attacks and severely wounds her, and goes in search of Danny, who has managed to escape and hide. Halloran, the summer chef, had told Danny to call him with his shine (his psychic telepathic gift) if Danny should ever need help. When Halloran, in Florida, gets the boy's terrified summons, the man rushes to Colorado, arriving at the Overlook during a terrible snowstorm. Wendy is badly hurt; Jack, insane and unable to do anything except rage for Danny's death, has forgotten to adjust the furnace boiler. Danny confronts the monster that had been his father and drives it back. The three of them—Danny, Wendy, and Halloran—escape the explosion that destroys Jack and reduces the Overlook and its ghosts to a pile of rubble.

Themes and Meanings

As long as Jack Torrance is in a civilized setting, among people and off alcohol, he is more or less able to keep his anger and self-loathing bottled up. At the start of the novel, Jack's marriage functions on a shaky basis, and he gets along with his child. Yet, when he feels himself trapped, he lashes out, as he did to the student who slashed the tires on his car. Placed in a closed environment such as the snowbound Overlook Hotel, all Jack's flaws combine and are magnified, bringing on his madness and causing his eventual destruction. Jack cannot handle isolation, for it forces him to confront himself and his weaknesses.

Danny, Jack and Wendy's sensitive and extremely bright son, reacts to his father's aberrant behavior, even before the family arrives at the Overlook. The child has visions of what is to come but is unable to interpret their meaning. Because he is a child, his parents ignore his reactions. They pass off his fevers and convulsive fits as manifestations of his strong imagination when, in fact, his nightmares are a direct result of his having "seen" the violent aura surrounding and threatening to destroy both his father and mother.

The Overlook Hotel becomes the prison in which Jack must face his weaknesses; the ugliness buried within him surfaces in the form of the grotesque long-dead people he hallucinates when he gets drunk on nonexistent liquor. Danny, too, sees these people. The Overlook is reaching out to capture all three members of the family and, ironically, the child is the only person strong enough to act to save them. Danny, however, is too late to redeem his father. In a very real sense, the seeds of Jack's destruction were present in his personality well before he brought his family to spend the winter at the Overlook. Yet, before he was walled in by the snowstorm, he had been able to avoid his demons, always managing to deny his own weakness— blaming his faltering marriage, his writer's block, or his failed teaching career on others instead of examining what in himself contributed to these problems.

Context

The Shining is a haunted house story in the tradition of Edgar Allan Poe's "The Fall of the House of Usher" (1839) or Charlotte Perkins Gilman's "The Yellow Wall Paper" (1892), stories that are more psychological than they are phantom hauntings. In all three instances, the demons are as much manifestations of the troubled psyches of the persons living within the houses as they are of free-floating demons that possess the structure. In the case of *The Shining*, there are definitely creatures that live on at the Overlook Hotel independent of the Torrance family; author Stephen King makes it clear that any number of violent, sordid events have taken place during the Overlook's long history. In fact, from the beginning, the Overlook seems to have functioned almost as a magnet that attracted violent individuals and prompted acts of rage.

In this novel, King also explores the powerlessness of the child. Danny is extremely sensitive to the unspoken tensions that rise and fall between his parents, yet until the conclusion of the novel, he is unable to do anything to prevent disaster after disaster from occurring. Furthermore, although he is psychic and a gifted child, his ability to interpret what he sees is often limited—as, for example, when he cannot make sense of the word "REDRUM," which should have warned him of his father's increasing inclination toward violence.

Finally, King has capitalized on the contemporary appetite for horror fiction, on the desire to be shocked by acts of violence. Generally in pulp fiction, such events are the result of some supernatural intervention or action. What makes King's stories all the more shocking, however, is that many of the most violent or repulsive events have their source or are set in the context of the everyday: The most horrifying monsters are sometimes the people themselves, as in the case of Jack Torrance, whose interior demons drive him toward greater anger and violence. In some respects, the ghosts of the Overlook's past horrors are only window dressing for the real monster, Jack's own psychosis.

Melissa E. Barth

SHUTTERED WINDOWS

Author: Florence Crannell Means (1891-1980)
Type of plot: Social realism
Time of plot: The 1930's
Locale: Landers School and Gentlemen's Island, near Charleston, South Carolina
Principal themes: Poverty, race and ethnicity, family, and friendship
First published: 1938; illustrated
Recommended ages: 13-15

A young black girl, Harriet Freeman, travels from Minnesota to her great-grandmother's home in South Carolina. Shocked by the poverty there, she stays to help her people.

Principal characters:
> HARRIET FREEMAN, a young, talented, privileged, and educated black girl, orphaned in Minnesota, who travels to South Carolina and is compelled to stay
> GRANNY FREEMAN, Harriet's warmhearted great-grandmother, who is the only living link to her heritage
> RICHARD CORWIN, a sensitive and intelligent but poor black boy from Gentlemen's Island who becomes Harriet's close friend
> MR. and MRS. TRINDLE, Harriet's foster parents in Minnesota, who encourage her to return North, where life for blacks is easier
> LILY, an impish, orphaned black child, who was taken in by Harriet's Granny
> MOSSIE CLAPP, Harriet's roommate at Landers, who is a shy, poor, black girl from rural South Carolina
> JOHNNIE LA ROCQUE, a young girl from Jamaica, who, like Harriet, feels out of place at Landers

The Story

The circumstances presented in the plot of *Shuttered Windows* provide an effective vehicle for realistic fiction. The protagonist, Harriet Freeman, faces events both beyond and within her control, and adolescent readers will identify with Harriet as she struggles with internal conflicts. An orphan, Harriet wishes to visit her proud and independent great-grandmother, Granny Freeman, her only living relative, who lives on Gentlemen's Island in South Carolina. Mr. and Mrs. Trindle, Harriet's foster parents, know that the South is not a welcome place for blacks, yet they understand Harriet's desire to meet her great-grandmother and agree to drive her there. Harriet's great-grandmother has asked her to spend her senior year at Landers, a school for girls. Eager to go, Harriet has romanticized visions of the island, the school, and even Granny. Upon her arrival in South Carolina, however, Harriet is shocked by the poverty and the strict segregation, revelations for which life in Minnesota had not prepared her. Finding Landers beneath her, Harriet decides before completing a tour that she will not enroll there. Daunted by her impression of Landers, Harriet is still eager to meet her great-grandmother. Harriet's first impression of Granny is one of bewilderment: She dresses strangely, speaks in a dialect almost unrecognizable as English, and lives in a shack by the sea with Lily, a young orphan. Harriet is greeted affectionately by Granny and Lily, and quickly responds in kind.

At a picnic, Harriet notices an attractive young man Lily identifies as Richie; Harriet has no idea that he is Richard Corwin, the one who handles her great-grandmother's correspondence. Richard, a helpful and sensitive boy, means little to Harriet until he tells her that he is the R. Corwin mentioned in her great-grandmother's letters. Harriet discovers that Granny's letters were written by Richard, not because her vision is failing, as Harriet had assumed, but because Granny is illiterate. Harriet is humiliated. When she learns that Granny's house is to be sold for back taxes, however, her shame is replaced by a desire to help. Harriet decides to stay nearby, attend Landers, and find a way to help Granny keep her home; she will return North for college when the school year is over.

Harriet is shocked when she meets her roommate, Mossie Clapp, a poor and timid rural girl. Full of contempt, Harriet rudely requests that Mossie be replaced with Johnnie La Rocque, a girl from Jamaica. In Harriet's opinion, she and Johnnie have much in common: Johnnie dresses properly, speaks proper English, and does not plan to remain in the South.

The other students resent Harriet and Johnnie because of their attitudes, and life at Landers is miserable for the pair. Harriet later discovers that, but for circumstances of birth, she, too, might be like these girls. Her feelings of superiority give way to a sense of identification with those she realizes are her own people: Harriet now wishes to help Mossie refine her behavior and style of dress. With Granny's house secured and the school year completed, Harriet decides to stay and help Richard educate the local blacks.

Themes and Meanings

In *Shuttered Windows* the themes of race, poverty, family, and friendships are perhaps constructed to appeal to a largely white audience. Harriet is from Minnesota, and readers can easily identify with her. This identification makes it easier for the reader to make the same discoveries and come to the same understanding as does Harriet.

The small insurance fund she receives from her parents' estate secures Harriet's future. Until she goes to visit Granny, Harriet is unaware of the many advantages in her life. The local people in South Carolina make a subsistence living at best, and Harriet is shocked by this. Harriet's academic interests include literature, music, and the fine arts, but most of the girls at Landers are concerned with more practical pursuits. As Harriet learns more about her great-grandmother and her family, she begins to understand just how different her life has been.

Aware of her racial origin, Harriet never really understood the ramifications of being black while living in Minnesota, where she attended school with whites, played on a white basketball team, and enjoyed complete freedom of movement; however, things were different in South Carolina.

Formal education is important to Harriet, but she soon recognizes how wise, independent, and proud her great-grandmother is. Florence Crannell Means has invested the character of Granny with the qualities of the archetypal earth mother, a woman without formal education whose function is to nurture and bind the family together. Means also utilizes another ancient figure, in a character long dead before the action of the novel takes place. Black Moses, Harriet's great-great-great-grandfather, was a leader among slaves, intent upon freeing his people from bondage. Harriet idealizes him, and follows his example by staying in South Carolina to help her people escape the bondage of ignorance.

Means shows well how the protagonist learns the true value of friendship: Harriet at first dismisses Mossie Clapp as unworthy of notice, but as her attachment to Lily grows, so does her understanding and compassion for Mossie. As her friendship with Richard develops, Harriet begins to identify with all black people. Instead of feeling superior and separate, she gains a sense of identity and belonging.

Context

Means was a prolific author who wrote more than thirty books for young readers, as well as plays, short stories, and adult fiction. Although white, Means devoted most of her efforts to writing about minority groups, such as blacks, Hispanics, and Native Americans. In an effort to make the lives of minority individuals understandable to a white audience, she emphasizes character, with the belief that people relate to people, regardless of race.

Now considered a period piece—blacks are called Negroes or colored, and whites and blacks live in a strictly segregated world—*Shuttered Windows* nevertheless has much to offer its readers. The central conflicts contained in the novel are common to all people: Harriet's struggle to find her place in the world is a universal adolescent experience.

Means helps white readers identify with a black protagonist in a novel way. Because Harriet's parents moved to Minnesota before she was born she knew no other life, and although black, she was never subjected to the sort of life-style that Southern blacks during the 1930's had to endure. Harriet finds the setting of the Deep South as alien as might most readers, because her experience has been one outside a poor and segregated community. Harriet's values with regard to education, art, music, and literature are more like those of middle-class whites than of Southern or urban blacks. Those readers who sympathize with Harriet must consider and eventually accept an alternative set of values.

Jon D. Peterson

THE SIBLINGS

Author: Roy Brown (1921-1982)
Type of plot: Domestic and social realism
Time of plot: The mid-twentieth century
Locale: London
Principal themes: Crime, family, and social issues
First published: 1975; also as *Find Debbie*, 1976
Recommended ages: 13-15

Debbie, an emotionally disturbed fourteen-year-old, has disappeared from the family flat in the middle of the night. Inspector Bates tries to find Debbie and untangle the mystery of her disappearance.

> *Principal characters:*
> DEBBIE SHEPHERD, a psychotic teenager whose erratic behavior
> has scarred her whole family
> INSPECTOR BATES, the police officer assigned to the case
> IAN, Debbie's twin brother
> MR. SHEPHERD, Debbie and Ian's father, a social worker who
> copes with his family problems by staying away from home
> MRS. SHEPHERD, their mother, who uses drugs as her escape
> TERRY, the twins' older married brother
> BRENDA, the twins' older sister, still living at home

The Story

Set in the dreary back alleys of London, the story of Debbie Shepherd is told almost in a stream-of-consciousness fashion, as Inspector Bates interviews each member of the family and seeks to understand the background of Debbie's disappearance.

Debbie's father, Jack Shepherd, is an administrator for Social Services. His concern is to quash the investigation and any probing into the way that the family handled Debbie's psychosis. Rather than seeking help through social service agencies, Mr. Shepherd chose to hide Debbie's plight by having her cared for at home by his wife and other children, in spite of the highly destructive effects this has had on the family.

The main burden of Debbie's care has been borne by her twin brother, Ian, who is apparently the only one who can quiet or control her in her rages. Ian shares a room with Debbie, both because of lack of space and because of his ability to control her. The room is dirty and barren and has a boarded-up window. Debbie destroys everything she touches and cannot be left unattended. Ian seems to be the only family member who has not given up on Debbie. He alone can communicate with her.

Brenda and Terry are the two oldest children. Terry has married and left home, while Brenda lives at home and works at a library. Both of the older siblings feel guilty in the knowledge that their mother and brother bear the brunt of Debbie's care, but neither knows what to do. It is left to an exhausted, defeated mother and to Ian, Debbie's twin, to manage the situation. As Inspector Bates, an almost retired detective, starts to build his case, unexpected roadblocks appear as a result of Jack Shepherd's influence. The grime and despair of life in London's slums, the problems of urban living, the politics of the human-services bureaucracy, and the hopelessness of the family situation add to the tension.

Themes and Meanings

The principal themes in *The Siblings*—family, crime, and social issues—became popular for junior novels during the 1970's. Roy Brown's background as a special education teacher brought credibility to these themes in *The Siblings*, as well as in his other stories. His experiences at the Helen Allison School for Autistic Children gave him an unusual understanding of the familial problems associated with the severely disturbed.

The Shepherds are a family under intense stress because of Debbie's psychotic behavior. The descriptions of this behavior by each member of the family, understated as these accounts are, build a chilling picture of what family life was like in the Shepherd household. The absent father, afraid that Debbie's disappearance will reflect on him, the ineffectual, worn mother, the resentful older brother and sister, and finally Ian, who has managed until now to control and protect his sister, all flesh out a picture of a family that no longer works.

The central theme, crime, is examined through the activities of about-to-be-retired Inspector Bates and the young Sergeant Holmes. At first the case is treated as a simple missing child case, but the politics of social issues begin to cloud the investigation as Jack Shepherd tries to quash the investigation. Nevertheless, Inspector Bates continues to interview each member of the family. His methodical approach heightens the suspense. The why and how of Debbie's disappearance from the family flat in the middle of the night continue to be intriguing even as the reader sympathizes with the family's dilemma of what to do if Debbie is found. The reader is deftly brought into the difficulties society has in handling the problems of the criminally insane and the destruction of people and families that results. Each family member has been scarred in a different way, and the resolution of the story's suspense does not resolve these issues.

In addition, the bureaucratic maneuvering of Mr. Shepherd, as he attempts to influence the outcome of the investigation in order to cover his culpability, lends a chilling sense of doubt regarding the effectiveness of many human service agencies.

Context

Under the title *Find Debbie*, *The Siblings* was rated by *School Library Journal* as one of the best books of 1976. Gloria Levitas, in her review, found that "it celebrates the triumph of life and of human spirit against the ever-present threats of death and madness."

The story of Debbie is a disturbing one. Care of the insane is a continuing social problem. The Shepherds' attempts to cope are very graphically presented in a lean, spare manner that adds to the realism and drama of the story. Although the reader never meets Debbie, the grimness of her life as the prisoner of a distorted mind leads the reader to a better understanding of psychosis. Although Debbie is always just out of reach, Brown's skillful touch with characterization keeps the reader focused on finding out just exactly what is going on.

Oddly, at first it is Ian who seems the least concerned about Debbie. As the story builds, however, so does his anxiety and suspense. Ian seems the least believable of the characters. Even a twin would balk at the burden of Debbie. The final resolution of Debbie's disappearance is unexpected and horrifying, but quite believable.

The Siblings, considered by many to be Brown's best work, exemplifies his major interests. The story includes a city background, deviant youngsters, and the difficulty people have in behaving in a humane manner. *The Collision Course* (1980), a later book by Brown, is probably the most similar in theme. This story is not a suspense tale, however, but rather a social commentary.

In the mystery line, Brown produced the Chips Regan series, which used urban settings and exploited his knowledge of London. Brown's books all deal with the problems of the disadvantaged, the alienated, or the social outcast, in keeping with the concerns of the 1970's. His books were popular and were very effective in acquainting young people with urban and humanitarian concerns.

Several of Roy Brown's junior novels have been translated into German, French, Italian, and even Japanese. He produced over thirty junior novels, as well as several plays and radio scripts. His first book, *A Saturday in Pudney* (1966), was based on his teaching experiences; these experiences proved to be a nondepletable resource that he used again and again.

Dorothy E. Carlson

SIDDHARTHA

Author: Hermann Hesse (1877-1962)
Type of plot: Moral tale
Time of plot: The sixth century B.C.
Locale: India
Principal theme: Religion
First published: 1922 (English translation, 1951)
Recommended ages: 15-18

Siddhartha undertakes a quest to find spiritual self-fulfillment. After first becoming an ascetic monk and then a rich businessman, he still feels empty and takes up the menial job of a ferryman. Listening to the wisdom of the river, he attains true serenity and inner bliss.

Principal characters:
SIDDHARTHA, a young man destined to be a Brahman priest
GOVINDA, his childhood friend, also a Brahman monk
KAMALA, a beautiful courtesan
VASUDEVA, a wise old ferryman

The Story

The quest that drives the plot of the novel is initiated when the young Brahman monk, Siddhartha, realizes that the teachings of the Brahman religion will not lead to his salvation, so he undertakes to find the true spiritual meaning of life. He and his friend Govinda live with the Samanas, an ascetic sect that practices fasting and yoga, for three years. Dissatisfied with this way, they go to the great teacher, Gotama the Buddha, with whom Govinda remains as a disciple, but Siddhartha continues his path of seeking. Siddhartha believes that he should experience the world of the senses, so he crosses a river and enters a large city where he meets the beautiful Kamala, a famous courtesan. She helps him to become a wealthy businessman, and he learns of the material, sensual pleasures of life.

After several years, Siddhartha realizes that the world of the senses is also a mere illusion and not the truth of existence. Unaware that Kamala is pregnant with his child, he leaves the city. He goes back to the river and, in his despair, tries to commit suicide. This alternative, he sees, is—because of the doctrine of rebirth—also an illusion. He decides to live a humble existence with the ferryman, Vasudeva, and from him, Siddhartha learns the truths of spiritual knowledge. After twelve years, Kamala and her son appear in search of the Buddha. She dies of a snake bite, and Siddhartha must care for his young and spoiled son. Although he loves the boy very much, Siddhartha must learn the lesson of unselfish devotion. When the boy runs away to return to the city, Siddhartha must allow him to go. After the realization of this final truth, Vasudeva dies, and Siddhartha takes his place as ferryman. Govinda, now an old man as is his friend, comes to the river one day and realizes that Siddhartha, in his own way, has become such as the Buddha and has attained a state of absolute bliss and harmony with existence.

Themes and Meanings

Hesse's work deals with the painful process of spiritual growth. In part, the novel retraces the legendary life of the Gotama the Buddha—the name "Siddhartha" was one of the Buddha's own appellations—and presents central teachings of Buddhist thought. The name of the beautiful courtesan—"Kamala"—for example, contains the Sanskrit word *kama* that means desire, and in the Buddha's teachings, desire is the force that causes and perpetuates the suffering that is existence. In order to gain spiritual salvation, the individual must learn to renounce the veil of illusion, or maya, that is generated by desire. Thus, Siddhartha leaves Kamala and his luxurious life in the city because he recognizes that such pleasures only bind him further to desire and are in truth ultimately ephemeral.

From Vasudeva and his observation of the eternal flow of the river, Siddhartha learns the central Buddhist teaching that existence is impermanence and that therefore the attempt to cling to it (or to reject it) only produces suffering. One of the illusions produced by desire is that there are static and permanent entities, including the notion of an ego that seeks to possess people and things. In order to achieve liberation, or nirvana, the individual must lose the ego that tries to clutch to itself what is ultimately illusory. That is the lesson of impermanence, the constantly changing "flow" of being. Thus Siddhartha, despite his love and concern for his son, must let the boy go in order to surrender his ego-based desires.

Hesse's novel also illustrates his own independent and iconoclastic nature. As a young man, Hesse was a rebellious and free-thinking individual who would not bow to authority. He was once even thrown out of his school for his nonconformist activities. This behavior is in fact alien to Eastern cultural traditions, which stress respect for the wisdom and authority of elders and the duty of the individual to fit into social norms. Hesse's own personality is evident in Siddhartha's independent attitude, which makes him reject the teachings of others, including those of the Buddha himself, and go out on his own to experience existence—and its suffering—for himself. This is evidence of the existential dimension of Hesse's writing, that is, his rejection of truth expressed in conceptual, intellectual terms in favor of truth that is subjectively felt or experienced by the individual.

Context

Siddhartha is an expression of Hesse's long-standing interest in Eastern culture and philosophy and in his lifelong quest for spiritual fulfillment. His grandfather had been a Christian missionary in India for thirty years, and Hesse became well acquainted as a child with aspects of Hindu and Buddhist thought. In 1911, he and a friend actually journeyed through India. He spent much of his life reading intensively in Eastern philosophy and seeking in its wisdom the truths he felt were valid for his own life. *Siddhartha*, as well as the later novel *Die Morgenlandfahrt* (1932; *The Journey to the East*, 1956), directly reflects this preoccupation, although all of his writings are concerned with this Eastern-influenced quest for spiritual release.

Much of existential fiction such as Hesse's *Siddhartha* deals with issues that are of particular relevance to the period of late adolescence: the definition of self as separate from family and society as well as the search for a personal meaning to life. During the late 1960's, Hesse's works, especially *Siddhartha*, were extremely popular among young American college students. Thus, his novel can be seen in the context of other well-known works from American literature—such as J. D. Salinger's *The Catcher in the Rye* (1951) or S. E. Hinton's *The Outsiders* (1967)—that treat aspects of the adolescent search for identity. Hesse rightly suggests in *Siddhartha*, however, that such existential questions are (or should be) in truth lifelong occupations. Unlike his friend, Govinda, Siddhartha never joins the religious establishment but continues his solitary quest for spiritual meaning.

Thomas F. Barry

SILENCE OVER DUNKERQUE

Author: John R. Tunis (1889-1975)
Type of plot: Historical fiction
Time of plot: May/July, 1940
Locale: Dunkerque, France, and environs; Dover, England
Principal themes: War, death, and friendship
First published: 1962
Recommended ages: 13-15

Surprised by the German invasion of France, the British Expeditionary Force at Dunkerque is pushed into the sea and must be quickly evacuated. When a sergeant and one of his men are left behind, they soon realize their survival depends on the friendship and courage of a young French girl.

> *Principal characters:*
> SERGEANT EDWARD WILLIAMS, a brave, dutiful soldier, who is marooned in France
> RICHARD and RONALD, his fifteen-year-old twins, who never doubt he will return
> THREE-FINGERS BROWN, with only three fingers on one hand, the sergeant's driver and companion
> MADAME YVONNE BONNET, a raging woman who is hostile to the British soldiers but later befriends them
> GISELE BONNET, her teenage daughter, courageous, resourceful, who repeatedly risks her life for the soldiers
> MARCEL DUPONT, Gisele's grandfather, a veterinarian, who hides Williams and Brown in his house and doctors their dog
> "OLD" BILL BENNET, the gruff but congenial captain of the *Shropshire Lass*, on which the twins stow away to search for their father

The Story

When the British Expeditionary Force at Dunkerque is evacuated to the mainland of Great Britain after the German invasion in May, 1940, Sergeant Edward Williams and Three-Fingers Brown are stranded in France. The two men are awakened at once to the frightening conditions under which people must live in wartime. Failing in two earlier escape attempts, Williams and Brown board a British destroyer, which is soon sunk by an enemy mine. Without regard for his own safety, Williams pulls the wounded Brown through a mile of open water to the beach. He sees no sign of Candy, however, a homeless Airedale dog he had found in the ruins of Dunkerque the day before. Exhausted, the men sleep that night hidden on the beach.

Meanwhile, at Dover, the brave, impetuous Williams twins, Ronald and Richard, grow anxious about their missing father. They decide to stow away on "Old" Bill Bennet's *Shropshire Lass*, which crosses the channel to look for survivors. Discovering them, Bill scolds the boys thoroughly but lets them continue, secretly admiring their bravery and devotion. Unfortunately, they return to England empty-handed.

A series of harrowing adventures follows, during which the soldiers just manage to avoid capture. First, they are found and led from the beach by fourteen-year-old Gisele Bonnet, who hides them in the hayloft of her mother, Madame Yvonne Bonnet. Unfortunately, Gisele's loyalty to the allies of France is not shared by her bad-tempered mother, who hates the British for deserting the French at Dunkerque and who threatens to expose Williams and Brown to the Germans.

Next, after barely missing detection by German troops who poke their bayonets through the floor of the hayloft, Gisele decides to move her friends to the house of her grandfather Marcel Dupont, a kindly old veterinarian at Calais. Disguised as peasant fishermen with fake identification credentials, the trio start for Calais. They are halted en route by a German squad, whose commander is distracted from searching them by the unexpected appearance of Williams' lost Airedale. Touched by this warm reunion of dog with master, the squad leader lets them pass.

Marcel Dupont receives the party at his house and arranges for them to depart France disguised as fishermen with a fleet that the Germans have allowed to fish offshore. The plan is nearly ruined before it is implemented by the enraged Madame Bonnet, who has followed Gisele and her friends to the Dupont house. Bonnet threatens to report them to the Germans, who have served notice that anyone harboring British soldiers will be shot together with his household. The noisy old matron relents, however, when she finally discovers in her daughter a kind of Joan of Arc valor and an unstinting determination to save these true friends of France. Thus, Sergeant Williams and Three-Fingers Brown are returned safely to England, but not without the clear conviction that they do so because of the courage and resolve of an ordinary young French girl, who, through the trauma of war, has metamorphosed into an extraordinary heroine.

Themes and Meanings

The central theme of *Silence over Dunkerque* is war. It dramatizes the ravages and immorality of war, its effects on the lives of people, its power to kill, and its capacity to create heroes and heroines from common people in and out of uniform. The terrible debacle of war is revealed through the suspenseful experiences of Sergeant Williams, who, ironically, is cast along with death as a by-product of war. In this case, war has given birth both to death and the common foot soldier, who emerges from the violence of war as a hero. Such a contrast invites comparison to the Homeric epics, *Iliad* (c. 800 B.C.) and *Odyssey* (c. 800 B.C.), in which violent deaths and memorable heroes abound.

A similar irony exists in the characters of Gisele and Madame Bonnet, who each respond in totally different ways to the circumstances of war and death. Bonnet, embittered by the British Expeditionary Force, whom she thinks deserted France in its darkest hour, takes an "eye-for-an-eye" point of view and seeks immediate satisfaction by exposing Williams, Brown, and her own family to the Germans. Contrarily, Gisele, even at fourteen, understands her role as a human being as one demanding much more than merely exchanging good for good and evil for evil. She also grasps the practical solution to her country's problems: In a free Great Britain lies the surest hope for a free France. Never wavering from her principles, she boldly places the values of humanism and patriotism above even her own mother, whom she believes is mistaken. She thereby emerges as an unsung heroine in her own right. Happily, if belatedly, Madame Bonnet, who has been tangled up throughout most of the novel in her own distorted notions of patriotism, is won over by her daughter in time to avoid total disaster for everyone.

Finally, war is also a powerful force in the shaping and cementing of friendships that might not otherwise have come to pass. Throughout the novel, closer relationships are seen to develop between the Williams twins and between them and their father; between Williams and Three-Fingers Brown, who are thrown together in battle, captured, and nearly killed; and among Marcel Dupont, Gisele, and ultimately Madame Bonnet. While all may have known that friendships in ordinary times are to be cherished and valued highly, they come now to realize that friendships in time of war are crucial to their very survival.

Context

John R. Tunis' best-known books are not about war but about sports for young people. Yet his only two war novels, *Silence over Dunkerque* and *His Enemy, His Friend* (1967), reflect essentially the same central values as his other works— goodness, honesty, fair play, and the right way to live and behave. These are all couched in what critic Ken Donelson calls "a quiet and realistic account of what war does to soldiers and civilians alike." If, as Donelson suggests, "Tunis believed in clean-cut, intelligent, clean-living, honest, young men, not perfect heroes," and "not the use of sports to win or gain acclaim or money" in his sports novels, he has conveyed essentially these same qualities in the central characters of this novel about war.

All these characters are indeed "not perfect," least of all Madame Bonnet, but, at one stage or another throughout the novel, they emerge as decent human beings with a respect for what is right and for human life. In Sergeant Williams and Three-Fingers Brown are seen classical warriors, whose character is fine-tuned by strict military discipline and high moral values. Purists neither as soldiers nor human beings, they nevertheless perform admirably under the pressures of war.

The courage and coolness of Gisele Bonnet is made more astounding by the fact of her youth. Radically different from dozens of her female counterparts in literature, yet a personification in some ways of many of them, she rises abruptly to the occasion of war, not hesitating to place her life on the line for her friends and country. The author draws other such believable portraits of daring human behavior in time of war. Sometimes such behavior is motivated by personal and emotional factors. The Williams twins, though brave and adventurous, would not likely have made such a foolish attempt to rescue someone other than their father from a combat zone. Likewise, Madame Bonnet's turnabout was certainly inspired by the heroism of her remarkable daughter.

Thus, from one of the most horrible and infamous wars in the history of mankind, Tunis has gathered from among the hundreds of thousands of its victims a handful of fictitious participants to demonstrate artfully how heroes and heroines are born. *Silence over Dunkerque* is a fast-paced adventure story of war; more than that, however, it contains worthy role models for all readers, especially the younger generations for "goodness, honesty, fair play, and the right way to live and behave."

W. Wayne Alford

SIMPLE GIFTS

Author: Joanne Greenberg (1932-   )
Type of plot: Psychological realism
Time of plot: The early 1980's
Locale: A farm on Croom Mountain near Bascom, Colorado
Principal themes: Social issues, family, and emotions
First published: 1986
Recommended ages: 15-18

An inept, socially ostracized family accepts a government scheme to use their farm as an "authentic" 1880's retreat for wealthy visitors. This produces a hilarious disregard for legality, building to a climactic Fourth of July picnic where a stampede of longhorns disrupts a riot and the whole experiment.

Principal characters:
   KATE FLEURI, a fifteen-year-old girl who apologizes for her
      family, yet tries to keep their secrets
   ROBERT LUTHER FLEURI, her older brother, who takes much of the
      responsibility, but finds maturity
   JANE and LOUISE FLEURI, her younger sisters, each with a special
      talent, who remain somewhat aloof from the action
   MARY BETH and AKIN FLEURI, her parents, who are judged
      retarded and weird
   MR. KELVIN, the government agent through whom all blessings
      flow, or cease to flow
   ONE-EYE, the demanding, horribly scarred man who markets the
      "popscull" and knows the family secrets

The Story

The Fleuri family is slipping deeper into poverty on their mountain. The farm will not produce sufficient cash crops to keep things repaired. If it were not for the income from Daddy's "popscull" (illegal whiskey) and the illegal herd of longhorns, the family would not have food. Their social status in Bascom has always been tenuous, to the dismay of Kate, who so wishes to be like normal folk.

Mr. Kelvin arrives on this scene with an offer from the government: turn the farm into an 1880's retreat for wealthy visitors. All modern conveniences would have to be discarded (or at least hidden). Daddy takes some persuading, but Robert Luther and Kate see this proposal as the only possible way to save the farm. Mama dreams of lawn parties and Japanese lanterns; Louise scorns the idea without words, but Jane falls in love with Mr. Kelvin.

The main problem the family foresees is hiding the family secrets: the still, the longhorns, and Daddy's sleeping fits. Yet the family members ingeniously work together and almost succeed. Their attempts to be authentic lead to illegal trapping and to killing deer out of season. Then Mama establishes "Anglus": When she rings the farmbell at six each evening, all work stops for a moment of silent prayer.

The guests come and go in a variegated display of temperament, abilities, and problems. The first visitors enthusiastically take part in all activities; from that point, however, things begin to go downhill. Squeamish visitors, lazy children, and intolerant parents begin to rub off the glamour. Still, the project makes it through the first winter in spite of being snowed in.

When the thaw arrives, Mr. Kelvin appears along with the spring flowers. The family is proud to show him everything they have learned, but he ignores all their sacrifices and expresses horror at the illegal activities, especially the prayers. Now the Fleuris learn that "authentic" does not mean "real."

The Van Houtons arrive: tough, authoritarian Dr. Richard, sex-starved Dorothy, and two pink, flabby daughters. In only one week Daddy's fits are discovered and scrutinized, the longhorns get loose, Robert Luther loses his virginity, and the two girls consume as much popscull as they can until they are scared out of their wits by One-Eye.

In an effort to make up for the disastrous visits, Mama suggests a Fourth of July picnic for the whole community. Mr. Kelvin agrees, on condition that it not cost a thing. Plans proceed well, and the day arrives. By noon there are already more guests than the hundred the Fleuris had anticipated. Soon the crowd polarizes at each end of the field. One set holds signs such as "PRAYER—EVERY CHILD'S RIGHT," while the other side proclaims "PROTECT THE FIRST AMENDMENT." Soon the angry buzz takes on a humming sound; then a feeling like a throbbing breaks out, and longhorns stampede, running down the whole crowd. In a minute it is over, and people begin rising from the ground, checking to see whether they are really still alive. No one has been killed; cattle are very sure-footed.

This fiasco seems to spell the end to the project, what with lawsuits, threats of jail, Internal Revenue Service agents, and the like. The project has failed—or has it? Kate sums it up this way: "But we had gone back; we had been as clever and strong as those real pioneers. We had made it through summer and winter and hard visitors, and we had showed Bascom we could be more and do more than it ever thought we could."

Themes and Meanings

Only one year transpires in *Simple Gifts*, yet the struggle for individuality against a collective mentality seems to span the whole century from 1880 to 1980. The Fleuris appear to be losing the battle: Only "normal" Kate is accepted socially in Bascom. By the end of the book, even Kate decides that it is better to be part of an insane family than of a sane society.

Each chapter is told from a different point of view, and each character struggles with a different theme: Robert Luther, coming of age; Kate, family versus social status; Mama, reality; Daddy, poverty; Louise, intellectualism; Jane, loss of love.

Together they coalesce into "us" against "them" and come out the winners in spite of legal hot water. They never lose their spirit and, like true pioneers, find their meaning in the land and in the family.

In the struggle to be authentic and to re-create the 1880's, the family shows the absurdity of some laws and how personal rights have been trampled by these laws. They also show how progress has brought improvement. Daddy reminds the children that an authentic re-creation of the past would mean lynching, rabies, poverty, and anthrax. Dr. Van Houton, though referring only to the "Anglus," puts his finger on the whole work when he says, "It was absurd, all of it, seen separately, but it was a part, in some way, of the Fleuri family and what they were trying to do."

The folk song alluded to in the title, but not mentioned in the book, neatly expresses the thrust of the book: " 'Tis a gift to be simple, 'tis a gift to be free,/ 'Tis a gift to come down where we ought to be."

Context

The rollicking flow of the plot of *Simple Gifts* is unlike most of Joanne Greenberg's books. Generally she deals with emotional distress, as in *I Never Promised You a Rose Garden* (published under the pseudonym Hannah Green in 1964), or with handicaps such as blindness and deafness, as in *Of Such Small Differences* (1988). As in *Simple Gifts*, however, her characters always strive for normalcy and acceptance, experience rejection, yet emerge stronger and more self-reliant. Many of her short stories reflect the struggle of an underdog, whether pushed down by race, handicap, or family. Her characters are real and multidimensional. They may be the only one of "that kind" ever met by the reader, but identification is so strong that the insults heaped on the protagonists are taken personally.

Greenberg has the Fleuri family and their guests tell their own stories. This use of many points of view almost makes the book a collection of short stories. Yet each part is necessary for the whole story. This technique was often used by William Faulkner; reading *Simple Gifts* may make his style easier to understand.

Greenberg highlights a society torn between pride in scientific progress and a desire to return to the "good old days." She shows flaws in each approach. Only the individual emerges with worth, and that is enough to make the struggle valuable.

Hayden McClung
Lee McClung

SISTER

Author: Eloise Greenfield (1929-   )
Type of plot: Domestic realism
Time of plot: The 1970's
Locale: Suburban America
Principal themes: Family, emotions, love, and coming-of-age
First published: 1974; illustrated
Recommended ages: 10-13

A young girl reads through her diary of the past four years and relives each spe-cial memory she has recorded. She realizes that, through her family's emotional struggles, she has gained the strength to develop her own identity.

Principal characters:
    DORETHA FREEMAN, thirteen, who is the narrator for most of the
        story
    ALBERTA FREEMAN, sixteen, Doretha's sister
    THELMA FREEMAN, Doretha and Alberta's mother, who becomes a
        widow when Doretha is ten years old
    CLEMONT FREEMAN, Doretha's father

The Story

Sister begins when Doretha is thirteen, eagerly awaiting a concert by Lonnie and the Liberations. Doretha and her friend Shirl attend the concert, and both girls leave the show mesmerized. Upon returning home, Doretha finds that her sister Alberta is again out late, her whereabouts unknown. Doretha's mother Thelma expresses her worry that Alberta could possibly be lying somewhere dead. Doretha tries to con-vince her mother that Alberta will return unharmed, as she always does. Doretha retires to her room and opens her journal, which she calls her "Doretha Book." She plans to write about the concert but instead starts reading the pages she has written over the past four years. She makes a bet with herself: Alberta will be home by the time she is finished reviewing the diary.

The first scene from the diary recalls a nine-year-old Doretha with a broken an-kle, sulking in the family's living room. Her father comes home from work and is determined to raise her spirits. He brings out a cardboard box containing high school memorabilia. Doretha is fascinated and asks him if she can keep a worn notebook, most of which is unused. This notebook later becomes her diary.

The next memory Doretha has recorded is that of her father's death. Relatives, neighbors, and friends have gathered for Clemont's annual birthday picnic. After an enthusiastic rendition of "Happy Birthday to You," Clemont laughs. His laugh con-torts his face, he drops his paper plate, and he beats a fist against his chest. He then falls face forward into the dirt. Doretha remembers her uncle turning her father over onto his back, and she remembers seeing the unblinking eyes stare directly at the sun. She is shocked that she and the others had been so happy just moments before, and now her father is dead, taken away in an ambulance.

An observant ten-year-old Doretha notices many changes in her sister after Clemont's death. While her mother plays a sad song on the piano to express grief, her sister seems to withdraw from the family and stays out of the house more often, wandering the streets with friends. Her mother takes a job at a towel laundry, and Doretha feels even more lonely than she ever remembers. One night before going to sleep, she promises her sister Alberta that she will never leave her. Alberta is obviously awake but makes no response to Doretha's pledge.

Doretha visits with her maternal grandfather, who tells her that people must laugh even when life seems painful. Doretha applies her grandfather's theory to Alberta's actions and believes that she can better understand what Alberta is experiencing. Doretha even emulates Alberta in an argument with a substitute teacher at school. She screams at the teacher and then coolly saunters back to her seat.

When Doretha is twelve, her mother appears to be seriously involved with a man named Turner, whom she has been dating. As Thelma readies herself for a date one evening, Turner's wife telephones, and a shocked Doretha speaks with the woman. Turner never calls or appears that evening. Doretha and Alberta sit on the sofa with their mother, comforting her as she cries and laments the loss of Clemont.

At thirteen, Doretha becomes interested in African heritage and joins a group that studies and teaches the culture. Doretha also tries to assist Alberta, who is involved in a violent fight with another girl. After the fight and a visit to the hospital, Alberta leaves home with bags packed, explaining to Doretha that she chooses to laugh at everything so that no one hurts her feelings. Doretha knows that it will be her responsibility to comfort her mother after Alberta's departure. For a brief moment, she wishes she could also leave. Alberta's independent life lasts only three days. She returns and Doretha notices that her sister looks tired and sad. This episode brings Doretha to the end of her diary, and Alberta has not yet come home. Doretha realizes that the memories she has just relived have molded her into the person she has become. She has gained strength, and she vows to share that strength with her sister.

Themes and Meanings

The title *Sister* provides a clue to the central themes of the book. Not only does the title refer to a worldwide black family made up of brothers and sisters, but it also refers to Doretha's role in her own family. After her father's death, Doretha's role changes and adjusts to fit the actions of her mother and sister. Doretha is no longer simply a daughter: She is now part of a family of women; as a result, her role has changed to that of a sibling, a helpmate. Doretha, Thelma, and Alberta are a family of sisters.

The distinction between parent and child has become hazy. Doretha assumes greater responsibility when her mother takes a full-time job. Doretha worries about Alberta's safety and tries to protect her from harm. Doretha comforts and reassures her mother, as a parent would a confused child. Doretha's source of strength and stability is her family. She knows that she has become a stronger, more capable person because she has endured domestic heartaches. Her sense of maturity has developed from the events she has recorded in her journal, and those events have all directly involved her family. Doretha's psychological and emotional growth is dependent upon the changing nature of her family. Thelma and Alberta similarly experience emotional growth, reacting to Clemont's death and the resulting changes in their lives.

Context

Eloise Greenfield states that her goal in writing is "to give children words to love, to grow on." The novel *Sister*, which depicts the endless trials and small joys of everyday family life, seems aligned with that goal. Her novel *Talk About a Family* (1978) is another work with a similar focus.

Greenfield has been an active member of the Washington, D.C., Black Writers Workshop for many years, working with both the adult fiction and children's literature divisions. Much of Greenfield's writing focuses on the experiences of blacks, especially black children, but her works speak to young readers of all races and ethnic backgrounds. *Sister* examines the ordeals one black family faces, but the issues of death, grief, and adolescence are issues which must be faced by everyone. Greenfield adds elements of African heritage and culture to the story, to remind her young black readers that there is an extended, worldwide family to which they belong. The elements of African culture in the story also distinguish *Sister* from other young adult novels similar in subject matter and theme.

Greenfield's writing has been described as sensitive, and *Sister* is no exception. The book's simplicity is deceptive, however, for behind the simplicity is truth. Adolescence brings with it many conflicting emotions, and in Doretha's case, adolescence carries additional burdens. As an author, Greenfield has a gift for making life both dramatic and realistic at the same time. She creates believable situations and identifiable characters. *Sister* is a novel about growing up in the modern world. It is a novel for all young people; not only blacks, and not only teenage girls. It pinpoints emotions common to everyone.

Angela Bushnell Peery

THE SKATES OF UNCLE RICHARD

Author: Carol Elizabeth Fenner (Carol Williams, 1929-   )
Type of plot: Domestic realism
Time of plot: The 1970's and the 1980's
Locale: An ice-covered lagoon in Michigan
Principal themes: Sports, race and ethnicity, family, and friendship
First published: 1978; illustrated
Recommended ages: 10-13

Through the help of Uncle Richard, nine-year-old Marsha begins the work of becoming the black champion figure skater who performs in her head.

Principal characters:
   MARSHA, a chubby, clumsy, black nine-year-old with dreams of
      becoming a thin, graceful ice skater
   MARSHA'S MOTHER, who tells Marsha that skates can come after
      she learns to stop being clumsy, who complains about her
      brother Richard's infrequent visits, and who gives Marsha the
      black skates once belonging to Richard
   LEONARD, Marsha's elder brother who calls her "Fatty," changes
      the television station when Marsha is watching figure skating,
      and is generally unsupportive of his sister
   UNCLE RICHARD, who finally appears on the scene and lovingly
      gives Marsha the first lessons she needs

The Story

The Skates of Uncle Richard, a didactic story, shows Marsha's progress from a clumsy, chubby black child to a girl who makes her first efforts toward becoming the dazzling figure skater of her fantasies. Marsha, at the beginning of the story, is a dreamer. She escapes from her chubbiness and feelings of awkwardness by watching television—especially figure skating—and daydreaming of one day becoming a champion ice skater. To escape the ridicule of Leonard, her elder brother, Marsha imagines her future performances with her brother attending and regretting ever having called her names.

Marsha goes with Leonard to the lagoon on one of his rare days of being kind. Although she runs and skids about in her boots, Marsha believes that her goal of being a beautiful, champion skater is quite distant. Marsha's mother asks her not to drop things and to be less clumsy. Because of Marsha's success, for Christmas her mother gives her a heavy pair of black skates from the attic. Although Marsha is disappointed with the style and color of the skates, she accompanies Leonard to the lagoon. Through foreshadowing, Fenner gives a hint of the trouble that is to come. "All sizes of shoes and boots were scattered near the benches on the bank. To Marsha they looked cold and lonely sitting in the snow. . . . Marsha felt a shiver of fear nip and tremble in her stomach." Fenner displays limited omniscience when she describes Marsha's thoughts and feelings after her initial failure at ice skating. "She wanted to go home, but she didn't know how she would ever get back across the ice. . . . She dropped her head, full of cold and misery."

When things seem at their worst, Uncle Richard appears to encourage and give Marsha some hints on how to lace the skates, how to push and glide, and how to rest her ankles. Uncle Richard praises Marsha profusely and makes a promise to return the next week in order to give Marsha another lesson. He is also hopeful that he can put himself back in his sister's good graces. The book ends with some last-minute instructions for Marsha to oil the skates' runners. The reader senses that Marsha has become a more dynamic character, who is ready to take her destiny into her own hands and achieve her goals.

Themes and Meanings

The sport of figure skating is the central focus of *The Skates of Uncle Richard*. It is not only the obsession of young Marsha but also representative of hope and unity. The skates themselves become a symbol of hope for a girl who has low self-esteem. The sport of figure skating is the vehicle through which Marsha is able to achieve some feeling of self-worth for the first time in her life. She need only strap on the skates and race across the ice to find herself.

The skates are also, as relics of the family's past, a symbol of the cohesiveness that once existed in the family but that has now been shunted aside. The revival of the skates also brings about a revival of her family, in that Uncle Richard returns to his family with hints that he will stay. With unity achieved, Marsha can now build on the base of her now-whole family and push ever forward with her dreams.

Although Marsha is a young black girl, race and ethnicity is not a predominant theme in this work. Fenner does express, however, that, no matter who you are, if you have a sense of purpose and a firm base of family and friendship, anything is possible. The novel tells the reader to reach for his dreams and never get discouraged.

Context

Carol Fenner's *The Skates of Uncle Richard* fits into the tradition in children's literature of a young protagonist achieving a sense of self-worth through sports. Strictly in the ice-skating realm itself is Mary Mapes Dodge's *Hans Brinker: Or, The Silver Skates* (1865), which is another story of a skater who was daring enough to try. Dodge's work was a landmark in the history of children's literature for its realism, and *The Skates of Uncle Richard* follows in this vein. Marsha's family is presented as realistic and not at all as an example of perfectionism. Because of this realism, a young adult reader finds it easy to relate to this story. For example, Marsha's mother supports her family alone and is not economically well-to-do, Marsha's brother treats his younger sister badly, and Uncle Richard is estranged from the family, circumstances that are not unfamiliar to the young adult reader.

The Skates of Uncle Richard is an excellent book for bibliotherapy—treating problems with books. Young girls of all colors can learn from Marsha, who dares to try and not merely to dream of success. Older females who wish to read of black girls who also have the courage to try may wish to read Louise Fitzhugh's *Nobody's Family Is Going to Change* (1974), which focuses on Emma, who wishes to be a lawyer.

Anita P. Davis

THE SKELETON MAN

Author: Jay Bennett (1912-   )
Type of plot: Thriller
Time of plot: The mid- to late twentieth century
Locale: An unnamed town a short drive from Atlantic City, New Jersey, and a nearby
   town named Louisville
Principal themes: Crime, death, family, and suicide
First published: 1986
Recommended ages: 15-18

*Ray Bond's Uncle Ed gives him thirty thousand dollars for his eighteenth birthday,
swears him to secrecy, and the next day falls to his death from a hotel window. Soon
Ray is coolly pursued by Albert Dawson, the gangster who loaned his Uncle Ed the
money.*

   Principal characters:
   RAY BOND, a hardworking, reserved eighteen-year-old,
      determined to attend law school
   ED BOND, Ray's uncle, a gambler, who loves Ray and gives him
      thirty thousand dollars for law school, at the cost of his life
   MR. BOND, Ray's father, whom he last saw when he was two
      years old, a compulsive gambler, who died in jail after being
      convicted of bank embezzlement
   MRS. BOND, Ray's mother, with whom he has a caring but
      strained relationship
   LAURIE, Ray's girlfriend, who becomes angry with him when he
      refuses to confide in her
   ALBERT DAWSON, a gangster, who is as efficiently even-tempered
      as he is calculatingly ruthless in his "business" dealings
   ALICE COBB, Ed Bond's longtime mistress, who has a history of
      psychological problems and is killed when she claims to have
      proof that Albert Dawson had Ed murdered
   PETE WILSON, a treasury agent, whom Ray mistakes for a gangster
      and who eventually saves Ray's life

The Story

Like the central characters of most thrillers, Ray Bond is something of a self-
reliant loner who begins to feel dangerously isolated as events overtake him. Unlike
the situations in most adult thrillers, however, in which each new event and revelation serves to heighten the terror, the situation in *The Skeleton Man* incorporates few
brief acts of violence that go largely unnoticed. The terror then is subtler and more

pervasive, undermining for Ray Bond—and the reader—the sense of personal security and community justice that is a basic assumption of ordinary life in small towns.

The story line of this novel consists of a series of conversations between Ray Bond and the other characters. Although he has more than one conversation with each character, each character becomes a prominent figure at different stages of the novel's development.

The Skeleton Man begins with Ray's Uncle Ed taking him to the deposit-box vault of the bank to show him the thirty thousand dollars he is giving Ray to finance his dream of going to law school. Uncle Ed swears Ray to secrecy concerning the source of the money, which becomes for Ray a gesture representative of his occasional, restrained, yet somehow special relationship with his uncle.

After Uncle Ed's apparent suicide, Ray has several difficult conversations with his mother. During one, he presses her to tell him precise details about his father's gambling, embezzlement of bank funds, divorce from his mother, and death in prison. Afterward, Ray reflects that his desire to become a lawyer has its source in some underlying sympathy for his father, much like his fondness for Uncle Ed. As later conversations with his mother make clear, however, he somehow cannot be completely open with her.

That night Ray agrees to drive to Atlantic City with his girlfriend, Laurie, but he refuses to go inside the casino with her. She becomes angry with him for his seemingly pointless obstinacy: He has not told her anything about his father's or his uncle's gambling. Later, as the strain of keeping his secret becomes apparent, Laurie becomes more exasperated by his refusal to confide in her.

Albert Dawson, the gangster who loaned the thirty thousand dollars to Uncle Ed, does not at first openly threaten Ray. Instead, he arranges isolated meetings with Ray and implies the threat with his knowledge of Ray's background and movements. When Ray seems determined to resist his pressure to return the money, Dawson makes the threat more pointed—first by shooting a resting cat with his gun equipped with a silencer and then by leading Ray to find Alice Cobb's corpse in the closet of her hotel room.

Although Ray agrees to return the money, Dawson decides that he must kill him as well to avoid being implicated in the death of Alice Cobb. Ray is saved by the intervention of Pete Wilson, a treasury agent who has been following Ray and whom Ray assumed was one of Dawson's hired guns.

Themes and Meanings

On the surface, the central conflict in *The Skeleton Man* is simple: Ray Bond can return the thirty thousand dollars his Uncle Ed borrowed from Albert Dawson and continue with his life; Ray can refuse to return the money and hope either that Dawson will decide that recovering the money is not worth the risk of harming Ray or that circumstances will somehow allow him to bring Dawson to justice. Ray's decision against immediately returning the money is, in part, a demonstration of his naïveté: It is also the result of a combination of complex motives and impulses that Ray does not have the luxury of sorting out.

Ray has ambivalent feelings toward both his parents. He resents his father for, in effect, abandoning him and his mother, yet he feels a sense of loss. Similarly, he appreciates his mother's sacrifices in rearing him properly and devotedly, yet he resents her hardened attitude about anything relating to his father. At the center of these conflicts, Uncle Ed has become a surrogate father for Ray—even though his visits are infrequent and Ray's mother dislikes him. Uncle Ed matches Ray's vague memories of his father, and so, when he asks Ray to accept the thirty thousand dollars in secrecy, Ray is affected by his uncle's gesture of love and confidence.

Ray refrains from confiding in his mother and Laurie concerning his dealings with Albert Dawson not because he is afraid of endangering them but because he does not believe that they will understand why he is compelled to keep his word to his uncle. Ray's apparent self-reliance is not merely the reflection of some foolhardy self-confidence. Rather, it is a mask for his confusion—in effect, a delay tactic that might allow circumstances to sort themselves out. Ray's error concerning Pete Wilson demonstrates the limitations of this tactic; Pete Wilson's arrival in time to shoot the gun out of Albert Dawson's hand demonstrates the terrible dangers in it.

Context

Jay Bennett's *The Skeleton Man* is his seventeenth novel, his eighth for young adults. All but two of his novels for young adults have been mystery-thrillers. The success of these novels in particular are reflected in the awards Bennett has received. He was the first to win the Mystery Writers of America's Edgar Allan Poe Award for Best Juvenile Mystery in successive years—in 1974 for *The Long Black Coat* (1973) and in 1975 for *The Dangling Witness* (1974).

In its characters, its narrative structure, its mood, and its themes, *The Skeleton Man* is representative of Jay Bennett's best work. Like Ray Bond, the central characters of Bennett's mysteries for young adults are usually older teenage boys who view themselves as loners and have difficulty confiding in family and friends. As in *The Skeleton Man*, the characterizations are usually more suggestive than exhaustive; succinct descriptions of settings and character movements establish an effective context for the long passages of constrained, edgy dialogue that are the most consistently remarkable element of his narratives. The reader is led to wonder what will be said next, and not only left to wonder what will happen next.

Reviewers often praise Jay Bennett's novels for their suspenseful plot structure, yet criticize them for sketchy characterizations. In *The Skeleton Man*, however, the suspense is built upon a series of small events to create a mood of genuine foreboding; the reader's interest lies more in Ray Bond's reaction to events than in the events themselves. Furthermore, the novel remains satisfying despite its convenient ending, which suggests that the most integral conflict is internal, and not external. The reader focuses upon Ray Bond's mixed loyalties, regrets, resentments, and self-doubts, and not merely the exchanges between Ray Bond and Albert Dawson. In

The Skeleton Man, Jay Bennett demonstrates how a simple surface can be made to suggest deeper issues that the reader cannot easily define.

Martin Kich

THE SLAVE DANCER

Author: Paula Fox (1923-   )
Type of plot: Historical fiction
Time of plot: 1840
Locale: New Orleans, a slave ship en route to Africa and back, and the Mississippi coast
Principal themes: Race and ethnicity, and social issues
First published: 1973; illustrated
Recommended ages: 10-13

Thirteen-year-old Jessie Bollier, kidnapped from his New Orleans home to provide music while slaves on a slave ship exercise, learns of human cruelty and of friendship and trust.

> *Principal characters:*
> JESSIE BOLLIER, a young fife player, who is kidnapped by the crew of *The Moonlight*
> CAPTAIN CAWTHORNE, the captain of *The Moonlight*, who is noted for cruelty to slaves and crew members
> NICHOLAS SPARK, the ship's mate, who is thrown overboard
> CLAY PURVIS, a sailor, whom Jessie admires
> CLAUDIUS SHARKEY, a sailor, who befriends Jessie
> BENJAMIN STOUT, a hard man, who replaces Spark as mate
> RAS, a young slave boy, whom Jessie befriends
> DANIEL, an escaped slave, who runs a stop on the underground railroad

The Story

The Slave Dancer, a Newbery Medal winner (1974), is the tale of *The Moonlight*, a slave ship that took part in a triangular pre-Civil War trade route. Ships on this route changed cargo three times: from rum and tobacco to slaves, from slaves to molasses, and from molasses to rum.

The human toll of the illegal slave trade is evident early in the story: Jessie Bollier, a thirteen-year-old fife player from New Orleans, is the victim of a "gangpressing." Returning from a late-night errand for his mother, Jessie is trapped and bound in a canvas tarp by sailors who, earlier that day, offered him pennies for a few notes from his fife. Captain Cawthorne's cruelty is apparent when he intimidates Jessie the first time they meet: He bites Jessie's ear so hard it bleeds. There are no slaves in the hold on the way to Africa, and it takes Jessie some time to realize what type of ship he is on. When he does, the reason for his own kidnapping becomes clear: His job is to play music, not to give the slaves pleasure, but to give them the exercise they will need to remain healthy and bring good prices when Captain Cawthorne sells them during the second cargo exchange.

Jessie's mother has taught him to feel more than average compassion for slaves, and he recoils more and more as he learns how they will be treated. Nothing—not even the cruelty of his shipmates to one another—prepares Jessie for what will occur when *The Moonlight* makes its first trade. In spaces too small to hold two dozen people, ninety-eight slaves are shackled below the deck. Thirty or more will die or be killed before they reach Cuba, where the second cargo exchange is scheduled to occur.

Not only will slaves die from sickness and mistreatment, but several of *The Moonlight's* crew will also die of these causes. When Nicholas Spark, the Mate, shoots a slave who becomes angry after a beating, the captain throws Spark overboard as an example to the other crew members. Because of the prices they bring, Captain Cawthorne values the lives of slaves more highly than he does the lives of his crew.

The slaves, however, become disposable when the stakes are the captain's freedom. During the second cargo trade, the captain and the Spaniard, a Cuban merchant who buys the ship's illegally captured slaves, are apprehended by an American Coast Guard ship on patrol. Healthy slaves by the dozen are quickly tossed into shark-filled waters so that the Captain and his business partner will not be caught.

Themes and Meanings

Throughout *The Slave Dancer*, Paula Fox explores the dark side of human nature, detailing the potential of human imperfection in one of its more extreme historical manifestations. Although she avoids some of the more graphic details of slave ship atrocities, careful characterization heightens the realism, as do the complex and lifelike interactions among characters. Captain Cawthorne is painted as evil; however, the character of the amoral Benjamin Stout is a bit more complex. Stout, who seldom seems to care how his deeds affect others, takes a liking to Jessie at first, but becomes spiteful when the young Jessie fails to reciprocate. Stout sets Jessie up for trouble as a result, an act consistent with his treatment of other crew members.

Clay Purvis and Claudius Sharkey are more complicated. Although they kidnapped Jessie and are responsible for his plight, they begin to care about him and earn his trust in return. The rough Purvis, to whom Jessie is drawn from the beginning, vows to help the discouraged boy find his way home safely; and Sharkey warns Benjamin Stout, who replaces Nicholas Spark as mate, that he and Purvis will track Stout down if Stout harms Jessie again. Jessie slowly builds a rapport with Ras, a slave boy about his age, with whom he has no way of speaking, even were it allowed.

Against a backdrop of cruelty to both slaves and shipmates, trust finds a tentative foothold. The dark side of human nature, then, is not this book's only focus. In fact, the tale is one of hope surviving adverse conditions, of confidence that compassion and trust can overcome ill will. This triumph is shown emphatically in the final section when Jessie helps the slave boy and both in turn are helped by an escaped slave. While she honors the risks just people will take on behalf of others, Fox illustrates fragility of trust in an unjust world.

Context

Paula Fox writes of the passage from innocence to moral knowledge, an initiation that results from suffering. *The Slave Dancer* reflects this preoccupation and offers readers an opportunity to develop a more refined understanding of right and wrong. Not only have Ras and the other slaves been torn from their families and tribes to make the cruel voyage that initiaties them into submission, but young Jessie also suffers a similar fate when stolen from his mother and "gangpressed" by the crew.

The story does not unfold along clear-cut lines of good and evil even though right and wrong are drawn with special clarity. Young people struggling to define themselves and their values should identify with Jessie and Ras as they are drawn, each into partial awareness and from complementary perspectives, of how power and greed breed inhumanity.

Knowledge of good and evil sets humans apart from the beasts, however; and coming to terms with truth is the basis of moral development. In a world where racial, sexual, and ethnic abuses tend to be sealed from historical view rather than acknowledged head on, books like *The Slave Dancer* expand awareness of a shared history of humiliation and shame, offer a point of departure for coming to terms with a painful past, and lead to the gradual disassembling of the walled-off parts of their mutual heritage that for many years have kept people apart.

Marie Wilson Nelson

SMOKY, THE COWHORSE

Author: Will James (1892-1942)
Type of plot: Adventure tale
Time of plot: The early twentieth century
Locale: Western Montana
Principal themes: Animals, nature, friendship, and education
First published: 1926; illustrated
Recommended ages: 10-13

A young colt gradually matures into an expert cow pony through the patient effort of a cowboy friend.

Principal characters:
SMOKY, a mouse-colored colt, who experiences a series of
adventures on the Western Range
CLINT, a kind and dedicated cowboy who trains Smoky to be the
most skilled cow pony in the country

The Story

Smoky, the Cowhorse depicts the lifelong education of a common range colt named Smoky. Foaled on a wild Montana hillside, Smoky is educated first by his loving "mammy," who teaches him how to survive in the wilderness by pawing for grass in the snow and avoiding dangerous "critters." As he runs free on the range, Smoky's early life is nearly idyllic. It is important to note that Smoky's contentment is derived mostly from the freedom of the open range, a factor that continues to influence Smoky throughout his life.

Later, when Smoky is nearly five years old, Clint assumes the task of training the buckskin gelding to be a working cow pony. At first, Smoky resists his "education," but because he is especially fond of Smoky, Clint painstakingly works with him until he is the best cow pony at the Rocking R Ranch. While herding cattle together on the range, Clint and Smoky develop a strong bond of friendship, and Smoky is happy to be Clint's favorite mount. Unfortunately, Smoky's happiness is shattered when a half-breed thief kidnaps him and takes him to Arizona. Unlike Clint, the half-breed is cruel and often beats Smoky to subdue him. Because Smoky must fight to defend himself, the half-breed indirectly teaches Smoky how to be vicious. Indeed, far away from the open range, Smoky's character slowly deteriorates until he turns into an uncontrollable "outlaw." Soon Smoky is sold to a rodeo, where he is billed as the ferocious "Cougar." For several years the Cougar bucks high in the rodeo ring, until his strength is spent. At that point Smoky is sold to a livery stable, where he is ridden by anyone who can afford the fee. After carrying hundreds of anonymous riders who all urge him to gallop, Smoky grows very tired, and his health begins to fail.

Long removed from the open range, Smoky's free-roaming spirit sinks to the bottom of his soul when he is turned over to a chicken-feed dealer and hitched to an open wagon. The cruel "black-whiskered" wagon driver likes to whip Smoky, who is now too weak and brokenhearted to resist. The once sleek and proud gelding is now a dull-eyed bag of bones. Sadly, the only lesson Smoky learns from the wagon driver is how to surrender his spirit. Thus, during a particularly harsh beating one day, Smoky lies down on the street for what appears to be the last time. Luckily, Clint suddenly appears on the scene and rescues Smoky from a certain death. Clint hopes to cure Smoky by shipping him home to the open range of Montana. There, Smoky gradually returns to good health. More important, however, Smoky's spirit is renewed, thereby allowing his heart "to come to life again."

Themes and Meanings

Like many other horse characters in American literature, Smoky symbolizes the high value that American culture places on individual freedom. *Smoky, the Cowhorse*'s central theme is the tension created when personal freedom is threatened by captivity. Born in the wilderness, Smoky desires to be free and shows his desire through certain actions and physical characteristics. When Smoky is young and roams free on the range, his body is sleek and vital. Later, when Smoky is captured by Clint, he signals his disenchantment by using his vitality to buck Clint to the ground the first time he tries to mount him. True to his own American ideals, Clint admires Smoky's resistance and labels his bucking "fighting for his rights." By allowing Smoky to keep some of his individual "rights," Clint maintains an agreeable balance for Smoky between freedom and outside control. Smoky flourishes under this arrangement, eventually developing into the best cowhorse on the ranch. When Smoky is robbed of his freedom, however, he responds first with defiance and later with reluctant submission. Smoky's broken-down state near the end of the book poignantly reflects his reaction to his long lack of freedom. It is important to note that when Smoky is finally revived, it is not through Clint's love, but through returning to the freedom of the Montana range.

Smoky's story also reflects humankind's desire to tame nature and to make use of its might. This universal human trait is most directly apparent when a person attempts to civilize a free-spirited animal, particularly a horse. In the case of Smoky, Clint corrals a free-ranging colt and ultimately trains him to labor as a cow pony. In American literature the characters who desire to conquer nature often display a cultural ambivalence toward their task of subjugation, despite their desire to harness nature's powers. Clint's admiration for Smoky's resistance to the reins, for example, reflects this ambivalence toward taming a once-wild animal. The ultimate illustration of Clint's ambivalence occurs near the end of the book, when Clint voluntarily returns Smoky to the wilderness instead of confining him in a stable.

Context

Smoky, the Cowhorse won the Newbery Medal in 1926 as the year's most distinguished contribution to American literature for children and has been in print continuously since 1926. *The New York Times* once referred to *Smoky, the Cowhorse* as "the *Black Beauty* of the cow country." Indeed, the two works share a theme of growth toward maturity which at least partially accounts for their classic status and lasting popularity among the young. Smoky, for example, passes through experiences resembling those of a young child: His mother rejects him, Clint trains or "schools" him, and he ultimately must learn to accept discipline and perform useful work. Young readers are probably attracted to *Smoky, the Cowhorse* because they can easily identify with Smoky as a youth suffering through the trials of growing up.

Without a doubt, *Smoky, the Cowhorse* is Will James's most successful book among all readers, young and old alike. Much of the book's success can be attributed to its authentic Western language, its realistic setting, and James's skillful illustrations. James wrote his book in the only words he knew, a jargon that is now referred to as "cowboy vernacular." According to James, his vernacular was simply the way "anybody would talk who got his raising and education outside, where the roofs is the sky and the floors prairie sod."

Smoky, the Cowhorse is set during the days before World War I, when most of the terrain from the Great Plains to the Pacific Ocean was livestock country. It was an era dominated by cattle, horses, and leather-clad cowboys, not the cowboys glamorized by Hollywood myth, but the actual working wranglers of the open range. James expertly re-creates this bygone era by meticulously recounting Clint and Smoky's everyday cattle-raising activities.

Finally, James placed *Smoky, the Cowhorse* in a special class among books about the West by including his own illustrations. Before becoming a writer James was an artist, and he originally sold his stories in order to make his artwork more marketable. As in the case of his writing, James's experiences of the range contribute to the detailed realism of his paintings.

Pamela Kay Kett

SO THE WIND WON'T BLOW IT ALL AWAY

Author: Richard Brautigan (1935-1984)
Type of plot: Psychological realism
Time of plot: The 1940's and August 1, 1979
Locale: Western Oregon
Principal themes: Emotions and death
First published: 1982
Recommended ages: 15-18

Through stream-of-consciousness memories, a man attempts to find meaning and purpose in his role in a shooting accident that occurred in his youth.

> Principal characters:
> THE BOY, the narrator, who tells his story from the perspective of the man he becomes
> A COUPLE, a man and woman who reconstruct their living room on the shore of a small pond where they fish every night
> A SAWMILL WATCHMAN, a middle-aged alcoholic man, who gives the boy his empty beer bottles
> A RECLUSE, an eccentric, much feared by other children but whom the boy befriends
> THE BOY'S MOTHER, an emotionally crippled woman, who merely tolerates her son
> DAVID, the popular, talented, and intelligent boy who is accidentally shot by the narrator

The Story

So the Wind Won't Blow It All Away is an absurd and nostalgic narrative of youth, imagination, and the end of innocence. The tale is an attempt by the narrator, an unidentified man, to come to terms with a shooting accident that occurred when he was twelve years old, an incident that has become the medium through which the narrator interprets his life.

Although the narrator writes from the present, the story is a series of jumbled flashbacks which interrupt the main plot, set on a summer evening in 1947, when the narrator, who is twelve, waits for a man and a woman to arrive at a local pond. Each evening, the couple has arrived in a pickup truck loaded with furniture which they then set up at water's edge to reconstruct a fully furnished parlor, complete with electric lamps that have been converted to kerosene. The couple habitually prepare a meal on their woodstove and spend the evening eating their dinner and fishing from their sofa.

While he is waiting for the couple, the boy visits an alcoholic sawmill watchman and, later, an old recluse who lives in a shack near the pond; both are isolated characters whose mysterious pasts intrigue the boy. Yet, as if walking to visit each of these characters again as an adult, the narrator also indulges in a series of flashbacks similar to the daydreams of youth. Many of these flashbacks focus on the narrator's prolonged fascination with the deaths of children: The reader is informed of the secret viewing of a child's funeral when the narrator is five years old, of the later death of a boyhood chum in a freak auto accident, and of a neighbor girl who succumbs to pneumonia. Other flashbacks detail the narrator's childhood loneliness and his dysfunctional relationship with his emotionally distant mother.

In one flashback, which foretells the emotional wreckage wrought by the shooting, the narrator tells how, in a childish attempt at self-therapy, he becomes obsessed with the hamburger he realizes he should have bought with the same money he spent on a box of bullets, one of which kills his young friend, David. The only character in the novel who is ever identified by name, David is a very popular, talented boy who befriends the narrator in secret because David is somewhat ashamed to be seen with him. Yet the narrator is the only person in whom David can confide his nameless dread of a vague future event. Toting his rifle and the newly purchased bullets, the narrator makes a rendezvous with David, who also packs a rifle. They bicycle together to an abandoned orchard to shoot rotten apples. While the boys are separated, David shoots at a pheasant but misses. Reflexively, the narrator also shoots at the pheasant, but he misses badly. As he soon discovers, his wide shot has mortally wounded David.

Despite a court acquittal, the incident leads to such social censure that the narrator's mother, who has finally found work as a waitress, is forced to move her family to a distant location. There, to save his sanity, the boy focuses obsessively on the hamburger which, he feels, would have saved him. Had he spent his money on the hamburger he craved when he bought the hollow-nosed .22 bullets, he would have spared himself unfathomable guilt and pain. With only the slightest awareness of her son's regret at not having bought a hamburger instead of the bullets, his mother acknowledges that indeed he should have bought the hamburger. The next day, the boy is able to end his obsession and burn the copious notes he has amassed in research on hamburgers throughout his long battle to save his sanity.

Finally, the narrator explains, he is able to release from his memory the man and woman who arrive in their pickup truck to fish at the pond on that summer evening months before the shooting. While the boy watches, they establish their living room and cook their supper, mourning loved ones they have lost. As the evening progresses, the narrator finds himself diminishing, "getting smaller and smaller . . . and more unnoticed . . . until I disappeared into the 32 years that have passed since then. . . ."

Themes and Meanings

Throughout *So the Wind Won't Blow It All Away*, author Richard Brautigan adheres to central themes of child death, guilt, psychological isolation, and the role of imagination. These themes are rendered by a character who is utterly self-absorbed, one who cannot interpret an incident or a relationship except as it can be linked to his own role in the accident that has molded his life.

The many digressions in the narrative, the flashbacks, are symptomatic of a mind probing painfully into the memories of a youth which, after the apocalyptic shooting, is now colored by the narrator's sense of guilt and his struggle with the conundrum of whether the actions leading to the shooting of David were deliberate or the product of chance. It is this struggle which leads him to his obsessive research on hamburgers, his imagined variations on what might have happened if he had bought a hamburger instead of the bullet that killed David, as well as his scrupulous recounting of child death that he has known or witnessed.

Yet, within this morbid recounting, the narrator struggles to recapture his youth, a time when his imagination served to render an incomprehensible world more sensible. Thus, the absurd man and woman who fish from their sofa come to represent the author's nostalgic recollection of the magical powers of the innocence of youthful imagination. The summer day in 1947, which is the point of reference for the entire novel, is spent waiting for them to appear—yet even here the imagination is not controlled, for the narrator wanders from recollection to recollection without volition. In fact, as the narrator points out, his imagination will not allow the couple to appear until he has thoroughly explored his youthful obsessions and the shooting. Yet the narrator never finds the answers he seeks. That he passively accepts the tyranny of his own imagination is the profound and central irony of the book.

Context

So the Wind Won't Blow It All Away is Richard Brautigan's last published novel. Two years after the book's appearance, its author committed suicide. The least successful of his published works, it sold fewer than fifteen thousand copies and was taken lightly, if not largely ignored, by the critics, in part because the book appears to be without the cynical humor of Brautigan's earlier fiction, notably *Trout Fishing in America* (1967) and *In Watermelon Sugar* (1968). Yet, *So the Wind Won't Blow It All Away* is quite similar to Brautigan's earlier novels in its anecdotal, conversational style; its use of eccentric characters; and its themes of escape. Like Brautigan's other late novel, *The Tokyo-Montana Express* (1980), *So the Wind Won't Blow It All Away* presents a darker rendering of Brautigan's earlier theme that the imagination provides a healthy escape from an unbearable reality. As the narrator is forced to relive interminable sequences of action leading to the shooting of his friend David, memory is a prison for the boy-become-a-man.

So the Wind Won't Blow It All Away is the first of Brautigan's works that is not directly engaged with American frontier dreams, except as these are posed through a youth spoiled by one fatal bullet. Also unique to the book is Brautigan's broad and valuable use of autobiographical experience. In part, the book recaptures much of Brautigan's nomadic and poverty-stricken childhood in Washington and Oregon with his mother, Lula Mary Keho Brautigan.

Brautigan's earlier works were widely popular, particularly with collegiate audiences. Many critics have suggested that by the time of publication of *So the Wind Won't Blow It All Away* in 1982, Brautigan's original audience had grown disenchanted with his style and themes, all of which had seemed so characteristic of the 1960's counterculture movement. Others, such as Edward Halsey Foster and Marc Chenetier, propose that Brautigan has been too quickly dismissed by critics and audiences alike. Despite its small audience and mixed reviews, *So the Wind Won't Blow It All Away* retains interest for those readers who seek a better understanding of an unconventional writer and his distinctive body of works.

William Hoagland

THE SOUL BROTHERS AND SISTER LOU

Author: Kristin Hunter (1931-   )
Type of plot: Social realism
Time of plot: The 1960's
Locale: A black ghetto in Philadelphia
Principal themes: Poverty, race and ethnicity, and social issues
First published: 1968
Recommended ages: 13-15

Fourteen-year-old Louretta helps her older brother obtain an abandoned church building for his printing business, talks him into letting young male gang members use part of it for a clubhouse, and reaps tragedy followed by unexpected glory.

Principal characters:
   LOURETTA HAWKINS, a talented black teenager who lives in an
      urban ghetto
   ROSETTA HAWKINS, her strict, religious mother
   ARNEATHA HAWKINS, her sister, an unwed mother
   WILLIAM HAWKINS, her older brother, the head of the household
   PHILIP "FESS" SATTERTHWAITE, a brilliant, owl-eyed poet and gang
      member
   JETHRO JACKSON, an epileptic tenor who also belongs to the
      Hawks gang
   OFFICER LAFFERTY, a white policeman who brutalizes Southside
      males
   CALVIN, an artist who is new in the neighborhood

The Story

   Boys, singing in an alley behind Louretta Hawkins' house, are threatened by a policeman named Lafferty, who regularly beats, arrests, and shoots black ghetto males. Lou helps them escape. She and her mother live in a five-room house with seven other people. Lou often takes care of the younger children, including sister Arneatha's out-of-wedlock baby. The whole family lives on brother William's post office salary, because their father has deserted them.

   William has been saving money to buy a printing press, and against his mother's wishes, he rents the vacant Baptist church building down the street to set up a printing business for supplemental income. Lou begs him to let the gang members use part of it as a clubhouse, to get them off the streets so that Lafferty cannot harass them.

   A blind blues singer, who has fallen on hard times, and some teachers come to help the boys with their music. Lou plays the piano for them. A new boy, the most talented member of the Hawks gang, is so intelligent that he goes to a special school, but he hates whites and leads a secret group that wants to overthrow the establishment. Called "Fess" for professor, he writes beautiful poetry and song lyrics. Another new boy in the neighborhood is Calvin, an artist who letters William's sign for him.

When the group holds a dance to raise money for musical instruments, Officer Lafferty and several other policemen force their way in to search the boys for weapons. They find nothing, but a young rookie overreacts and shoots the tenor, Jethro, whose fear has thrown him into an epileptic seizure. After Jethro is taken to the hospital and everyone is gone, William and Lou find weapons hidden in the piano.

Arneatha steals the dance profits and, when William insists that she pay the money back, runs away. Louretta is disillusioned and leaves school. She tries to give blood to help Jethro, but cannot. At a night meeting of Fess's secret group, her light skin and reddish hair are suspect, so she leaves and is followed by Fess, who tries to rape her. She bites him and runs home.

William is fired, and Calvin is seriously beaten by gang members, who blame him for tipping off police about a planned fight with the Avengers gang on the night of the dance. He is innocent, but is seriously hurt. When Jethro dies, Avengers team up with Hawks to write about the murder in their newspaper; Fess composes verses entitled "Lament for Jethro."

Lou thwarts the youths' planned ambush of Lafferty and plays the piano to get them singing. She takes Jethro's tenor part, and they work on music for Fess's poem. At the funeral, television news cameras record them as they sing "Lament for Jethro." The next day, promoters sign them up to make a record, which becomes a hit. William does well in his print shop, Officer Lafferty is suspended from the police force, and all ends happily.

Themes and Meanings

Soul is the central theme of *The Soul Brothers and Sister Lou*. The anger and rebellion of the 1960's are present, but the ugliness and poverty of an urban ghetto is softened by the warmth of family love and the support of friends. Religion is important as an inherent feature of the quality called "soul."

The plot is patterned after melodrama, with red-faced police officer Lafferty as the villain and members of the gang as the virtuous objects of his mistreatment. Officer Lafferty sets the action in motion.

Characterization in melodrama is subordinate to plot, so incidents such as Jethro's shooting are sensationalized. Political revolution is treated in a shallow way, but social revolution is a strong theme. The secret meeting Lou attends where the group considers her skin too light and so identifies her with the white establishment, and Fess's newspaper article about racist cops who have small brains and big feet are examples of the characters' social concerns. The behavior of Fess after he becomes successful shows a lack of commitment to the black cause. Instead of using his money in a political way, he drops his leadership role in the militant group and saves for college.

Romance plays a minor part in melodrama. The romantic interest in *The Soul Brothers and Sister Lou* is provided by Fess, whose romantic attentions to Lou are rebuffed, and Calvin, to whom Lou is attracted. Neither romance goes anywhere.

Other characteristics reminiscent of melodrama are the interspersed songs, the rhymed speaking that William does with Lou, and the happy ending with virtue triumphant. The villain gets exactly what he deserves, and the reader wants to cheer. The windfall or "accident of fortune" is provided when the singing group is discovered and becomes a success.

The novel's most powerful symbol is the piano. Its music brings all the characters together and unites them. It hides the gang's weapons, and it enables Lou to control events after Jethro's death.

The work might be called a tragicomedy, since it develops tragically but ends happily. It is optimistic and harks back to the turn of the century, when adolescent literature was marked by platitudinous morals—for example, hard work leads to material success, evil will be vanquished, honesty brings happiness, piety is rewarded. Such messages may have been hopeful ones to young blacks of the 1960's but are fantasy to later generations.

Context

This is the first juvenile book written by Kristin Hunter, who has also written several books and numerous poems, short stories, book reviews, and articles for adults. In addition, she wrote a play that was produced in Philadelphia and a CBS television documentary, *Minority of One*, for which she won a prize. Hunter also won the Book World Festival Award in 1973 and the Christopher Award in 1974.

The Soul Brothers and Sister Lou won awards from the National Council on Interracial Books for Children and the National Conference of Christians and Jews. It is an important book, because it was one of the first to give young people a true picture of ghetto life in American cities. It shows the beginnings of Afro-American pride in the race, which culminated in the slogan "Black Is Beautiful," and of the intensifying anger that led to a penetration of the wall of American segregation. Family values, speech patterns, habits, and religious practices are faithfully portrayed. The ending has been criticized as unrealistic, but when it is viewed as part of the melodrama formula the author chose as the pattern with which to tell her story, no other ending is possible.

Lou in the Limelight (1981) continues Louretta's story. It was written to satisfy readers' requests to know what happened to the characters.

Josephine Raburn

SOUNDER

Author: William H. Armstrong (1914-   )
Type of plot: Social realism
Time of plot: The early twentieth century
Locale: The rural South, probably western Virginia
Principal themes: Animals, education, family, race and ethnicity, and social issues
First published: 1969; illustrated
Recommended ages: 10-15

A man is sentenced to the chain gang for stealing food for his impoverished family. His faithful son and dog wait patiently for the man's return over the next six years.

Principal characters:
THE BOY, a sensitive ten-year-old, who learns to endure life's
unexpected cruelties
THE BOY'S FATHER, a black sharecropper who, unwilling to see
his family go hungry, steals food for them and is caught and
sentenced to prison
THE BOY'S MOTHER, kind, loving, and long-suffering, who
struggles to keep her family together when her husband is
imprisoned
SOUNDER, the dog, a mixture of Georgia redbone hound and
bulldog, maimed during his master's capture

The Story

In terms of its setting and subject matter, *Sounder* could perhaps be described as a protest novel; yet the story is told with such delicacy and control that it transcends mere protest. *Sounder* is at once an animal fable of sorts—a story of the proverbial dog as man's best friend—and the story of the coming-of-age of a small boy who faces a multitude of hardships. Furthermore, *Sounder* examines certain realities of being black and poor in rural America during the early part of the twentieth century.

After the father has been caught and imprisoned for stealing a ham and pork sausages to feed his hungry family, the responsibilities of the man of the house fall to his ten-year-old son. The young boy cares for the younger children and shoulders most of the chores around the house, while his mother tries to keep food on the table by selling shelled walnuts in town. When the father is put to work on a road gang, the boy goes in search of him day after day, hoping to bring home word of his father's well-being. In the meantime, the boy waits patiently for the return of the family's beloved dog, Sounder, who, severely wounded during the arrest of his master, has run off, either to die or to heal himself.

During the course of the six-year period covered by the novel, the family suffers numerous heartbreaks but remains together as a family unit, hopeful that someday the father will rejoin them. One day the boy meets a kindly schoolmaster who invites him to attend school in town and work in exchange for room and board. This is one of the boy's happiest moments, and one of the family's greatest triumphs. Also, Sounder returns, having healed himself in the woods, but still carrying the scars from the sheriff deputy's gunshot. Gone, too, is Sounder's deep, melodious bark, but he has nevertheless returned to wait for his master.

One hot August day, the boy and his mother spy a figure limping toward them in the distance. To them the figure is unrecognizable, but Sounder immediately recognizes him as his long-lost master, and, regaining his voice in a loud bark of its former richness, limps out to welcome his master home. The father is now paralyzed on the left side from being caught in a blast of dynamite, and the remainder of his prison sentence has been commuted because of the extent of his injuries. The family is reunited, although briefly, for the father soon dies, as does Sounder, and the boy returns to town to finish school.

Themes and Meanings

Numerous themes abound in *Sounder*. First, because the story is set in the rural South during a time when the sharecropping system exploited many black families in particular, the story is a gentle but firm protest against conditions that force a man to resort to thievery simply to feed his family. Furthermore, there is mild protest against the ruthless treatment of the father during the arrest by the white sheriff and his deputies, and against the lengthy prison sentence, which was far too harsh for the crime.

On another level, *Sounder* is a story of strength of family and the family's eventual triumph over great odds. The story also posits that everyone must undergo his or her own personal tragedies and struggles; this theme is underscored and made more poignant by the lyrics of the song, "That Lonesome Road," a recurring metaphor for life. Furthermore, *Sounder* suggests that life is indeed a journey. This theme is informed by a number of biblical accounts, especially the story of Joseph. On yet another level, *Sounder* is the story of a dog, faithful to the end to his master, a modern version of the classical story of Argus, the faithful canine companion to Odysseus. In *Sounder*, the dog sets the example of friendship and devotion that the author seems to want his readers to emulate.

Finally, it is important to note that none of the human characters is named. This technique rescues the novel from mere protest and sentimentality and helps to establish certain of the themes as universal.

Context

Sounder is William Armstrong's first novel for young readers. Having spent a career in education and publishing scholarly matters, Armstrong has turned to his own experience as a child growing up in Lexington, Virginia, as the chief motivation for writing the story. The author, who is white, writes of having been greatly influenced by an old black man, who was both teacher and friend in his community. *Sounder*, according to Armstrong, is this man's story.

The book's chief importance lies in its treatment of its various themes. It concludes, especially through the character of the boy, that the good things in life can be achieved through faith, determination, and persistence. Furthermore, there is a timeless quality to *Sounder*, for even though the story is set during a particular era, it holds that life's tragedies and triumphs are ageless and applicable to all people, in all places, at all times. This universal quality probably accounts not only for *Sounder*'s original acclaim but for its perennial popularity with readers, especially young readers, and critics as well. *Sounder* is an enduring work of classic proportions.

Warren J. Carson

STEFFIE CAN'T COME OUT TO PLAY

Author: Fran Arrick (Judie Angell, 1937-   )
Type of plot: Social realism
Time of plot: The 1970's
Locale: Clairton, Pennsylvania, and New York City
Principal themes: Coming-of-age, emotions, sexual issues, and social issues
First published: 1978
Recommended ages: 13-15

Fourteen-year-old Stephanie Ruff is lured into prostitution by a handsome pimp who promises to protect her but instead uses and abandons her when trouble arrives.

Principal characters:
STEPHANIE "STEFFIE" RUFF, a pretty but naïve girl from a
    Pennsylvania mining town, who falls in love with a pimp and
    his offers of security and fancy clothes
FAVOR, a New York pimp, who lures Steffie into prostitution
GLORY, Favor's "Main Lady," who is an experienced prostitute
BRENDA, Steffie's New York roommate, who is another young
    prostitute
CAL YARBRO, a police officer, who helps Steffie escape city life
ED FELCHER, Yarbro's younger partner

The Story

Steffie Can't Come Out to Play begins with fourteen-year-old Stephanie Ruff's good-bye note to her family, who, she believes, cannot understand her desire to leave and seek fame as a model in New York. The conflict begins as soon as Steffie steps off the train in New York. She experiences her first taste of fear but is then approached by the handsome and understanding Favor, who assures her that she will be safe if she goes home with him. Steffie's desire for independence and her dream of becoming a model conflict with her desire for security, love, pretty things, and someone to take care of her.

From the start readers see through Favor, the smooth-talking pimp; they also foresee the jealousy that erupts among the women who work for Favor. It takes Steffie longer to catch on, however; and by the time she does, she has convinced herself that she loves Favor, that he loves her, and that she will marry him. The situation is ironic, however, because Favor is honest with her: He promises to protect her and give her a chance to enjoy nice things; he never lies to her. Favor does not offer her drugs, nor does he touch her sexually, until she has slept with other men. It is Steffie who reads love and marriage into Favor's words. It is her own dependence and self-deception that bring her rapidly under Favor's control.

Feeling safe and protected in Favor's expensive rooms, Steffie suspects that she is not unique when another young woman named Brenda telephones. Favor's actions with other women confirm Steffie's fears, but she clings to her fantasy of marrying him. Once she acquiesces to Favor's insistence that she make money to pay for her fancy new clothes and jewelry, however, Steffie is quickly removed from Favor's rooms. He places her under the instructive wing of Glory, who is known as his "Main Lady" on the street; it is her responsibility to make certain Steffie understands the pecking order. Steffie moves further from her dream when Favor moves her into Brenda's tiny apartment. Dependent and anxious to please her increasingly distant protector, Steffie works harder. Her success increases the tension between her and Glory, until she finds herself set up with a client who slips a powerful dose of LSD into her drink.

Themes and Meanings

In this modern, working-class Cinderella tale, Fran Arrick paints a grim but not entirely hopeless picture of a situation common to many runaways: They become prostitutes because they have few skills with which to support themselves. At home, while her parents worked, Steffie took care of the house by cooking, washing, scrubbing, and caring for the other children. They lived in a Pennsylvania mining town, so one of her duties was wiping coal soot from walls and furniture. One difference between Steffie and Cinderella, however, was that Steffie never lacked love.

Developing themes more fully than characters, Arrick shows Steffie's gradual awakening from innocence. Blame falls squarely on Steffie's conflicting dreams—one to be taken care of, the other to have a career—both fairly common in a changing society that is still uncertain where its values lie.

Although Steffie is innocent, she cannot be considered a victim; although Steffie is a prostitute, she cannot be considered bad or evil. And although she can be viewed as a victim of sexual and economic oppression, Steffie is ultimately responsible for the choices she makes. Conditioned to want a glamorous career, past experience offers her little knowledge of how to turn that dream into an attainable goal. Bombarded by television advertisements and features in fashion magazines, Steffie naïvely believes that her beauty will make her rich, and that a handsome prince exists who will transport her from poverty to luxury.

Context

This story is consistent with the body of Arrick's work which includes other novels about social issues: *Tunnel Vision* (suicide) in 1980, *Chernowitz!* (racism) in 1981, and *God's Radar* (religious fundamentalism) in 1983. All show young protagonists struggling to define their identities while attempting to cope with the sometimes overwhelming problems of daily life.

Taking its place in the realistic tradition, this book explores the problems of teenage runaways, forcing Arrick to deal with an issue all young adult writers face: How much explicit detail should an author include? Arrick handles sexual matters discreetly. She develops emotional themes, describing with intensity and detail Steffie's situation and the pain she brings upon herself.

For young readers, Arrick demystifies a profession about which information has often been withheld. She does not portray Steffie as unredeemable, but she puts responsibility on Steffie herself. Hometown flashbacks show Steffie as a hardworking, innocent teenager. The unflappable Officer Yarbro draws attention to her youth and innocence (symbolized by the bear she carries when times get rough). Steffie has an unexpected effect on the seasoned Yarbro: He intervenes when Favor abandons Steffie, in effect giving Steffie a second chance. Whether she now deals realistically with her choices is a question readers must decide for themselves.

Marie Wilson Nelson

THE STORY CATCHER

Author: Mari Sandoz (1901-1966)
Type of plot: Historical fiction
Time of plot: The late nineteenth century
Locale: Nebraska and other parts of the Great Plains
Principal themes: Coming-of-age, family, and race and ethnicity
First published: 1963; illustrated
Recommended ages: 13-18

Young Lance, son of Good Axe, goes through many trials and adventures as he tries to find his place in the Sioux tribe.

> *Principal characters:*
> YOUNG LANCE, a young brave whose differences make it difficult for the men of the tribe to accept him
> GOOD AXE, a respected warrior and family leader, the father of Young Lance
> SUN SHIELD, the village leader
> LITTLE REE, a young Pawnee whom Young Lance finds and brings home with him
> FEATHER, Young Lance's second mother
> BLUE DAWN, the young maiden of Young Lance's choice
> CEDAR and
> DEER FOOT, friends Young Lance's age, with whom he shares adventures

The Story

Young Lance, a Sioux Indian lad and a member of Sun Shield's village who lives on the Great Plains, has great difficulty living by the philosophy of his people. The Sioux are taught from childhood that doing things impulsively without thinking of the good of the family and the tribe is a selfish way of life, not to be tolerated. Young Lance, however, is continually straying to find what lies beyond the hill, to go back and look at danger in more detail.

Once, for example, he brought home a young Ree, a little Pawnee boy. (Rees are a branch of the Pawnee Nation, enemies of the Sioux.) Young Lance went back to a battleground where they had fought and found the little Ree, about five years old, naked, hungry, and hiding. Without thinking about the burden to his family tribe— that the widow of the warrior killed in the battle might choose to kill the little one to avenge her husband, as she has a right to do—Lance captured the Ree and took him back to camp. Jumping Moose, leader of the scouting party, told him, "You are a leaky kettle in which to cook the soup of responsibility!"

Several times in the growing years, Young Lance must be punished for his impulsiveness, but he learns independence and develops keen senses of tracking and scouting, which proves valuable to his people. He wins some favor, while having to remain behind when a hunting party leaves one spring, by trapping and killing a bald eagle with only his hands. The span of the eagle's wings is more than six feet.

The young Sioux's greatest talent is in observing, drawing, and painting pictures of events in the life of the tribe. He paints on animal hides given to him by Feather. At first they have no value, but as his talents develop, he shows them and recounts the story that goes with the picture. The old historian of the village criticizes him until he learns to be accurate.

On his first buffalo hunt, he kills three buffalo. It is in the fall of the year, when the village is trying to kill and preserve by drying and making wasna for the winter. (Wasna is a food made by grinding dried meat and mixing in some dried berries and tallow.) They need hides for their beds, their tents, and their robes, as well as the meat for food. Young Lance is proud to be able to present meat to his second mother, Feather. (Boys of the tribe have second mothers, who chose them as babies. The blood mother is not allowed to speak directly to a son after he is seven years of age because by doing so she ties him to her too closely. The second mother is free to express the care that is denied to the blood mother.)

Young Lance wants to win the favor of Blue Dawn, a popular young maiden of the village, but he is too shy to court her, as others have done. Winning her hand and learning to draw the pictures that will tell the history of his people are motivations for many of his adventures. The rigors of survival for himself and his people demand many sacrifices. Speaking to Paint Maker, Young Lance tells of his dreams about making pictures and his hopes to see things as if from a high hill and into tomorrow. Days later, Paint Maker looks at some of Young Lance's pictures and says that he must learn to observe things in the natural world and record the wisdom of Mother Earth.

After many adventures and wounds, winters, battles, and white men's measles, Lance finally hears Good Axe and Paint Maker chant his deeds and declare his new name, Story Catcher, to the tribe. He is honored and determined to live up to the honor.

The Story Catcher depicts the harshness of life on the plains before the comforts brought by civilization. Young readers can identify with Young Lance, who is a very believable character, and feel pride when he finally wins recognition and a name from his people.

Themes and Meanings

Only through dedication and loyalty to the village are the Sioux of the story able to survive. The good of the group is valued above individual wants. The Indians in Mari Sandoz's story care for one another with loving concern shown in very humble ways. The older women and men teach the younger ones the customs and train them in ways of hunting, fighting, and endurance. The dedication of the men to the family and to their children is clear.

Sandoz also understands the emotional reactions of the young people. Story Catcher is taught independence and interdependence, because only through both can he and his people survive the harsh winters on the plains. Sandoz makes the young reader understand and admire the courage of the Sioux, giving meaning to their sense of values and regard for life. Her story awakens a sense of adventure and allows young readers to identify with people of another age and of a different culture.

Context

Expert, painstaking research went into the writing of *The Story Catcher*. Sandoz was born in the Sand Hills cattle country of northwest Nebraska. The rigors of land and climate about which she wrote were a part of her nature, but her knowledge went beyond experience. She said, "When I was nearly 14 my brother and I had to dig our cattle out of the snowdrift of a May blizzard, and by night I was snowblind, totally blind for around six weeks. Then I discovered I had only one eye left. But it's very useful to me, so it doesn't matter." In *The Story Catcher*, Sandoz shows that same kind of determination and outlook toward life to Young Lance. He does what must be done and is thankful for all blessings.

In *The Cattlemen of the Rio Grande Across the Far Marias* (1958), a nonfiction book written for an adult audience, Sandoz shows similarly thorough and extensive research. The same is true of *Cheyenne Autumn* (1953), the story of the heroic attempt to preserve the Northern Cheyenne Indians from disease and starvation. This novel was adapted for film in 1964.

Sandoz calls upon her own experiences for the descriptions of the plains. One critic, W. H. Hutchinson, speaks of "the singing voice and nobility of soul this woman has brought to her writing." Sandoz depicts the spiritually rich, physically stark life of the Plains Indians, showing a complex, mystic people facing life with dignity and faith in their customs. To understand the evolution of culture among the Native Americans and their contributions to the history and to the culture of all Americans, *The Story Catcher* is a story to cherish.

Mary Joe Clendenin

THE STORY OF A BAD BOY

Author: Thomas Bailey Aldrich (1836-1907)
Type of plot: Domestic realism
Time of plot: The first half of the nineteenth century
Locale: Rivermouth (Portsmouth, New Hampshire)
Principal themes: Coming-of-age, friendship, family, and nature
First published: 1869, serial; 1870, book; illustrated
Recommended ages: 13-15

Tom Bailey, a young boy, returns to his native town of Rivermouth to be educated and to live in his grandfather's house. At school, he makes a number of friends with whom he shares various adventures, most of them happy ones.

> *Principal characters:*
> TOM BAILEY, a lively boy, who lives with his grandfather
> CAPTAIN NUTTER, Tom's kindly maternal grandfather, a veteran of the War of 1812
> MISS ABIGAIL, Captain Nutter's unmarried sister, who supervises his household
> KITTY COLLINS, a good-natured maid
> PEPPER WHITCOMB, Tom's schoolmate and best friend

The Story

Narrated by Tom Bailey, *The Story of a Bad Boy*, though realistic in tone, nevertheless sounds the kind of sustained note of nostalgia that one would expect to find in a work that is largely autobiographical and that deals with a chiefly happy childhood. At eighteen months of age, Tom had been taken from his native Rivermouth to New Orleans, where his father had gone into banking. Now that it is time to begin his schooling, his parents take him to live in his Grandfather Nutter's house back in Rivermouth. In the large, cheery old Nutter house, Tom is made to feel at home by his grandfather, the maid Kitty Collins, and Captain Nutter's unmarried sister, Miss Abigail. An additional solace in times of homesickness is Gypsy, the almost humanly wise and sympathetic pony that Tom's father had shipped from New Orleans for his son's use.

Enrolled by his grandfather in the academy, or Temple Grammar School, Tom quickly makes friends among his schoolmates, though Tom must later beat a bully named Conway. Tom starts a theater in his grandfather's barn, but an accidental injury to Pepper Whitcomb, though not serious, brings an end to the theater. One Fourth of July, Tom and his friends drag a long-idle mail coach from its barn into a roaring bonfire. Caught by the watchmen, they are apprehended and locked up. They escape but are made to compensate the owner of the coach.

A highlight in Tom's life is his induction into the Rivermouth Centipedes, to which many of his schoolmates belong. The induction occurs following a comical though frightening initiation. Somewhat later, in winter, Tom and his friends at the academy turn Slatter's Mill into Fort Slatter and engage in a prolonged snowball fight with boys from another part of town. When, contrary to their own rules, both sides put marbles in the snowballs and serious injuries ensue, the constabulary and citizenry demolish the fort and end the fight.

About a year later, a boat puts into Rivermouth, and Tom discovers that one of its sailors is Sailor Ben, whom he brings home with him and who turns out to be Kitty Collins' long-lost husband. A tearful but happy reunion ensues. Now an adolescent, Tom is intrigued by the girls at a nearby all-female academy, but his mild flirtations come to nothing. Not until his grandfather's nineteen-year-old niece comes to visit does Tom know love, and when the young man who comes to fetch her away is identified as her fiancé, Tom is inconsolable for a long time.

Gloomy news arrives from New Orleans: His father's banking business is folding, and cholera is raging in the city. Longing to be reunited with his parents, Tom runs away by train to Boston, intending to ship from there to New Orleans as a cabin boy. Aware of the boy's plan, Grandfather Nutter orders Sailor Ben to shadow the boy and bring him back. When the two do return home, Tom learns that his father has died of cholera. Since the family has experienced financial ruin, Tom can no longer think of going off to college. Instead, he accepts the offer of an uncle in New York of a job in a counting house. Tom's boyhood days are behind him forever.

Themes and Meanings

The Story of a Bad Boy is an account of a boy's coming-of-age. After a brief history of his life in New Orleans, Tom tells the reader of what it is like to grow up in a relatively small town, where a boy is close to nature. In fact, a number of episodes are tied to the seasons. For example, one comical episode takes place in summer, on the Fourth of July. Another episode concerns the snow fort and snowball fight; Binny Wallace's death in a boating accident is the next important episode, and that occurs in spring. Tom's infatuation with his grandfather's niece occurs in the warm days of September.

The magic and beauty of a snowfall and the lure of the sea for the boys of Rivermouth are lovingly described. The author has a strong sense of place, which is firmly linked with the importance of family and friends. Captain Nutter's affection for his grandson is always evident, and when he has to discipline Tom, as in the Fourth of July episode, it is clear to the reader that the old man has in no way lost his love for the boy. When Tom mopes following the departure of his first love, Pepper Whitcomb's concern for his friend's well-being is apparent, and the universal affection that Binny Wallace enjoys is what makes the description of his death so moving.

Context

The Story of a Bad Boy is in the tradition of "bad boy" books, a fact that a number of critics have noted. Thomas Bailey Aldrich's book was preceded by Thomas Hughes's English work, *Tom Brown's Schooldays* (1857), and followed in America by Mark Twain's *The Adventures of Tom Sawyer* (1876) and *The Adventures of Huckleberry Finn* (1884). Also to be mentioned are George Wilbur Peck's *Peck's Bad Boy and His Pa* (1883), William Dean Howells's *A Boy's Town* (1890), and, in the twentieth century, Booth Tarkington's *Penrod* (1914) and J. D. Salinger's *The Catcher in the Rye* (1951).

Unlike Twain's Huckleberry Finn or Salinger's Holden Caulfield, however, Tom Bailey does not feel alienated from society; he is not trying, consciously or unconsciously, to develop a moral code of his own—one which might conflict with that followed by the society in which he lives—and he is not aware of any hypocrisy in the people around him, as Huckleberry Finn and Holden Caulfield are. *The Story of a Bad Boy* continues to be of interest because of its ability to evoke vividly what boyhood was like in the early years of the twentieth century and because of the clear picture Aldrich paints of a younger and more innocent America.

Seymour Eichel

THE STORY OF THE TREASURE SEEKERS
Being the Adventures of the Bastable Children in Search of a Fortune

Author: E. Nesbit (1858-1924)
Type of plot: Adventure tale
Time of plot: The late nineteenth century
Locale: Lewisham, England
Principal themes: Family, poverty, and social issues
First published: 1899; illustrated
Recommended ages: 10-13

When the family fortunes fall, the six Bastable children take it upon themselves to restore them. Their adventures are amusing, warm, serious, and sometimes dangerous, but always lively.

> *Principal characters:*
> DORA, the eldest child, who tries to take care of the other children
> OSWALD, an intelligent child who conceives the idea of looking for treasures and excels in Latin
> DICKY, who is good at math and wants everything precisely thought out and stated
> ALICE, a twin, the adventuresome sister
> NOEL, her twin brother, a poet
> HORACE OCTAVIUS, the youngest child
> ALBERT-NEXT-DOOR, the unfortunate child who lived next door
> ALBERT'S UNCLE, a novelist, the friend and protector of the Bastable children

The Story

The Story of the Treasure Seekers is a series of stories told by Oswald Bastable. Each one is filled with realistic mischief, subtle humor, and the sometimes pathetic, sometimes charming adventures of this nineteenth century family. Some of the events seem to be based on childhood remembrances of the author; others are perhaps from her wide readings and her fertile imagination.

A series of events leads the children to believe that they need to restore the fallen fortunes of the Bastable House. First, the mother dies. Then, while the father is very ill, his business partner leaves with the business' money. The servants leave, the family silver is gone, and there are no more fancy dinner parties. The children no longer attend boarding schools, bill collectors are constantly at the door, and a policeman leaves a warrant for their father. At this point, the children decide to look for treasure. Their search begins in the garden. Albert-next-door helps them to dig.

The ground caves in on him, and Albert's uncle gets him out. After telling the children that no treasure more than a half-crown has ever been found in the yard, Albert's uncle finds two half-crowns that he divides among the children.

The children next decide to become detectives. Alice thinks that burglars may be in the house next door because the neighbors are supposed to be away. Oswald looks through a window, falls, and makes enough noise to alert the "burglars." The "burglars" are really the people next door, who are pretending to be gone to the seaside.

The next scheme the children decide to undertake is for Noel to sell his poetry to the newspapers. On their way to London, he and Dora meet Mrs. Leslie. She befriends them and gives them two shillings. Dora and Noel try several newspaper offices before they locate an editor who will talk with them. The editor pays Noel one pound seven for the poetry.

They next plan an ambush on the Heath. Their victim turns out to be Albert. They send a ransom note to Albert's mother. Albert's uncle pays an eightpence ransom for his nephew after he explains the seriousness of kidnapping, even in play. Albert's uncle then suggests that journalism could provide a permanent money source. The children edit a newspaper. Instead of selling their newspapers, the *Lewisham Recorder*, they give them away. Next, after reading about a money-lender, Mr. Rosenbaum, the children decide that he must be a generous benefactor. He lends them fifteen shillings and sells a bottle of perfume to them, but charges a very high rate of interest. Even though they do not get money, they get their father's attention after Mr. Rosenbaum contacts him. The children continue to try new schemes for making money, but these plans inevitably fail or get them into trouble.

The last episode of the story involves the children's befriending the "poor Indian Uncle" who visits the family. They serve rabbit and currant pudding when he comes to dinner and recount their efforts to restore the Bastables' fortune. Because the children believe him to be very poor, they offer him what little money they have. This selfless offer brings treasures to the family. First, Uncle brings gifts to them, and then he extends an invitation to a party. Finally, he offers to share his home.

Themes and Meanings

Beginning when Oswald Bastable is about ten years old and continuing for several months, *The Story of the Treasure Seekers* is a series of stories of family, poverty, and social issues. The central theme is the love of family, as portrayed by the Bastable children. This theme is developed through the leadership of Oswald and the boldness of Alice, the children. They live in a home with an absent father and a household helper who appears to have little to do with caring for the children. They appear tattered, torn, and generally unkempt. With the occasional exception of Albert's uncle, there is no constant adult role model or authority figure to guide the children. Those adults who do appear during their search for riches are either unscrupulous or unconcerned with the general well-being of the children. Still, although the children meet with failure after failure, their sense of loyalty to one another and their trust in adults never falters. They continue to look after one another, allow a rather loosely defined democratic code of decision making, and thoroughly enjoy each adventure.

Even though Arthur-next-door is not one of the Bastables, the children include him in most of their adventures that occur at home. They also stake a claim to his uncle. Of the adult characters, Albert's uncle is dominant. He supports them in their efforts to find a fortune, and he also is the only guiding force in shaping their characters, offering assistance in their journalism adventures. When Albert is "buried" in the garden, it is his uncle who comes to the rescue. Later, when Noel gets very ill, it is Albert's uncle to whom the children send a telegram. Nevertheless, Albert's uncle is the only adult who plays a positive role, and he is not a central character.

Deception forms a subtheme that ties the children's adventures together: The neighbors only pretend to be away on vacation. Deception greets the children's second attempt to secure money; on their way to sell Noel's poetry, they meet a patron of the arts who reads Noel's poetry, gives them the name of an editor, and two shillings. When the editor pays one pound seven for the poetry, it is the second time during the adventure that adults have placated the children. During the next adventure, they learn of class distinction when they are not welcome to play with a princess. Later, Mr. Rosenbaum lends them money at a very high rate and then sells them perfume. Equally abusive are the butcher, the lady from the orphanage, the minister, and a burglar. The children get no real help until they befriend an old Indian.

Despite these mishaps, the Bastables are not innocent victims. During their adventures, they participate in theft, in selling goods not belonging to them, in kidnapping, in the illegal sale of wine, and in the production of quack medicine. Yet all of these ill-fated undertakings are well-intentioned, motivated by the love for one another that the Bastable children share. They know that they have no money and no one to care for them, but as long as they have one another, they are content.

Context

The Story of the Treasure Seekers appears to be have been written during a turning point in the career of E. Nesbit. Her extensive writings include several genres—poetry, short stories, novels, retold stories of William Shakespeare and English history—but her venture into children's books blossomed with the appearance of *The Story of the Treasure Seekers*. It was not only well received by readers, but also one of her first profitable works. Moreover, beginning with this book, Nesbit's writing began to exhibit greater discipline and organization, and in it she used dialogue in an entirely new style. *The Story of the Treasure Seekers* continues to be listed among favorites of children. Other novels for which Nesbit is known are *The Woodbegoods* (1901), *The Phoenix and the Carpet* (1904), *Five Children and It* (1902), and *The Railway Children* (1906).

Anna Hollingsworth Hovater

STRANGER IN A STRANGE LAND

Author: Robert A. Heinlein (1907-1988)
Type of plot: Science fiction
Time of plot: An unspecified but not too distant future, after World War III
Locale: The Poconos and other locations in the United States; and Heaven
Principal themes: Religion, sexual issues, and politics and law
First published: 1961
Recommended ages: 15-18

Valentine Michael Smith, born on Mars and reared by Martians, is brought to Earth by a rescue party when he is in his early twenties, bringing with him many of the beliefs and powers of the ancient Martian race. He spends several years learning the ways of Earthlings and eventually forms a religious cult that is condemned as immoral and blasphemous.

> *Principal characters:*
> VALENTINE MICHAEL "MIKE" SMITH, a human born on Mars and reared by Martians
> JUBAL E. HARSHAW, a wealthy physician, author, lawyer, and philosopher who becomes a father figure to Mike
> GILLIAN "JILL" BOARDMAN, a nurse who becomes Mike's constant companion and his lover
> BEN CAXTON, a newspaper columnist who becomes a member of Mike's cult

The Story

Valentine Michael Smith was born the illegitimate son of members of the first Earth expedition to Mars. After his parents die, he is reared by Martians until a search party discovers him and brings him to Earth. Because of his heritage and birthplace, Mike is considered to be the sole owner of the planet Mars and therefore the richest man on Earth. This identity makes him valuable to the political system known as the Federation. Newspaper columnist Ben Caxton fears for Mike's life and begins questioning the reasons behind his sequestration in a heavily guarded hospital room. Ben's girlfriend, nurse Gillian Boardman, befriends Mike and kidnaps him from the hospital. When Ben mysteriously disappears, Jill and Mike flee to the secluded home of Jubal Harshaw.

Mike displays unusual talents of discorporation, telekinesis, telepathy, and total recall of what he has heard or read. He performs an ancient Martian ritual of water sharing, which bonds the participants together in a lifelong brotherhood of unconditional, irrevocable love and trust.

Mike and Jill remain at Jubal's paradisiacal home until Mike feels ready to see more of the world. The two travel across the country working odd jobs, keeping Mike's identity secret. Mike becomes fascinated by Earthlings' religions and finally forms a cult of his own. As in the popular Fosterite religion, members are given a chance for advancement into the elite inner circle made up of water brothers. Those in this select inner circle are taught the ancient Martian powers and learn to worship themselves and one another as God. They live together as one family, devoid of jealousy, malice, or unhappiness. They believe in free and open sex.

Before long, the public becomes aware of Mike's new religion and judges it a threat to and a mockery of the Fosterite faith. Mike's doctrine that all humans are divine is deemed blasphemous and the sexual sharing immoral, and Mike is soon arrested and imprisoned. The church is burned down, but Mike teleports the members of the inner circle to a church-owned hotel to await his return. Before long Jubal and his house guests are informed of Mike's arrest, and they join their water brothers at the hotel. Mike escapes from the jail and appears among them.

Mike confides to Jubal his recent discovery that he has been an unwitting spy for the Martians, sent to determine whether Earth should be destroyed for its own sake. He grows doubtful about his teachings and the future of Earthlings, but is then able to regain his vision. He presents himself to an angry mob outside the hotel, smiles at them, and opens his arms, telling them, "I love you, Thou Art God." The crowd hurls rocks, bricks, and bullets at him as he discorporates.

His water brothers make a broth from his remaining body parts to "grok" him fully. They do not believe that Mike is truly dead; rather, they are calm and almost joyous over what has happened.

Mike goes to heaven and becomes Archangel Michael. There he joins the founder of the Fosterite religion and his successor, and together they monitor the universe. Members of the inner circle of Mike's church disperse to various parts of the country to continue Mike's teachings. Jubal begins work on a new book, *A Martian Named Smith*.

Themes and Meanings

In *Stranger in a Strange Land* Robert A. Heinlein uses Jubal Harshaw as his mouthpiece to present a satirical and perhaps somewhat cynical view of religion, politics, and morality in contemporary society. Harshaw's explicit cultural criticism is paralleled and dramatized by Mike's actions, which provide positive alternatives to these negative social institutions. Mike represents the ideal or utopian norm to which socialized human behavior can be contrasted. He is the unblemished, unadulterated clean slate, the natural state of all humans if not warped by society, especially by political and religious institutions.

Mike's role as a semiallegorical figure is implicit in his emblematic name: Valentine, suggesting his doctrine of universal love, and Michael, recalling the biblical archangel, but also, and just as significantly, Smith, symbolizing his function as a sort of Everyman, the character who would in fact be normal and average rather than unusual in a better world. Mike's primary function at the level of allegory is that of a martyr, a Christ figure, a savior. In attempting to teach Earthlings the ways of the Martians, he, like Christ, meets with opposition from narrow-minded people who crucify him. After his discorporation Mike is shown in heaven, still able to play a role in Earth's destiny by monitoring the world's progress.

Heinlein uses these satirical and allegorical frameworks to dramatize his concern over the restrictions that education, law, and religion can place on the public's freedom and knowledge. In using a superhuman character, however, Heinlein seems to be suggesting that the alternatives open to Mike may not be available to others. For some readers, his failure to offer more realistic alternatives suggests an underlying hopelessness. Certainly Heinlein is not offering any detailed blueprint for concrete social reforms. Rather, he is pointing out contradictions and weaknesses in cultural institutions and showing the need for changes.

Context

Stranger in a Strange Land was the first science-fiction novel to make the bestseller list of *The New York Times*; it also won for Robert Heinlein his third Hugo Award. Despite negative reviews, the novel quickly established itself as one of the most popular science-fiction novels ever written and certainly proved to be one of the most influential. While cultural criticism had long been a thematic staple of science-fiction writing, *Stranger in a Strange Land* initiated an entirely new handling of sexual themes. What had once been taboo now became a primary thematic concern in the genre. The book is generally regarded as having moved science fiction from a juvenile to an adult genre.

There was a change taking place in the entire structure of life in the United States in the early 1960's, especially for young adults, and Heinlein, as if on cue, delivered in *Stranger in a Strange Land* a book that came to be read as something of a "howto" handbook for a whole range of new movements. People were bonding together in cults and communes much like the inner circle of Mike's temple. Everywhere across North America people were taking part in a change of moral, social, political, and sexual values. Communal living, promiscuity, sharing, and loving seemed to be a way for people to unite and protect themselves and one another against the sterile, uncaring world. The fear of the atomic bomb and the Cold War was wearing off, and the world seemed ready for freedom from political and moral fear.

The more durable power of the work to attract young readers and hold their interest seems to lie in Heinlein's ability to take the reader beyond real life by offering imaginative plots and characters. Valentine Michael Smith is uprooted from his familiar surroundings and taken to an alien world. He is expected to adapt to and function in this new and confusing world, a thematic concern with which a wide spectrum of readers, especially young adults, seem to identify. The fantasy and utopian elements introduced by Mike's Martian upbringing and special abilities make him a superhero of sorts, but he remains a symbol for anyone who has ever been the stranger.

William Nelles
Lori Williams

STRAWBERRY GIRL

Author: Lois Lenski (1893-1974)
Type of plot: Domestic realism
Time of plot: Early 1900's
Locale: Southern Florida
Principal themes: Poverty, family
First published: 1945; illustrated
Recommended ages: 10-13

Two Florida farm families face poverty and other hardships, and deal with them in sharply contrasting ways

>*Principal characters:*
>BIRDIE BOYER, an industrious, intelligent, about twelve-year-old girl who earns the nickname "strawberry girl" from growing and selling crops
>PA and MA BOYER, her Christian parents, who overcome hardships with work and dedication
>PA and MA SLATER, non-Christian parents, who are slovenly and lazy but who later change
>SHOESTRING SLATER, a teenage boy, who changes from illiterate and uncaring to a concerned young man trying to better himself

The Story

Set in the rural backwoods of southern Florida in the early 1900's, this brief novel opens with foreshadowing of immediate conflicts between the principal family characters, the Slaters and the Boyers. Pa Slater is warned by daughter Essie that one of their cows is about to go down to the orange grove that belongs to their new neighbors, the Boyers. She tells him that the destruction of the orange trees by their cow will cause trouble, and his reply is that she is "mighty right." Slater refuses to stop the cow and refuses to allow his daughter to do so either. This opening scene sets the novel's tone of sharp and vivid contrasts between the two families.

The Boyer family—Pa, Ma, Birdie, and several other children—have migrated from northern Florida. They buy a home, paint it, plant flowers, and enjoy such luxuries as a comb, a looking glass, and a tablecloth. They grow many diverse crops and raise cattle. Pa Boyer is a loving, gentle giant of a Christian man, who provides for his family; he is quickly established, however, as someone who will stand up for his rights and be pushed only so far. Slater, on the other hand, is depicted as a lazy, abusive drunk who shames his family. The two men have opposite philosophies about work, education, religion, and family life.

Birdie and her family plant strawberries, which they later harvest. Birdie sells them, earning the nickname "Strawberry Girl," after the crops are almost destroyed by severe cold, storms, and feasting robins. The women are vivid and realistic, as strongly portrayed as the men. Each is the mother of many children and subservient to her husband. Ma Boyer's obeisance, however, is loving, whereas Ma Slater is quelled through fear of her husband's drunken brutality. Ma Slater is influenced favorably, albeit reluctantly, by Ma Boyer. When Ma Slater's husband shoots all of her chickens in a drunken rage and then leaves, she invites the Boyers over for chicken pileau. Prior to the Boyers' coming, she would have been far too intimidated to commit such a daring act.

When the barbed-wire fence that Boyer erects to protect his crops from Slater's pigs and cows becomes a symbol to Slater that his squatter's rights have been violated, Slater cuts the fence. Boyer kills three of Slater's hogs and leaves them on his porch. With the battle lines drawn, the feud accelerates until a mysterious fire in the woods threatens the Boyers' home. The Slaters refuse to help fight the fire, but other neighbors rally. Boyer saves two of his children and two of Slater's. Slater later disappears in a drunken rage, his answer to all life's problems.

Shoestring Slater is Birdie's counterpart. While the Boyer children walk several miles to their one-room schoolhouse, Shoestring's elder brothers beat the teacher so badly that the school closes. The story, however, finishes with a nicely rounded happy ending for all.

Themes and Meanings

The harshness of dirt-poor poverty, struggling for the barest necessities, and triumph of perseverance over adversity are the bases for this sharply drawn saga of two distinct families. The age-old theme of good versus evil is depicted in three relationships: between the fathers, the mothers, and the children. Right prevails every time, but only after serious tragedies—such as animals killed, crops destroyed, and the schoolhouse burned—have occurred.

The author provides provocative glimpses of the goodness of Ma Slater, which has been hidden under layers of fear that are gently pulled back by Ma Boyer. Shoestring has two dramatic chances to show decency of character: when he agrees to try to keep his animals away from the crops, and when he betrays the presence of the pliers that his papa carries.

Yet it is the conversion of Pa Slater to Christianity that is the ultimate victory and marks the turn of the whole family's attitudes and fortunes. There are significant changes in the characters of Pa Slater and Shoestring. Pa Slater's changes are the most dramatic, but Shoestring's conversion to education heralds a brighter future for the coming generation.

Context

This extremely prolific author has written more than two dozen books, fourteen of which have a regional flavor and deal with juveniles. *Cotton in My Sack* (1949) is set in Arkansas and was written after Lenski had made a brief spring visit, and an extended fall visit, to the state. She actually dragged a nine-pound cotton sack and picked cotton with the children. *Houseboat Girl* (1957) developed from a six-week stay with shanty boaters in Luxora, Mississippi. *Texas Tomboy* (1950) and *San Francisco Bay* (1955) were also based on personal, on-scene research.

It was *Strawberry Girl*, however, that was awarded the Newbery Medal. The dialogue, mannerisms, and customs of the characters are based on the author's personal experiences with real Florida crackers. The dialogue is realistic and captures that period of time as well as the characters' intellectual development. Today's ten-year-old might have some trouble with the dialogue, but the theme of the story is well worth the effort to understand it.

Though Lenski's books are regional studies, they deal with problems that are universal in nature. A struggle for survival is a struggle whether it exists in an Arkansas cotton patch, a Mississippi houseboat, or a Florida farm. Her characters have human foibles as well as virtues. A climactic scene in *Strawberry Girl*, when Pa Slater returns home after a drunken spree and finds Ma Boyer there, shows human nature at its worst. He orders her out of the house.

Billie Taylor

STREET ROD

Author: Henry Gregor Felsen (1916-   )
Type of plot: Moral tale
Time of plot: The early to mid-1950's
Locale: Delville, Iowa
Principal themes: Coming-of-age, death, social issues, and sports
First published: 1953
Recommended ages: 15-18

Teenager Ricky Madison must show his parents, peers, girl friend, and local authorities that he is competent to modify his car into a "street rod" that he will drive responsibly. He does so for a time but meets a tragic end.

> *Principal characters:*
> RICKY MADISON, a sixteen-year-old fighting to show his parents and community that he is ready for his first car
> MERLE CONNOR, a down-on-his-luck garage operator, who teaches Ricky how to work on a car
> LINK ALLER, a bigger, stronger sixteen-year-old, whom Rick desperately wants to outrace
> ARNIE VAN ZUUK, a local policeman sensitive to the needs and desires of teenage drivers
> SHARON BRUCE, a sensible sixteen-year-old girl, who prefers Ricky's company to that of Link
> MR. and MRS. MADISON, the concerned and earnest parents of Ricky

The Story

Although set in rural Iowa, the events depicted in *Street Rod* typify suburban America of the 1950's as the period in which the teenage car culture is born. The novel not only demonstrates the importance to a teenager of owning a car but also shows how the normal developmental process of adolescence is complicated by the threats posed by a potentially dangerous machine. *Street Rod* effectively establishes context and setting for a young man learning to develop his own identity in relation to those of his family and peers. Ricky fears being a "car suck," someone without his own car who has to ask others for rides. Worse yet, he fears he will not be admired by his male peers or attractive to girls like Sharon without his own vehicle. When Ricky withdraws his savings to buy a 1939 Ford coupe from Merle Connor, he begins a new period in his life.

After living through the frustrations of learning that his car needs extensive repairs and is far less impressive than he had thought originally, he gradually learns about how to work on cars. As assistant at Merle's second-rate garage, Ricky begins to see how he might extend his interest in fixing up his own car to a career as a car designer and customizer. Once he rebuilds his engine and refurbishes the body, Ricky has a "street rod" that brings him respect. Although Ricky has on one level the normal adolescent insecurities related to dating, on another level he displays boundless confidence, impervious to the sort of tragic accidents that befall other teenage drivers.

After a young couple from the area is killed in a hopped-up car, the parents of Ricky's classmates become concerned. When the parents of the girls in Delville forbid their daughters to ride with youths outside the city limits, Ricky and his pals decide to show the town that they are capable and safe drivers by establishing the Delville Timing Association (DTA), an organization that will oversee the safe and reputable operation of a drag strip outside town; the book clearly states that this sort of arrangement is the safest way to deal with teenagers' fascination with cars. In working to have a local road periodically open as a carefully and responsibly monitored drag strip, the youths promise to obey all traffic rules and serve as examples of courtesy and safety on the road. When the city council rebuffs this request at a public meeting, the youths are frustrated. They realize that individual council members may like to brag about how fast their new luxury cars will go, but they frown on any idea of a teenager using a drag strip, even a sanctioned one. Arnie realizes the boys are right, but he is afraid to incur the council's displeasure by championing the boys' side.

Ricky's father, a sensitive and responsive man who begins to share his son's interest in cars, convinces him to rethink the idea of abandoning the DTA. Instead, he encourages Ricky by telling him that the idea of establishing a drag strip is sound. With Sharon's encouragement, Ricky channels his disappointment at the failure of the proposed timing association into the building of his car into a custom job worthy of a prize at a big regional competitive meet in Des Moines. He believes that if he can win the show and impress people with his car, he will then be able to build credibility and ensure the success of the DTA.

After winning first place in the show with the 1939 street rod designed and built with the cooperation and help of not only Sharon but also other, professional, auto workers, the couple's mood is highly elated as they return to Delville from Des Moines. Link follows them back, however, determined to prove that he can still beat Ricky's car, even if it did just win first place in the custom car show. With the new speed equipment Ricky has installed on his engine, he is easily able to outrace Link. Yet a terrible tragedy ensues when the feelings of power and speed overcome Ricky. With Sharon asleep at his side, he cannot stop himself and continues to drive faster and faster even though Link's headlights are no longer in sight. As the car begins to go out of control, Sharon wakes up; the coupe flies off the road and into the river. Just as the coupe sinks, Link speeds over the bridge, grimly determined to catch Rick. The novel ends abruptly with this unexpected punch.

Themes and Meanings

The basic plot of the *Bildungsroman*, or the coming-of-age of a young man, is evident in *Street Rod*, but even more critical is the moral tale that derives its strength from the needless death of the two principal characters. The tragedy arises not so much from the recklessness of youth—though that factor is certainly present—as it does from the unwillingness or inability of the older generation to comprehend and take action to deal with the problems of youth. Although the families of the two young lovers are not at odds with each other, the generational gap presented in this novel echoes William Shakespeare's treatment in *Romeo and Juliet* of a pair whose elders do not understand the depth of the young people's emotional needs.

While Sharon is sensitive to Ricky's frustrations and sees his considerable strength of character, her affection is not by itself sufficient. Ricky's insecurities run deep; perhaps only another ten years of living would reveal to him that the acne, feelings of inferiority, and dismay at not being taken seriously by adults are temporary stages and not absolute conditions of his life. His coupe represents an opportunity to show the world his true abilities because as he takes a tired, beat-up old castoff and transforms it into a solid machine, powerful and dependable, he is demonstrating how he has the expertise to craft from something virtually worthless a custom car that reflects his personality and values. In the end, his fascination at finally being able to see how the new speed equipment boosts his engine's performance turns to horror as he loses control, and the car flies off the curving downhill slope.

The real tragedy, however, goes beyond the limits of the narrative. Readers will imagine how the Bruce and Madison families will cope with the loss, and they will also wonder how the Delville city council will now regard the proposal for a timing association to run time trials on a deserted road.

Context

Street Rod is the second in a series of books related to hot-rodding that Henry Gregor Felsen wrote from 1950 to 1960; in that decade as well as the following one, his popularity with teenage readers was considerable. From the first novel, *Hot Rod* (1950), through *Boy Gets Car* (1960), Felsen was read by young people because they recognized in his books the frustrations of adolescence as well as the ways in which a teenager would have to go about customizing or hopping up an old car. He could describe convincingly a young boy's dilemma over whether to accept sweets from a pretty girl for fear that his face would break out, and he was equally adept at chronicling the proper order in which a budget-minded enthusiast would decide to add high-performance parts to his Ford or Merc flathead engine. With this versatility, Felsen demonstrated that his talents as a novelist were well-suited to the time in which he wrote.

Not only does Felsen present adolescent affection honestly, but he also confronts such typical problems as bullies in his treatment of Link Aller in *Street Rod* and such archetypal characters as the young girl from a modest background who dreams of Hollywood, memorably embodied in LaVerne Shuler of *Hot Rod*. Her illusions of stardom parallel in some ways the goals of Ricky Madison in his attempts to build a car that will take the automotive world by storm; in attempting to get Bud Crayne to take her out of Avondale and drive to California, LaVerne evokes the pathos of teenagers living in drab small towns whose dreams tell them of greater lives and greater adventures beyond the horizon. Felsen's novels are explicit about the dangers of using cars as the means of realizing dreams. Built and driven responsibly, cars are the concrete manifestations of a young driver's latent ability; the slightest lapse of caution, however, sends the car spinning off the road and dooms its occupants. Perhaps because no other popular young adult novelist knew as much about hot rodding as Felsen, no other writer has surpassed him in capturing adolescent fascination with building a car of one's own.

Peter Valenti

STUDS LONIGAN
A Trilogy

Author: James T. Farrell (1904-1979)
Type of plot: Social realism
Time of plot: 1900-1933
Locale: Chicago
Principal themes: Coming-of-age, family, gender roles, love and romance, poverty, and race and ethnicity
First published: 1935: *Young Lonigan: A Boyhood in Chicago Streets*, 1932; *The Young Manhood of Studs Lonigan*, 1934; *Judgment Day*, 1935
Recommended ages: 15-18

The coming-of-age, maturity, and death of an Irish Catholic boy on the South Side of Chicago are told within his stream of consciousness, emphasizing the way in which society shapes his way of looking at the world.

> *Principal characters:*
> STUDS LONIGAN, a small but tough boy who grows up yearning to be a hero
> LUCY SCANLON, a pretty young girl he loves but cannot seem to woo successfully
> PATRICK LONIGAN, his father, a benevolent man who takes his son into the painting business
> MARY LONIGAN, his mother, a devout Catholic who vainly hopes that he will become a priest
> FRANCES LONIGAN, his sister, a proper, fussy girl
> LORETTA LONIGAN, his sister, who marries Phil Rolfe, a Jew who converts to Catholicism in order to please her
> MARTIN LONIGAN, his younger brother, who grows up to sneer at him
> HELEN SHIRES, a tomboy who befriends him
> CATHERINE BANAHAN, a pretty, conventional Irish girl engaged to be married to him

The Story

Studs Lonigan traces the growth and demise of an Irish Catholic boy on the South Side of Chicago. He smokes, drinks too much, goes to "cathouses" (brothels), fights to prove his courage, and dreams of distinguishing himself as the toughest guy in his neighborhood. He does not want to finish high school and can barely tolerate the Catholic grammar school he attends. His parents do not know how to control him: His father cannot keep him off the streets, while his mother is tender with him but knows nothing about his desires or feelings and nurtures the unrealistic hope that he will become a priest. Studs does have a tender streak. He is infatuated with Lucy Scanlon, a provocative young girl with whom he manages to spend a day but who then teases him about the episode, so that he stays away from her even as he yearns to resume their intimacy.

Studs's emotions are very much hemmed in by his environment. Except for his parents, there is little encouragement to stay in school or to understand the world outside his immediate neighborhood. After he quits school, he goes to work for his father and spends his spare time with the neighborhood toughs. For a brief period he is the reigning tough, having beaten Weary Reilley, a particularly big and vicious bully, in a street fight. Studs's victory is short-lived, however, as he becomes more and more frustrated at his inability to attain his dreams. Lucy seems beyond his grasp, and then she is married to another man. Studs's experiences with sex are rather sordid, and his heavy drinking and carousing take a toll on his health. By his mid-twenties, his father's business begins to fail, and jobs become more scarce. As Studs matures, he sees his world become transformed; he moves with his father out of the old neighborhood, which is now mostly black. His sisters make good marriages and are content, but Studs and his father face financial ruin.

The one note of hope in Studs's life is Catherine Banahan. She is not as pretty as his ideal, Lucy, but she loves him and is excited by his lovemaking. She gives in to his sexual needs, even though her loss of virginity leads to a pregnancy and plans for a hasty marriage. Neither Catherine nor Studs seems to have the power to rise above circumstances. With his modest investments virtually worthless and his father's business hitting a new low, Studs desperately seeks other employment, ruining his health in the process by ignoring several debilitating heart attacks. Approaching the age of thirty, he is a physical wreck. Weakened by a long day's search in the rain for a job, he catches pneumonia and dies.

Themes and Meanings

Studs Lonigan longs to be a hero, to be recognized for his unique self, to be admired for his courage, and to be loved by all the beautiful women he sees on the street. Mooning over Lucy, who has spurned his love and teased him, he dreams of his better self, but Lucy stands there laughing at him: "He tried to think of himself as a hero. He was a hero in his own mind. He was utterly miserable." These words sum up the plight of Studs Lonigan. He is capable of imagining the great man he might become, but he is powerless to effect any real change in himself or in his surroundings.

James T. Farrell is careful to show how Studs's vision of things is bounded by his family, his friends, and his neighborhood. At home, his parents caution him to stay in school, but schooling has only an abstract value in their minds. There is never a word exchanged about what an education might actually bring him. His father merely expects his son to work for him; his mother expects him only to be well-behaved and religious. Studs reacts strongly against the narrowness of his home life. He cannot abide his sister Fran's prissy scolding, for he does not want to be a conventional, dutiful brother and son. There is no excitement, no challenge in domestic life, no reason for believing the platitudes of his parents.

At the same time, there is little recognition in Studs's world that people can rise above their upbringing, their prejudices, and peer pressures. Danny O'Neill, the one boy from the neighborhood who goes to college, is looked upon as a freak. He does not conform to the gang mentality. The irony Studs does not see is that Danny represents the route out of provinciality. Danny's is the distinctive voice that Studs does not hear in his preoccupation with making himself into the hero of his immediate milieu. Only much later, toward the end of his life, does Studs vaguely understand that quitting school has been a disaster for him.

Studs Lonigan is essentially the victim of the societal forces that make for ethnic neighborhoods, race prejudice, and unemployment. His father's only explanation for the economic depression is the chicanery of the international Jewish bankers. When the neighborhood begins to deteriorate and housing values go down, it is a result of the fact that Negroes have moved in. This may be the proximate cause of the area's decline, but the Lonigans do not realize that their racism actually contributes to their economic undoing.

In sum, Studs lacks self-consciousness and an awareness of how he has been placed in society. Until the very last years of his life, he persists in believing that somehow he can change everything around, that somehow he will emerge triumphant:

> He remembered when he licked Weary Reilley, that other day when he had sat with Lucy in the tree, and that day when he had gone home from work with his first pay, how on all those times, he had felt that life was going to start being different for him. This time, though, it had to be.

Yet each time, life is not different for him, because he does not have the means to take control of his life. Rather, he imagines that he will distinguish himself through some terrifying deed, like those of the gangsters in the films he admires.

When Catherine Banahan takes an interest in Studs, she revives his romanticism; with her, he is "going to get everything that he wished for, all that he deserved." This is Studs's American Dream: that he will be able to fulfill all his wishes for himself and that life, indeed, exists for the pursuit of his happiness. It is an incredibly sentimental, unrealistic, and, in the end, melancholy hope. All Studs has are these intense moments of yearning, of projecting what it might be like actually to feel satisfied with his life. Catherine herself is a disappointment. She is not as pretty as Lucy. Her main value is that she adores Studs and makes him feel proud that he has the power to excite a woman. In her social attitudes, she is not much different from his sister Fran; indeed, Catherine is annoyingly banal on the subject of men and is tiresome in her constant teasing regarding Studs's male code of behavior.

That Studs should die after a day's walk in the rain looking for a job after the failure of his father's painting business is particularly apt. He has ignored his health most of his life and never known how to seize opportunities. He has ignored the warning signs—his heart attacks, his unwise investment in a bad utility stock that he keeps until it is virtually worthless—and has dreamed that if he finds the right girl, if he joins a Catholic fraternity or some other gang or group, his talents will finally be recognized. It is no wonder that his young brother Martin sneers at him, for by the logic of Studs's own life he is not much more than a used-up stud.

Context

Studs Lonigan is a classic of American literary naturalism. Farrell was the first American author to portray the life of an ethnic neighborhood with realistic specificity, giving a clear sense of the language, the prejudices, the whole mind-set of a people. Farrell stays close to Studs's perceptions of things, so that even his racial slurs and sexual fantasies are seen from his point of view as natural, taken for granted. While Farrell does not condone or endorse these opinions, he shows how they become the unexamined part of a person's experience.

Farrell is often compared to Theodore Dreiser, his distinguished predecessor in literary naturalism. While both writers stress the way individuals are shaped by society, Farrell is more concerned with the quality of the minds that are produced by environment than with the environment itself. There is relatively little physical description in Farrell's works, for he was greatly influenced by James Joyce's stream-of-consciousness technique, in which the concerns of a society are filtered through a close reading and representation of individual mentalities. Nevertheless, Studs is clearly kin to Dreiser's Clyde Griffiths in *An American Tragedy* (1925), who has the same romantic longings, seeing in Roberta Alden the ideal representation of womanhood that Studs finds in Lucy Scanlon. The two characters are dogged by the same nebulous and unfounded belief in their own greatness which is their American tragedy.

Young readers might find it helpful in their attempt to grasp the significance of Farrell's achievement not only to read Dreiser but also to compare the coming-of-age story in *Studs Lonigan* with Mark Twain's *The Adventures of Huckleberry Finn* (1884) and *Billy Bathgate* (1989) by E. L. Doctorow. All three stories center on young boys who reject schooling, are attracted to romantic or criminal figures, and are the complex products of their society's values even as they apparently rebel against its mores. Each author tries to render American speech realistically, to capture the times his characters inhabit, and to assess the extent to which Americans are capable of achieving the individuality they so zealously prize.

Carl Rollyson

SULA

Author: Toni Morrison (Chloe Anthony Wofford, 1931-   )
Type of plot: Social realism
Time of plot: 1917-1965
Locale: Medallion, Ohio
Principal themes: Friendship, and race and ethnicity
First published: 1973
Recommended ages: 15-18

Two black women, Sula and Nel, become friends in the small Ohio town where they live. When Sula chooses a life of rebellion and promiscuity and Nel chooses marriage and respectability, they learn the bounds of their love for each other.

Principal characters:
SULA PEACE, an inconsistent, emotional girl, who grows up to be a rebellious, wanton woman
NEL WRIGHT, Sula's strong and steady best friend, who chooses traditional marriage and motherhood
HANNAH PEACE, Sula's mother, a promiscuous woman
EVA PEACE, Hannah's mother, a tough woman, who rules the family home from her wheelchair
HELENE SABAT WRIGHT, Nel's mother, the daughter of a prostitute, who is determined to teach her children respectability

The Story

Set in the small town of Medallion, Ohio, *Sula* is a story of black women in America. Although the novel opens with accounts of men's actions, it quickly turns to the women who are its center. Men, black and white, may shape the external trappings of the world in which *Sula* takes place, but women move through the world on their own power.

Nel Wright is the daughter of the beautiful, dignified Helene and a frequently absent father. Taught to be obedient and unimaginative, Nel takes her one trip out of Medallion when she is ten. This trip takes Nel out of the all-black sections of Medallion into the segregated South, where Helene's mother is revealed as a beautiful, gardenia-scented whore. Nel is fascinated with all she sees and dreams of other places she will visit one day.

Once Nel becomes attached to Sula Peace, however, her longings for travel cease. She finds that having a friend gives her the strength and excitement she had thought travel would provide. Sula's home is as unconventional as Nel's is conventional and as untidy as Nel's is neat. Her family is dominated by Sula's mother, Hannah, and Eva, her one-legged grandmother; no men of any strength appear to challenge the women's authority. Helene does not approve of Sula's family: Eva's past is scandalous and mysterious, and Hannah has had sexual encounters with most of the married men in town. Sula herself is undisciplined, emotional, and daring—all that Nel wishes she could be. Yet Nel's discipline gives her strength that Sula lacks, and the two become best friends.

At twelve, the girls discover together the first yearnings for sex, walking daily past a crowd of boys to hear their whistles and jeers. As conflicts with their mothers intensify, so does their interdependence. They compare notes on the sexual talents of boys in town and share experiences and feelings without quarreling or jealousy. Nel marries just after high school graduation, and Sula leaves Medallion to find a new life.

Ten years later, Sula returns, having attended college and experienced big-city life. Nel realizes suddenly that, while she has enjoyed her husband and children, her friendship with Sula is the most rewarding and empowering relationship in her life. As before, the two women completely accept each other: Nel remains stable and respectable, while Sula is rebellious and promiscuous. Sula becomes widely thought of as an evil presence in the town, but Nel loves and supports her.

When Sula takes Nel's husband as her lover, however, everything changes. Nel cannot understand how Sula could hurt and betray her; Sula honestly cannot understand why Nel's husband should be the one thing they do not share. For years, they do not speak, and Sula sinks ever lower in the town's estimation. Finally, when Sula lies dying, Nel is the only person who will come to her. The two quarrel bitterly, and Nel leaves Sula to die alone. It is only after Sula's death that Nel realizes again how important her friend was to her.

Themes and Meanings

Telling the story of two women, one "good" and one "evil," *Sula* is a story of friendship and an exploration of what good and evil mean. Toni Morrison has commented on the special nature of friendship between black women and her belief that her novel was the first to treat such a friendship as a central theme. This friendship is more powerful, more enduring, than blood or marriage ties; it is what gives women strength.

For Nel, her friendship with Sula is the only relationship in her life that enables her to realize her truest self: Her mother manages merely to stifle liveliness in Nel, her father never appears in the novel, and although her husband and children are loving and enjoyable, they do not satisfy nor do they stay. When Sula dies, Nel realizes that it has been her friend—not her husband—whom she has missed during the years of their bitter quarrel.

For Sula, too, no relationship is as deep or empowering as her friendship with Nel. Her mother and grandmother cannot love her, and her many fleeting unions with men provide only temporary satisfaction. That is not to say all other relationships in the novel are destructive or hurtful; they provide different kinds of reward, but none is as important as the bond between the two women.

The nature of good and evil is also questioned in this novel. Sula is clearly an evil figure in her town, yet her presence there causes much good. Seemingly kind acts bring evil results, and acts that appear evil to others are done with the best intentions. A mother lovingly burning her own child to death, a daughter watching curiously as her mother also dies in flames—how is a reader to interpret these acts? The world of *Sula*, like the real world, is complicated, uncontrollable, and ultimately unknowable.

Context

Although all Morrison's novels focus on the relationships between black characters, *Sula* stands alone in its lack of attention to these characters' interaction with whites. Unlike Pecola in *The Bluest Eye* (1970), who dreams of having blue eyes and blond hair, or Sethe in *Beloved* (1987), who has been owned and tormented by whites, Nel and Sula live in a small town populated only by blacks. Whites appear infrequently in the background—as a slave owner who tricks the blacks into accepting the poorest land or as the contractors who will not hire black laborers—but the focus of the novel is the friendship between the two women, and their foils are their own families and lovers.

It is important to note, however, that Morrison does open *Sula* with an account of the slaveholder responsible for the creation of Medallion. While the history of slavery is not as central to the action here as it is in Morrison's *The Song of Solomon* (1977), *Beloved*, or even *Tar Baby* (1981), the author insists that the reader approach the story with this essential background reality in mind.

Sula might be compared with such works as Gloria Naylor's *The Women of Brewster Place* (1982), Alice Walker's *The Color Purple* (1982), and other works by younger writers who have explored with Morrison the special empowering nature of friendship between black women. In *Sula*, however, the friendship transcends sexuality (there are no hints here of homosexuality as there are in the Naylor and Walker novels), separation, and betrayal.

While the frank descriptions of sexual matters may make this novel unsuitable for some younger readers, *Sula* has much to recommend it to more mature young adults. The give-and-take leading to gradual understanding between mothers and daughters, the conflicting yearnings for adventure and for stability, and the final lesson about the strength and importance of nonsexual friendship are dealt with honestly and sensitively, revealing all their complexities. *Sula* provides young readers with important and fascinating issues with which to grapple.

Cynthia A. Bily

THE SUMMER BIRDS

Author: Penelope Farmer (1939-   )
Type of plot: Fantasy
Time of plot: The late 1950's to the early 1960's
Locale: A rural English village not far from the seaside
Principal themes: Coming-of-age, emotions, friendship, nature, and social issues
First published: 1962; illustrated
Recommended ages: 10-13

A mysterious boy teaches a group of schoolchildren to fly, but his attempts to lure the children to his remote bird world fail when Charlotte Makepeace persuades the children to stay. Charlotte's choice, however, produces in her a sense of personal loss.

Principal characters:
   CHARLOTTE MAKEPEACE, a reserved, thoughtful twelve-year-old, who lives with her grandfather
   EMMA MAKEPEACE, her ebullient ten-year-old sister
   THE BOY, the birdlike stranger who teaches the children to fly
   MAGGOT HOBBIN, the girls' shy friend, who establishes a special rapport with the boy
   JOHN "GINGER" APPLE,
   THOMAS "TOTTY" FEATHER,
   ANNIE FEATHER,
   MARLENE "MARLY" SCRAGG,
   MOLLY SCOBB,
   ROBERT "BABY" FUMPKINS,
   WILLIAM "BANDY" SCRAGG,
   GEORGE "SCOOTER" DIMPLE, and
   JAMES "JAMMY" HAT, the girls' schoolmates

The Story

When twelve-year-old Charlotte Makepeace and her ten-year-old sister Emma first encounter the mysterious birdlike boy on their way to school, little do they anticipate the summer of adventure that awaits them. Charlotte will face the dilemma of choosing between the exciting world of carefree flight and romance as represented by the boy and the workaday world of responsibility to her family.

The boy accompanies the girls to school, but later in the day when he and Charlotte escape, he reveals the secret that he can fly. One by one over the ensuing days, the charismatic boy teaches all the children to fly. The children meet on the Downs to revel in their newfound freedom to soar and skim over tree and lake.

As the summer wears on, a power struggle between the boy and the former class leader, Totty Feather, intensifies. Totty questions the boy's authority to make deci-sions for the group and probes into the boy's mysterious background. The tension leads to a fight between the two boys. Charlotte proposes a tournament to settle the dispute. The children will support either the boy or Totty Feather in a game of "French and English," a flag capture game. If Totty wins, the boy agrees to reveal his mysterious background and leave the group. If the boy wins, he claims the right to stay through the summer as part of the group.

Before the tournament, Charlotte, Emma, Maggot Hobbin, and the boy share an idyllic interlude of increasing friendship climaxed by an exciting adventure at the seaside. The boy convinces Charlotte to come with him to imitate the seagulls' freefall plunge from the high cliffs. Charlotte must jettison the safety of her life, reach out to trust in the boy and in herself, and make a plunge toward the sea that could result in her death. Terrified and yet not wanting to disappoint the boy, Char-lotte leaps from the cliff in a breathless, ecstatic fall that nearly ends in catastrophe. Only the boy's admonition to "Stop!" keeps her from plunging to her death. She swoops over the waves in a giddy arc, aware that she has just experienced life to its fullest, an experience she will never again capture.

The group of classmates reassembles at the end of the summer for the long-anticipated tournament. In an exciting struggle, the boy's side finally wins, and the children's final days of summer extend into glorious days of flight and exploration. Two days before school resumes comes the crucial revelation of the boy's intent in being with them that summer. The boy invites all the children to fly away with him to a special place. He reveals that he is a bird, the last of his species. The Phoenix, the mighty birdlord, has granted the boy the summer to entice the children back with him to his island, where they will be transformed into birds and help the boy to perpetuate his species.

Charlotte, in agony over her need to choose between the boy and his promise of perpetual flight and the human world of duty to family and friends, chooses to stay. She convinces the others that a carefree world in which they will not have to worry about the human pains of growing up also brings with it the heartache of giving up parents and home and the guilt over causing their families pain. Only Maggot, who has always lived an isolated life with her gamekeeper uncle in the woods, consents to go with the boy to perpetuate the species. Before the boy and Maggot fly away, he explains privately to Charlotte that she was his first choice. Charlotte turns toward the upcoming days and years with a sense that she has made the correct choice, but that it is nevertheless a sad one.

Themes and Meanings

The Summer Birds looks through the eyes of Charlotte Makepeace as she changes from the "prig" of the first chapters to the wise leader who is more receptive to new experience and more willing to take risks. The role of leader and decision maker is new for Charlotte and unexpected by the other children. Charlotte continues to grow in confidence and assertiveness as the novel progresses. Through the friendship and love of the boy, with its hints of a romantic relationship, Charlotte begins to open up to the joys of life lived to its fullest. She learns to fly and even to plunge off the cliff like the gulls. She asserts her views in the group, and they turn to her for advice and guidance. She makes choices that she believes to be morally responsible even when they also lead to personal pain. Her friendship with the shy Maggot enables her to probe the hidden resources of a girl she had never known well. Charlotte is able to look beyond the surface and to become more sensitive to the emotions and needs of others around her.

The very ability to fly opens up new perspectives. Now all the children are able to see their world from the rooftops, from the trees. They perceive their world differently and also come to appreciate the skills of those nonhuman creatures who live in the world. Author Penelope Farmer uses the group of children to explore issues of loyalty and social order. Children must choose between two potential leaders and observe the conflicts that arise when the new leader threatens the power of the old. Members of the group must explore the reasons for their loyalties either to Totty or to the boy, with a number of surprising results.

Context

The Summer Birds was British author Penelope Farmer's first full-length work, adapted from a short story that was intended for her first book, *The China People* (1960). The novel, one of three about the Makepeace children, was a runner-up for the Carnegie Medal in 1963. The second novel, *Emma in Winter* (1966), features a flight through time by Emma Makepeace and one of the other schoolchildren. *Charlotte Sometimes* (1969) is a timeshift fantasy involving Charlotte and the girl Clare, who lives during World War I.

The evocation of flight is one of the most striking achievements of *The Summer Birds*, as it is in *Emma in Winter* and a later Farmer work, a retelling of the Greek myth of flight, *Daedalus and Icarus* (1971). Indeed, the novels have often been compared to Sir James Barrie's *Peter Pan* (1904), which revolves around the fantasy of flight, but critics are also quick to notice that Farmer is particularly adept at portraying the difficulty that humans might have in mastering its complexities. Although all the children in *The Summer Birds* learn to fly, some are more skillful than others, and each child has his or her own idiosyncrasies of flight. Arms become tired, landings are not always smooth, and intense concentration is required.

The Summer Birds echoes Peter Pan's concern over taking one's place in the adult world. Peter Pan desires to remain a child forever in Neverland. Although the issue is not quite identical in *The Summer Birds* (after all, becoming a bird on a remote island probably does not ensure immortality), the question of growing up is still central. Charlotte recognizes the pain involved in giving up her fantasy life with the boy and her ability to fly, but she chooses the human world with all its foibles nevertheless. *The Summer Birds* also resembles Robert Browning's retelling of *The Pied Piper of Hamelin* (1842) in its story of the boy luring the children away from their village and families. Farmer frequently forces her characters to choose whether to stay in the fantasy world; in most cases, the characters choose the real world.

Penelope Farmer has written works complex in both theme and style. Generally recognized as possessing a unique and hauntingly beautiful style that creates intensely tangible settings, Farmer allows thoughtful readers to penetrate introspective worlds that are often hypnotic and hauntingly memorable.

Ann M. Cameron

SUMMER OF MY GERMAN SOLDIER

Author: Bette Greene (1934-   )
Type of plot: Psychological realism
Time of plot: The early 1940's
Locale: Jenkinsville, Arkansas
Principal themes: Family, friendship, race and ethnicity, and war
First published: 1973
Recommended ages: 13-15

A young Jewish girl, Patty Bergen, whose parents do not like her, helps a German soldier who is being held as a prisoner of war. After he is killed and Patty is punished, she tries to understand and like herself.

Principal characters:
  PATTY BERGEN, a talkative, friendly twelve-year-old Jew, who
    helps a German soldier
  ANTON REIKER, the young German soldier who helps Patty realize
    how special she is
  RUTH HUGHES, the Bergens' black maid, one of Patty's only
    friends
  HARRY BERGEN, Patty's father, who owns a department store and
    mistreats his older daughter
  PEARL BERGEN, Patty's mother, who wants a cute, popular
    daughter
  SHARON BERGEN, Patty's six-year-old sister, who is winsome and
    popular

The Story

Patty Bergen, the Jewish heroine of *Summer of My German Soldier*, lives with parents who favor her sister, Sharon, and find fault with her. Mrs. Bergen criticizes Patty's wavy auburn hair and forces her to undergo a permanent wave, which frizzles her daughter's best claim to beauty. The hot-tempered Mr. Bergen, who fears poverty and works nervously to make his department store in Jenkinsville, Arkansas, prosper, beats Patty for accidentally breaking a car window and associating with a poverty-stricken boy, Freddy Dowd.

Patty's story resembles "Cinderella." In her father's department store, Patty meets and instantly recognizes as her Prince Charming Anton Reiker, a German prisoner of war. When Anton escapes from camp near Jenkinsville, Patty hides him in a garage apartment behind her parents' house. Forced to decide between her father and Anton, Patty chooses Anton, and expresses her decision by giving him the expensive blue shirt she had given to her unappreciative parent on Father's Day. In turn, the soldier leaves Patty his grandfather's gold ring, his most valued possession, to show how much he cares. Both the ring and the shirt, which bears the initials "H. B.," help the Federal Bureau of Investigation discover that Patty has helped him.

Ruth, the black maid, serves as Patty's fairy godmother. At first she encourages Patty to be sweet, neat, and well dressed, in the hope of pleasing her parents. When Ruth discovers Anton, who comes out of hiding while Mr. Bergen is beating Patty, she feeds him breakfast; however, she also encourages him to leave. From the beginning of the story, Ruth recognizes both Patty's need for compassion and the love that exists between Patty and Anton. By the end of the book, Anton has been killed in New York, and Patty has been sent to reform school. Patty's parents do not visit her, and when Ruth rides the bus there one Sunday, she tells the girl that her parents are "irregular seconds folks," not worth the high price Patty has been paying for them. Although Patty cannot marry her prince, she hopes to find his family in Germany when the war ends. With Ruth's help, she glimpses the strength required to make such a journey.

The forces of good and evil are represented by those who help Patty and those who mistreat her, although a few characters are indifferent toward her. Her mother's parents support her, her grandfather by praising her intelligence and her grandmother by buying her books and clothes. A reporter from Memphis introduces her to journalism, stands by her during the trial, and sends her a gift subscription to the *Memphis Commercial Appeal* when she is in reform school. The Jenkinsville sheriff refuses to let her father take away her gold ring, and the man who drives her to reform school stops to buy her a hamburger and a piece of pie, even though he is breaking a rule. In contrast to these friendly characters is Patty's Memphis lawyer, who tells her that she has embarrassed all Jews and caused their loyalty to be questioned. Also depicted as evil is the reform-school supervisor, who calls Patty greedy and spoiled and refuses to let Ruth stay longer than thirty minutes. These good and evil characters either help or harm Patty in her quest for love.

Themes and Meanings

During Patty's Cinderella-like search, she either discovers for herself or naïvely reveals to the reader three obstacles to compassion. Neither Patty's immediate family nor that of her father and mother has provided enough love and approval to at least one of the children. After Patty's father has beaten his daughter, he mutters to himself that no one ever loved him; Mr. Bergen probably dislikes Patty because she resembles his mother. When Patty's mother, Pearl, complains that her father gives everything to her brothers, Pearl's mother dismisses her daughter's feelings. Her parents' upbringing and poor family relationships scar Patty.

Patty finds that patriotism can also interfere with love. Patty's father, her grandmother, and the majority of the residents of Jenkinsville are shocked that Patty has knowingly aided "the enemy." In fact, at the trial her lawyer refuses to let Patty reveal her true feelings for Anton. The townspeople and the girls at the reform school call her "Nazi," thinking that to like the enemy is to become the enemy. Only Ruth informs Patty that people and their feelings mean more than do mere ideas, such as patriotism.

Above all, it is racism that keeps people from being able to love. Patty's first clue comes when Chu Lee, who had owned a grocery store in Jenkinsville, leaves town without notice. Later, she finds a large hole in his plate-glass window, broken from the outside. Jenkinsville is segregated, and the white townspeople believe that blacks are ignorant and satisfied with their lot. The townspeople's hidden racism toward Jews becomes obvious when they discover that Patty has helped Anton: They shout "Jew Nazi" and spit on her. Patty's compassion for Anton helps reveal the narrowness of the white American family and of patriotism during the 1940's and the intolerance of American racism.

Context

In *Summer of My German Soldier*, which received three book awards in 1973 and was made into a television film in the late 1970's, Bette Greene has created a female Huckleberry Finn. Patty and Ruth are friends in some of the same ways as are Huck and the Negro Jim. Yet Greene blends her criticism of society with her story of friendship more smoothly than Mark Twain does in *The Adventures of Huckleberry Finn* (1884). The Cinderella tale of Patty's growth in some ways parallels that of Huck, although Patty becomes involved in thoughts of romance, which Huck scorns. Huck searches for his ideals among unspoiled nature, away from "civilization," but Patty looks toward Europe for her ideal society.

In her next book about Patty, *Morning Is a Long Time Coming* (1978), Greene shows Patty at age eighteen, traveling to Germany to look for Anton's family. In *Them That Glitter and Them That Don't* (1983), the author again depicts realistically some of the tensions and problems that mid-twentieth century young people experience. Greene uses concrete details and believable dialogue in these books also.

Patty is as intelligent, determined, and outspoken as the heroine of Charlotte Brontë's *Jane Eyre* (1847). Her curiosity and developing maturity can be compared to that of the main character in Anne Frank's *Het achterhuis* (1947; *The Diary of a Young Girl*, 1952). Patty's defiance of the laws of her family and country brings to mind the Greek heroine Antigone, in Sophocles' play by the same name.

Greene has combined the simplicity of the moral tale with the sophistication of psychological analysis and social criticism. She has also woven a seamless story that contains both realism and optimism. *Summer of My German Soldier* shows that love between members of different races and cultures can exist in spite of society's sicknesses, and can perhaps help cure some of them.

Shelley Ann Thrasher

THE SUMMER OF THE SWANS

Author: Betsy Byars (1928-   )
Type of plot: Domestic realism
Time of plot: The early 1970's
Locale: A small town in West Virginia
Principal themes: Coming-of-age, emotions, and family
First published: 1970; illustrated
Recommended ages: 10-13

In addition to the customary trauma of growing up, Sara Godfrey must cope with the special problems of her younger brother Charlie's mental retardation.

> *Principal characters:*
> SARA GODFREY, a bright, observant fourteen-year-old girl who is
>   dealing with the problems that accompany adolescence
> CHARLIE, her ten-year old retarded brother
> WANDA, her pretty older sister, who is studying to become a nurse
> AUNT WILLIE, who has reared the three children since their
>   mother died six years ago
> MARY WEICEK, Sara's best friend
> SAM GODFREY, Sara's father, a defeated man
> JOE MELBY, a boy Sara regards as a thief and tormentor of her
>   brother Charlie
> FRANK, Wanda's red-haired, fun-loving boyfriend

The Story

Because of the simplicity of both its plot and its setting, *The Summer of the Swans* might be dismissed as just another coming-of-age novel, were it not for the particular nature of the adjustments the protagonist must make. Along with the usual problems of teenage adjustments, Sara Godfrey must deal with the fact that her ten-year-old brother is not and never will be "normal." Charlie is mentally retarded.

At fourteen, Sara is undergoing great changes, though she cannot seem to find any particular detail that distinguishes this summer from the last, or the one before that. She visits the local Dairy Queen with her best friend Mary, watches television, and babysits for the neighbor. The design of the summer is all too familiar, yet the texture is different. Sara finds herself on an emotional seesaw; one moment she is ecstatically happy, and the next she is disconsolate. She hates the orange sneakers that until recently were her pride and joy. She hates her height, her big feet, her crooked nose. She feels a new resentment toward her beautiful older sister and absolutely chafes at any show of authority on the part of Aunt Willie.

Woven into this tapestry of Sara's discontent is a new thread of feeling that she has long denied—her ambivalence toward Charlie and his special problem. Stricken by fever at the age of three, Charlie is brain-damaged and severely retarded. He is incapable of speech yet somehow manages to print letters of the alphabet. He brandishes his wristwatch at the slightest provocation, yet he cannot tell time. As Sara matures, as her body grows and her emotions evolve, she is struck by the realization that Charlie cannot change. He will forever be the little boy who cannot place his sticky sucker back on its stick, who cannot tie his own shoelaces or find his way around town without the aid of another person. He is trapped in a world of simple pleasures and can while away an entire afternoon digging a hole in the yard or lying beneath a homemade tent.

Combined with Charlie's inability to develop (and thus adding to Sara's misery) is the community's growing awareness of Charlie's shortcomings. The larger his body grows, the more apparent it is that his mind cannot keep pace. Other children tease him and call him "retarded" (a word Sara hates). A neighbor asks Charlie the time, knowing that he will gladly show his watch though he cannot begin to read it. Even Wanda talks about Charlie in a psychology class, reemphasizing to Sara that Charlie is different and that that difference is worthy of note.

The single event that most forcefully hammers home the nature of Charlie's uniqueness is the incident from which the book takes its name. Sara escorts Charlie to a nearby pond to observe a flock of swans during their migration. Later that same night, Charlie mistakes a neighbor's white cat for the swans and imagines that they have come for him. He leaves the safety of his bedroom in pursuit of the birds and soon becomes lost in a wooded ravine on the outskirts of town. Charlie's absence goes unnoticed until the following morning, when a search party is mobilized. The frantic search for her little brother forces Sara to realize how dependent and helpless he truly is. In the process she reexamines her relationship with Joe Melby, the boy she suspected of stealing Charlie's watch, and with her father, whose absence she has long equated with disinterest.

Though Sara and the searchers eventually locate Charlie, the young people's lives will never be quite the same. Sara has been forced to confront her brother's vulnerability, but at the same time she has learned that not everyone is allied against him.

A subsequent invitation to a young people's party is also an invitation for Sara to get on with her life.

Themes and Meanings

On one level, *The Summer of the Swans* is a classic coming-of-age novel, or a story about adolescent growth and development. Sara is possessed of all the foibles, fears, and doubts that teenagers face. She is overly concerned with her appearance— her feet are too big, her nose crooked, her height towering. She resents both the dominance of her aunt and the hours of the day that must be given over to the care of her younger sibling. She dislikes boys for their baser qualities yet is annoyed with herself for wanting them to like her. Until this summer, she loved her family and did not envy her sister's beauty or find her aunt coarse or her brother an object of pity.

The discontent of her fourteenth summer, however, has spilled over into every aspect of her life.

Sara's trauma at the disappearance of her brother leads her to reexamine her relationships in a positive light and to conclude that every human being, including her absentee father, beautiful sister, and retarded brother, has his or her own particular challenges. Also, she realizes that the single quality that distinguishes her father from other people in her life is that he is no longer trying to raise himself up. It is life that has beaten him down.

In tandem with the coming-of-age theme is the social issue of mental retardation. This issue is not the common stuff of fiction. Just as the real world tends to ignore mental impairment, so fiction writers tend to skirt it. Betsy Byars, however, confronts retardation. She affords the reader glimpses of the workings of a retarded mind—Charlie's fascination with the watch he cannot read, his preoccupation with a missing button on his pajamas, his nighttime restlessness, his confusion, and his inability to verbalize the simplest needs.

Further, Byars supplies insights into the pained reality of family members who love the retarded person unconditionally yet find their strength sapped by the need for constant care and vigilance. Nowhere is this captured more graphically than in Aunt Willie's call to the police to report a missing child, who is lost even if he is only three blocks from home, and, furthermore, one who cannot speak to ask for help.

Context

The Summer of the Swans was the recipient of the Newbery Medal in 1971 and has become one of Byars' best-known novels. She tells a good story in a smooth, succinct style and addresses the universal emotions of childhood with sympathy and humor.

Byars is recognized as a popular and prolific author of contemporary realism for both middle grade and junior high readers. She writes about children who are loners or those who have problems with peer or family relationships. In *The 18th Emergency* (1973) she deals with a boy's emotional battles as he works through his fears and accepts life as it is rather than as he would wish it to be. In *The Pinballs* (1977), a story of child abuse, she follows three lonely foster children as they move into a supportive environment and begin slowly to comprehend the idea of caring for others.

Aside from dealing with human fears and relationships, Byars addresses the experience of the relationship between human beings and nature in *The House of Wings* (1972). In this work she explores the theme of persons in need of nature to restore spiritual needs. In *The Winged Colt of Casa Mia* (1973), she deals with the relationship of a boy and a man, intertwined with a boy's love for an animal. Here she combines realism and fantasy.

Even though the main body of her work is contemporary realistic fiction, Byars wrote and illustrated a picture book, *The Lace Snail*, with a valuable message to the young reader: Just as the snail's gift is to make lace, the most generous gifts are those that are given naturally. It is a powerful message.

Byars' works have been translated into Danish, Dutch, Finnish, German, Japanese, and Norwegian. *The Summer of the Swans* was dramatized and presented on national television and is only one of her books that remain popular with young readers.

Elizabeth Crosby Stull

SUNSHINE

Author: Norma Klein (1938-1989)
Type of plot: Domestic realism
Time of plot: The early 1970's
Locale: Near Spokane, Washington, and in Vancouver, Canada
Principal themes: Health and illness, death, and family
First published: 1974
Recommended ages: 15-18

In her late teens, Kate Williams learns that she has terminal cancer. Attempting to understand her ordeal and to leave something of herself for her daughter, she records her thoughts and reminiscences over the last two years of her life.

Principal characters:
> KATE WILLIAMS, an eighteen-year-old mother, who learns that she has terminal cancer
> JILL, Kate's energetic infant daughter by her first husband
> SAM HAYDEN, Kate's boyfriend and later, second husband, a witty, good-natured musician
> DAVID, Kate's first husband, a conservative, college-educated geologist
> WEAVER, Sam's music partner and Kate's cousin, who resents Kate for intruding in Sam's musical career
> NORA, Kate and Sam's earthy neighbor, known for her many male friends and fondness for health food
> DR. GILLMAN, Kate's primary doctor, young and in her thirties, whom Kate regards as a substitute mother

The Story

Based on the true story of Jaquelyn M. Helton, *Sunshine* is a first-person account of Kate Williams' battle with bone cancer. As she describes the final two years of her life, she intersperses enough of her past to present the biography of a girl strongly influenced by the ideology of the late 1960's.

When Kate learns that she has a very serious cancer in the bone of her leg, she is living with her boyfriend, Sam Hayden, and her six-month-old daughter, Jill, in the mountains near Spokane, Washington. Having been incorrectly diagnosed and treated for bursitis, Kate has lost precious time; she is advised to have her leg amputated. Realizing that she cannot care for Jill with only one leg, Kate refuses the operation, planning to seek a second opinion in Vancouver, Canada.

At this time, Sam proves his commitment to Kate and Jill. Because her illness may become a burden, Kate suggests that Sam should leave her. Sam met Kate while she was pregnant with Jill, yet he chose to live with her, even listing himself as

Jill's father on the birth certificate. Sam refuses to abandon Kate and Jill. While Kate is still in the Vancouver hospital, they are married.

Prior to their departure for Vancouver, David, Kate's first husband, makes an inopportune appearance. Kate had married David at the age of sixteen, while he was still in college. Realizing that she was not the traditional housewife, and acknowledging that she married as an escape from her mother, she had left David without telling him that she was pregnant. David now demands custody of Jill. After a tense evening, Sam takes David aside and explains that Kate has cancer; David leaves immediately and does not interfere again. Though brief, this scene quickly establishes the relationships of the characters, reinforces Sam's commitment to Kate and Jill, and reveals much of Kate's past.

In their apartment near the Vancouver hospital, Kate keeps house and cares for Jill between chemotherapy treatments. The previous diagnosis has been confirmed, with amputation of her leg being the most hopeful treatment, but not guaranteeing a cure.

As a result of the medication, Kate's personality changes. She becomes short-tempered with Jill and Sam. After an honest discussion with her doctor, Kate realizes that medication is only prolonging her life while making life less desirable. Dr. Gillman supports her decision to end medication and live a fuller, though shorter, life. Sam is less understanding. Calling her decision "suicide," he leaves for several days. Though sympathetic to his reaction, Kate longs for him. They reunite, after which Sam, thus far unemployed, finds a job. As Kate's health quickly deteriorates, neighbor Nora helps care for Jill while Sam works. Kate frequently worries about who will care for Jill after her death, though Sam has legally adopted her.

Eventually the cancer spreads to Kate's lungs, and she must enter the hospital for her final days. She continues to record her thoughts on a tape recorder loaned to her by Dr. Gillman. Throughout her ordeal, she reveals little fear of death, finding separation from Sam and Jill her greatest concern in dying. Her last recorded thoughts are of Jill.

Themes and Meanings

Coping with illness and death is clearly the central theme of *Sunshine*, but it is important only to the extent that it interacts with the theme of family relationships and friendships. Kate faces death squarely, resenting more than fearing it, at the same time confessing that she does not understand it. To her, Heaven seems a dull place. She briefly discusses burial versus cremation. Commenting on reincarnation, Kate decides that she would prefer to return as a cat.

The effect of her cancer and imminent death on those she loves becomes her major concern and ultimately the purpose of the book. When she becomes angry with God, questioning His existence, it is because of His unfairness in leaving Jill motherless. Kate's response is to keep Jill close and to leave behind on paper and tape anything that may help Jill answer life's questions. An outgrowth of this is an exploration of the mother-daughter relationship: Kate wants Jill to receive the open-minded understanding that Kate's own mother never exhibited.

Prolonged illnesses can have profound effects on spouses. Marriages may fall apart, or partners may be drawn together. Both effects are portrayed in Sam's relationship with Kate. As they face her illness, Sam's commitment deepens. When Kate decides to end her treatments, however, death becomes a reality to Sam, who suddenly expresses his vulnerability by running away. Even at her death, Sam is not nearby to comfort her. He cannot face losing her.

Context

When author Norma Klein is mentioned, the title *Mom, the Wolfman, and Me* (1972) springs to mind. *Sunshine* is not her best-known work, but it is representative of her straightforward approach to issues concerning juveniles and young adults. In contrast to much adolescent fiction, in *Sunshine* Klein offers no black-and-white resolutions to the issues raised.

This broad-minded approach to life, accompanied by a "free love" doctrine, environmental concerns, and antiwar sentiments, firmly places *Sunshine* in the early 1970's. For example, Kate lives with her boyfriend, considering marriage too confining. She wants her body to return to the earth when she dies. Her poetry often condemns the war in Vietnam. These ideas are in many ways timeless, but American youth culture of the 1960's and 1970's embodied and extolled them. As Irene Hunt's *Across Five Aprils* (1964) allows the reader to experience the issues of the Civil War through Jethro Creighton's eyes, *Sunshine* conveys the philosophies of a time in American history through Kate's own life applications.

More than simply portraying a historical culture, however, *Sunshine* challenges the reader to face life's most perplexing questions: Why do young people sometimes die? How should one face death? What comes after death? *Sunshine* is certainly not the only young adult book to discuss death. *Bridge to Terabithia* (1977) by Katherine Paterson, *Rumble Fish* (1975) by S. E. Hinton, and even *Little Women* (1868-1869) by Louisa May Alcott present central figures who must deal with the death of a loved one. John Gunther's *Death Be Not Proud* (1949) and Jeannie Morris' *Brian Piccolo: A Short Season* (1971) both discuss the illness and death of the main character. Yet *Sunshine* is unusual for its first-person narration.

One feature *Sunshine* shares with other memorable books dealing with death is that its overall message does not focus on death at all. Rather, Kate asks, in effect, "When death is impending, how should one choose to live?" Subtly, the reader finds himself or herself asking, "But should I not live this way all the time?" *Sunshine*, rather than a morbid account of the progression of a terminal disease, becomes an unromanticized commemoration of a life.

Karen Ann Ebert

SWALLOWS AND AMAZONS

Author: Arthur Ransome (1884-1967)
Type of plot: Adventure tale
Time of plot: August, 1929
Locale: Lake District (Coniston Water), England
Principal themes: Friendship, family, nature, and sports
First published: 1930
Recommended ages: 10-13

The four Walker children meet the two Blackett girls while camping on an island in the Lake District. Together they have sailing adventures and prove to the Blacketts' Uncle Jim that piracy is more fun than being a stuffy native.

Principal characters:
>JOHN WALKER, the resourceful and dependable captain of the
>sailboat *Swallow*, who is about eleven or twelve years old
>SUSAN WALKER, the motherly first mate, who is about ten or
>eleven
>TITTY WALKER, a highly imaginative eight- or nine-year-old able-
>seaman
>ROGER WALKER, the ship's boy, delighted at age seven no longer
>to be youngest and to be allowed to participate
>NANCY BLACKETT, the eleven- or twelve-year-old captain of the
>sailboat *Amazon*, whose real first name is RUTH
>PEGGY BLACKETT, an Amazon pirate, who is nine or ten years old
>JIM TURNER, Nancy and Peggy's uncle, a writer and traveler called
>CAPTAIN FLINT by the children
>MRS. WALKER, the Australian-born mother of the Swallows, who
>is resourceful and imaginative

The Story

During their summer holiday, the four oldest children of a high-ranking British naval officer come with their mother, baby sister, and nurse to the Lake District, where they stay with a farm family. When they discover a sailboat named *Swallow* and an apparently uninhabited island on the lake, they immediately write to their father in Malta for permission to sail to the island and camp on it. His telegraphed reply reads, "BETTER DROWNED THAN DUFFERS IF NOT DUFFERS WONT DROWN," and the Walker children begin their preparations. John, the oldest, is to be Captain, and Susan is to be First Mate. The imaginative Titty is Able-Seaman, and Roger, no longer the youngest, is Ship's Boy. John and Susan are to be responsible for the younger two and take their responsibilities most seriously. The children draw up the ship's articles, gather their supplies (with help from their mother and the friendly natives who own the farm), and sail to the island.

There they discover evidence of earlier campers and settle into a fine campsite. The previous inhabitants, however, were Nancy and Peggy Blackett, local children who sail the *Amazon* and hoist the Jolly Roger. Nancy's real name is Ruth, but her Uncle Jim told her that Amazon pirates must be ruthless, and she quickly took a new name. During the previous summer, Uncle Jim had been a fine companion, teaching the girls to sail and even buying them *Amazon*, but this year he is busy writing a book and has forbidden them to bother him. The Amazons and the Swallows negotiate a "treaty of offence and defence," which will enable them to fight mock battles with each other whenever they like and combine forces to attack Uncle Jim, whom they dub Captain Flint.

First, though, comes the war between the Swallows and the Amazons over who shall be Commodore and which sailboat shall be Flagship. The two crews agree that whichever captain captures the other's ship shall win the honor, and the opposing captains plot their strategy. Meanwhile, burglars have broken into Captain Flint's houseboat and stolen a locked trunk containing his book manuscript, as the Swallows had been warned by friendly natives would happen. Captain Flint had rejected John's earlier attempted warning, suspecting him of a prank played on him by the Amazons. Titty, who captures *Amazon* almost by accident while playing at being Robinson Crusoe, overhears the thieves burying the trunk, but a search fails to reveal it. Captain Flint apologizes to John for his suspicions and for having wrongly called him a liar, and he agrees to join the pirate games as he had the previous summer.

The next day brings the battle, and Captain Flint is made to walk the plank. He then serves a sumptuous banquet and leads the Swallows and Amazons in singing sea shanties. Titty, however, has her heart set on retrieving the treasure she knows is still there. On their last day on the island, Titty and Roger go by themselves to find the trunk. When they do so, Captain Flint presents Titty with his parrot in gratitude. The Swallows and Amazons plan for their next year's adventure, and a rousing storm completes the perfect summer holiday.

Themes and Meanings

Arthur Ransome enjoyed the outdoors and spent his summers in the Lake District when he was a child. In *Swallows and Amazons* and its sequels, he has created an idealized British childhood, with emphasis on self-reliance, the discovery of nature, the joys of sailing, and the bonds of friendship and family. In this ideal world of games, sailing, clearly defined roles, familial harmony, understanding adults, and dependable friends, the child heroes have everything they could wish for. They have the excitement and delicious fear of danger without any real risk of injury, the thrill of discovery, emotional support and wise counsel when they need it, and the freedom to do as they like, when they like. It is a childhood that never was but as all wish it could be.

At the same time, Ransome makes it clear that integrity is the first principle of the ideal childhood. It is when Captain Flint calls John a liar that the otherwise steady captain of the *Swallow* is reduced to tears; John is shocked that his integrity has been called into question, and his brothers and sisters understand and sympathize. The discovery of this unjust accusation enrages the volatile Captain Nancy, and she immediately confronts Captain Flint and demands an apology for John, which (much to his credit) her Uncle Jim promptly delivers. Later, John confesses to his mother his misjudgment in a night-sailing episode during the war with the Amazons; she gently agrees that it was rash but supports his good sense in reporting it.

The other major theme of *Swallows and Amazons* is embodied by Titty, in many ways the most delightful of the children. It is her bountiful poetic imagination that keeps the plot moving forward, ties the pieces together, and suggests that the reader, too, can use his or her capacity for imaginative play. She continually sees possibilities that the more prosaic children overlook, and she persuades them to follow her example. It is surely no coincidence, for example, that she brings Daniel Defoe's *Robinson Crusoe* (1719) along on the voyage, while John brings a compass and Susan, a frying pan.

Ransome describes sailing and camping in realistic and loving detail, with the obvious intention of instilling a desire for these activities in his audience. While not all readers will respond, for many, *Swallows and Amazons* can become a treasured experience to which one can return again and again, with each reading recapturing the joys of childhood and imagination.

Context

Set in England in August of 1929, *Swallows and Amazons* portrays children of a particular class in a particular time. Between the world wars, England was struggling with the remnants of her empire, not yet having faced the inevitability of its decline. On the domestic front, the ancient class structure was still in force, though it, too, tottered on the brink of extinction. From a modern perspective, the reader sees strong elements of both problems in the text.

The Swallows are the children of a high-ranking naval officer. The boys attend private schools; the family takes its summers in the Lake District; they have a nurse to look after their baby sister. John and Roger automatically assume that they will follow their father into the navy; given the advent of World War II ten years later, this assumption takes on unintentional irony for a modern reader. Even the Amazons provide evidence of the class structure underlying the novel. Their family has a cook and presumably other servants. Their uncle gave them the expensive present of a sailboat the previous summer. These are not working-class people. At the same time, the working-class people whom one does see in the novel are all anxious to please their social superiors; there is even the young policeman who is bullied by Captain Nancy. While the children are not conscious of any class distinctions and treat everyone with the respect to which they are entitled, the reader cannot fail to notice the obvious distinctions that are drawn.

Similarly, the plot betrays a racism and mild paranoia that clearly marked England between the wars. There is much talk of "enemies," "natives," and "savages," and the children almost automatically fall into a quasi-military "treaty of offence and defence" in imitation of their elders. There is also a strong element of sexism in the rigid roles that the Walker children assume (John is captain, while Susan does all the cooking, for example), although this is mitigated somewhat by the introduction of the Amazons.

It must be noted, however, that seeing these things in the novel requires a modern perspective; without knowing what was to come, Ransome was simply presenting a loving portrait of an ideal English childhood, using many of the conventions of the pastoral. *Swallows and Amazons* is best seen as representative of its time. Ransome went on to write eleven other novels in the *Swallows and Amazons* series, from 1930 to 1947, nine of which focus on the characters introduced here. He has been often imitated but never equaled. The Swallows were apparently based on a real family, and Ransome, a journalist and world traveler, arguably makes his own appearance in most of the books as Uncle Jim.

David Stevens

A SWARM IN MAY

Author: William Mayne (1928-   )
Type of plot: Domestic realism/mystery
Time of plot: The mid-twentieth century
Locale: A cathedral boys' choir school in Great Britain, modeled upon the Canterbury Choir School in Kent
Principal themes: The arts, coming-of-age, education, and friendship
First published: 1955; illustrated
Recommended ages: 10-13

Owen refuses to serve as cathedral Beekeeper until he finds a small white ball that mysteriously attracts bees and the key to a room locked for four hundred years. His discoveries restore him to favor in the school, enhance his sense of self-worth, and revive an old cathedral ceremony.

Principal characters:
>JOHN OWEN, a cheerful, rather feckless Welsh youth, who is the youngest Singing Boy in the cathedral choir
>TURLE, the genial, psalm-quoting watchman, whom the boys fondly call TURTLE
>MR. ARDENT, the occasionally acid-tongued, sometimes indulgent headmaster, affectionately called TWEEDLEDEE
>DR. SUNDERLAND, the portly, good-humored organist and choirmaster, who also is known as TWEEDLEDUM
>MR. CHARLES UNWIN SUTTON, the elderly, sharp-tongued Latin Master, called BRASS BUTTON
>TREVITHIC, the adventurous, sometimes cheeky Head Chorister
>MADINGTON, a serious, officious senior boy, who is good at Latin
>IDDINGLEY, a junior singing boy, who reluctantly agrees to serve as Beekeeper but yields with relief to Owen

The Story

The novel's central conflict is indicated when usually good-natured, unassuming John Owen returns to cathedral choir school after spring holidays and is dismayed to discover that as youngest Singing Boy, he is expected to serve as Beekeeper one week later. Although the cathedral has kept no bees for four hundred years, the position holds ceremonial significance and falls automatically to the youngest boy, who must deliver a new wax candle to the bishop and sing the Introit on the Sunday after Ascension Day. Unwilling to expend the effort to learn the Latin and dreading to sing solo, Owen persuades Iddingley, next youngest, to replace him in return for the customary salary of five shillings.

Owen's refusal arouses the displeasure of Mr. Ardent, the school's perceptive, acerbic headmaster, who maintains that the boys should cheerfully assume whatever responsibilities come their way; of Mr. Sutton, the elderly no-nonsense Latin master, called Brass Button; and occasionally of the boys. Among them are Iddingley, who was not keen about the office in the first place and becomes less enthusiastic when he realizes how much Latin is involved; Madington, a conscientious senior; and Head Chorister Trevithic, a quick, clever, adventurous, fun-loving senior from Cornwall, who deplores Owen's dereliction of duty but remains loyal. In spite of pointed banter, barbed remarks, and increasing isolation, Owen refuses to change his mind.

Matters take a turn when, on a trip to the storage room in the old Norman tower to fetch Owen's Welsh dictionary from his trunk, Owen and Trevithic hear the music of the Beekeeper's Introit. They remember the legend about a beekeeper lost in the cathedral, shut in by mistake when, at the time of Henry VIII, old Prior Tollelege decided not to keep bees anymore and sealed up the bee room. They investigate, careful to avoid Turle, the slow-moving yet seemingly omnipresent watchman called Turtle, and find a key connected to a chain bearing a smooth white ball that exudes a mysterious, enticing odor when warm. They fit the key to the crumbling lock of a small room at the head of a spiral staircase and discover the remains of the Prior's beehives.

Invited to view the swarming bees of affable Dr. Sunderland, choirmaster and organist, Owen prevents a small swarm from leaving by singing to them and allowing them to cling to the little white ball, which holds a peculiar fascination for them. Now interested in bees, Owen gets the idea of reenacting the old ritual, in which the Beekeeper brings the bishop a swarm for the tower room as well as a candle for the service.

Trevithic and Dr. Sunderland help Owen gather the old wax and fashion a candle, and Madington and especially Brass Button help him learn the Latin. The Ascension Day Sunday service goes beautifully. Turtle leads the procession, Owen carries the swarm dangling from the white globe, the bishop is properly impressed, Mr. Ardent compliments Owen, the old ritual is reinstituted, Owen's self-esteem is restored, and his reputation with masters and boys is redeemed.

Themes and Meanings

Although it employs conventions of the English school story—in which the closed world of the boarding school becomes a microcosm of the larger society, an older youth mentors a younger, and group transcends the individual who is often bullied into acquiescence—*A Swarm in May* stresses friendship in the sense of affectionate acceptance and loyalty in helping a recalcitrant member adapt to regulations. These ideas appear both in the plot and in the interplay between the characters as Owen struggles to maintain his individuality as well as contribute to society. The music, the bees, and the legend also serve as catalysts.

Owen's viewpoint persists throughout, and the reader identifies with him as he leaves behind the outside world and readjusts to the school atmosphere replete with inside jokes, colloquial expressions, and the behavioral codes of masters and peers.

Willful and determined if lazy, Owen treads a tightrope to get his way, and even though in his innocence and ignorance he sometimes exaggerates incidents, he shows the stuff of which leaders are made in maintaining his position. The novel goes a step beyond the usual school story in not forcing him to admit he is wrong. Solving the mystery of the locked room and reinstituting the ceremony enable him to save face as he becomes a full-fledged member of society. This ending avoids the didacticism that an admission of shame would produce.

While rules are important and infractions incur expressions of scorn or even punishment, the extensive humor particularly evident in the dialogue relieves the tension of Owen's increasing estrangement. The masters are consistently respectful and supportive of the boys. The boys not only discipline one another in unabusive if strict ways but also, as in the case of Trevithic, do not hesitate to bend rules in the interests of adventure and to satisfy the healthy curiosity expected of right-minded youths.

The mystery and detecting add spice and contribute to the resolution of Owen's problem. Education, secular and religious, is another important aspect of the book. The cathedral resonates with both organ and vocal music. The church music and the frequent biblical and other literary allusions underscore the importance of maintaining tradition, and the good-humored tone provides an optimistic atmosphere in which Owen can work out his problems. Owen's recovery of the Beekeeper ceremony supports the importance of maintaining tradition as it also provides the opportunity for him to come of age gracefully.

Context

A Swarm in May is the first of William Mayne's several choir school novels that are loosely based on his own youth at the Canterbury Choir School. *Choristers' Cake* (1956), the best known of the sequels, employs the plot pattern of *A Swarm in May* in having a boy come of age by entering a club under the friendly but firm persuasion of peers and masters. Mayne's choir school stories enlivened a subgenre fallen from popularity.

Friendship and detecting or solving a mystery appear elsewhere in Mayne's books. In *The Blue Boat* (1957), two brothers united against an unsympathetic guardian enter into an unusual friendship with outsiders from society, circus freaks. In *The Member for the Marsh* (1956), four boys who have formed a singing group on their school bus seek the source of mysterious noises in the local marsh. *A Grass Rope* (1957) has two sisters and two schoolboys unravel the mystery behind a local legend involving a lost treasure. In *Ravensgill* (1970), two young people solve an old murder mystery and lay to rest the feud between their families, forming a friendship at the same time.

Regional or tightly restricted landscapes and local color assume importance in Mayne's stories. The music, religion, and traditions in the cloistered setting of *A Swarm in May* direct the lives of the inhabitants to such an extent that the cathedral functions almost as a character in its own right. Yorkshire dialect, ways, and outlook affect the action in *Ravensgill*, *A Grass Rope*, and *The Member for the*

Marsh, while the coastal setting of *A Year and a Day* (1976), about a strange foundling discovered on the Cornish shore, strengthens the book's mystical, fairy-tale quality. Highly regarded for realism, Mayne has also attained prominence for fantasy. *Earthfasts* (1966), which improvises on Arthurian legend, was named to the Lewis Carroll Shelf, *A Year and a Day* appears on the *Horn Book* Fanfare list, and *A Game of Dark* (1971), a shrewd psychological study tight with emotion, is an honor book for the Children's Literature Association Phoenix Award.

Alethea K. Helbig

SWEET WHISPERS, BROTHER RUSH

Author: Virginia Hamilton (1936-   )
Type of plot: Psychological realism
Time of plot: The 1970's
Locale: A city in southern Ohio
Principal themes: Health and illness, death, emotions, and family
First published: 1982
Recommended ages: 13-15

Brother Rush, a dead uncle, appears to fourteen-year-old Teresa Pratt in the form of a ghost. The visitations from the past help Teresa cope with the illness and death of her brother, Dabney.

    Principal characters:
      SWEET TERESA "TREE" PRATT, a lonely teenage girl who lives in an isolated apartment and takes care of her older brother
      DABNEY "DAB" PRATT, her older brother, who at seventeen years of age is retarded and physically ill
      VIOLA "M'VY" SWEET RUSH PRATT, their mother, a practical nurse, who lives and works in another part of the city
      BROTHER RUSH, a dead uncle who appears to both Tree and Dabney in the form of a ghost
      SYLVESTER "SILVERSMITH," M'Vy's friend and companion, whose physical and emotional strength help both M'Vy and Tree deal with Dabney's death
      MISS CENITHIA PRICHERD, an old woman without family who cleans the apartment

The Story

Viola (M'Vy) Pratt is a single parent forced to provide for her children by working as a practical nurse outside the home. For weeks at a time, Teresa (Tree) Pratt is burdened with the responsibilities of attending school, cooking and cleaning, and overseeing her older brother, Dabney Pratt, who is retarded and frequently ill. She retreats to a lonely and inward existence.

Tree first encounters Brother Rush as she is taunted by some young men on the street. Rush is standing on the corner dressed in clothes proper for a wedding or funeral. For the next three weeks she sees him now and again, but he is always in a fixed position. She discovers that Brother Rush is a ghost when she enters a small workroom in the house and sees him standing through the middle of a table. Peering into a space-mirror cupped in Brother's hand, she enters his time and space. She experiences events and people of the past.

An understanding of the family history takes shape over the next few days as Tree revisits the small workroom. She learns that her brother, a difficult and unmanageable child, was physically abused by her mother, who lacked patience and understanding. Brother Rush, her mother's brother, was killed in a car crash. Her vision, however, reveals that Brother Rush jumped to his death rather than endure the pain of a physical condition aggravated by sunlight, drugs, and alcohol.

These harsh family revelations are softened by the descriptions of Tree caring for her brother—communicating through touch, reading to him, and providing for his physical needs. Sharing the mystery of the workroom with her brother reveals that he, too, has the gift of seeing into the past, but his visions are of family funerals.

In the middle of the night M'Vy arrives at the apartment. Tree confronts her mother with the visions and Dabney's illness. M'Vy has no doubt that her daughter has inherited the *"mystery"* for seeing. Not until her son collapses on the floor, however, does she face the reality that Dabney has developed all the symptoms of the inherited family condition known as porphyria.

Enlisting the help of her friend Sylvester (known as Silversmith), M'Vy frantically gets Dabney to a hospital. Emotions abound. M'Vy must face the guilt of neglecting her son. Tree experiences anger toward her mother, anxiety over her brother, and ambivalence as she learns of her mother's close relationship with Silversmith.

Eagerly anticipating her brother's return, Tree is devastated to learn of his death. Her emotions erupt; she lashes out at the things and people around her. She is determined to leave home, especially when she discovers that her mother has already given Dabney's room to Miss Ole Lady Cenithia Pricherd.

Tree's anger and grief are tempered when she sees her lifeless brother at the funeral parlor and realizes that death has released him from a life of pain. The story ends on a note of hope: Tree begins to embrace M'Vy, Silversmith, his son Don, and Miss Pricherd.

Themes and Meanings

From the very first chapter of *Sweet Whispers, Brother Rush*, the main character's affection for a ghost named Brother Rush intrudes on the descriptions of a family caught in the complications of poverty. The ghost serves not merely as an invention of Teresa Pratt's imagination but also as a poetic device that allows Tree to understand and cope with present circumstances by visiting the family of the past. A theme of survival despite the "wasteland" of misfortune emerges from the intricate plot when Tree accepts the death of her brother Dabney and begins to establish new family relationships.

The love relationship between Tree and Dabney is central to the plot and theme of the story. While Tree's world is bounded by the obligations of caring for Dabney, it is enriched by her sense of closeness and their intuitive communication. Tree's relationship with Dabney is in sharp contrast to M'Vy's relationship with her son. M'Vy physically beat, isolated, and rejected her son; Tree finds comfort in touching, enjoys his companionship, and assumes the role of both mother and sister. It is only through his death, however, that Tree is freed from the role of mother. It is only through her vision of Dabney's release from his painful physical existence to live in an imaginative world with Brother Rush that Tree is freed to pursue new relationships, including a relationship with Silversmith's son, Don.

Sweet Whispers, Brother Rush is about a black family that struggles to endure in southern Ohio. At first it may appear incidental that the family is black; however, the two most important plot devices are traced to the African American heritage. The gift of the "*mystery*," which gives credence to the device of the ghost, is explained as "in the blood of centuries, comin down the line, just like health or sickness." The genetic abnormality known as porphyria is described as originally a white man's disease that was most likely passed on to the black population of North America via the slave trade. Hence, Virginia Hamilton has deftly rooted both the novel's fantasy and its realism in the black experience.

Context

Virginia Hamilton, author of numerous award-winning novels for young readers, is best known for *M. C. Higgins, the Great* (1974), which received the 1975 Newbery Medal and several other honors. *Sweet Whispers, Brother Rush* is her second most recognized book, having received the 1983 Coretta Scott King Award, the Boston-Globe Horn Book Award, and designation as a Newbery Honor Book and an American Book Awards Honor Book.

The granddaughter of a runaway slave, Hamilton has a deep sense of the generations of her ancestors and their struggles in southern Ohio. She draws upon her clan history and black heritage to create characters who manage to survive severe circumstances and in the process come to an understanding of self. The character of Tree Pratt, therefore, is in the tradition of M. C. Higgins, who survives a strip-mining spoil heap that threatens to bury his home, as well as that of Junior Brown (*The Planet of Junior Brown*, 1971), a 262-pound musical genius, whose hope for survival comes from his association with a streetwise buddy and a school janitor.

The author's sense of living in several time periods simultaneously by seeing the world through the eyes of her ancestors has resulted in her exploration of literary space-time imagery. While *M. C. Higgins, the Great* contains the subtle image of a "*feeling*" to convey the presence of the original ancestor to the mountain, the ghost in *Sweet Whispers, Brother Rush* and the psychic powers in Hamilton's Justice cycle (*Justice and Her Brothers*, 1978; *Dustland*, 1980; and *The Gathering*, 1981) demonstrate a bolder use of space-time imagery.

It is the use of space-time imagery in *Sweet Whispers, Brother Rush*, however, that reveals Hamilton's incredible talent for conveying "the illusion of reality." *Sweet Whispers, Brother Rush* is a high-wire act, balancing the imaginative yet realistic fiction of *M. C. Higgins, the Great* and the science fantasy of the Justice cycle. With its creation, Hamilton has explored a new genre that might best be described as "inventive realism."

Dorothy Ruth Troike

A SWIFTLY TILTING PLANET

Author: Madeleine L'Engle (Madeleine Camp, 1918-   )
Type of plot: Fantasy/science fiction/moral tale
Time of plot: The late twentieth century and medieval times
Locale: New England, Wales, and the fictional South American country Vespugia
Principal themes: The supernatural, science, and religion
First published: 1978
Recommended ages: 13-15

> *When Madog Branzillo, the dictator of the South American country of Vespugia, threatens to start a nuclear war with the United States, Charles Wallace Murry and the unicorn Gaudior return to the past through time travel and make use of an ancient rune to prevent Branzillo from carrying out his plans.*

Principal characters:
> CHARLES WALLACE MURRY, a precocious fifteen-year-old boy, chosen to travel back through time to stop the destruction of the world
> GAUDIOR, a unicorn, sent to help Charles in his perilous journey
> MEG MURRY O'KEEFE, Charles's older sister, who is able to communicate with her brother telepathically
> MRS. BRANWEN ZILLAH "BEEZIE" O'KEEFE, Meg's mother-in-law, who gives Charles the ancient rune of Patrick
> MADOG BRANZILLO, "EL RABIOSO," the dictator of Vespugia
> THE ECHTHROI, evil forces who try to thwart Charles and Gaudior

The Story

A fifteen-year-old boy, Charles Wallace Murry, and a unicorn, Gaudior, are called to travel back in time to intervene in past events in order to prevent a nuclear holocaust. To alter past events, Charles must use his powers of empathy to go within others in order to steer them toward goodness and prevent specific acts of evil from occurring. Charles and Gaudior must find the specific Might-Have-Been that has led to the present crisis. Throughout their time travels, they are harassed by the Echthroi, powers of evil who try to thwart them.

The Murry family are gathered in their country home for Thanksgiving dinner when Dr. Murry receives a call from the president. Madog Branzillo, dictator of Vespugia, has threatened to start a nuclear war with the United States in twenty-four hours. Somehow he must be stopped. With the help of an ancient rune taught to him by his sister Meg's mother-in-law, Mrs. Branwen Zillah O'Keefe, Charles has the means of stopping Branzillo, if he can find the precise Might-Have-Been and alter it in time.

Despite the cold rain, Charles goes outdoors to his favorite star-watching rock and recites the first two lines of the rune. Gaudior, a winged unicorn, appears, and the two ride the wind back into the past. On their first trip back in time, they witness the creation of the universe, when all was harmonious until some of the stars turned away from the good. After they observe the creation of the earth and the solar system, Charles enters the consciousness of Harcels, a young boy of the People of the Wind, in order to experience the sensation of being within another person.

As Charles and Gaudior ride the wind forward in time, they are thrown into a Projection, an evil possibility that the Echthroi want to make real. With the help of the rune, they escape and return to their mission. Charles enters the mind of Madoc, a Welsh prince who has come across the seas to the New World before the time of Leif Eriksson. On the day of his wedding, Madoc must vanquish his jealous brother, Gwydyr, who has unexpectedly appeared, before he can marry Zyll, the native princess. Madoc triumphs with the aid of the rune, and Gwydyr leaves for South America, to settle in what eventually becomes Vespugia.

Charles and Gaudior travel forward in time to New England during the Puritan era. Charles enters the mind of Brandon Llawcae, a young Welsh boy, just in time to prevent Zylle Llawcae, his sister-in-law and one of Madoc's descendants, from being hanged as a witch. Attempting to move in both space and time, Charles and Gaudior are almost destroyed by the Echthroi as they try to reach Vespugia. To recover their strength, they travel to Gaudior's home planet, where Charles witnesses the hatching of baby unicorns from eggs.

After their recovery, they return to Earth, having realized that Madog Branzillo's name is derived from Madoc and from Bran and Zillie, suggesting a connection with the Welsh settlers of Vespugia. Charles must ensure that Bran Maddox, who has emigrated to Vespugia from New England, will marry his American fiancée, Zillah, and not the Vespugian temptress Zillie, so that their descendant, the dictator Madog Branzillo, will turn out to be a man of peace and not of war. Charles manages this difficult task, although he is almost lost at the death of the sickly Matthew Maddox, Bran's twin brother, whose being Charles has entered. Mrs. O'Keefe and Meg hurry outside and say the rune to bring Charles back. As they return to the house, there is a call from the president saying that the threat of war has been averted.

Themes and Meanings

In the apocalyptic struggle between good and evil in Madeleine L'Engle's work, salvation often comes from the weakest and most unlikely sources, since everything in the universe is ultimately interdependent. Through her fictional narrative, L'Engle retells the story of creation and the primal disobedience of the rebellious stars, resulting in the creation of evil. The presence of evil disrupts the harmonies of the universe. Now humans live in an irrational, unpredictable world in which they must work actively to create peace and reason in their hearts, as the Murrys do at their Thanksgiving dinner. The powers of darkness may reach even into the sanctity of the home, as with the sudden telephone call from the president, informing Dr. Murry of the threat of nuclear war. Each act of goodness will somehow influence the future.

Prayer, courage, and faith are the weapons of choice of L'Engle's characters in the struggle against the powers of evil.

The particular evil represented by Madog Branzillo can perhaps be traced back to a reenactment of the story of Cain and Abel, brother fighting against brother. From the original enmity of Gwydyr and Madoc stems the Might-Have-Been that will influence Madog Branzillo's decision on whether to launch nuclear missiles. If he is to choose for peace, Gwydyr's children should not marry Madoc's, because it makes all the difference who Branzillo's ancestors were. In the center of this genealogical suspense is Mrs. O'Keefe, who proves to be distantly related to Branzillo. She is the one who finds the letters and diary entries that ultimately resolve the question of Branzillo's parentage.

Not only is genealogy important to L'Engle's plot, but names and naming are significant as well. The act of naming confers identity. As Mrs. O'Keefe points out, Branzillo is a combination of his parents' names, Bran and Zillah. The name Vespugia is perhaps derived (like the name America) from that of the explorer Amerigo Vespucci; Gaudior is Latin for "more joyful"; and the name of the Murrys' dog, Ananda, is Sanskrit for "the joy in existence without which the universe will fall apart and collapse."

Context

In *A Swiftly Tilting Planet*, L'Engle has virtually created a new genre that incorporates myth, fantasy, suspense, and science fiction. The novel derives its mythic quality from its retelling of Scripture, particularly the stories of creation, the Garden of Eden, and Cain and Abel. The fantasy element stems from the assumption that by traveling back in time, individuals can alter past events so as to prevent evil contingencies from occurring. Success in that struggle is by no means guaranteed, however, and several times Charles and Gaudior are almost lost in Projections thrown in their way by the Echthroi.

L'Engle is an accomplished children's writer who makes great demands upon her readers, but whose books offer equally great rewards for perceptive readers. She has acknowledged the influence of George Macdonald on her work, which at times also resembles that of C. S. Lewis and Ursula Le Guin. *A Swiftly Tilting Planet* is part of L'Engle's fantasy trilogy, which also includes the Newbery Medal-winning *A Wrinkle in Time* (1962) and *A Wind in the Door* (1973). In each of these works, Charles and Meg Murry, at various ages, embark on a series of fantastic adventures that involve them in the cosmic struggle of good and evil. In each book, their eventual triumph comes not through force or might, but through their quiet confidence and self-knowledge and their ability to name and to love, which link them with the ancient universal harmonies.

Andrew J. Angyal

SWIFTWATER

Author: Paul Annixter (Howard Allison Sturtzel, 1894-   )
Type of plot: Adventure tale
Time of plot: The late 1940's
Locale: The Maine wilderness
Principal themes: Nature, coming-of-age, and animals
First published: 1950
Recommended ages: 10-13

Bucky Calloway overcomes hardships of the Maine woods, the attack of a wolverine, and the death of his father to supply his family's needs and fulfill his dream of creating a wildlife refuge.

> *Principal characters:*
> BUCKY CALLOWAY, a fifteen-year-old boy, who is thrown into providing for his own family
> CAM CALLOWAY, Bucky's father, whose lessons of survival in the woods pay off when he breaks his leg and Bucky is able to run the trap lines
> LIDE CALLOWAY (MA), Bucky's long-suffering mother, who prefers life in town to the woods
> BRIDIE MELLOTT, Bucky's girl, who does not understand his intention to build a wildlife refuge
> WHIT TURNER, who fights Bucky for Bridie and the dream of a sanctuary for the migrating geese
> DEL FRASER, one of the townspeople, whose eye is turned by commercial interests

The Story

Although *Swiftwater* was published in 1950, several themes in the novel make it a timeless story for young adults. Bucky Calloway, the fifteen-year-old son of a local woodsman, faces family hardships, physical danger, and the insults of the people in the town of Swiftwater who do not understand the Calloways' way of life. A reverence for nature and a concomitant distrust of civilization; episodes of love, adventure, and combat; incidents in which emotion overcomes reason; and the devaluation of commercial interests make this junior novel a romantic tale.

Bucky's father, Cam, teaches the boy about hunting, trapping, and survival in the wilderness. Cam takes great—but silent—pride in the abilities of his son, and a strong mutual respect develops between the two. It is not long until Bucky must tend his father's trap lines by himself because Cam has broken his leg. On his first trip out to check the traps, Bucky finds stolen bait and devoured game that has been caught in the now-ruined traps. A porcupine that has been eaten—quills and all—

and the remains of a silver fox tell him that this destroyer is not the usual bear that raids the trap line. Cam and Bucky have been warned by Peter Nigosh, an old Indian, that there is a "bad dog" raiding the traps in the woods this winter. He suggests that they wait until next year to set their trap lines, but Cam is determined that nothing keep them from their livelihood.

Bucky faces the frightening prospect that this "bad dog" is a wolverine, the most mysterious and feared woodland creature. Doubling back along his trail, Bucky surprises the wolverine and is able to hit him with a hurried shot. Bucky follows a trail of blood to a large undergrowth through which he must crawl to get at the wounded animal. His rifle lost, Bucky must slay the wolverine with his ax and hunting knife. At sixteen, he has a pelt that most woodsmen only hear about from old-timers.

Bucky's skill in the woods contrasts sharply with his inability to communicate with others, especially Bridie Mellott, the girl in whom he has been interested for several years. Standing in his way is Whit Turner, a boy from town he has fought before and who is also laying claim to Bridie. Since this defeat, Whit has trained himself for revenge but is still no match for Bucky.

Whit's defeat opens the way for the beginning of a romance between Bucky and Bridie, and also for the inauguration of a wildlife refuge—a dream Bucky and Cam share. Cam, however, is killed by hunters who are indiscriminately killing the geese the Calloways want to preserve. Bucky has faced the wolverine alone, and now he is alone again, facing the objections of the Swiftwater citizens who see a hunting lodge as a quick way to bolster the town's faltering economy. Not until an enterprising newspaper reporter tells of the Calloways' efforts to make Swiftwater a safe stop for migrating geese is the town persuaded of the value of the bird sanctuary. Bucky not only has learned his father's skills but also has inherited the reality of his father's dream.

Themes and Meanings

To view *Swiftwater* as merely an adolescent's initiation into adulthood is to ignore other important statements. First, it is a story about a young man overcoming difficulties. Bucky faces the woods, the wolverine, his father's injury and death, and the insults of the townspeople, who fail to understand what his father has been trying to accomplish.

Second, *Swiftwater* makes a strong environmental statement. Paradoxical though it seems, the family that makes its living killing animals also champions a cause to preserve their lives. At the same time Cam teaches Bucky to trap successfully, he also teaches him not to take more from the woods than the family needs for survival. He also teaches his son to trap fairly, without using methods that will lead to unnecessary suffering or further harm to other animals. Cam's idea of creating a preserve is his way of replenishing the wildlife that has provided sustenance for his family. It is no accident that the loss of his life leads to the birth of his dream.

Third, the novel presents a pristine wilderness threatened by commercial interests. Hunting, with its lodges, stores, and need for local guides, will bring needed money into Swiftwater. The town loses its innocence when the hunters that Cam guides shoot down geese from a blind and let the wounded birds float downstream without claiming them. In his attempt to prevent the further slaughter of the geese, Cam is accidentally shot. It is ironic that the idea of a sanctuary becomes popular only when its commercial value is revealed by Matt Laird, a local newspaper reporter.

More than a record of Bucky's initiation into manhood, *Swiftwater* is the story of a struggle against both the threat of an encroaching civilization—hunting merely for sport—and the wantonness of the wolverine in the wilderness. It is also the story of death and rebirth. The last lines of the novel show how these ideas come together in Bucky: "In some way Cam had come to stay with him. He couldn't leave. Cam was rooted in his heart like a tree in the good earth."

Context

Howard Sturtzel published more than five hundred short stories before he wrote *Swiftwater* and has completed a number of books and short stories since then. He and his wife, Jane, have collaborated on many of the books published since 1955. Many of his stories, such as *Swiftwater*, focus on nature and life in the wilderness.

Swiftwater's appearance on reading lists was largely a result of the comments of Dwight Burton in an article in the *English Journal*, "The Novel for the Adolescent" (September, 1951). Burton, at one time editor of the *English Journal*, later praised the work in his several editions of *Literature Study in the High School* (1959, 1964, 1970). Burton believed *Swiftwater* to be an important novel because of the adolescent's confrontation with evil, symbolized by the wolverine. To Burton, Bucky represents all adolescents who must at some time fight evil. Burton was not the only one who recommended *Swiftwater* for reading, however. A survey of reading lists shows that *Swiftwater* was one of a number of young adult works of fiction that appeared most frequently.

Swiftwater has several qualities that make it attractive to adolescents. The adventures of hunting, trapping, and observing nature certainly absorb the reader. Bucky's education in nature and the achievement of his goal are as exciting as his victory over the wolverine. A boy's acceptance of increased responsibility is similarly appealing. In *Swiftwater*, Bucky progresses from merely completing chores to being forced to do his father's work, and finally to becoming responsible for his widowed mother. In addition, he becomes a leader in the management of the game preserve. An adolescent's struggles to become a man, confronting the difficult problems of life, the successful completion of a worthwhile goal, and suspenseful action make the book popular with adolescents.

Bill Yost

THE SWISS FAMILY ROBINSON

Author: Johann David Wyss (1743-1818)
Edited and adapted by Johann Rudolf Wyss (1781-1830)
Type of plot: Adventure tale
Time of plot: The late eighteenth century
Locale: An uninhabited Southern Hemisphere Pacific island named "New Switzerland" by the castaways
Principal themes: Family, nature, animals, and coming-of-age
First published: Der Schweizerische Robinson, 2 vols., 1812-1813 (*The Family Robinson Crusoe,* 1814); illustrated
Recommended ages: 10-13

Shipwrecked on an uninhabited island, a Swiss family—father, mother, and four sons—leads an adventurous, Robinson Crusoe-like life as they struggle to survive and create a new home by using the resources available and their own ingenuity.

Principal characters:
FATHER, the head of the family; he is the authority on issues both practical and moral
MOTHER (Elizabeth), expert in matters domestic, she is the loving support of her husband and sons
FRITZ, the eldest son, age fifteen as the story begins; he is his father's counterpart
ERNEST, the second son, two years younger; he is intellectually precocious but sometimes lazy
JACK, the third son, age ten; he is brave and impetuous
FRANZ, the youngest, nearly eight
JENNY MONTROSE, a young Englishwoman found shipwrecked on the island

The Story

From the time of their escape as the sole survivors of a shipwreck on the coast of an uninhabited island, the family (calling itself "The Swiss Family Robinson" after reading the book *Robinson Crusoe*) meets a series of crises and builds a new life with courage and resourcefulness. By salvaging materials from the wreck of the ship and making use of the abundance of the island, the family creates a kind of tropical paradise that they call "New Switzerland." The island, a geographically diverse (though scientifically implausible) repository of flora and fauna from throughout the world, is a rich source of subsistence and the setting for the episodic adventures of the family.

After successfully escaping from the shipwreck and reaching the island, the Swiss

Family Robinson sets about creating shelter, finding food, and exploring the island. While Father and Fritz return to the ship to salvage anything that might be useful, Mother and the remaining boys remain ashore and begin the process of creating a home. Ultimately the family develops a variety of living places, such as a tree house (Falconhurst), a farm (Woodlands), and a salt cavern. The ensuing years are given over to providing for the necessities of life and encountering a series of adventures, usually associated with ferocious or exotic birds and animals, such as ostriches, lions, bears, monkeys, and boa constrictors. All these activities occur in a context of thankfulness to God, who has provided for the family. Each of the boys grows and matures, exhibiting his special talents and coping with his faults. Ernest, for example, provides invaluable assistance through his knowledge of nature, while creating problems on occasion because of his aversion to work.

After ten years, the family has settled into a comfortable existence. One day Fritz discovers a message attached to the leg of an injured albatross. The message asks the finder to save an "unfortunate Englishwoman." Fritz locates and returns to the family with Jenny Montrose, marooned on New Switzerland as a result of another shipwreck. Shortly thereafter, a British brig of war, searching for survivors of the ship on which Jenny Montrose sailed, makes landfall on the island. Each of the family must now make a decision about staying or leaving New Switzerland: Father and Mother remain with two of their sons, Jack and Ernest, with the expectation that colonists will come to share their island; Fritz goes to England to seek permission to marry Jenny, and Franz returns to Europe to be educated and to remain as the family's representative.

Themes and Meanings

The Swiss Family Robinson is an example of a Robinsonnade, a tale of shipwreck and survival in the tradition of Daniel Defoe's *Robinson Crusoe* (1719). Presented in the form of Father's journal, the narrative is both romantic adventure and instructive text that exalts family relationships and the "thoughtful application of knowledge and science" under the protection of a beneficent God. Dramatic episodes that typically involve coping with natural phenomena or unusual animals are interspersed with disquisitions on practical matters, religious references, and parental dicta gently administered. This emphasis on virtuous behavior and instruction in a natural setting suggests the influence of Jean-Jacques Rousseau (whose own Émile is to read *Robinson Crusoe* as his first and always preeminent text) on Johann David Wyss.

Rather than a fully rounded portrayal, each of the members of the family is defined by a few dominant attributes. Father is the paterfamilias, the head of the family in matters spiritual and practical, while Mother exemplifies the virtues of domesticity. The four boys flourish in the island environment, becoming physically and morally strong while overcoming their childhood flaws, such as laziness or impetuosity, under the guidance of their parents. It is this family survival as a loving unit that distinguishes *The Swiss Family Robinson* from many other survival stories in which a solitary individual is the focal point. Yet *The Swiss Family Robinson* is more than a survival tale. The family not only endures, but it prevails through faith and hard work, turning the island into a prosperous and salutary Eden.

Context

The Swiss Family Robinson originated in an extended narrative created by Swiss pastor Johann David Wyss and his four sons for their own entertainment. The story content was influenced by Defoe's *Robinson Crusoe* and the report of the discovery of a Swiss family shipwrecked on an island in the Pacific. Years after its creation, Wyss's second son, Johann Rudolf, edited his father's handwritten copy of the manuscript and had it published.

The novel is a prototype of the survival story in children's fiction and continues to be one of the most popular of its genre, this despite its dated style, somewhat pedantic and moralizing tone, and factual implausibilities. Its primary appeal for children lies in the many adventurous episodes in which the four "real" boys participate with great exuberance, and its uniqueness is to be found in its focus on "communal" survival. Contemporary children's fiction such as Scott O'Dell's *Island of the Blue Dolphins* (1960) and Theodore Taylor's *The Cay* (1969) continue the tradition of the island survival story. Other books consider the survival theme in various settings, from the tundra of Jean George's *Julie of the Wolves* (1972) to the city subway of Felice Holman's *Slake's Limbo* (1974).

The popularity of *The Swiss Family Robinson* has spawned innumerable editions, many of whose authors have taken extensive literary license with the original. Thus, the book has had an independent life of its own in many versions, with significant differences in content (wording, translation, plot sequence, ending) and illustrations.

John J. Carney

TARZAN OF THE APES

Author: Edgar Rice Burroughs (1875-1950)
Type of plot: Adventure tale
Time of plot: 1888-1910
Locale: The African jungle
Principal themes: Nature, friendship, and love and romance
First published: 1914
Recommended ages: 13-15

An English orphan lives the first eighteen years of his life among jungle apes, to whom he is known as Tarzan. After having gradually differentiated himself from the apes, he comes into contact with humans, falling in love with an American woman, Jane Porter, and gaining the friendship of a French naval officer, Paul d'Arnot.

Principal characters:

TARZAN OF THE APES, an exceptionally strong and handsome man, who develops an animal's instincts for survival and furthers an inherent genius for learning

JANE PORTER, a beautiful American woman, who, rescued from death by Tarzan, falls in love with him

LIEUTENANT PAUL D'ARNOT, a ship's officer, who, rescued from cannibals and nursed to health by Tarzan, teaches him the French language and accompanies him to Paris

KALA, Tarzan's foster mother, an ape

PROFESSOR ARCHIMEDES Q. PORTER, Jane's absent-minded father, a widower

SAMUEL T. PHILANDER, his nearsighted secretary, general assistant and devoted friend

WILLIAM CECIL CLAYTON, Tarzan's cousin, an English nobleman in love with Jane Porter

ESMERALDA, the Porters' black maid and the devoted protector of Jane

ROBERT CANLER, a businessman, who offers the Porters financial security in return for the hand of Jane in marriage

The Story

Nature in *Tarzan of the Apes* is shown to be hostile to those who cannot adapt to it. Tarzan's parents, John Clayton, Lord Greystoke, and Lady Alice Rutherford Clayton, fail in their attempt to insert material nicety into the menacing coastal jungle where they have been marooned. Lady Alice dies within a year after bearing her son. Clayton is killed shortly thereafter by the mighty ape, Kerchak. Jane Porter, her father, and other persons from Europe and America prove to be singularly inept at meeting the challenges of the jungle, its beasts, and its cannibal inhabitants.

Lady Alice's orphaned son emerges as the grand exception. Reared from infancy by a female ape who had lost her own newborn, Tarzan, as his adoptive mother calls him, the name denoting "White-Skin," is prodigiously adaptable to his ever-challenging habitat. Among the apes, he learns that survival consists in making the jungle his own. He also learns, by means of the remnants of his human parents' possessions, not only to read and write English but also to discern those qualities of civilized life that are consonant with humaneness and moral compunction. To his great strength and highly developed physical agility, by which he adapts himself to the wilds, Tarzan adds the expert use of his dead father's hunting knife, of rope that had come from shipboard, and of a cannibal's bow and poisoned arrows.

When Jane Porter, her father, her father's assistant, her maid Esmeralda, and her suitor, William Cecil Clayton, who is Tarzan's own cousin, are marooned as John Clayton and Lady Alice had been, Tarzan saves them all from both mutineers and beasts. He falls in love with Jane and she with him, but Tarzan is as ill-adapted to love as the Europeans and Americans are to life in the jungle. Up to this point in his existence, he has experienced no love except the maternal love of an ape, which he requited in filial fashion. He does not force himself upon Jane, but his jungle surroundings offer him no fitting context for the expression of his love. Tarzan and Jane are of different worlds.

The two worlds are tentatively bridged when Tarzan rescues Lieutenant Paul d'Arnot from the cannibals. D'Arnot teaches Tarzan French, which, apart from the language of the apes, is Tarzan's first spoken language. Friendship between the two men develops without the inhibitions and complexities that preclude the consummation of love between Tarzan and Jane. D'Arnot takes his friend to Europe, and Tarzan, with his exceptional aptitude for learning, adjusts to the world of civility and gentility without, however, permitting it to supplant the world of the jungle, to which he will always belong.

It is precisely this world of the jungle that keeps Tarzan's pursuit of Jane from a successful conclusion. He traces her to northern Wisconsin, where he rescues her from a forest fire. Swinging through the trees, he is again in his element, but, again, the romance of dramatic rescue does not overcome the reality of Jane's practical world. Called upon to choose from among three suitors, she does not accept Tarzan, whom she loves, because their worlds are incompatible; nor does she accept Robert Canler, whom she detests, because he represents the venality of her world. She accepts the proposal of William Cecil Clayton, whom she does not love but who does love her and who is a true gentleman. Moreover, she and Clayton share the same world. The story ends with Tarzan's return to Africa and the author's promise of more to come. In *The Return of Tarzan* (1915), Jane will finally abandon her world for Tarzan's and become the mate of her beloved.

Themes and Meanings

Although Edgar Rice Burroughs stated that his idea for the character of Tarzan came from the legend of the she-wolf nursing Rome's mythic founders, Romulus and Remus, the figure of the jungle demigod most closely approximates a fusion of the principal figures in *Gilgamesh* (c. 2000 B.C.): the radiantly intelligent Gilgamesh and the wild Enkidu, whose initial rapport with animals was complete. There abides in the figure of Tarzan much of what eighteenth century Europe had propagated in its concept of the "noble savage," a morally good person living in harmony with nature and uncorrupted by the immorality inherent in European civilization; the noble Tarzan is at least a vestige of the later Romantic extension of this concept.

While *Tarzan of the Apes* may flout the shortcomings of Western civilization, it caters to the notion that breeding and sustained gentility contribute to the continuity of genetic superiority. Tarzan's simian upbringing enhances his physical mastery of the jungle, but his aristocratic English blood ensures his moral superiority to apes, cannibals, and mutineers. Burroughs constructs a gradation of classes: the irrational apes, capable of love, tribal identity, oral communication, and violent hate; the irrational humans, represented by white mutineers and black cannibals; the equestrian or business-oriented class comprising Robert Canler; and the patrician class, represented by the Claytons (including Tarzan), by Paul d'Arnot, and, in her ethereal beauty and moral transcendence, by Jane Porter. The figure of Esmeralda affirms, despite Burroughs' concessions to humanistic egalitarianism, the post-Civil War stereotype of the American black.

The ape-man is the embodiment of Burroughs' major themes. Tarzan's compatibility with the challenges and majesties of physical nature is complemented by his ideally noble capacity for true love and deep friendship. To his beloved Jane Porter and his genuine friend Paul d'Arnot, he is the selfless savior and protector. He is without guile in his human relationships. He displays in both his actions and his attitudes the qualities of the natural man who can adapt to civilization without being contaminated by those ambitions and drives which it shares with bloodthirsty mutineers and cannibals, both of which groups are shown in *Tarzan of the Apes* to devour their own kind. Burroughs makes Tarzan complex enough to weigh profoundly moral considerations, and the character of Tarzan proves that, in the contexts of nature, love, and friendship, inherent goodness can be both interesting and exciting.

Context

Tarzan of the Apes: A Romance of the Jungle first appeared in the October, 1912, issue of *The All-Story* magazine. The publication of *Tarzan of the Apes* in book form two years later initiated the international success of Edgar Rice Burroughs' modern hero. Twenty-one additional Tarzan books followed in the years 1915 through 1947, and two collections of Tarzan stories were published posthumously in 1963 and 1964. Burroughs also published ten novels about the planet Mars, four about the planet Venus, six about the interior of the earth, two Apache novels, and fourteen other novels of adventure, romance, and fantasy. It was the Tarzan figure, however, that contributed a new myth to the world, a myth that gained dimension in motion pictures, comic strips, and television series and even provided such place-names as

Tarzana, California, and Tarzan, Texas.

It is the mythic dimension of *Tarzan of the Apes* that has ensured its popularity with young people. The appeal of Tarzan is his exceptional physical ability coupled with an admirable predilection for morality and justice. The same kind of appeal sustains the popularity of Ulysses, Parsifal, Robin Hood, and Superman. The idea of a healthy mind in a healthy body lends itself to effortful discipline and rigor in formal systems of education and religion. Yet when his or her imagination is caught by the heroic figure of the jungle lord in the form of a suspenseful and stimulating story, the young reader effortlessly and voluntarily pursues the idea. Effective fictional exemplars must be larger than life without seeming to be so; a good storyteller smoothes away the semblance. Burroughs is a superb storyteller, and his Tarzan is a magnificently mythic exemplar of the sound mind in the sound body.

Roy Arthur Swanson

TEACUP FULL OF ROSES

Author: Sharon Bell Mathis (1937-   )
Type of plot: Domestic realism
Time of plot: The early 1970's
Locale: Washington, D.C.
Principal themes: Drugs and addiction, death, family, and race and ethnicity
First published: 1972
Recommended ages: 13-15

Seventeen-year-old Joe, who provides financial and emotional stability for his family, faces his family's problems and searches for solutions.

> Principal characters:
> JOE BROOKS, a former high school dropout, who believes that dreams and actions will create a happier future
> MATTIE BROOKS, his mother, who favors her oldest son and neglects the younger two
> ISAAC BROOKS, Joe's father, who is disabled and seldom confronts Mattie's preferential behavior
> PAUL BROOKS, Joe's older brother, who is a gifted artist and a heroin addict
> DAVID BROOKS, Joe's younger brother, who is an outstanding student and athlete
> ELLIE, Joe's sweetheart, who believes his stories of hope for the future

The Story

Teacup Full of Roses is a realistic novel that tells of a black family's strength and love, which allow them to face the problems of ghetto living. The characterization of the three Brooks brothers—Paul, Joe, and David—forms the basis of conflict and resolution in the novel. Paul, the oldest brother and a gifted artist, is a recovering heroin addict. As the story begins, he has returned to his family after spending seven months in a drug rehabilitation center. Mattie, his mother, overjoyed to have her favorite son home again, plans a family dinner to celebrate. The evening is a disaster because Paul, back on the streets once again, contacts a drug dealer. When he returns home it is nearly midnight and he is unable to eat any of the food Mattie has prepared. In the days that follow, it becomes obvious that Paul has returned to the streets and his drug habit. Mattie directs her efforts toward saving her son, but nothing changes the fact that Paul has given up hope.

Seventeen-year-old Joe, a dreamer who tells stories full of fantasy and hope, provides much of the family's emotional and financial stability. He shares none of his mother's illusions concerning Paul. Conversations with Paul convince him that his brother has no intention of giving up heroin.

Joe is faced with two questions that will affect his family and his own life: How can he help David, his younger brother, who is both a talented athlete and a scholar? What should he do after his own high school graduation?

Joe's first decision ensures that David will participate in a special program for gifted seniors. When his mother refuses to speak to the counselor, Joe has the permission papers notarized, takes them home for signatures, and gives them to David. Concern for David's future also influences Joe's second decision, regarding his own immediate future. Joe cancels plans to attend college with his sweetheart, Ellie, and decides to enlist in the Navy and give David the money he has saved. An old jacket in David's closet becomes an overnight hiding place for the money, which is to be deposited in David's account the following day.

Joe's high school graduation provides the setting for the climax of the novel. His father, Isaac, in the first show of strength in many years, insists that Mattie wear the dress Joe has bought for her and attend the graduation ceremonies. Joe's graduation is a proud occasion for the family: Joe, a dropout, has worked during the day and attended night classes for the past two years to earn his diploma.

Joe joins his family and friends after the ceremonies and learns that Paul discovered the money in the old jacket pocket, has taken it, and has disappeared. Angry and afraid, Joe finds Paul on the street in a deep nod, then locates the local drug dealer and fights his bodyguards in an attempt to retrieve his money. As the police arrive, one of the bodyguards aims a gun at Joe. David, to save his brother, leaps between the two young men and is fatally shot.

Lying beside his brother's body, Joe assures David (and himself) that his stories are true: There is a place where life is kinder and people are happy; David will soon be there. The reader is assured that Joe, too, will create for himself that happier life of his dreams.

Themes and Meanings

Set in a Washington, D.C., ghetto community, *Teacup Full of Roses* is a novel of hope and despair. Its central theme is the strength inherent in human nature that allows one to hope, even in the most troubled circumstances. This theme is developed by constrasting the characters of Joe, who believes that he can create a better life for himself, and his older brother, Paul, who abandons the hope he once felt.

Of the book's characters, only Joe is able to see beyond the hopelessness of ghetto life. For Ellie, his sweetheart, he creates a symbolic, magic place where there are no dirty streets and troubled lives: a teacup, full of roses. Joe's symbol allows them to imagine and believe that they will achieve their dream.

On one level, Joe appears to be a hope-filled dreamer, but there is another dimension to his character. A former gang leader, friend of a well-known hustler, and competent street fighter, Joe is aware of the reality that gives rise to hopelessness. He recognizes his mother's favoritism, but knows as well her love for him. When David is killed, Joe feels the painful loss, but he continues to rely on his dreams. Life, he believes, is made up of yin and yang, evil and good.

Paul's despair provides a contrast for Joe's faith in love and beauty. A gifted artist, Paul succumbs to drug addiction when his genius is unrecognized. Life is beautiful only when he is drugged; he exchanges his dreams for the needle.

Joe is a symbol of the strength that black men, and all men, can contribute to their families and communities, the strength of toughness, of love, and of magic. Paul, however, no longer believes that he possesses the power or means to move out of the ghetto.

Context

Teacup Full of Roses is Mathis' second critically acclaimed work and first full-length novel. As many critics, and Mathis herself, have noted, her writing is a tribute to the beauty, talent, and tremendous inner resources of black youth. She celebrates the positive aspects of African American culture without ignoring the problems of poverty, discrimination, and racism. In *Sidewalk Story* (1971), Mathis' first widely recognized juvenile book, Lilly Etta's determination and love provide a solution for her friend's evicted family. Muffin, the blind protagonist in *Listen for the Fig Tree* (1974), copes with her father's murder, her mother's grief, and an attempted rape without becoming hopeless or embittered.

Mathis' work can best be understood in the political context of the late 1960's Civil Rights movement. Black leaders believed that black people should value the qualities that make them unique and separate from mainstream culture. Black writers began to be recognized by publishers for their skillful portrayal of their culture; there was an interest in understanding black culture and in publishing the work of black writers. Mathis' work reflects pride in the uniqueness of her culture by creating strong protagonists with close family ties.

Strong family ties are evident in all Mathis' work. Joe's family, in spite of neurotic interaction patterns, is built upon a solid foundation of love. *The Hundred Penny Box* (1975), a Newbery Medal book, clearly demonstrates, through conversations and 101-year-old Aunt Dew's stories, the love and respect Michael has for his aunt. In addition, the language spoken by the characters in Mathis' work is unique to black culture. Considered taboo until the late 1960's and early 1970's, the use of black dialect became a technique for creating realistic characters.

Mathis joins many excellent black writers who describe the positive aspects of black culture to young audiences. Virginia Hamilton's *The Planet of Junior Brown* (1971) and Walter Dean Myers' *Fast Sam, Cool Clyde, and Stuff* (1975), for example, contain strong black protagonists who are proud of their heritage and who struggle successfully with the problems of poverty and racism. In Eloise Greenfield's *Sister* (1974) and Alice Childress' *A Hero Ain't Nothin' but a Sandwich* (1973), young black people give and receive family support. Pride in black culture is nourished by Mathis and writers like her who celebrate the beauty of young black men and women.

Muriel Rogie Radebaugh

TEENS

Author: Louise Mack (1874-1935)
Type of plot: Domestic realism
Time of plot: The late nineteenth century
Locale: Sydney, Australia
Principal themes: Friendship, education, and coming-of-age
First published: 1897; illustrated
Recommended ages: 10-13

A thirteen-year-old girl wins a scholarship to a prestigious private school. Here she forms the first strong friendship of her life, and the two girls encounter various adventures together. Eventually there is a heartbreaking separation because the friend is being taken abroad for several years.

> *Principal characters:*
> LENNIE LEIGHTON, a bright thirteen-year-old girl who lives with her middle-class family in suburban Sydney
> MABEL JAMES, her best friend at school, fifteen years old and equally intelligent and talented
> DR. JAMES LEIGHTON, her wise and loving father, a good provider for the family
> BERT LEIGHTON, her older brother, who likes to tease her but is indispensable as an escort
> FLOSS,
> MARY, and
> BRENDA LEIGHTON, her younger sisters, ranging in age down to seven, who all love and admire their sister

The Story

At age thirteen, Lennie Leighton has a happy life with devoted parents to look after her. When she wins a scholarship to attend a prestigious girls' school, it is the biggest event in her sheltered life. Her three younger sisters are thrilled and share vicariously in all of her new experiences.

At first Lennie feels lonely and unwanted. Then she makes friends with a girl named Mabel James. Mabel has also been feeling rejected, but she and Lennie quickly discover that they share many likes and dislikes. They become inseparable: They sit together in class and walk with their arms locked around each other's waists. Lennie invites her friend home for tea. Mabel is cordially liked by everyone in the family and soon becomes a regular visitor. Mabel's mother has been dead for five years. She has a father and three brothers, and her family's male-run domestic affairs are reminiscent of Charles Dickens' description of Mr. Pocket's chaotic household in *Great Expectations* (1861). Yet the unsupervised environment has made Mabel more aggressive and independent than the typical girl.

At school the girls follow the curriculum considered suitable for young ladies in the nineteenth century. They study English literature and composition, arithmetic, French, history, geography, and fancy sewing. Both Lennie and Mabel are inclined to daydream and are chronically behind in their homework. They like to sneak sweets into the classroom and sometimes get caught at it. The only serious trouble Lennie ever gets into, however, occurs when a teacher catches her surreptitiously reading a book entitled *The Beautiful Wretch*, which sounds far more lusty than it actually is.

Lennie and Mabel have only one falling out—not for any good reason but simply because of hot weather and moodiness. Both are lonely and miserable for days. Finally they are reconciled, as everyone knew they would be, and are happy again.

The two girls create a great stir by starting their own school newspaper; however, a schoolmate launches a rival paper that puts theirs to shame, because her father is a professional printer. The experience of being writers, editors, and entrepreneurs has a sobering effect on the two friends. They buckle down to their studies and achieve spectacular scholastic success.

At the end of the school year, Lennie is stunned and heartbroken to learn that Mabel is being taken overseas. She may not return to Australia for three years. The two girls spend their last night sleeping side by side. Lennie knows that she will never have another friend who will mean as much to her as Mabel. She has learned one of life's cruelest lessons: that everything changes. She will be a sadder but wiser person as a result of her relationship with her friend.

Themes and Meanings

By far the most important theme in this novel is friendship. In fact, Louise Mack stresses the importance of getting along with everyone. Lennie dislikes some of her schoolmates at first, because they seem affected, or stupid, or spoiled, or snobbish; however, through daily experience she learns that all of them have good qualities and that many of them are not aware of the image they are presenting to the world. Lennie's friendship with her three sisters has always been important to her, and it is especially valuable during the bleak period when she is a new girl at the intimidating private school and feels awkward, despised, and inferior. Her sisters love her in the old way and remind her that she is an important human being in her own domain.

When Lennie makes friends with Mabel, a sort of chemical reaction occurs, proving that in friendship one plus one adds up to more than two. Each is encouraged by the approval and affection of the other, so that each is able to blossom and display the full beauty of her personality. During this crucial period of adolescence, each helps the other to become an independent, self-reliant individual. The importance of their friendship to their development is seen during the period when they separate because of a petty quarrel. Each goes back into her old shell and becomes a colorless nonentity. When the quarrel is patched up—which they find very easy to do, since they miss each other's affection so much—they are both strengthened and renewed. It is after this experience that they go into bold new enterprises, such as starting a school newspaper. Mabel would never have considered publishing her poetry without Lennie's encouragement, and Lennie would never have tried to write at all without Mabel's example and support. Together they can do many things that neither could do by herself.

Teens resembles the world-famous novel *Little Women* (1868-1869) by Louisa May Alcott, a work that Mack regarded very highly. Like *Little Women*, the Australian novel stresses the importance of relationships as the source of most human happiness. The novels paint similar pictures of the protected but confined condition of women in the nineteenth century. *Teens*, however, is a far less complex work: It focuses on a single relationship and covers a much shorter period of time.

Context

Teens was originally published in 1897. It is interesting mainly as a historical document, giving an intimate glimpse into the lives of middle-class people, and particularly middle-class girls, in a world without radio, phonographs, television, motion pictures, telephones, automobiles, airplanes, or even electric lights. Social life centered on the family, and it was generally believed that a woman's place was in the home, where she could find her life's fulfillment by ministering to her husband and her children.

The novel shows the well-intentioned but relentless social forces that shaped middle-class girls into wives and mothers. They spent almost their entire lives either at home or at school. Their reading was heavily censored; they were shielded from knowledge of many of the realities of life, and particularly from any sexual knowledge. Lennie creates a sensation by being caught reading a book entitled *The Beautiful Wretch* in class. The middle-aged spinster principal does not even dare to look inside the covers for fear of being contaminated by exposure to the facts of life.

Reading was by far the most common form of entertainment for girls in late Victorian times. It was therefore quite natural that a career in literature might appeal to some individualistic young women, although they were handicapped in comparison to male authors by having so little worldly experience. The modern reader will sense that the object of a young lady's education in the Victorian era was not only to keep her pure but also to keep her ignorant, so that she would be content with the confinement and dependence that were the housewife's lot.

Lennie and her friend Mabel are gifted and intelligent, but their talents are not wanted in a "man's world." This was particularly true for girls growing up in Australia, which in the late nineteenth century was still very much a British colony with a small population and a narrow infrastructure. Lennie and Mabel would have had a bitter struggle to break out of the mold into which their socialization was designed to shape them. Their friendship gives them courage to pursue their literary interests, but when they are separated, they are in danger of losing faith in themselves and abandoning their literary aspirations. They were born a hundred years too soon.

Bill Delaney

THE TEREZÍN REQUIEM

Author: Josef Bor (1906-1979)
Type of plot: Historical fiction
Time of plot: 1944
Locale: Terezín Concentration Camp, Czechoslovakia
Principal themes: Death, religion, and social issues
First published: Terezínské rekviem, 1963 (English translation, 1963)
Recommended ages: 15-18

> *In the summer of 1944, as Adolf Hitler's "final solution" to the Jewish problem nears its climax, Raphael Schächter, a talented young conductor, produces a magnificent performance of Verdi's Requiem at the Terezín concentration camp. The Requiem is performed for Adolf Eichmann and other Nazi officials shortly before Schächter and the five hundred musicians are taken away from Terezín to the ovens of the death camps.*

Principal characters:
RAPHAEL SCHÄCHTER, a sensitive conductor, thirty-five years old
THE OLD BEGGAR, a lover of music and adviser to Schäcter in preparing the *Requiem*; also known as "The Court Councilor"
FRANCIS, a tenor and a Jewish cantor
ANNEMARIE (MARUŠKA), a Bavarian soprano
ELIZABETH, a formerly famous mezzo-soprano
ELIZABETH'S HUSBAND, crippled during the "Night of Broken Glass"
MEISL, a cellist
JOSEF, a bass
BETKA, a mezzo-soprano who replaces Elizabeth
MEPHISTOPHELES, a chimney sweep, a bass who replaces Josef
RODERICH, a cantor's son and a tenor, one-quarter German, formerly in the German army
HAINDL, a Schutzstaffel (SS) officer
THE CAMP COMMANDANT
ADOLF EICHMANN, chief architect of the "final solution"

The Story
 In the summer of 1944, as the German army begins to suffer shattering defeats, Adolf Eichmann converts the Terezín ghetto, in central Europe, into a disguised assembly camp for the newly constructed Birkenau extermination camp. Among the Jews at Terezín is Raphael Schächter, a brilliant young conductor who decides to embark on a study of the Giuseppe Verdi *Requiem*. Schächter is attracted to the project by the incredible availability of talent at Terezín, where the Nazis have as-

sembled thousands of artists to promote the image of Hitler's "model" camp. He is also drawn to the *Requiem* as a prayer for the dead that may comfort the prisoners of the concentration camp and help him answer profound questions about the meaning of life and death for Jews under Nazi rule.

Coached by a half-deaf, old beggar (who later turns out to be a musical genius), Schächter begins to assemble his choir and soloists. Chief among them are Francis, a cantor from Galacia who sings tenor; Maruška, a delicate soprano who has witnessed unspeakable Nazi atrocities; and Elizabeth, a famous mezzo-soprano whose crippled husband is the choir's first audience.

Because the Nazis are concealing the actual purpose of Terezín, they lead Schächter and his musicians to believe that they will be secure there. Nazi officials provide sheet music and instruments, confiscated from Jews all over Europe. They remove all the inhabitants of the local hospital and turn it into a rehearsal hall. They reassure all the musicans that they will not be separated. The performers rejoice in the hope that they will be spared the fate of their fellow Jews in the camps.

This confidence is shattered when the injured and disabled who have been evacuated from the hospital are taken away, and their relatives in the choir follow them to their doom. Schächter must start assembling musicians all over again. New soloists miraculously appear, including Roderich, the son of a Jewish father and a Roman Catholic mother who unknowingly sent him to Terezín for his own protection when the German army drafted him. Roderich finds the choir rehearsing while running away from Haindl, a particularly vicious SS man whom he has insulted and actually struck. Haindl cannot find his victim as Roderich blends into the choir, and Schächter is delighted to have found a tenor who can replace the departed Francis. Yet on the eve of the performance, Roderich appears again, distraught with fear. This time he cannot escape Haindl and the torture and death he knows await him. He asks Schächter to lead the choir in one last chorus for his sake and sings his solo in a trembling voice—his own farewell to his friends and fellow Jews.

At last Schächter succeeds in assembling a company of singers, and the premiere of the *Requiem* takes place before an audience of Jewish inmates. Eichmann himself arrives to inspect the camp, and the commandant summons a performance for the Nazi officials. Schächter's final gesture of defiance is to alter the last bars of the *Requiem*, "Libera Me," from Verdi's original soft whisper to a thundering drum roll, proclaiming the Jews' powerful longing for freedom. It is the last performance for Schächter and his musicians. The Nazi command keeps its promise not to separate the *Requiem* performers, and they are all led away to the ovens together.

Themes and Meanings

The overwhelming theme of *The Terezín Requiem* is the search for meaning in a world of unspeakable evil. Schächter ponders the purpose of his enterprise as he coaches the soloists in the various parts of the *Requiem*, always interpreting Verdi's prayers for the dead as pleas for his fellow victims. The final cry, "Libera Me," becomes a call for freedom, not only from the terrors of hell but also from the earthly hell of the death camps.

Schächter, as Bor's voice, is also preoccupied with expressing the meaning of Judaism as a means for understanding good and evil. He chooses the *Requiem* as an attack on Hitler's ideas of pure and impure blood—"Italian music with a Latin text, Catholic prayers, Jewish singers . . . studied and directed by an unbeliever." Yet it soon becomes apparent to Schächter that Verdi's Catholic sensibilites must be reinterpreted to make the *Requiem* meaningful to a Jewish audience. Jewish theology teaches that good and evil, rewards and punishments, take place here on earth, among the living. Verdi's Catholic concept of eternal retribution, as described in the "Dies Irae" portion of the *Requiem*, no longer means a Day of Wrath at the Last Judgment, but God's righteous anger, which is already sweeping over the Nazi empire in Europe and will exact historical justice in this world. Hell is no longer an otherworldly region to be feared after death, but rather, the living hell that is the camps.

Finally, *The Terezín Requiem* explores the question of how the powerless may respond to evil. Even at Terezín, where death is always waiting, Schächter and his musicians create meaning through their art. Roderich, the tenor, chooses to sing a last verse with the choir when he finds out that he is to be tortured and killed. Schächter himself rewrites the last verse of the *Requiem* to remind his listeners and his fellow inmates that they have not forgotten their desire for freedom. *The Terezín Requiem* is a reminder that human beings matter even in the shadow of certain death.

Context

Josef Bor, himself a survivor of three death camps, wrote *The Terezín Requiem* as a tribute to the five hundred Terezín musicians who did not live to tell their stories. As Israel Knox points out in the introduction to *An Anthology of Holocaust Literature* (1968), in which part of *The Terezín Requiem* is reprinted, the books of the Six Million are "a sort of cemetery," and in reading them, "we are reciting *Kaddish* [the Jewish prayer for the dead] for those who left none to say it for them."

Like other Holocaust memoirs—Elie Wiesel's *Un di velt hot geshvign* (1956; *La Nuit*, 1958; *Night*, 1960), Primo Levi's *Se questo è un uomo* (1947; *If This Is a Man*, 1959; revised as *Survival in Auschwitz*, 1961), Fania Fénelon's *Sursis pour l'orchèstre* (1976; *Playing for Time*, 1977)—Bor's book makes the unthinkable real by telling the story of a small group of people whom the reader comes to know as individuals. Studied in a history book, the sheer magnitude of the Holocaust may seem unreal, but in the story of Raphael Schächter, the reader encounters a vivid character with feelings and aspirations. As Schächter and the others meditate on the meaning of evil, the existence of God, and the nature of history, they become real people who can be believed, admired, and mourned.

Although it was not written primarily for adolescents, *The Terezín Requiem* is one of a small number of Holocaust memoirs that can be read and appreciated by young people whose only knowledge of the Holocaust comes from history books. The issue of appropriateness is an especially difficult one where Holocaust literature is concerned. Young readers may not be developmentally ready for graphic descriptions of torture and crematoria; yet, it is essential that they learn about the camps and ovens as they really were. Bor's book is a good choice for the mature, young adult reader; though the horrors are suggested, the focus of the novel is on the humanity of Schächter and his musicians. The book is tragic, even shocking, but never grotesque.

Critics have debated the value of historical memoirs over fictional accounts of the Holocaust, and some have concluded that, in this particular case, history is so powerful that it is a profanation to fictionalize it. Bor's book partakes of both approaches, starting with real characters known to the author, and embellishing with details to bring the story to life. Like Victor Frankl's powerful memoir *Ein Psycholog erlebt das Konzentrationslager* (1946; *Man's Search for Meaning*, 1959), *The Terezín Requiem* ultimately celebrates the greatness of the human spirit—that a prisoner could compose a work such as Verdi's *Requiem* and sing it in the midst of unfathomable evil. Most of all, in memorializing Schächter, Bor has created his own *Requiem*, not only for the Terezín musicians but also for all those who perished without graves in the ovens of the Holocaust.

Rita M. Kissen

THESE HAPPY GOLDEN YEARS

Author: Laura Ingalls Wilder (1867-1957)
Type of plot: Historical fiction
Time of plot: The late nineteenth century
Locale: DeSmet, South Dakota
Principal themes: Coming-of-age, family, and friendship
First published: 1943; illustrated
Recommended ages: 10-13

Laura Ingalls has been offered her first teaching position at the age of fifteen. Through her new experiences, she learns just how important her family is to her and must decide if she is willing to grow apart from them to start a new life with Almanzo.

Principal characters:
LAURA INGALLS, a sensitive, caring, determined, and dedicated girl, who has grown up on the prairies of the frontier
ALMANZO WILDER, bachelor farmer, who shows interest in and concern for Laura and who eventually becomes her husband
CHARLES (PA) INGALLS, Laura's "jack-of-all-trades" father, whose influence on her for strength and guidance is a mainstay in her life
CAROLINE INGALLS, Laura's mother and role model
MARY INGALLS, Laura's older sister, who attends a school for the blind in Iowa
CARRIE INGALLS, Laura's younger sister
GRACE WILDER, Laura's youngest sister
MRS. BREWSTER, a bitter, despondent farmer's wife, with whom Laura lives while teaching in her first school
MR. BREWSTER, Mrs. Brewster's farmer husband

The Story
These Happy Golden Years opens on a sunny winter morning on the prairies of South Dakota, with the protagonist, Laura, on her way to her first teaching position in a nearby settlement twelve miles from town and her home. During her ride in the open sleigh with her father, she expresses her concerns and fears to him about teaching. As they near the house in which she will stay, she begins to realize that life as she knew it is about to change. Once she enters the house, she is confronted with a family that is quite unlike the one she has known. Thus, Laura begins to make her transition from childhood to adulthood. Although she can understand the bitterness and hostility in the Brewster home, she cannot help but reflect upon the uniqueness and specialness of her own home and family. Yet this experience is merely the begin-

ning of her growth and reflection.

As she begins her first day as teacher in the one-room school, she is confronted with children who are reluctant to learn and eager to challenge her. She must now begin the process of gaining their trust and respect. When she returns at night to the Brewsters' house, she is faced with the misery and frustration of a woman who despises her life and living conditions; her infant son, who is neglected and unhappy; and her husband, whose only concern is survival for the family. To help her cope, she devotes all of her time to her studies in an effort to keep pace with her classmates back in town and remembers that her employment will allow her sister Mary to continue to attend a school for the blind in Iowa.

As her first week drags on, she comes to the realization that the twelve-mile trip there and back is too difficult for horses to make during this time of year. She is confronted with the fact that she will be confined with this family for two months and begins to fear the coming days. As school ends on the last day of her first week, she hears sleigh bells and looks to see two familiar horses pass the window. They belong to Almanzo Wilder. Thus begins the weekend trips to and from town with him and the beginning of a cautious relationship and another transition in her life.

Throughout the eight weeks of her employment, she gains confidence in herself as a teacher and begins to respect and appreciate Almanzo and his concern for her. More important, she gains new insights into the significance and closeness of her family and their dependence on one another. When she returns home, she notices the details of the touches her mother adds to the house and the love and caring that are reflected in the music of the fiddle and the words of the songs her father sings with them.

As she develops into her womanhood, she grows into a relationship with Almanzo that, in her independent way, she at first denies. Her free spirit and independence remain an important part of her character and an integral part of his attraction to her. Upon his eventual proposal, she is most concerned as to whether he will want her to "promise to obey" him. Their Sunday drives in his sleigh or buggy (depending on the time of year) eventually bring her to the realization that he is indeed someone special to her. She is torn between her commitment to and deep love for her family and her desire for a life with Almanzo but realizes that maturing and growing away is part of life, and she willingly looks forward to their life together.

Themes and Meanings

Beginning with Laura's transportation to a nearby settlement and ending with her first night in her new home with Almanzo, this story is one of a series of transitions. Throughout this novel, the reader sees Laura growing up and into her various new roles as teacher and financial contributor to her family and eventually relinquishing these roles to become a wife.

The initial setting of winter and harsh, unpredictable weather conditions symbolize and forebode the changes in her life and the conflict of emotions that are about to take place. As she glides over the snow in the opening scene on the way to her first teaching position, she seeks her father's advice. As the story progresses, the reader sees her returning to her family members for advice and guidance in helping her define herself and her future. Much of the book deals with her reflection on her past: the security she has known throughout her happy childhood and the importance of her family in her life. This reflection and the confidence she gains from it help her in making her transitions.

In one important episode near the end of the book, she and Almanzo encounter severe weather while on one of their Sunday rides. It proves to be a tornado, and in her effort to escape its ravages, Laura must rely on Almanzo to prevent them from being overtaken by it. Her confusion and trepidation about her relationship with him are dramatized and symbolized by this episode. Almanzo proves himself by returning her safely to her home. Thus, a major transition is made by her placing her trust in him and accepting him as a part of her family. She is now ready to commit to a relationship with him. As the story closes, the reader finds Laura and Almanzo on the doorstep of their new home, and she expresses her contentment with her world. She in essence has made the transition to womanhood and is satisfied.

Context

These Happy Golden Years is the last "complete" book written by Laura Ingalls Wilder in a series. Although *The First Four Years* (1971) was written as a sequel to this novel, it was never finished by her for publication but was instead released after her death. In essence, *These Happy Golden Years* marks the end of her truly happy and idyllic childhood as portrayed by the series. Her life immediately following her marriage was fraught with hardships. Drought, crop failure, sickness that eventually left Almanzo permanently lame, the death of her infant son, and the destruction of their house by fire finally forced them to move. She did, however, have a daughter, Rose, who eventually became a writer herself and encouraged Wilder to write an account of her childhood.

The Wilders were eventually to settle near Mansfield, Missouri, where they were content to farm. Her success with farming and her ability to express herself in writing led to her first published article in the *Missouri Ruralist* in 1911. One year later, she became the editor of the home section for the magazine and a contributing author to other recognized national publications.

The "Little House" books stand alone for their portrayal of family life in the expanding American West during the late 1800's. Her characters, though flawed and each with his or her own peculiar weakness, demonstrate the strength of character and determination that helped the pioneers to survive and eventually conquer the frontier. The writing in *These Happy Golden Years* is an example of Wilder's direct, uncluttered, and simple style that reflects the direct, uncluttered, and simple lives of the time. This style not only adds to the force of the book but also makes it accessible to readers who are just learning to tackle writing of this length. The book's topic and content parallel the initial studies of the westward expansion in the school curriculum, thus potentially making both the study and the reading more meaningful. Finally, *These Happy Golden Years* is a satisfying conclusion to the series in presenting the successful transition of Laura Ingalls from childhood to adulthood.

Donna C. Kester Phillips

THIMBLE SUMMER

Author: Elizabeth Enright (1909-1968)
Type of plot: Domestic realism
Time of plot: The Depression
Locale: Rural Wisconsin
Principal themes: Family and nature
First published: 1938; illustrated
Recommended ages: 10-13

Nine-year-old Garnet and her family experience a hot, drought-filled summer on a Wisconsin farm during the Depression.

Principal characters:
GARNET LINDEN, a nine-year-old tomboy
JAY LINDEN, her eleven-year-old brother
CITRONELLA HAUSER, her best friend
MRS. EBERHARDT, Citronella's great-grandmother
ERIC SWANSTROM, a homeless thirteen-year-old
MR. FREEBODY, a kindly neighbor, who often rescues Garnet from the consequences of her actions
TIMMY, a piglet, the runt of the litter

The Story

In the tradition of family stories, *Thimble Summer* consists of a series of episodes rather than a linear plot. The reader first meets Garnet and her family at the beginning of a hot, dry summer in Esau's Valley, Wisconsin, during the Depression. In the course of that summer, Garnet begins to grow up, the Linden family expands and its fortunes change, and the perennial rhythm of the seasons works its magic.

Discovery is a motif in many of the episodes, starting with Garnet's finding an old silver thimble in a stream one oppressively hot day. Ever hopeful, Garnet is sure that the thimble is an omen; that very evening the drought breaks, and a spectacular thunderstorm heralds the renewal of all the crops in the valley. Also at the beginning of the summer, Garnet feels sorry for the runt piglet, Timmy, and begins paying him special attention. Where others take the familiar for granted, Garnet can often see something new and important.

Garnet's discoveries are not limited to the here-and-now. In imagination, she goes back to the Indian days of Esau's Valley through the reminiscences of her friend Citronella's aged great-grandmother, Mrs. Eberhardt. So, too, she broadens her life vicariously through the adventures of Eric Swanstrom, a homeless vagabond who turns up one night when Garnet's family and Mr. Freebody are firing lime for their new barn. Eric stays on and eventually becomes part of the family, and Garnet discovers much about how a family grows and changes.

Several of Garnet's discoveries involve journeys. A trip to nearby Blaiseville leads to her being locked in the town library with Citronella; a trip to New Conniston, eighteen miles away, introduces her to people outside the valley and to the experience of running out of money far from home. A day at the county fair brings another emergency when Garnet and Citronella are trapped on the Ferris wheel. On all these excursions, Garnet's resourcefulness, as well as the generosity and helpfulness of those around her, pull her through.

By summer's end, the Lindens have a new barn and a new member of the family, the crops are safely gathered, and Timmy has won a blue ribbon. Garnet, reflecting on what has happened in this memorable summer, sees a magnificent blue heron, which seems to symbolize her happiness; the heron takes flight, and Garnet crosses the pasture turning handsprings in her exuberance.

Themes and Meanings

Thimble Summer is a book about farm and family. The rhythmic cycle of the seasons controls life in Esau's Valley, as it did in Mrs. Eberhardt's girlhood and as it will in generations to come. Author Elizabeth Enright makes this continuity explicit, linking the valley's present to its past through Citronella's great-grandmother and to its future through Eric, who wants to become a farmer as much as Jay wants to escape. Mr. Freebody, their kindly old neighbor, has had a series of dogs named Major and a series of horses named Beauty; the individuals change, but the part they play remains constant. Every year has its summer, and Enright is careful not to invest this one summer with too much symbolic importance.

Family, too, represents stability amid changes. There is always room for growth, whether literally, by taking in another person such as Eric, or figuratively, by giving members of the family room to learn from their own mistakes, as when Garnet runs away to New Conniston. The family in *Thimble Summer*, as in Enright's other books, is a place where people can try out new roles (for example, when Garnet wants to become a sailor) yet where, at the same time, there are always plentiful reminders of reality.

Unlike many favorite books for older children and young adults, *Thimble Summer* presents growth and change as gradual and incremental. There is no single rite of passage in this story, no turning point after which things are forever different. Indeed, Garnet grows through repeated experiences; her thoughtlessness causes her to be trapped first in the library, and later on the motionless Ferris wheel. In the trip to New Conniston, which forms a central section of the story, she goes from the initial mistake of running away from a bungled task to the more serious one of running out of time and money in a strange town. In all these crises, Mr. Freebody rescues Garnet and admonishes her; three near-disasters call for three appearances by Mr. Freebody. So, too, there are two chapters in which Garnet listens to people's life stories, two journeys that she makes, and two scenes—one at the beginning of the summer, one at the end—in which she thinks about the silver thimble she has found and gives it special meaning in her life and that of her family.

Context

Thimble Summer marks a turning point in Enright's career. Originally trained as an artist, she had illustrated several books (for one of which she also wrote the text) before returning to her own experiences in Wisconsin for material. Enright's mother (sister of the architect Frank Lloyd Wright) came from a place known among her family as "the Valley." The author, an only child brought up in the city and suburbs by a single parent, enjoyed many visits to rural Wisconsin; later, she took her own children there and incorporated their experiences into her stories. The myth of the countryside as a place of permanence, to which one can always return, meant much to Enright. (Later, another city-bred writer—E. B. White—would use similar material—farm, girl, and pig—in *Charlotte's Web*, 1952.)

All Enright's books after the Newbery Medal-winning *Thimble Summer* deal with families, and most employ the same kind of episodic plot, interspersed with stories of interesting people's lives in other places and other times. During the 1940's, Enright brought out a very popular series of books about the Melendy family. In *The Saturdays* (1941), she recounts the adventures of the four Melendy children on their Saturday-afternoon outings in Manhattan. In *The Four-Story Mistake* (1942), the family moves to the country and has more adventures, including an acting career for Mona and the discovery of a diamond ring in a brook by Randy. *Then There Were Five* (1944) describes the arrival of an orphan boy, Mark, who joins the family. A later book, *Spiderweb for Two* (1951), continues the story of the younger two Melendy children, after Mona and Rush have gone to school.

Some years later, Enright introduced the Blake family, in *Gone-away Lake* (1957) and *Return to Gone-away* (1961). Again, an episodic series of adventures leads to a permanent move to the country, and again, well-drawn child characters enjoy a number of different experiences and learn from one another, as well as from some odd but likable older people.

Among writers of family stories, Enright has most often been compared to Eleanor Estes, author of the Moffat books. Like Estes, Enright portrays the family as stable, traditional, and almost infinitely flexible. Both authors show families headed by a single parent and frequently short of money. The Moffat children live in the shadow of World War I, the Linden children in the anxiety of the Depression, and the Melendy children in the rationing and shortages of World War II. Few other writers of family stories equal Enright and Estes in their careful handling of the political and economic background.

Where Enright excels is in her delicate and varied prose style, in her descriptions of nature, and in the psychological complexity of her characters. Enright chose to write in essentially the same style she had used in her adult stories for *The New Yorker* magazine. In this respect, she invites comparison with another great prose stylist who wrote for children of all ages, E. B. White.

Caroline C. Hunt

THINGS FALL APART

Author: Chinua Achebe (1930-   )
Type of plot: Social realism
Time of plot: The late nineteenth century
Locale: The Ibo region of eastern Nigeria
Principal themes: Race and ethnicity, social issues, politics and law, and religion
First published: 1958
Recommended ages: 15-18

The Ibo village of Umuofia enjoys a routine traditional life until the arrival of Christian missionaries and the British colonial government. The clan must adapt or, like Okonkwo, face a tragic end.

Principal characters:

OKONKWO, a respected man of title in Umuofia, whose pride is unyielding against overwhelming odds

EKWEFI, Okonkwo's second wife

EZINMA, their daughter and Okonkwo's favorite

IKEMEFUNA, a boy, given by Mbaino to Umuofia in compensation for a murdered Umuofia girl, who is reared in Okonkwo's household

UNOKA, Okonkwo's father, who is remembered for his cowardice and laziness

NWOYE, later called Isaac, Okonkwo's first son, who fails to live up to his father's expectations

CHIELO, the priestess of Agbala and chief oracle of Umuofia

OBIERIKA, Okonkwo's friend and confidant, a voice of reason in the community

UCHENDU, Okonkwo's uncle, the wise elder of Mbanta, who graciously receives his exiled nephew

MR. KIAGA, an Ibo interpreter from a different clan, who heads the Christian church in Mbanta

MR. BROWN, the first Christian missionary to Umuofia

REVEREND JAMES SMITH, Brown's intolerant, uncompromising replacement

The Story

Set in the Ibo region of what is now eastern Nigeria, *Things Fall Apart* re-creates the life of an African people before and during the early colonial period, at the end of the nineteenth century. While the novel attempts to capture typical features of daily and yearly routines and, indeed, focuses attention on the village as a communal character, the primary focus is on one character, Okonkwo, whose self-definition is dependent on the survival of the clan. Son of the cowardly Unoka, who spent his time talking and playing the flute instead of working his farm, Okonkwo dedicates his own life to hard work and to achieving the four highest titles of the land. As the novel begins, he has already attained two of them and is one of the nine spirits of the clan who adjudicate civil disputes; he has a prosperous farm, three wives, and several children.

The future, however, will not be so kind. A series of misfortunes will prevent him from realizing his final goal. The first misfortune stems from his character and his status within the traditional culture. When someone in the neighboring village of Mbaino kills a young woman from Umuofia, the two villages come to a political settlement to avoid war. Mbaino agrees to send the widower another wife and the village a young boy, Ikemefuna, as compensation. Okonkwo is to keep him until his fate is decided. After three years, Okonkwo learns that Ikemefuna must die. Though he is warned discreetly not to participate in the execution, a fear of cowardice drives him to strike the fatal blow; the emotional effect on him is significant and lasting.

The second misfortune seems totally accidental. At a wake in honor of Umuofia's eldest dignitary, Okonkwo's gun explodes, killing the dead man's son. According to the law of the land, Okonkwo must, for this inadvertent killing, suffer seven years of exile in his mother's homeland. As a matter of custom, his entire compound is destroyed. He must start a new life in Mbanta. He is thus cut off from the community which might one day have afforded him its highest honor.

The third misfortune is the loss of his son Nwoye. Being the eldest, Nwoye would be expected to carry on Okonkwo's name, but he never measures up to his father's rigid standard. Okonkwo's disappointment is no secret. Ezinma, the daughter of his second wife, has much greater strength of character than Nwoye, but a female cannot fulfill a social role reserved for males. Already rejected as a suitable heir, Nwoye spiritually withdraws from the household after his father kills Ikemefuna. Like others who cannot prosper within the Ibo way of life, Nwoye eventually abandons father and mother to follow the new Christian god.

Thus, it would seem that Okonkwo is doomed by character and circumstance to fail. His uncle in Mbanta, Uchendu, tries to restore his confidence. Indeed, in spite of all three misfortunes, when Okonkwo returns to Umuofia after his exile, his fighting spirit returns as well. He soon discovers, however, that times have changed. During those seven years not only the Christian church but also the British colonial government have begun to replace the old authority that gave his ambition meaning. Things move too rapidly for him. While his two grown daughters may find suitable husbands, his sons will have to wait two years to earn their *ozo* titles. He has become materially prosperous again, but the spiritual significance of prosperity is lost. Christian converts multiply; an elder is even sending a son to the British school, and the people are quickly adapting to a British economic system. Neighboring clans hold a conclave to decide their future course, but when Okonkwo senses that they will not go to war, on his own he kills one of the messengers who have come to break up the meeting. His life over, Okonkwo commits suicide and becomes both an obscure paragraph in a district commissioner's book about primitive tribes and a prominent symbol of cultural and ethnic vulnerability in the twentieth century.

Themes and Meanings

Behind the story of Okonkwo and the pictures of Ibo culture, slightly disguised but clearly audible, echoes the voice of the author, a philosophical voice; in the measured tone Achebe adopts toward his character, his people's history, and the new order there is humor and equanimity. His main character, Okonkwo, reflects the voice negatively by his failure to achieve philosophical detachment in his quest for personal fame, to evaluate personal desire within a wider frame of reference. Ibo proverbs, which record traditional wisdom, can guide the individual, but as in any society, the individual must be wise enough to apply them.

The proverbs themselves are likely to be, not surprisingly, contradictory on controversial matters. On the one hand, for example, the Ibo of *Things Fall Apart* acknowledge the presence of fate in human character, designated by one's personal god, or *chi*. On the other hand, the Ibo recognize individual ambition that makes success possible. After his return to Umuofia, his fortunes temporarily improve; Okonkwo seems more reliant on fate than on his own strong will: "His *chi* might now be making amends for the past disaster." The seven-year exile has thus had a humbling effect, but it does not grant Okonkwo inner strength. His perception of manly dignity is still inseparable from public honor within a provincial order.

While Okonkwo bases his very identity on the absoluteness and immutability of his culture's values, other elders, more cosmopolitan in their outlook, recognize that what is true in one part of the world is not true in another. Obierika, the primary voice of reason in the novel, suggests a moderate response to the changing times. Uchendu asks the exiled Okonkwo not egotistically to consider himself a unique case but to observe the tragic suffering others endure. The new order with the white man must be seen within a larger tragic sense of life. The final authorial attitude would seem to be close to the philosophical stoicism of Obierika and the tragic awareness of Uchendu as they watch their world fall apart about them.

Context

Things Fall Apart is the first of four novels by Chinua Achebe tracing the recent history of the Ibo people as they become part of the Nigerian state. *Arrow of God* (1964) takes up the story twenty-five years later, in the confrontation of an Ibo priest and a firmly entrenched British colonial power. *No Longer at Ease* (1960) presents the experience of a Western-educated Nigerian during the 1950's, and the satirical *A Man of the People* (1966) focuses on political instabilities in the postindependence period of the 1960's. Such historically oriented novels about traditional life and the impact of colonialism are typical of African literature since World War II. They are, at the same time, Western in language, form, and preoccupation; generally suspicious, however, of Western civilization; and genuinely concerned about losing a way of life, a cultural heritage, and an ethnic identity.

Of all these and other attempts to re-create Africa's past, *Things Fall Apart* is probably the best known and most widely read. Though not intended specifically for young audiences, it not only is accessible to the adolescent reader but also provides an introduction to a non-Western culture through an entertaining medium. Achebe takes seriously Uchendu's warning that all stories are true and proves that not only proverbs but also novels "are the palm-oil with which words are eaten." He raises Ibo culture to life through a management of English prose and the novel form. The narrative abounds in Ibo proverbs and repeatedly uses turns of phrase and an indirect manner of speech to achieve an African vernacular. Further, Achebe employs a narrative technique characteristic of the Ibo—"skirting around the subject and then hitting it finally"—that not only reproduces the mentality of the people but also allows him to survey the culture while gradually narrowing the focus onto the fate of Okonkwo, an appropriately African strategy since the fate of the individual is intimately tied to the fate of the community. Equally important is the corollary message for a Western audience. Achebe manages to break the stereotype of so-called primitive, that is, nontechnological cultures. He gives a convincing, realistic portrayal of intelligent human beings living within a complex social system.

Thomas Banks

THIS STRANGE NEW FEELING

Author: Julius Lester (1939-   )
Type of plot: Historical fiction
Time of plot: The pre-Civil War period
Locale: The American South
Principal themes: Love and romance, and race and ethnicity
First published: 1982
Recommended ages: 13-15

Based on actual people and historical fact, three different love stories are related of black men and women born into slavery but willing to risk their lives for freedom. Their heroic endurance contributes to their sense of racial pride.

> *Principal characters:*
> "This Strange New Feeling"
> RAS, a strong young slave, whose outward appearance belies a
>   bright, sensitive man
> UNCLE ISAAC, an old slave, who reared Ras
> SALLY, a young, female slave, who captures Ras's affections
> THOMAS MCMAHON, a Maryland plantation owner, who frees the
>   slaves he "inherits"
>
> "Where the Sun Lives"
> MARIA, a house slave, who has endured unjustified whippings
>   from her mistress
> FORREST YATES, a free black man, who by reputation is one of the
>   finest blacksmiths in Virginia
> MASTER PHILLIPS, a man who chooses law and politics rather than
>   the distasteful task of managing his wife's plantation
>
> "A Christmas Love Story"
> ELLEN CRAFT, a slave, who has inherited the appearance of a
>   white woman from her white father and master
> WILLIAM CRAFT, Ellen's husband, a slave and a carpenter, whose
>   trade gives him some independence
> THE REVEREND THEODORE PARKER, a noted Boston abolitionist

The Story

This Strange New Feeling is a novel that is composed of three entirely separate stories involving different characters. The first story, "This Strange New Feeling," opens as Ras helps to build a tobacco shed with a visitor from the North, who arouses Ras's desire for freedom. Uncle Isaac, moved to action, arranges Ras's escape with Thomas McMahon, who owns a neighboring plantation. Ras settles in the North, where his appearance and demeanor are transformed by two months of freedom. Recognized by the Northerner, who is now in financial difficulty, Ras is returned to Maryland for twenty-five silver pieces.

Ras is saddened to learn of the gruesome death of Uncle Isaac, who, rather than reveal Ras's whereabouts, endured hanging upside down and bleeding to death from whip lashes. Ras plays the dumb and repentant slave who is disdained at first by those who loved Isaac. Their scornful looks turn to laughter when Ras, with the help of McMahon, aids in the escape of numerous slaves.

His master, however, deduces Ras's role in the escape plots and, in the middle of the night, comes after him with a pistol. Warned by the house butler, Ras, with Sally, manages to reach the bridge. He and his master struggle in the rainy night. Sally intervenes by grabbing the pistol and killing the master, whom Ras then tosses into the raging river. Together Ras and Sally experience "this strange new feeling of freedom" before moving on.

In "Where the Sun Lives," the mistress of the plantation dies just prior to her thirtieth birthday. Neither Master Phillips nor the slaves mourn her passing, since she was a harsh and embittered woman. Master Phillips makes a feeble attempt to persuade Maria to live with him in Richmond, but she refuses.

Approximately a month later, Master Phillips sells Maria to Forrest Yates, who by Virginia law may not marry nor free her. Instead, they live as if married, and for several years, Maria enjoys a life of freedom with a loving "husband." Tragedy strikes, however, when Forrest is killed while shoeing a horse. His will, which frees Maria, becomes meaningless when she must be sold to cover his debts. Remembering Maria's refusal, Master Phillips does not volunteer to pay the debts, and Maria will not beg. Maria returns to slavery with the proud knowledge that she knows "now where the sun lives."

The protagonists of "A Christmas Love Story," Ellen and William Craft, decide to escape their onerous lives as slaves by disguising themselves as "Mr. William Johnson" and his manservant, who are traveling to Philadelphia. Swathed in bandages and wearing green spectacles, Ellen will appear to be a young man requiring medical treatment. Their journey begins in Macon, Georgia, where they secure a four-day Christmas pass to visit family. Many transfers back and forth from train to steamer are required as they travel to their destination via Savannah, Charleston, Richmond, Washington, D.C., and Baltimore. Almost detected in Macon by William's master, the couple face mounting tension as they encounter various people and obstacles along the way. On Christmas Day, they safely arrive in Philadelphia.

The Crafts move to Boston, where William gets involved in the antislavery crusade. Ellen is apprehensive and somber as William travels the state of Massachusetts, telling their story of escape and publicizing their whereabouts. After two years of freedom, their return to slavery appears imminent when the passage of the 1850 Fugitive Slave Bill brings William's master to Boston to secure his lost property. With a contingent of sixty white men, the Reverend Theodore Parker confronts the master and a slave catcher in the United States Hotel and persuades them to leave rather than risk their lives. The Crafts are persuaded to journey to England to escape any future slave hunts.

Themes and Meanings

These three stories based on actual people challenge several fallacies related to slavery and slaves. They consequently reveal the overriding theme that Afro-American men and women were willing to risk their lives and even their bond of love to secure the rights of freedom.

One predominant fallacy is that slaves were content when they lived under benevolent masters. The story of Ellen and William Craft refutes this myth. Both had relatively easy and independent lives compared to the majority of slaves; however, for freedom, they risked being separately sold into more servile slavery. Maria, of the story "Where the Sun Lives," poignantly reveals a universal truth when she tells her husband-master that she does not miss the plantation: "It don't make no difference how good a master is, you still a slave."

There continues to exist the misconception that slavery provided many Afro-Americans with a secure life, free from worry and financial hardship. These stories, however, reveal that security was always tenuous, since in the future lurked the threat of the auction block, separation from loved ones, a new harsh master or overseer, vile living conditions, and cruel physical punishment.

The myth that slaves were basically unintelligent is also debunked. The institution of slavery shaped Ras into a man with rounded shoulders and a mute tongue, but two months in freedom revealed his true character and intelligence. Not only was William Craft a skillful carpenter, but within two years after his escape, he also was reading essays by Ralph Waldo Emerson and lecturing throughout the state of Massachusetts. The creative escape plot of the Crafts is sterling testimony to the ingenuity of Afro-Americans and their fierce desire for freedom.

The falsehood that slaves were primitives who lacked human emotions and principles is exposed by these tales of love and commitment. Uncle Isaac's wife smothers her three babies rather than have them endure slavery, and Uncle Isaac suffers a martyr's death rather than betray Ras. The bond of love between Ellen and William Craft engenders in each courage and determination. "A Christmas Love Story" returns to the point that love of freedom transcends the bonds of human love, since William was ready to choose freedom for himself and others over his love for Ellen. "Where the Sun Lives," however, reveals that there is something even more important than freedom: Maria chooses self-respect over compromised freedom.

Context

While all three stories are based on true accounts, the story of Ellen and William Craft is the most widely known and documented. Information about the Crafts is included in books about the abolitionist movement and Boston African Americans, as well as in William Lloyd Garrison's newspaper, *The Liberator*. In 1860, William

Craft recorded the escape story in a book entitled *Running a Thousand Miles for Freedom: Or, The Escape of William and Ellen Craft from Slavery.* In 1971, a version for children by Florence B. Freedman was published under the title *Two Tickets to Freedom: The True Story of Ellen and William Craft, Fugitive Slaves*.

Julius Lester is the author of two other books written for young adults on the topic of slavery. *To Be a Slave* (1968), a Newbery Honor Book, presents the narratives of former slaves, as recorded by abolitionist groups in the 1800's and the Federal Writers' Project in the 1930's. *Long Journey Home* (1972) contains six stories from black history, all true accounts of ordinary people living during or after the slave period. Both of these books are good companions to *This Strange New Feeling*.

Basically, Julius Lester has chosen to record the slave experiences of the ordinary but, in his mind, great men and women who forged the freedom movement by escaping the bonds of slavery. These stories can be read in combination with those of the famous leaders, such as Frederick Douglass, Harriet Tubman, and Sojourner Truth.

Julius Lester's interest in preserving the cultural history of Afro-Americans is evident in several other books that he has written for the benefit of both children and adults. *Black Folktales* (1969) contains twelve tales of African and Afro-American origin, *The Knee-High Man and Other Tales* (1972) contains six tales told originally among slaves, and *The Tales of Uncle Remus* (1987) and *More Tales of Uncle Remus* (1988) retell the Afro-American folktales of Brer Rabbit important to American culture and folklore.

Dorothy Ruth Troike

THE THREE MUSKETEERS

Author: Alexandre Dumas, *père* (1802-1870)
Type of plot: Historical fiction
Time of plot: c. 1625, the era of Louis XIII and Cardinal Richelieu
Locale: Paris; La Rochelle, France, and London
Principal themes: Friendship, love and romance, and politics and law
First published: Les Trois Mousquetaires, 1844 (English translation, 1846)
Recommended ages: 15-18

*D'Artagnan, a Gascon, comes to Paris to join the king's musketeers. He is be-
friended by three of them—Athos, Porthos, and Aramis—and embarks upon a series
of exciting adventures in the service of the Queen, Anne of Austria.*

> *Principal characters:*
> D'ARTAGNAN, a shrewd young Gascon, who eventually becomes a
> musketeer
> ATHOS, a serious and noble musketeer with a secret past
> PORTHOS, a pompous, sometimes comic musketeer
> ARAMIS, a secretive musketeer, who longs to become a priest
> MILADY (LADY DE WINTER), a dangerous, wicked woman, who is
> a spy for Richelieu
> CONSTANCE BONACIEUX, the mistress of d'Artagnan
> JOHN FELTON, the assassin of Buckingham
> RICHELIEU, the cardinal, who is active in political intrigue
> ANNE OF AUSTRIA, the queen, who is involved in a quarrel with
> Richelieu
> DUKE OF BUCKINGHAM, the queen's English lover

The Story

The Three Musketeers, a historical fiction filled with adventures, romance, and
suspense, takes place in France and England during the time of Louis XIII and
Cardinal Richelieu. Alexandre Dumas imbues the novel with a guise of historical
reality by centering it on three important historical events of the period which resulted from the conflict between Richelieu and the Queen of France, Anne of Austria. These events are the incident of the Queen's diamonds, the siege of La Rochelle, and the assassination of the Duke of Buckingham.

Interwoven with these happenings is the story of d'Artagnan, a young Gascon
nobleman whose most ardent desire is to become a musketeer, and of his friends
Athos, Porthos, and Aramis, three of the best of the king's musketeers under Monsieur de Tréville. Throughout the novel, the exploits of d'Artagnan and his friends
continuously place them upon the side of the queen and against Richelieu. Their
military allegiance is to Monsieur de Tréville, who is constantly at odds with Richelieu. Even before d'Artagnan arrives in Paris, he encounters agents (later identified

as Count de Rochefort and Lady de Winter) of Richelieu. Once he is in Paris, he becomes involved in a duel between the musketeers and the cardinal's guards.

His next adventure in the company of his three friends is the retrieval of the queen's diamonds from the Duke of Buckingham, her English lover. The four start for England, but only d'Artagnan arrives there, as Richelieu's agents detain the others en route. This mission successfully accomplished, d'Artagnan returns to France, finds his friends, and encounters Lord de Winter, an Englishman who introduces him to his sister-in-law, Lady de Winter, and entangles him in a deadly love affair. This beautiful woman is the infamous Milady, who carries a criminal's brand on her shoulder, was once Athos' wife, poisoned her second husband, and is now a spy for Richelieu. D'Artagnan makes the mistake of offending her and is almost killed.

The scene then moves to the siege of La Rochelle. Here, the historical events and the personal lives of the characters become even more tightly interwined. Milady attempts to have d'Artagnan killed. Athos discovers her plot with Richelieu to assassinate Buckingham, and the musketeers attempt to thwart the plot with the help of Lord de Winter. They fail, however, as Milady, imprisoned by Lord de Winter, corrupts her jailer, John Felton, who not only helps her to escape but also assassinates Buckingham. Milady returns to France and manages to commit one final odious act, the poisoning of d'Artagnan's mistress, before d'Artagnan, Athos, Porthos, Aramis, and Lord de Winter capture, try, and execute her in a macabre night scene. Dumas's characters return to Paris as the story closes.

Themes and Meanings

Although *The Three Musketeers* is far from a moral tale (Dumas often excuses his characters' behavior or motives by the manners of the times), it does develop a basic theme of conflict between good and evil. Richelieu and his agents, especially Milady, represent that which is sinister and dangerous. D'Artagnan and the three musketeers embody high ideals, heroism, devotion to duty, and loyalty. Alexandre Dumas uses this theme in both the historical and personal aspects of his novel through the character of Milady. She harms everyone who is unfortunate enough to be involved with her. She is no one's friend.

By contrast, d'Artagnan, Athos, Porthos and Aramis share a truly devoted and loyal friendship. They share their wealth and both their good and bad fortune. They are always ready to come to one another's assistance. Their friendship is based upon certain basic ideals in which they all believe. The qualities of courage, honor, and loyalty bind them together as they find in one another these characteristics that they most admire. They are not, however, merely carbon copies of one another; Dumas individualizes each character by giving him a distinctive quality and by repeating it in the man's servant. D'Artagnan's servant is Planchet, a brave and loyal Picard; Athos is served by the silent Grimaud; Porthos employs Mousqueton, who enjoys the table as thoroughly as does his master; and Aramis has Bazin, who, like Aramis, longs for the life of a priest.

This mode of parallelism appears again in the treatment of love and romance.

D'Artagnan has love affairs with three different women. His romantic relationship with Constance Bonacieux is mirrored in Aramis' relationship with his mistress. His less than admirable conduct with Milady's maid Kitty is similar to Porthos' love affair with Madame Coquenard; just as Kitty is a means to gain access to Milady, so Madame Coquenard is the way to her husband's money chest. The almost deadly affair with Milady is shared with Athos, who was married to her.

Context

While most critics do not view Dumas's novels as great literary works, the novels remain significant as some of the best and most popular escape literature ever written. Dumas was a master storyteller. His aim as a writer was to invent a good story filled with adventure and excitement and then place it in a historical setting. He was particularly interested in creating individual characters through action and dialogue, all of which he accomplished in *The Three Musketeers*. Since Dumas was not particularly interested in literary innovation and used the same basic techniques in all his novels, *The Three Musketeers* is not only an excellent introduction to his fictional works but also representative of them.

In addition, *The Three Musketeers* introduces the reader to the Romantic novel. It contains all the elements of this genre: high ideals, desire for glory and conquest, devotion to noble causes, and the willingness to risk everything for love or friendship. During the Romantic period, a special kind of novel developed: the serial novel, which appeared in installments in the newspapers. The serial novels enjoyed enormous success and greatly increased newspaper circulation. Dumas published *The Three Musketeers* as a serial novel in *Le Siècle*. Thus, the novel is also an example of this phenomenon of the nineteenth century. These novels had to hold the reader's attention and pique his curiosity in such a way that he was eager to purchase the next newspaper edition in order to find out what was to happen next. Alexandre Dumas, a consummate storyteller, was able to create such novels.

By combining his storytelling talents and the facts of history, Dumas created novels which are enjoyable reading and at the same time give the reader a feel for various periods of history. *The Three Musketeers* has enjoyed universal popularity. The novel's rapid-paced action and exciting adventures, coupled with its larger-than-life heroes, appeal to both the adult and the adolescent reader.

Shawncey Jay Webb

THROUGH THE LOOKING-GLASS
And What Alice Found There

Author: Lewis Carroll (Charles Lutwidge Dodgson, 1832-1898)
Type of plot: Fantasy
Time of plot: Mid-winter in 1859 or the early 1860's
Locale: The dream world of an imaginative child
Principal themes: Coming-of-age, education, animals, and travel
First published: 1871 (dated 1872); illustrated
Recommended ages: 10-13

*Young Alice steps through the mantelpiece mirror into a world of bizarre charac-
ters and transformations, finding herself part of a Looking-glass chess game. At the
last, becoming a queen, Alice awakens.*

> *Principal characters:*
> ALICE, a seven-and-a-half-year-old English girl
> DINAH, a cat
> SNOWDROP, the white kitten, and
> KITTY, the black kitten, Dinah's children
> THE WHITE KING, the memorandum maker
> THE WHITE QUEEN, who is slow and befuddled
> THE RED KING, the snoring dreamer
> THE RED QUEEN, a pedantic governess
> THE RED KNIGHT, who claims Alice as his prisoner
> THE WHITE KNIGHT, who frequently falls off his horse
> TWEEDLEDUM and
> TWEEDLEDEE, a pair of mirror-image brothers
> HUMPTY DUMPTY, the wordsmith and overbearing egghead
> THE LION and
> THE UNICORN, who are perpetual enemies

The Story

The playing-card motif in *Alice's Adventures in Wonderland* (1865) is replaced by
that of a chess game in *Through the Looking-Glass*. Young Alice, having just finished a game of chess with her sister, is drowsily playing with Dinah's black kitten,
which is unwinding a ball of yarn Alice is trying to wind up. Alice, in a "let's pretend" mood, fancies Kitty is the Red Queen, though the animal seems reluctant to
oblige—which brings a threat of punishment from the girl to put Kitty into the
Looking-glass House in the mirror above the fireplace.

Mesmerized by her own speculations about the mirror-world, Alice climbs the
mantel and steps through the Looking-glass into a room of living chess pieces, some
having fallen into the fireplace cinders. Alice, invisible, restores the White Queen

and White King to the table so that they may tend to their daughter, a White Pawn, and in so doing causes much consternation among the royalty. It is then that Alice spots a Looking-glass book in which she reads the nonsense poem "Jabberwocky" by holding its backward printing up to the mantelpiece mirror. Unable to puzzle out the meaning of its strange words, Alice begins her exploration of the rest of the Looking-glass House by floating down the stairs and out onto a path, where, after several attempts to walk away from the house (only to find herself back at the front door), she comes upon the garden of live flowers.

Watched over by the edgy Tiger-lily, the flowers find Alice to be a queer creature. It is here that Alice first encounters her nemesis, the Red Queen, and together from the hill, they survey the country of the Looking-glass. Green hedges cut the land into squares with streams running parallel from side to side. "It's a great huge game of chess that's being played," Alice says, "—all over the world. . . . I wouldn't mind being a Pawn if only I might join—though of course I should *like* to be a Queen, best."

Subsequent chapters are episodic yet patterned after a more or less orthodox chess game (as the author diagrammed in a preface added in 1896). Running downhill, Alice reaches the wood of forgetfulness, where she loses her name for a while, and as the day draws on, she comes to the brothers Tweedledum and Tweedledee, plump little men who tell her the story of the Walrus and the Carpenter. East of Alice, the Red King snores away, and Tweedledee tells the girl that she is only an image in the King's dream. Soon, the White Queen's shawl blows past, with the White Queen herself in hot pursuit. Helped by Alice, the Queen regains her shawl, and Alice learns of the giddy Queen's backward living, where memory works both directions and, as the Queen boasts, she can believe "as many as six impossible things before breakfast."

Impossibly, an egg Alice is about to buy becomes Humpty Dumpty as Alice approaches it, and once again, Alice is lectured on the meaning of names, with Humpty pridefully allowing that he makes words mean whatever he wants them to mean. It is Humpty who more or less unpacks the meaning of the odd words of "Jabberwocky," but his own nonsense rhyme, which he recites to Alice, ends in midsentence. Amid the King's horses and men scurrying to help put poor Humpty back together again, Alice finds the White King writing his memo book. Then she sees the Lion and the Unicorn, perpetually fighting for the White King's crown—until the time for plum cake rolls around. In a world where the bizarre is normal, Alice seems to them to be a monster. The next moment the ensemble is gone, and the Red Knight, tumbling from his horse, claims Alice as his prisoner. The White Knight, tumbling off his steed even more frequently, eventually prevails and befriends Alice. Critics have seen in the Knight (with all his silly inventions) the author himself, and Alice says that it is the scene she remembers best in the Looking-glass world.

As the Knight departs, Alice finds herself with a golden crown on her head and, eventually, at a banquet. Chaos reigns, however, as the table service comes to life. Alice grabs the Red Queen to shake her for all the trouble she has caused and finds the Queen small and kitten-shaped. As Alice relays the story later to her sister, the big question upon her awakening was whether she had dreamed the adventure—or whether the Red King had.

Themes and Meanings

Through the Looking-Glass is neither an allegory nor a morality play. On one level, it is simply a brilliant nonsense tale, stitched together from stories told to entertain the young female friends of the author, a deacon at Christ Church and a lecturer in mathematics. The silly characters capture the attention of younger readers as Alice tries to make sense of this strange world beyond herself and to communicate with "adults" (such as the brothers Tweedle) who seem to be operating out of their own illogic in their concern for trivialities.

Older readers find delight in the intricate puns and logical riddles in the Looking-glass world, a world which, in its very unpredictability, appears to have some of the properties of the subatomic universe postulated by quantum physics. Humpty Dumpty's wordplay and the very flow of the dream tale anticipate the modern novel and especially the works of James Joyce (1882-1941). Some commentators suggest that Lewis Carroll's work is at least mildly subversive of the Victorian sense of order; others, that the transformations in the Looking-glass world were socially acceptable releases of repressed imagination.

Yet the poems that frame the work suggest also an air of melancholy. Carroll writes in his preface that "the shadow of a sigh/ May tremble through the story,/ For 'happy summer days' gone by," and the closing poem, an acrostic spelling out "Alice Pleasance Liddell" (for whom the heroine is named), views the young friends of Carroll "Dreaming as the days go by,/ Dreaming as the summers die . . . / Life, what is it but a dream?" In *Through the Looking-Glass*, Alice begins to mature as she moves through a series of tests and contests, facing the hostility of the Red Queen, the violence of the Lion and the Unicorn, the condescension of Humpty Dumpty, and for a time even the loss of herself in the wood of forgetfulness. Yet Alice is determined never to lose her name again, despite a Humpty Dumpty world that arbitrarily defines and redefines words (and people) and considers her something of a monster.

Almost petulant at times, Alice finds that she must knit her own reality in the face of others who would twist her up in their own logical yarn. In the Looking-glass world, sanity is treated as insanity, but Alice prevails; she becomes a queen, triumphant in the end over the Red Queen. Yet, in passing from girlhood, Alice must inevitably put away girlish things, and it is to this loss that Lewis Carroll alludes: both the loss to Alice of those summer days and the loss to Carroll of his child friends.

Context

Alice's Adventures in Wonderland and *Through the Looking-Glass* are Lewis Carroll's triumphs, and together with the illustrations of Sir John Tenniel (1820-1914), with whom the author worked closely, the works are among the world's greatest nonsense literature. Phrases from Carroll's poetic burlesques and parodies, such as "Jabberwocky" (which may parody an old German ballad), "The Walrus and the Carpenter" (in the style of poet Thomas Hood), and "The Aged Aged Man" (a parody of the subject matter of a poem by William Wordsworth), have become part of the culture.

The Alice books had their genesis in 1862, when Carroll and a colleague rowed Alice Liddell and her two sisters up the Thames River to return home that evening with Carroll's fairy tale of *Alice's Adventures Underground* (later published in 1886). Carroll published other works of nonsense verse, most notably *The Hunting of the Snark* (1876), and, as the prosaic Charles Lutwidge Dodgson, produced mathematical works such as *Euclid and His Modern Rivals* (1879) and *Curiosa Mathematica* (1888-1893). Said by some to be unsettled that his most successful work contained no Christian moral, Carroll sought to rectify the situation with a two-volume novel of fairy tales and ethical reflection, *Sylvie and Bruno* (1889) and *Sylvie and Bruno Concluded* (1893).

Carroll's era produced other nonsense literature, such as Edward Lear's *Book of Nonsense* (1846), and other fantasy stories for children, such as Charles Kingsley's *The Water-Babies* (1863). Yet it is the Alice books of Lewis Carroll, free of moral didacticism, whimsical and amusing, touched with melancholy, which continue to claim the hearts and minds of adults as well as children.

Dan Barnett

THUNDER AND LIGHTNINGS

Author: Jan Mark (Janet Marjorie Brisland, 1943-   )
Type of plot: Domestic realism
Time of plot: One summer in the late twentieth century
Locale: The village of Pallingham, Norfolk, England
Principal themes: Friendship, family, education, and social issues
First published: 1976; illustrated
Recommended ages: 10-13

Newcomer Andrew feels lonely and isolated until he makes friends with Victor, who is obsessed with airplanes and believed to be mildly retarded. When Andrew learns that Victor's favorite plane, the Royal Air Force Lightning, is to be phased out, he tries to soften the blow.

> Principal characters:
> ANDREW MITCHELL, an intelligent, compassionate schoolboy of
>   twelve, who is new in Norfolk
> VICTOR SKELTON, his awkward, good-natured classmate, who has
>   a passion for airplanes and is believed retarded by teachers,
>   classmates, and parents
> MRS. MITCHELL, Andrew's very tall, easygoing mother, who was
>   a librarian
> MR. MITCHELL, Andrew's understanding, helpful, nondirective
>   father, who is a computer specialist
> MRS. SKELTON, Victor's fussy, house-proud and socially conscious
>   mother

The Story

At first, *Thunder and Lightnings* appears to be the story of a boy's adjustment to a new environment. When Andrew Mitchell's family moves from London to Tiler's Cottage in rural Norfolk, he is struck by the openness of fields and sky, but especially by the almost constant rumble of aircraft from the Royal Air Force field at Coltishall.

Andrew is a loner, because his family moves often. Bored with school, he becomes acquainted with Victor Skelton, a classmate who is also isolated. Andrew soon discovers that Victor is believed to be backward and unable to learn and, indeed, is barely literate. He is scorned by classmates because he is clumsy and dresses eccentrically, wearing seven layers of garments at a time. Andrew also discovers that Victor is fascinated with airplanes. Both boys are pleased to learn that they live in the same neighborhood and soon become close friends.

During the summer holidays, the boys visit each other and go for jaunts about the neighborhood. Andrew finds the formal atmosphere and emphasis on cleanliness that Victor's meticulous, nagging mother maintains vastly different from his mother's messy housekeeping and the amiable banter that goes on at home. He learns that Victor's mother also believes her son is backward and denigrates him. The boys play with the model planes that decorate Victor's room, run errands for Andrew's mother, and visit the RAF airfield to watch the planes take off and land.

Andrew discovers that Victor is very knowledgeable about aircraft; he talks about them with atypical confidence and authority and without his usual country accent and incorrect grammar. Victor is particularly enamored of the Lightning, an important fighter plane used during World War II.

The central problem arises one evening when Mr. Mitchell announces that he has read that the Lightnings are to be phased out. Reluctant, Andrew passes the news along to Victor. Although Andrew's mother remarks that Victor may be tougher than he thinks, he sets about helping Victor accept the loss by suggesting that they do a project on planes for Victor's term report. When Victor resists the idea, Andrew believes that Victor simply refuses to accept the truth.

At Coltishall one Friday, they watch the Jaguars arrive to replace the Lightnings. When Victor remarks that nothing in life stays the same, Andrew realizes that Victor understands the phaseout, but he remains uneasy. The following Monday, a Lightning roars over the village in a magnificent, low-soaring dive and Victor announces with a grin, "What a way to go out, eh?" Andrew concludes that he has worried unnecessarily and realizes that Victor is a realist capable of accepting the inevitable with grace.

Themes and Meanings

Although the tone is light and sometimes humorous, *Thunder and Lightnings* invites a serious examination of the nature of friendship, the rearing of children, and the educational system. The activities in which Andrew and Victor engage catch the reader's interest, but they are of less import than why the boys are friends. Both boys reveal qualities more significant in a friendship than merely doing things together. The story suggests that opening one's self to another person and displaying compassionate respect and genuine appreciation for the other person constitute real friendship.

The boys' friendship also develops against their contrasting home life. Andrew's home is warm and inviting, with a comfortable messiness; conversation is free and easy. Victor's home, however, is silent; conversation is almost nonexistent. His mother cherishes her immaculate house; his father is abstracted and addicted to television. The brutality beneath their remote behavior comes out when Victor's mother strikes him viciously because Andrew has accidentally dropped a clean sheet. The blow is symbolic of the many Victor has received, just as the layers of clothes he wears represent his attempts to protect himself from the world.

School is uncomfortable for both boys. Both have adjusted, however, to a situation they can do little about. Teachers and classmates ignore Andrew because he is new. He has been treated this way at other schools and believes that school is generally a wasteland. Victor is also overlooked. The teachers assume that, because he makes little progress in what they ask him to do, he must have a learning disability. Victor, however, says he does not want to have to learn things. He simply wants to find out about them. Learning is not fun; finding out is.

Context

Thunder and Lightnings, Jan Mark's first book, catapulted her to fame in children's literature when it won the Carnegie Medal in England. Seven years later, *Handles* (1983), for a somewhat older audience, also received the Carnegie. Although Mark has written fantasies, such as *Aquarius* (1982, winner of the Young Observer Teenage Fiction Prize) and short stories, she is best known for her novels of domestic realism.

Mark commonly explores the themes of friendship, social obligations, the necessity to confront issues and accept the truth, and the importance of self-assertion. These aspects unfold gradually and convincingly within her works without sentimentality or explicit statement and without the pedantry often found in children's books where the adult's viewpoint rather than the child's predominates. Her protagonists tend to be loners, isolated by circumstances and their own inclinations or failings. In *Handles*, an adolescent girl who is interested in motorcycles simply does not fit into her aunt's rigid, traditional family. Viner, in *Aquarius*, knows what it is to be ostracized and scorned, yet is too emotionally scarred, or perhaps too unfeeling or too pragmatic, to provide the support his king needs.

Critics acclaim Mark's ability to create convincing images of home life and interpersonal relationships, especially within families and between peers. Her characterizations, her economical use of language, her believable dialogue, and her skillful use of humor are all evident in *Thunder and Lightnings*.

Alethea K. Helbig

TIGER EYES

Author: Judy Blume (1938-   )
Type of plot: Social realism
Time of plot: The 1970's
Locale: Atlantic City, New Jersey, and Los Alamos, New Mexico
Principal themes: Death, family, friendship, social issues, and race and ethnicity
First published: 1981
Recommended ages: 13-15

Davey Wexler's father is killed during a robbery of his 7-Eleven store in Atlantic City. Davey and her mother and brother move to Los Alamos, New Mexico, where they all learn to live with their loss and rebuild their lives and their family.

> Principal characters:
> DAVEY WEXLER, the fifteen-year-old narrator
> ADAM WEXLER, her father
> GWENDOLYN WEXLER, her mother, who suffers a nervous
> breakdown after Adam's death
> JASON WEXLER, her seven-year-old brother
> BITSEY and WALTER KRONICK, her overprotective aunt and uncle
> MARTIN "WOLF" ORTIZ, who has come home from college to Los
> Alamos to be with his dying father

The Story

Tiger Eyes is a book of contrasts, of varying views of reality. Before her father's death, Davey Wexler spends her free time with friends on the beach and the boardwalk in Atlantic City, New Jersey. Adam Wexler is a trusting parent who paints portraits and listens to classical music. After he is shot and killed during a robbery of his 7-Eleven store, Davey, her mother (Gwendolyn), and her brother (Jason) move to the desert community of Los Alamos, New Mexico, to live with Bitsy and Walter Kronick. After learning that the 7-Eleven has again been robbed, Gwendolyn suffers a nervous breakdown. The Kronicks assume the role of well-meaning but overprotective parents to Davey and Jason. Walter Kronick is a nuclear weapons engineer at the laboratory where the nuclear bombs dropped on Japan had been developed during World War II.

Jason seems to adjust well to his new family. Bitsy teaches him to cook, and Davey wonders whether he could support them in New Jersey selling his cookies on the boardwalk. Davey, however, does not fare so well. Walter will not let her go skiing because it is too dangerous, and he will not let her take driver's training in school because automobile accidents are a leading cause of death among teenagers.

In order to get away from the overprotective Kronicks and to understand her anger and frustration in the wake of her father's death, Davey escapes to a beautiful canyon. Here she meets Martin Ortiz, who introduces himself only as Wolf. She introduces herself to him as Tiger. He sees and comments on her sad eyes but does not force her to talk; instead, they make each other laugh. It is only after meeting and hiking together several times that Davey tells Wolf that her dad has died, and he tells her that his is dying. The hikes into the canyon and Wolf's friendship begin to replace walks on the beach with friends in New Jersey.

Wolf has come back to Los Alamos from college in California to be with his dying father, a man Davey has befriended at the hospital where she volunteers as a candy striper. Mr. Ortiz has earned his living working as a maintenance man at the laboratory where Walter Kronick is an engineer. While Los Alamos has one of the highest numbers of Ph.D.'s per capita of any town in the United States, most of the engineers are Anglo, while those who clean and run errands are Hispanic.

One day Davey finds Wolf in Mr. Ortiz's room and learns that they are father and son. A few days later Mr. Ortiz dies, and Wolf leaves town. He leaves her a note telling her to remember Mr. Ortiz as a man full of life and love. Davey begins to understand that that is the way she must remember her own father, as a man full of life and love. Wolf promises to meet Davey again in the canyon "cuando los larar-tijos corren" — when the lizards run, in the spring. It is through Wolf and his father that Davey begins to accept the death of her own father.

Gwendolyn Wexler, through the help of counseling and the care of the Kronicks, also recovers and begins to take charge of her own and her children's lives. She takes a job at the laboratory and begins to date. Finally, she decides to take her family back to Atlantic City. A few weeks before they leave, she explains to Davey why she was not able to be a parent: She had been afraid that Davey would ask questions about her father's death and that those questions would hurt too much. Gwendolyn now feels ready to talk about her husband's death. Davey says, "But now I don't need to."

Themes and Meanings

Tiger Eyes explores social issues through the eyes of fifteen-year-old Davey Wexler. The power of this novel is that there is no sudden revelation, there are no easy answers.

Time is the thing that helps Davey and her mother get on with the business of living after Adam Wexler is killed. Davey feels guilty: Somehow she should have done something that would have saved her father. It is only through time that she is able to see that others, such as Martin Ortiz, also suffer the death of parents. She learns to accept that she cannot change the fact of her father's death; instead of remembering him as dead, she resolves to remember him as full of life and love.

Another but more subtle theme of *Tiger Eyes* is that of racism. Davey sees racism and the fear it causes. Her best friend in New Jersey is Lenaya, an Afro-American girl who wants to be a scientist. New Mexico is unusual in that it is made up of three cultures: Hispanic, Anglo, and Native American. Anglos are not a majority through-out the state, although in Los Alamos they are. Walter Kronick always takes a loaded gun in his car when he leaves town, saying that he would rather be safe than sorry. On a shopping trip to Santa Fe with a school friend, Davey hears her friend worry that the Hispanic boys might try to rape them because they are Anglo. When Martin gives Davey a ride home from the hospital, Bitsy Kronick asks whether Martin is a dropout, whether he is Spanish, and whether he works in maintenance at the laboratory. She is relieved when Davey tells her that Martin is taking a semester off from college to be with his father.

The fear, lack of trust, and misunderstanding of others is balanced. Davey is more concerned with her uncle's contradictory nature than with his fear of people from other cultures. She questions how he can be so concerned about the immediate safety of those in his custody while developing weapons that have the potential to destroy the world. Lenaya offers Davey friendship and support after her father dies, and Davey has to tell the reader that her best friend is Afro-American. It is only through their last name and the occasional use of Spanish that the Ortizes can be identified as Hispanic. She hears Mr. Ortiz, as a concerned parent, planning a successful life for Martin much as the Kronicks try to do for her. *Tiger Eyes* makes no attempt to solve the problems of race relations; it only observes those relations through the eyes of a sensitive adolescent girl.

Context

Realism for young adult readers can be traced back to 1967 and the publication of *The Outsiders* by S. E. Hinton. Up to that time it had been generally believed that fiction for young readers should be humorous and have happy endings. Kenneth Donelson and Alleen Nilsen make the case that young adult readers use novels with realistic problems to examine issues that cannot be so closely examined in real life. While few experience the loss of a parent during their teenage years, and fewer yet suffer the loss in the tragic way Davey does in *Tiger Eyes*, some do, and all know of someone who has.

Judy Blume has written books for all age groups. *Tales of a Fourth Grade Nothing* (1972), *Blubber* (1974), and *Superfudge* (1980) were written for younger children and are full of humor. *Tiger Eyes*, however, is not the least bit humorous. Blume knows and respects her audiences. She knows that younger readers respond to humor, but she also knows that her young adult audience is able to explore serious matters in serious ways.

For her honesty, some have found Blume controversial, and her books have been attacked by censors. *Are You There, God? It's Me, Margaret* (1970) has been attacked because it explores a girl's thoughts as her body changes during puberty. *Are You There, God? It's Me, Margaret* and *Tiger Eyes* both draw readers in to identify with the problems that face the two protagonists. Davey in *Tiger Eyes* is not a heroic character. She comes through a crisis in her family life, and like others, many others, she is able to go on with her life.

Blume makes no judgments; believing that there is more than one answer to most questions, she does not offer simple solutions. She lets readers come to their own conclusions about social issues. Because of this approach, the books written by Judy Blume will continue to be popular with young adult readers.

Don Melichar

THE TIME MACHINE

Author: H. G. Wells (1866-1946)
Type of plot: Science fiction
Time of plot: The late nineteenth century; A.D. 802,701; and thirty million years into the future
Locale: London
Principal themes: Science, social issues, and travel
First published: 1895
Recommended ages: 15-18

Solving the mysteries of time travel, the Time Traveler spends eight days in the year 802,701, but what he learns about the ultimate destiny of the human race is disturbing.

> *Principal characters:*
> THE TIME TRAVELER
> WEENA, a female Eloi, who becomes the Time Traveler's friend
> HILLYER, the narrator

The Story

At a dinner party in London, the Time Traveler is attempting to convince his six skeptical guests that Euclidean geometry is based on a misconception. He outlines a four-dimensional geometry in which time is understood to be the fourth dimension of space. He claims that it is possible to travel through time, and he shows them his Time Machine, made out of brass, ebony, ivory, and quartz.

One week elapses. A number of guests are again assembled at the Time Traveler's home. The Time Traveler arrives late, and his haggard and pale appearance is startling. It transpires that he has indeed succeeded in his mission: he has spent eight days in the year A.D. 802,701.

He tells of how he encountered a small, beautiful, but frail-looking race known as the Eloi, who were clad in rich silk robes. They garlanded him with flowers of a type he had never seen before, and he shared a meal of strange fruit with them in a great hall. In this new world he soon discovered that the earth had become a garden of fruit and flowers, and he saw no evidence of disease. The next night, however, he received his first hint that life in 802,701 was not confined to the languid existence of the Eloi. Encountering white, apelike creatures who appeared to live underground, he realized that mankind was now split into two species, inhabiting an Upperworld and an Underworld.

Guessing that it was the underworld Morlocks who had hidden his Time Machine (the loss of which had driven him into a panic the previous day), the Time Traveler clambered down one of the several wells he had discovered to find them. The air was full of the sound of machinery and the atmosphere was unpleasant. Three Morlocks approached him, but he made them recoil by striking a match. Still they thronged around him, plucking at his clothing, and he escaped with difficulty.

He had made one discovery: The Morlocks were cannibals and fed on the Eloi. He resolved to arm himself against them. Exploring the countryside by day with his new friend Weena, a young Eloi whom he had saved from drowning, he discovered a vast, Oriental-style building that he called the Palace of Green Porcelain. In this ruined museum, they found skeletons and fossils, broken-down machines, the remains of a library, matches, and some camphor in a sealed jar. That night he and Weena slept in the open air, building a fire for protection against the Morlocks. Yet as they slept the fire went out, and they were attacked. The Time Traveler hit out with an iron lever, and the Morlocks were finally frightened away by a forest fire. In the confusion, Weena died in the fire.

After sleeping through most of the next day, he returned to a huge marble figure of a White Sphinx, in which he was convinced the Time Machine had been hidden. He found that the pedestal of the Sphinx had been opened, and the Time Machine stood inside. He knew that the Morlocks had tried to trap him, but as he heard them closing in on him he pulled the vital lever and was gone.

Racing forward in time, he came to rest on a desolate beach. The air was thin and the vegetation was a poisonous-looking green. He saw a monstrous, crablike creature moving toward him; another crab touched him with its antenna and was ready to devour him. Horrified, but curious about the ultimate fate of the world, he hurried thirty million years into the future. The same beach seemed completely lifeless, save for the green slime that covered the rocks. It was bitterly cold, dark, and eerily silent. Then he saw something hopping fitfully across the beach—it was round like a soccer ball, black, and trailing tentacles. The Time Traveler felt nauseated contemplating such a dark and awful scene, but he managed to struggle back into his machine and return to the present.

Having heard the Time Traveler's story, the dinner guests hardly know what to make of it. The next day Hillyer visits the Time Traveler again, who says that he intends to prove his story. He goes to his laboratory equipped with a camera and knapsack. When Hillyer goes to investigate, the Time Traveler has gone, and Hillyer reveals that he has never returned although three years have elapsed.

Themes and Meanings

Although the opinions of the Time Traveler are not necessarily to be equated with those of H. G. Wells, the vision of the world of the future presented in *The Time Machine* is directly linked to social and economic conditions in nineteenth century England. The Eloi and the Morlocks are the distant descendants of the haves and have-nots, respectively. The haves were the capitalists, whose wealth and comfort was secured through the work of the have-nots, the working-class laborers. Eventually, the separation between the two classes became so great that the have-nots were driven underground and became resigned to their role of providing for the wealthy. Each class became adapted to its own way of life, and a long period of quiet security followed. Eventually, however, the Eloi, no longer possessing the restless energy and intelligence that had helped them to overcome nature, became too secure. Their size, strength, and intelligence diminished. By 802,701, the established order was becoming reversed. The Morlocks needed strength for their work with machinery (through deeply ingrained habits, they still served the needs of the Eloi) and had remained carnivorous. Animals having become extinct, the Morlocks were forced to turn to devouring the Eloi to meet their needs. Now the Eloi were to fear the Morlocks, rather than the other way around.

Some critics have interpreted this aspect of *The Time Machine* in Marxist terms. Marx believed that all history was dominated by a class struggle. In industrial societies, the struggle was between the capitalists and the proletariat. According to Marx, there would eventually be a social revolution in which capitalism would be overthrown and a classless society would emerge. Other critics have argued that Wells's story is more anti-Marxist than Marxist. They point out that the society depicted is very different from what Marx envisaged, and that Wells emphasizes the idea of Darwinian evolution and adaptation—the survival of the fittest—rather than the Marxist concept of the class struggle.

Another theme is Wells's comment on the aesthetic movement, which flourished at the end of the nineteenth century and is associated with writers such as Walter Pater and Oscar Wilde. The slogan of this movement was "art for art's sake," regardless of its social utility, and it was characterized by sensuous indulgence, eroticism, and lassitude. The Eloi are clearly the embodiment of such ideals, which the Time Traveler regards as highly dangerous: "Energy in security . . . takes to art and eroticism, and then comes languor and decay."

The Time Traveler emphasizes that he is going to undermine some of the beliefs that his guests take for granted. This refers not only to their disbelief in the possibility of time travel but also to the general Victorian belief in social progress and the permanence of human civilization. The Time Traveler emphasizes the inevitability of change, and his vision of the future is deeply pessimistic, although this is slightly mitigated by the final lines of the epilogue: The narrator Hillyer looks on the two flowers that Weena had given to the Time Traveler and reflects that "even when mind and strength had gone, gratitude and a mutual tenderness still lived on in the heart of man."

Context

The Time Machine was Wells's first published work of fiction. It was an immediate success, has never been out of print, and has been translated into innumerable languages. Not only was it the first significant dystopia, it was also the first book to discuss time travel scientifically. It has had a large influence on later science fiction: Fans of the television series *Dr. Who* will recognize many plot devices that echo Wells's story. Like *Dr. Who*, *The Time Machine* appeals equally to young people and adults. Understanding of the political, economic, and scientific themes and allusions is not necessary for the enjoyment of what is essentially a simple and gripping adventure story, in which an admirable hero explores a strange new environment, battles monstrous villains, and lives to tell the tale.

The most important literary influence on *The Time Machine* was probably Jonathan Swift's *Gulliver's Travels* (1726), in which a traveler confronts a strange civilization and uses it to pass judgment on his own. Other novels, such as Mary Shelley's *Frankenstein* (1818) and Robert Louis Stevenson's *Dr. Jekyll and Mr. Hyde* (1886), both of which feature scientists whose inventions produce unexpected results, may also have been in Wells's mind.

Scientific influences were as important as literary ones. Wells had had some scientific training, and he drew on contemporary biology, geology, and astronomy. The cosmogenic theories of Pierre-Simon Laplace can be found in chapter 11, and Wells also demonstrates the workings of the second law of thermodynamics, which had been formulated by Lord Kelvin. *The Time Machine* shows on a cosmic scale the tendency of entropy to increase. The most important scientific influence was that of Wells's teacher, Thomas Henry Huxley, under whom Wells studied biology and zoology. Huxley was one of the foremost interpreters of the evolutionary theories of Charles Darwin and was noted for his pessimistic view of human evolution and destiny. Huxley's influence can perhaps be seen in Wells's own comment on *The Time Machine* as "a glimpse of the future that ran counter to the placid assumption of that time that Evolution was a pro-human force making things better and better for mankind." Wells never, however, preached a philosophy of despair. He once wrote, "I think the odds are against man, but it is still worth fighting against them."

Bryan Aubrey

TIME OF TRIAL

Author: Hester Burton (1913-   )
Type of plot: Historical fiction
Time of plot: 1801
Locale: London and the Sussex coast of England
Principal themes: Coming-of-age, family, friendship, love and romance, and social issues
First published: 1963
Recommended ages: 13-15

During her father's imprisonment for publishing his ideas on social reform, Margaret Pargeter learns to cope with loss and to welcome the unexpected pleasures that can accompany change.

Principal characters:

MARGARET PARGETER, an educated and intelligent young woman who loves London and her father's bookshop

MR. PARGETER, a widowed bookseller who advocates social reform to improve the lives of the poor and uneducated

JOHN PARGETER, his son, who hates bookselling and his father's values

MRS. NEECH, the Pargeters' housekeeper

ROBERT KERRIDGE, a medical student from Sussex who lives with the Pargeters and falls in love with Margaret

DR. KERRIDGE, Robert's father and Mr. Pargeter's godson, a self-confident, self-centered man

The Story

At the beginning of *Time of Trial*, when Margaret Pargeter awakens with pleasure to the chiming of bells from the city's various churches, her love of London and her life there becomes immediately apparent. Yet St. Sepulchre's repeating monotone bell reminds her that on Mondays Newgate criminals hang. With this juxtaposition, author Hester Burton sets the tone—love and beauty coupled with visible poverty and strife. Margaret, seventeen, and her unhappy brother John, nineteen, live behind their widower father's bookselling shop on Holly Lane. Mrs. Neech, the housekeeper, and Robert Kerridge, a medical student who is the grandson of Mr. Pargeter's good friend, live with them.

A tenement on Holly Lane collapses, killing its inhabitants, and Mr. Pargeter rushes to write his horrified response to this result of government irresponsibility, in a tract called "New Jerusalem." He thinks that children should learn literature and mathematics, with no physical labor before the age of fourteen; tenant farmers, instead of wealthy landowners, should own the land they farm; and government should support physicians and provide free medical care to all. The volatile government condemns him. Even though Dr. Kerridge, Robert's father, comes from Herringsby in Suffolk to defend his godfather (to repay an old debt), the jury convicts Mr. Pargeter of sedition. John departs, deploring the ignominy of his father's beliefs, before hearing about the six months' sentence in the Ipswich prison.

A mob of the uneducated and poor whom Mr. Pargeter wants to help rush to destroy his shop. Old Mr. Stone, Mr. Pargeter's loyal friend, arrives first, however, and helps Margaret save such valuable books as originals of William Shakespeare and John Milton. The mob wrecks the printing press and sets the place on fire. When Mr. Pargeter hears, he regrets that these people have misunderstood his ideas.

Dr. Kerridge offers lodging for Margaret, Mrs. Neech, and Elijah (a young orphaned boy the family had rescued from the tenement) at Herringsby, near the Ipswich jail. Before they leave London, Robert kisses Margaret on the cheek, and she realizes that she loves him. When they arrive in the lonely town, they move in with a widow, whose smuggler husband had been a victim of the dangers of the secret but flourishing coastal trade. When the murder of a soldier searching for smugglers brings the army to infiltrate the area, John, Margaret's brother, arrives. Not knowing of the family travails until Margaret recounts them, John regrets his desertion and immediately goes to reunite with his father.

Soon Robert's parents summon Margaret and accuse her of plotting to marry Robert for his money. Unaware of Robert's letter to them declaring his intentions to marry her, she must protect herself. Confused, but knowing that Robert will arrive within a day, she says that Robert must make the decision about marriage. He requests Mr. Pargeter's approval, and they are married within three days, with Mrs. Kerridge's blessing after the ceremony.

When Margaret and Robert visit Mr. Pargeter immediately after the wedding, he tells them that Mr. Stone has negotiated the purchase of a new London bookshop. He explains his plans for teaching children to read with Margaret helping and Robert giving medical attention adjacent to the bookshop.

Themes and Meanings

Time of Trial clearly illustrates a concept that dates back to the Egyptians and that Lord Edward Bulwer-Lytton clearly states in *Richelieu* (1838): "The pen is mightier than the sword." When Mr. Pargeter writes and publishes his beliefs, his government imprisons him. In 1801 his ideas seemed preposterous, yet today one would be appalled at children working with no medical care or welfare. Then, Mr. Pargeter's ideas threatened the illiterate because they did not understand that education could free them from their bleak lives.

Margaret survives a progression of trials. She remains steadfastly faithful to her father throughout the ignominy of his incarceration and endures the pain of Robert's parents' rejection. She learns that few friends remain when trouble arises and gains new appreciation for old Mr. Stone's loyalty. She begins to appreciate Mrs. Neech's unsung contributions to the family during her lifetime. She finds that people such as

Lucy's family can have beauty, culture, and money, while living not in London but on a farm near Herringsby.

Others also overcome hardship. Mr. Pargeter never wavers from his beliefs; throughout his prison term, he prepares to help those who ruined his bookshop. Mrs. Neech, family supporter since Mrs. Pargeter's death, continues to comfort Elijah and chaperon Margaret. Robert recognizes his father's dishonesty and possible involvement with the lucrative smuggling trade when his father denies his Hippocratic oath by refusing to help a dying man. Dr. Kerridge foils Mr. Pargeter: His disdain of integrity, his selfishness, clearly contrasts with Mr. Pargeter's selflessness.

The novel's three-part division mirrors three major thematic strains. Chapters 1 to 7 reveal the costs of expressing and living one's convictions if they conflict with a censorious government. In part 2, chapters 8 to 15, the mob destroys that which would help it. In chapters 16 to 21, Margaret sees Robert's home and makes strides toward adulthood. She discovers that one needs to observe the worlds of others before making judgments, and she comes to understand that a man must find job security before he declares his love.

Mrs. Neech serves the additional role of surrogate mother. She keeps the family united until Margaret leaves with her new husband. Her memory of Mrs. Pargeter on her own wedding day gives depth to the ritual of dressing for the marriage ceremony. The symbolism of the new gown readying the wearer for change and the old (Margaret's mother's amethyst necklace) connecting the wearer to the past acknowledges the value of both embarking on growth and continuing traditions.

Context

Hester Burton has said that she searches for a small event in history, tries to find all she can about it, and then places her characters there to see what they can do. Her favorite period is 1790-1805, the time of Lord Horatio Nelson and of England's lonely fight against Napoleon Bonaparte, which she compares with England's struggle against Adolf Hitler in 1940. *Time of Trial*, which won the Carnegie Medal for the best British children's book in 1963, is set in this period (in 1801). Burton's childhood in East Anglia also influenced the setting of *Time of Trial*: She sends Margaret and Mrs. Neech there while Mr. Pargeter serves his prison sentence.

Since the American Revolution of 1776 and the French Revolution of 1789 had just occurred, the British government of 1801 feared that civil war might erupt in England with the peasants following their French model and guillotining the nobility. The government, like the smugglers, had its own secrets which it did not want revealed. Its fears were reasonable, considering the squalid living conditions of the poor, such as those whose tenement collapses in *Time of Trial*. Government censorship thwarts change and allows corruption to continue; therefore, one can assume that singular voices such as Mr. Pargeter's or his friend Tom Paine's (*Common Sense*, 1776) were often silenced before reforms began.

Burton wrote four other novels, *No Beat of Drums* (1966), *The Rebel* (1971), *Riders of the Storm* (1972), and *To Ravensrigg* (1976), in which she presented the inherent dangers of advocating social reform. Persons become so quickly adjusted to a better life that they forget the struggles and loss of lives to attain it. *Time of Trial* reminds the reader that people, even in the face of persecution, must stand up for their beliefs if they hope to improve their lives and those of others.

Lynda G. Adamson

THE TIMES THEY USED TO BE

Author: Lucille Clifton (1936-   )
Type of plot: Social realism
Time of plot: 1948
Locale: Cold Spring, a neighborhood on the outskirts of an urban area
Principal themes: Religion, coming-of-age, sexual issues, the supernatural, and race and ethnicity
First published: 1974; illustrated
Recommended ages: 10-13

An adult black woman recalls the summer of 1948 and relates the story to her children.

>   *Principal characters:*
>   SYLVIA (SOOKY), twelve, who is the narrator of the story
>   TALLAHASSIE (TASSIE), thirteen, who is Sylvia's best friend
>   MAMA, Sylvia's mother
>   DADDY, Sylvia's father
>   UNCLE SUNNY JIM, Mama's younger brother, who is a World
>   War II veteran
>   GRANNY SCOTT, Tassie's grandmother and legal guardian

The Story

The narrative of *The Times They Used to Be* is told by an adult Sylvia to her own children, who are begging to hear of their mother's childhood. Sylvia begins by introducing the two events which, by the end of the narrative, will have changed her entire life. The reader is told that Uncle Sunny and Tassie are the principal characters in this dramatic summer of Sylvia's twelfth year. Sylvia briefly describes the setting of the story: her family's duplex, shared with her best friend Tassie and Granny Scott, and her Uncle Sunny's cottage in the rear, all located in one of the predominantly black neighborhoods of the city. Sylvia describes the characters who will be important to the plot. Tassie's father is in prison in Florida, and she has been left in the care of her grandmother. Uncle Sunny has returned from World War II, where he was a soldier in the ninety-second division, an all-black unit of the military forces.

One favorite family activity is listening to the radio and Sylvia recalls how she enjoyed the programs. She also remembers how she and Tassie would sit outside and wait for the streetlights to be turned on in the evenings. Television is relatively new in 1948, and one evening everyone goes down to the hardware store to watch through the windows: Sylvia and her neighbors are excited yet frightened.

Uncle Sunny has a peculiar habit of driving back and forth across the Grider Street bridge, and insists that he sees a nun. He says that he wants to catch her so he can return the kindness the Italian nuns showed him when he served in Europe.

Mama and Daddy discuss the fact that Uncle Sunny was never baptized; therefore, he is not saved. Tassie is also not saved, and often expresses her worry that she is a sinner who will never be forgiven. Her grandmother often warns her that she must be saved or face the harsh consequences.

On the same night that Sylvia sees television for the first time, her Uncle Sunny drives off the Grider Street bridge and drowns. As his body is being readied for his funeral, Tassie insists that her body is infected by sin, and she must run away from home. Sylvia and Tassie decide that they will soon run away to Florida.

Sylvia and Tassie go to view Uncle Sunny's body, and Granny reminds the girls that even young people die. Sylvia tells her friend that Uncle Sunny was never saved, and Tassie reacts with a shiver. She then runs to the coffin, throws herself over it, and asks to be blessed. Sylvia notices a cross-shaped bloodstain on the seat of Tassie's pants, and rushes outside, colliding with Mama. Mama picks Tassie up, ties a scarf around her waist, and walks the two girls home. Mama explains menstruation to them, and reprimands Granny Scott for hiding the facts of puberty from Tassie.

Themes and Meanings

Religion plays a prominent role in the story. Sylvia and her parents are churchgoing people to whom faith is essential. Uncle Sunny and Tassie have not been baptized, and they feel some confusion about the fact that they are not saved. What Sylvia's father dismisses as a case of shell shock is really Uncle Sunny's quest for salvation. The nunlike ghost on the bridge represents redemption, and Uncle Sunny must catch her in order to attain salvation and eternal life.

Uncle Sunny's death brings with it rebirth. Convinced that her body is filled with sin, Tassie does not understand the process of menstruation, a process that signifies fertility and new life. Tassie begs to be blessed as she throws herself over Sunny Jim's coffin, because she does not want to die unsaved as he did.

Minor references to supernatural phenomena appear, most notably in the image of the nunlike ghost who repeatedly smiles at Uncle Sunny and then vanishes. The reader is told that Uncle Sunny can see spirits, because he was born "with a veil over his face." This statement demonstrates the family's somewhat superstitious nature. Sylvia's mother and father are wary of television when they first see it, and believe it may be an evil that must be avoided. Their superstitious nature and deep sense of religion are related: They are spiritual people in many ways, and their spirituality molds their daily lives.

Race is a minor theme in *The Times They Used to Be*. Sylvia refers to several prominent black Americans of the time period, thereby placing her story in a historic frame as well as identifying role models of her generation. Otherwise, she does not dwell upon specific racial issues. Her story's purpose is to inform and to entertain while also making a statement about God's way of overseeing life and death.

Context

Lucille Clifton is best known as a contemporary poet who explores the issues of the black and female experiences. In *The Times They Used to Be*, Sylvia experiences life as both a black person and a woman. Indeed, her friend Tassie's passage from child to woman is one of the most significant events of Sylvia's childhood.

Clifton says that being a black woman and having a family have greatly influenced her writing. In *The Times They Used to Be*, Clifton explores many facets of family life: religion, maturity, and death. The character of Sylvia is a young Lucille Clifton, an adolescent black girl dealing with the realities of everyday life in the postwar era.

Like Clifton's poetry, her fiction is autobiographical in some respects. American poetry has tended toward a more personal focus since World War II, and Clifton's work is no exception. Her style, however, is distinguishable from that of many of her contemporaries; in it, there is a rhythm reminiscent of black spirituals. Although her style is compact, it is at the same time musical and descriptive. Her characters are vivid despite her economic use of the language. Even though Uncle Sunny, for example, appears very briefly in *The Times They Used to Be*, he is a fully developed and pivotal character.

Clifton creates unique children's books by combining her poetic talents with her storytelling ability. She draws upon her experiences as a mother and wife, and uses them to construct believable stories. Several other notable poetic picture books she has written include *Some of the Days of Everett Anderson* (1970), *Everett Anderson's Christmas Coming* (1972), and *All Us Come Across the Water* (1973). The simplicity of her fiction makes her books accessible to a very young audience, while the subject matter lends itself to deeper understanding.

Angela Bushnell Peery

TO KILL A MOCKINGBIRD

Author: Harper Lee (1926-   )
Type of plot: Social realism
Time of plot: The early 1930's
Locale: The small northern Alabama town of Maycomb
Principal themes: Coming-of-age, race and ethnicity, and social issues
First published: 1960
Recommended ages: 13-15

Scout and Jem Finch grow up amidst the warmth of small town friendships, the biases of a racially divided society, and the strain of being hounded because their lawyer father takes an unpopular stand by defending a black man accused of rape.

> *Principal characters:*
> JEAN LOUISE "SCOUT" FINCH, six when the story begins, eight
>   when it ends, from whose viewpoint the narration unfolds
> JEREMY ATTICUS "JEM" FINCH, her brother, four years older
>   than she
> ATTICUS FINCH, their father, a lawyer
> CALPURNIA, the Finches' cook, a black woman
> CHARLES BAKER "DILL" HARRIS, a summer visitor Scout's age
> ARTHUR "BOO" RADLEY, the Finches' mysterious neighbor
> MRS. DUBOSE, the Finches' less mysterious neighbor
> TOM ROBINSON, a black man accused of raping a white woman
> BOB EWELL, the father of the woman Tom Robinson is accused of
>   raping

The Story

To Kill a Mockingbird opens on a summer of innocence in Maycomb, a lazy town in northern Alabama. Scout and Jem Finch are devising a plan with Dill Harris, in town from Meridian, Mississippi, visiting his aunt, Miss Rachel, to lure a mysterious neighbor, Boo Radley, out of the house he has not left for many years. Boo allegedly has stayed inside because he became violent once in the murky past and stabbed his father with scissors. It was agreed then that his family would keep him inside. The narrator is Scout, who, although she does not deviate from her six-year-old's point of view, has shrewd insights into life and people. Harper Lee does not confine Scout's narration to a six-year-old's vocabulary.

The Finch children are being reared by their father, Atticus, a lawyer with a strong social conscience and a zeal for unpopular causes. Their mother died of a sudden heart attack when Scout was two. Calpurnia, the Finches' black cook, helps to raise the children and mediates their frequent squabbles, infusing her admonitions with folk wisdom and unstinting love.

The arrival of Dill Harris provides Lee with the opportunity to apprise her readers of much background information as Scout babbles on introducing herself, her family, and her neighborhood to the new arrival. The Finch children have imbibed some of their father's spirit, characterized by trust, service, and a strong sense of justice. Atticus is the small-town lawyer who knows everyone in Maycomb, serves those who need him, and trusts them to pay him when they can—as most of them eventually do. The children, who call their father by his first name, have long, serious discussions with him about such social issues as the treatment of blacks in their town.

When Tom Robinson, a black man, is accused of raping a white woman, Mayella Ewell, Atticus takes his case, and Tom Robinson is barely saved from an angry lynch mob by the unwitting intervention of Scout and Jem. Meanwhile, many townsfolk turn against Atticus for taking on this unpopular case. In the months before the trial occurs, Scout and Jem are badgered by their schoolmates because of their father's association with Tom Robinson.

The beginning of the trial evokes a carnival atmosphere. Scout and Jem watch the proceedings from the gallery, generally reserved for blacks, fearful that their father might see them and not approve of their attending. Predictably, although Atticus proves that Tom could not have committed the rape, community prejudices surface; Tom is adjudged guilty. This miscarriage of justice is highly and troublingly instructive to the Finch children, who have inherited much of their father's sense of right.

After the trial, Tom tries to escape from prison and is killed in the attempt. When Tom Ewell attacks the Finch children in a drunken rage, furious over their father's defense of Tom Robinson, it is Boo Radley who rescues them and teaches them the all-important lesson that appearances can be deceiving, a pervasive theme throughout the narrative.

Themes and Meanings

To Kill a Mockingbird functions on several thematic levels. The novel is essentially about justice, but justice run amok rather than justice fulfilled. Still, the implication is that a better society is emerging. Scout and Jem are relatively color-blind despite the environment in which they were reared. They also learn through their encounters with Boo Radley not to make hasty judgments about the people they know only through rumor or slight contact.

In one scene, an unaccustomed snow falls in Maycomb. Scout makes a snowman, but there is not enough snow to make a very good one, so she fashions one of mud and pats snow onto it to create the effect. Soon the air warms and the snow melts, leaving the muddy frame of her snowman. When it snows again, the frame is covered, re-creating the snowman she had made earlier. Much of the thematic structure of the novel is found in this scene in which the snowman is both white and colored and in which its color is a superficial quality. That Tom's trial cannot go well is a foregone conclusion. Through this failure of the justice system, however, Scout and Jem both come to realize that one must not give up fighting for the rights of the oppressed and for equal justice for all people, as their father has done in this case.

The Finch children go to school, but that is not where they receive the bulk of their education. They learn from their father and from the society surrounding them the lessons they need to internalize to function one day as productive adults. It has been pointed out that this novel creates its dramatic tensions by presenting opposing themes and exploring them simultaneously. Among these themes are prejudice and acceptance, appearances and realities, fear and courage, blind adherence to social norms and informed, conscientious deviation from them.

Context

To Kill a Mockingbird is Harper Lee's only novel. When it was published in 1960, it attracted considerable admiration. Lee was awarded a Pulitzer Prize for it in 1961, after which it was made into a successful film, which won an Academy Award in 1962.

Because of her penetration of a child's psyche and because of her easy, free-flowing style, Lee is often compared to Mark Twain. She is apparently directly indebted to him for the courthouse balcony scene in her novel, which is reminiscent of the scene from *The Adventures of Tom Sawyer* (1876) in which Tom and Huck, crouching in the church balcony, witness their own funerals. The book has also been compared to Twain's *The Adventures of Huckleberry Finn* (1884) for its easy dialogue and natural style.

Among her contemporaries, Harper Lee reminds one of Carson McCullers, both for her choice of social issues about which to write and for her understanding of how children think. McCuller's *The Member of the Wedding* (1946) is the work that comes most immediately to mind when one thinks of this parallel, one that might also legitimately be made with Reynolds Price's *Kate Vaiden* (1986) and with the early portions of his *Clear Pictures* (1989).

In her consistency of portraying the point of view of a young child, Lee can be compared to James Agee, whose Rufus in *A Death in the Family* (1957) shows insights remarkably similar in essence to Scout's. One finds similarities, as well, to Bob, the youthful narrator in Jack Schaefer's *Shane* (1949), and perhaps even more closely to Mattie Ross, the fourteen-year-old heroine in Charles Portis' *True Grit* (1968).

These similarities should not suggest any direct influence of other authors upon Lee or of Lee upon other authors, although her debt to Mark Twain is clear. Rather, they demonstrate a widespread literary interest in writing from the point of view that she adopts in *To Kill a Mockingbird*. If Lee derived any direct benefits from another contemporary author, they probably came from Truman Capote, her next-door neighbor and childhood companion (Dill in this novel) during her early days in Monroeville, Alabama, the Maycomb of her novel. Lee was his constant companion during an influential part of her life, one in which she was highly impressionable.

Despite her slim bibliography, Harper Lee is remembered as a significant contributor to regional literature in the United States and as a writer about childhood. In *To Kill a Mockingbird*, she writes with an ease and credibility that make her unique. The propitious combination in this novel of timely social concerns, the authenticity of the local color, the capturing of northern Alabama speech patterns, and Lee's obvious ability to assume and maintain the point of view of a young girl have assured the place of this novel in the curriculum of many secondary schools and accounts for its continued popularity among young readers.

R. Baird Shuman

TOM BROWN'S SCHOOLDAYS

Author: Thomas Hughes (1822-1896)
Type of plot: Moral tale
Time of plot: The first half of the nineteenth century
Locale: Berkshire, Rugby, and Oxford, England
Principal themes: Education, emotions, friendship, religion, and sports
First published: 1857, anonymously; 1858, with full authorship
Recommended ages: 15-18

Tom Brown, the eldest child of an honorable Berkshire family, survives the terrors and trials of Rugby public school to emerge a young hero, inspired by the humanist Christian ideals of its headmaster.

Principal characters:
> TOM BROWN, a robust, combative boy sent to Rugby for character shaping
> SQUIRE BROWN, his father, who believes in being a brave, true, Christian English gentleman
> HARRY "SCUD" EAST, Tom's friend, a witty lad with a propensity for practical jokes
> FLASHMAN, the cruel school bully, who is a coward at heart
> BROOKE, the best football player at Rugby and the school leader
> GEORGE ARTHUR, a clever young boy befriended by Brown and East
> DOCTOR ARNOLD, the kind, humane headmaster
> DIGGS (THE MUCKER), a brave, large-sized loner who challenges the school bully
> MARTIN, the untidy school eccentric
> WILLIAMS (THE SLOGGER), a rough but generally good-natured leader of his form
> THE NARRATOR, a middle-aged alumnus of Rugby

The Story

Thoroughly Victorian in its social and moral tenor, *Tom Brown's Schooldays* has as its hero a young boy whose character is tested at a renowned public school. The novel begins with painstaking geographical and genealogical details that create a legendary pedigree and context for Tom Brown. The novel is divided into two parts, with the first given to the boy's pastoral idylls and mischief, including pony rides, cricket, football, wrestling, illicit angling, quarrels with his nurse, and escapades with old Benjy, a cheery, gossipy septuagenarian.

When a fever epidemic cuts short Tom's days at a private school run by two poorly educated masters, his father sends the boy to Rugby, where he can be turned into a true Christian English gentleman. Upon arriving at Rugby, Tom meets East, a frank, hearty boy, who instructs him in the rules of football. In entering the game, however, Tom is winded, though he catches the eye of head boy Brooke. Recovering, he relishes roast potatoes in East's company at Sally Harrowell's. Here he gets his first look at Flashman, the school bully who delights in tossing young boys in a blanket. Tom's hectic first day ends with tea in the lower fifth school, supper song, a glimpse of Doctor Arnold at prayer, and a tossing in a blanket.

Tom quickly learns that Rugby can be either a noble institution for the training of Christian Englishmen or a place of evil bullying in which Flashman holds sway. Brown and East, with counsel from Diggs, defy the tyrant and his cohorts, but Tom's greatest manliness and thoughtfulness come to the fore when he takes nervous George Arthur under his wing and defends the boy against Williams "the Slogger." At sixteen, Tom is a new boy who learns from Arthur's meekness and piety and who overcomes his own vanity, which has made him believe that he is more important to Rugby than either Doctor Arnold or any other person.

By the end of his eight years at Rugby, Tom is won over to Doctor Arnold's Christian humanism, and upon bidding farewell to the school, he has honest regrets about leaving behind this stage of adolescence. In the final chapter, set during the summer of 1842, Tom, now a student at Oxford, learns of Arnold's death and cuts short a Scottish holiday to return to Rugby. In the chapel, thoughts flood back to him of his old schoolfellows, nobler, braver, and purer than he.

Themes and Meanings

Written as an edifying entertainment for juveniles, *Tom Brown's Schooldays* was created as "an old boy's" reminiscences of his own public school days when a radically new philosophy of education was taking hold. Thomas Hughes was intent on depicting the old evils of boarding school life, such as fagging and bullying, before Doctor Thomas Arnold's Christian humanism came to be the dominant shaping influence.

When Tom Brown arrives at Rugby, he is quick to note that the condition of a small boy at school is one of peculiar suffering, virtually as if all the proper supports of civilization were suddenly and cruelly denied him. Although young, Brown swells with pride at his new social position and shows enthusiasm for cricket, football, and his relative independence as a boarder. Yet he quickly becomes the target of the predatory bully Flashman, and his school career has to balance between the friendship and example of cohorts such as East, Brooke, Diggs, and Martin on the one hand and the hostilities of Flashman's gang on the other. Flashman's harrowing mistreatment of weaker boys is Brown's greatest physical and moral test in part 1, but Brown triumphs by virtue of his own pluck and tenacious resolve.

These virtues are sharpened in the second part of the book, when Brown becomes a guardian to George Arthur, the vulnerable new boy, whose Christian meekness and piety give Brown a new reference point for his own developing character. It is Arthur who stirs Brown's moral purpose in life, for Arthur shows him what it means to be charitable, kind, and sympathetic in a rough world. Brown also learns moral strength from the example of Doctor Arnold, who, though usually a background figure rarely seen in focal action, remains a spiritual presence at Rugby. Doctor Arnold enables everybody to feel of some importance at school, and he makes school seem like a microcosm of the outside world.

Brown and his friends all undergo crucial moral developments. Arthur loses his old timidity and becomes a figure of quaint fun. East goes off bravely to a military regiment in India. Brown, however, changes in a truly startling way once he overcomes the vanity of his own self-importance and acquires a mission to be useful to his fellowman.

The book is decidedly moral in tenor and purpose. It is as if every episode and conflict were meant to lead to a single epiphanic moment of Brown's conversion, when he is finally able to put aside the old boy of false pride and mere combativeness and take on the character of a new youth rounded by Christian gentlemanliness. The spirit of Doctor Arnold's humanism triumphs, and the novel becomes an expression of the best results of English education and character building.

Context

Lamenting the lack of good books for his eight-year-old son, who was about to enter boarding school in 1847, Thomas Hughes, then a young lawyer, decided to write his own novel for young readers. He found in his own experiences at Rugby (1833-1842) a perfect topic and fund of incidents and characters. Although Hughes himself was never particularly close to Doctor Thomas Arnold, the famous father of poet and critic Matthew Arnold, he never forgot the headmaster's influence on Rugby. Arnold stressed that the primary objective of the education was not the instruction of Latin and Greek but the production of good English boys with well-rounded characters.

Tom Brown's Schooldays first appeared anonymously on April 24, 1857, but was so popular that five printings were required within the first year of publication. Charles Kingsley, the author of *The Water Babies* (1863), lent his enthusiastic endorsement, and so did the American critic William Dean Howells.

Hughes's novel was eventually printed under the author's own name in 1858 and started a new run in children's literature. It also began a new genre—that of the boarding school story from a young person's point of view. Although Hughes's novel was frankly autobiographical—Brooke, for example, is modeled after the author's elder brother, George; Arthur is a version of Hughes's daughter Evie, who died of scarlet fever; and the narrator is a thinly veiled disguise for Hughes himself—one of its characters, Flashman, became the spin-off for an entire series of burlesque picaresque novels by George Macdonald Fraser, beginning in 1969 with *The Flashman Papers*. Some of the literary descendants of Hughes's novel are J. D. Salinger's *The Catcher in the Rye* (1951), John Knowles's *A Separate Peace* (1960), and Robert Cormier's *The Chocolate War* (1974), all written in a contemporary idiom much more relevant to young readers of the modern age.

Keith Garebian

TOM'S MIDNIGHT GARDEN

Author: Philippa Pearce (1920-   )
Type of plot: Fantasy
Time of plot: The mid-twentieth century and the late Victorian era
Locale: East Anglia
Principal theme: Friendship
First published: 1958; illustrated
Recommended ages: 10-13

Lonely during his brother's illness, Tom at first finds little to interest him while confined to his aunt and uncle's dull apartment. Then he finds his way into the dreams of old Mrs. Bartholomew, who lives at the top of the "flats." In her Victorian garden, he discovers friendship and the mystery of time.

> *Principal characters:*
> TOM LONG, a boy who loves the outdoors
> PETER LONG, Tom's brother, sick with the measles
> UNCLE ALAN, Tom's uncle, a very reasonable, unimaginative man
> AUNT GWEN, Tom's aunt, who cooks rich food and means to be kind
> MRS. BARTHOLOMEW, an old woman with a strange clock
> HATTY, an imaginative Victorian girl who loves her aunt's garden
> AUNT GRACE, Hatty's aunt, who favors her three sons and resents Hatty

The Story

While *Tom's Midnight Garden* includes ghostly figures and passages through time, the book's magic does not depend on the conventions of either the Gothic or the historical novel. The ghosts here are alive, and time past still lingers in dreams and in the figure of an old woman.

Mrs. Bartholomew's dreams are set against a landscape where houses crowd out trees and Victorian houses are cut up into modern flats. Tom sees his aunt and uncle's home as empty, cold, and dead, but when Mrs. Bartholomew's clock strikes a thirteenth hour, he is led to explore the "midnight garden" of her dreams. It is a magical and mythic place, alluring with its paths, great lawn, and towering fir. At first the garden is static, from its gravelike mounds of asparagus to the dark oblong of the pond to the sleeping summerhouse. Dewy footprints tell Tom that he is not alone, and, as he will learn, the child Hatty watches his explorations. On later nights when he meets Hatty, he is introduced to special hiding places, lively names for the trees, and mythic and spiritual images and lore—Hatty's initial appearance with scepter and orb, apple and sprig; her childish note to King Oberon; the burning bush she claims was grown from a slip cut from the original; her tales of the gardener

Abel's murderous brother. Events of importance occur in this Edenic garden. There Tom satisfies his deep love of nature and shares it with Hatty. There Tom develops a friendship with this little girl. There Tom enters into Hatty's sorrows when Aunt Grace shows her only cruelty.

Tom comes to feel that Hatty has made the garden into a timeless kingdom. Yet it proves to be a region like the reader's own world, ruled by time. Mrs. Bartholomew's clock in the hall shows an angel with a book, pointing to Revelation 10:1-6 and the motto "Time No Longer." Yet Tom comes to see that Hatty grows older in the garden. As her childhood's loneliness is replaced by her love for "young Barty," Tom becomes less distinct to Hatty. At last Tom loses his dream garden, and in his dismay he cries out for his former companion. Mrs. Bartholomew hears him call out her name; the dream-child Hatty, now an old woman, is still his friend. The separations of time are "no more" when "then" and "now" link.

Themes and Meanings

Tom's Midnight Garden presents a seemingly timeless, mythic realm in which, paradoxically, a boy encounters and must come to terms with time and change. Through the midnight garden, Tom learns that the gulf of age and historical time may be bridged by friendship.

The dream garden is colored by biblical and mythic elements. It is truly a kingdom ruled by the Victorian Hatty: by Mrs. Bartholomew's haunting dreams. First shown as sleeping, the garden awakes to the play of Hatty and Tom. This magical place transforms the barren world in which Tom lives during the day. Whether exploring Hatty's storied walks or skating down the river to Ely during the Great Frost, Tom feels more awake and alive than during his dull days.

Mythic and apparently supernatural elements in the story are bound to daily life. Loneliness draws both Tom and Mrs. Bartholomew to dreams; awakened, they continue their friendship under the ordinary light of day. Time, which separated the Victorian Hatty from the modern Tom, joins them. Tom has seen a little girl grow up, become a woman, and then become an old woman in whom the former child still lives. He has accompanied her from the sheltered garden of childhood to the free sweep of the young woman's countryside. In the process he has begun to think about time, timelessness, and change.

Context

Winner of England's Carnegie Prize for 1958, *Tom's Midnight Garden* is notable for its handling of setting, style, and character. Difficult to categorize, Pearce's best-known book has won praise for its lyrical and imaginative writing. The book creates a precise dream, a magical Eden in which friendship is born. The author's achievement is her blending of a realm of mystery with psychological truthfulness and the realism of the daily world. Readers have noted with interest Pearce's intricate and evocative landscape, and British critics have praised her ability to capture the East Anglian countryside, a region pictured in most of her books.

Philippa Pearce develops a familiar archetypal setting—the garden—in a striking manner, artfully blending theme and landscape. The backdrop strongly reinforces the theme of time and change in several interesting ways. Pearce creates a sense of historical time and place, contrasting the enclosed Victorian garden and open countryside with a cramped modern world of walls and barriers. The secret hours of childhood pass within the garden's shelter; during Hatty's childhood the two children play in its bounds, but as she grows older time moves more quickly and the garden gives way to the long sweep of fields and river.

Reviewers immediately connected this haunting tale set in a garden with books for children such as Frances Hodgson Burnett's *The Secret Garden* (1911). The bond is clear: a magical, renewing garden; young characters with mythic overtones; a focus on friendship between boy and girl. Critic Sheila Egoff describes *Tom's Midnight Garden* as an example of fantasies which stress character and human time, creating an "enchanted realism." For similar examples, she points to stories such as William Mayne's *A Year and a Day* (1976), Lucy Boston's Green Knowe series, and Natalie Babbitt's *Tuck Everlasting* (1975). Hatty's unhappy state as ward of her scornful aunt and the comfort she takes in stories and romantic nature may also suggest Charlotte Brontë's *Jane Eyre* (1847).

Marlene Youmans

TRAIN RIDE

Author: John Steptoe (1950-   )
Type of plot: Social realism, adventure tale
Time of plot: The 1960's
Locale: New York City
Principal themes: Race and ethnicity
First published: 1971; illustrated
Recommended ages: 10-13

Charles, a young black boy in New York City, leads a group of his friends on a train ride downtown, where they see things previously unknown to them; after returning home late, they receive beatings from their parents.

Principal characters:
CHARLES, a black youth living somewhere in the ghettos of New
     York City
FREDDY, Charles's neighbor and best friend, another black who
     takes the train ride
BILLY and
TERRENCE, two other friends who accompany Charles on his
     excursion downtown

The Story

One summer day in New York City, Charles and his friends tire of playing on the streets and decide to do something different. They notice, as usual in the extremely hot weather, people emerging from the train station at the corner of their block. None of the boys in the group has ever been on the train before, but Charles—who identifies himself as "the smartest one"—knows that the train goes into the city, although no one is sure of what "the city" is. Charles is the only one who has been there, but he does not know directions nor does he realize what the city truly is.

Acting on an impulse and primarily because they have nothing else to do, the four children decide to go for a train ride. All of them are scared as they realize they are disobeying their parents in leaving without permission. They have no money, so they sneak over the iron gate to the train station and manage to smuggle themselves aboard the next train.

They exit the train at Forty-second Street, where they see things previously unknown to them. First, they notice a block full of motion-picture houses, many of which are showing "dirty movies"; they also see clothing stores that carry what they call "dynamite" clothing. Their main activity and object of interest, however, is an arcade full of game machines and guns. Two or three of them have some coins in their pockets, and so they quickly use their quarters in attempts to win prizes, but fail to do so. Their money goes quickly; they then watch others play games until they become bored with this, and so they return to the street, where they simply watch people, look at the signs, and display interest for the films in the theaters.

Eventually someone realizes that the four boys must return to the train station and attempt to go home. There is a sudden realization that it is late and that all of them are in trouble, and they deal with this by insulting and blaming one another for the difficulties. They are in luck, however, when the train station clerk, realizing the desperateness of their plight, lets them board the train for the trip home, even though they have no money for fare. The trip is mostly a sad one, as they realize a beating awaits each of them when they do return to their parents. The next day, all of them meet on the street again, where they discuss and brag about their excursion the night before. All of the boys agree that the train trip was worth the beating, and each resolves to go back to the city again, but such a trip is seen as happening in the distant future.

Themes and Meanings

John Steptoe has written this book essentially to show how black youths live in large cities. His first intention was to show, realistically, the day-to-day existence of youngsters in the ghetto who, here at least, have something of an adventure. Their trip to New York City's Forty-second Street at night serves to entice his target readers: black children in similar circumstances. The story does not attempt to explain what it is like to be a child in the ghetto. Rather, it is taken as a given that readers will already understand this; they will then, perhaps, have more reason to read the story.

Surprisingly, there are no racial tensions depicted in this 1960's story. All the main characters are black, and other characters are not identified by race. Life unfolds, whether fairly or unfairly, on its own terms. While race is surely one of those terms, it is never a problem for anyone.

The trip itself becomes something of a mini-odyssey, a trip into the unknown, where some fair amount of growing up occurs. The four youths explore an unknown world, have adventures, go through trials and tribulations, and return home the better for it. That they have disobeyed their parents in so doing is not so important as what they learn and experience. They now know something of the vastness and strangeness of the world as well as something of its kindness.

The fact that the youths must return home to receive beatings shows that a price must be paid not so much for disobedience as for learning. They all accept their punishments as just, although none of them can be expected to receive these fondly. They all declare that they will make yet another trip to the city, a place of knowledge, evil, and bright lights, even though they were scared when there, because they were out of their own domain and territory. This, of course, is what is required for any escape from childhood: a willingness to enter adult territories on unknown terms and to pay the price for so doing.

Context

Train Ride is a book written by a black author specifically calculated to accommodate the reading desires of lower-income black children living in large cities. Steptoe accomplishes this objective in several ways: First, *Train Ride* is written in black dialect; the author not only records dialogue in dialect but also tells the entire story in this manner. Second, the setting is entirely "black," which is to say that the location described and the activities depicted are all commonplace in the black environment of large urban centers in the late 1960's. Third, all the characters are black; at least all the main ones are, while the race of other characters is indeterminate and inconsequential. Finally, the moral of the tale—that blacks must pay a price (in this case a beating) for knowledge of the mainstream society—comes from a particularly ethnic frame even if its application is in no way limited to the black outlook.

In addition to being a product of black America written for young black urban readers, *Train Ride* is also an outgrowth of the 1960's. Steptoe makes every attempt to capture the reality of life as these children experience it. It is a time when everyone, specifically children coming of age, must take chances—do the daring—to work effectually for the improvement of self and the social all. Thus society itself is shown to be a place replete with pornographic films and unseemly game arcades and, more immediately, a place were the youths must return home to accept beatings from their parents. Steptoe's effort is to record the world as it is likely to reveal itself to his target audience.

Thus the train ride itself becomes, vaguely, a metaphor for the movement of the individual within his immediate society and then within the society in general. The boys are wrong to take the trip in defiance of reason and in disobedience to their parents; moreover, they take it for the wrong reason—to escape boredom. Yet they are correct in wanting to learn, to see, to do, and to have new experiences. It becomes the right choice.

Carl Singleton

TREASURE ISLAND

Author: Robert Louis Stevenson (1850-1894)
Type of plot: Adventure tale
Time of plot: The mid-eighteenth century
Locale: A small village on the coast of England near Kent; Bristol, England; and a
  fictitious island in that part of the Caribbean Sea known as the Spanish Main
Principal themes: Friendship, coming-of-age, crime, and social issues
First published: 1883
Recommended ages: 10-12

*The orphaned son of an innkeeper discovers a map to the treasure buried by a
dead pirate. Aided by wealthy gentlemen, he joins a company who quest for the
treasure in the South Seas, where they encounter surviving members of a pirate crew.*

Principal characters:
> JIM HAWKINS, a bright and resourceful twelve-year-old boy whose
> parents run the Admiral Benbow Inn at the beginning of the
> story; he is soon orphaned by pirates and becomes a cabin boy
> aboard the ship *Hispaniola*
>
> BILLY BONES, an old, rough-hewn seaman who takes up residence
> at the Admiral Benbow Inn
>
> DOCTOR DAVID LIVESEY, the local physician and a sponsor of the
> treasure quest
>
> SQUIRE JOHN TRELAWNEY, a wealthy landowner, magistrate, and
> the primary investor in the vessel *Hispaniola*, who first
> suggests the enterprise
>
> LONG JOHN SILVER, a fifty-year-old one-legged seaman who is
> hired as cook on the treasure quest and as agent in selecting
> the crew
>
> CAPTAIN ALEXANDER SMOLLETT, the master of the *Hispaniola*, a
> strict, no-nonsense type of individual
>
> BEN GUNN, a wild, half-demented resident of the island who was
> marooned there three years before by the pirate crew that left
> the treasure

The Story

Treasure Island established the pattern of the classic adventure tale for young
people in that it features an adolescent hero who narrates his own story. This was
standard practice in adventure magazines for young readers when it first published. Yet the quality of the writing and the appeal of the themes make Stevenson's
novel an international enduring success.

Jim Hawkins helps his parents operate an inn called the Admiral Benbow on an unfrequented stretch of English seacoast. An old, tyrannical seaman, Billy Bones, takes up residence there, terrorizing everyone. Dr. Livesey attends Jim's father, who is gravely ill, and stands up to the ruffian alone. One day, another wayfarer who happens by forces Jim to bring him to his "mate Bill." After driving him off, Bill collapses from a massive stroke, from which he recovers slowly. In the meantime, Mr. Hawkins suddenly dies. The same day, a blind man, Pew, arrives to summon Bill to a meeting. Bill suffers a second stroke and dies. After searching the chest, Jim and his mother barely escape before the pirates attack. While they are ransacking the inn, the watch surprises and scatters them. In the melee, Pew is ridden down and killed.

One of the items salvaged from the chest turns out to be a map of an island, complete with latitude and longitude, and a notation reading "bulk of treasure here." Squire John Trelawney immediately proposes that he and the doctor commission a ship and find the treasure. He invites Jim to be cabin boy. The squire leaves for Bristol, where he purchases a ship, the *Hispaniola*, for the voyage. In due time, he calls Jim there, and hires Long John Silver, the proprietor of a pub and former seaman who wears an artificial leg, to raise a crew and act as cook and agent of his interests when the ship gets under way. Some things seem vaguely suspicious. Captain Alexander Smollett has just replaced Captain Flint as skipper, and he objects to everything about the enterprise. His first order is to stow the arms and powder where the crew cannot get at them.

The voyage to the island is uneventful. Then, just before landfall, Jim climbs into a barrel to get an apple, and from within he overhears Silver plotting mutiny with other former members of Captain Flint's crew. At that moment, the island comes into view. Jim reveals his secret to the captain, who permits the crew to go ashore the next morning. Jim slips away with them to spy.

On land, Silver kills two of the sailors who refuse to join the mutiny, stunning them with his peg leg and then impaling them with it before shooting them dead. Attempting to escape, Jim runs into the old man of the island, Ben Gunn, marooned three years before. He leads Jim to the island stockade, where the outnumbered captain and crew have been forced to seek refuge. The *Hispaniola* now flies the Jolly Roger skull and bones.

The loyalists hold off the first attack, after which Jim joins them. Their supplies are dangerously low. Silver calls for a truce, offering liberty in exchange for the map, but the captain scorns him. Before long, the pirates mount a full attack, which is just barely repelled. The doctor then sets off to find Ben Gunn, and Jim decides to reconnoiter on his own. After finding Ben's homemade boat, he paddles it to the *Hispaniola*'s portage, and cuts the ship adrift to deprive the pirates of a means of escape. A gale swings the vessel about, however, and with billowing sails it makes headway directly in the path of Ben's little boat, which it destroys. Jim clambers aboard the ship again, and beaches it to keep it safe. He strikes the sails, but not before shooting its one remaining sailor, who wounds Jim with a knife.

Jim returns to the stockade, where he is captured by the pirates, who have captured it. The company, meanwhile, has taken refuge in Ben Gunn's cave. When Jim tells them he has taken the ship, the men reject Silver's authority and plan to kill him. Silver, however, is able to win them back and save Jim's life. Dr. Livesey appears the next morning to treat the ill and wounded—part of a pact with the pirates. Although the doctor encourages him to do so, Jim refuses to try escaping— he has given his word. Silver vows to protect Jim, and the doctor in return promises to do what he can to keep the pirate from hanging. Ben Gunn intimates to Dr. Livesey that, early in his stay on the island, he had stumbled upon the treasure and brought it to his cave. Livesey gives the worthless map to Long John Silver, warning him for the sake of appearances not to use it.

The pirates will not leave the island without the treasure. At first, the signs of finding it seem good: They find a skeleton deliberately laid out as though to act as a pointer. Then Ben Gunn holds them up for a bit by playing the ghost of Flint. Finally, they arrive at the site, only to find it empty. Fearing retaliation, Silver arms Jim and saves his life again. The doctor and his company kill two of the pirates and drive the others to flight. Squire Trelawney's party returns to Ben's cave, captures the prize, and makes for the ship accompanied by Long John Silver and Ben Gunn. Three of the buccaneers are deliberately marooned on the island. During the return voyage, the *Hispaniola* anchors briefly in the West Indies, where Long John escapes with a sack of coins. The rest arrive safely in Bristol, where they fare variously.

Themes and Meanings

Treasure Island has many of the earmarks of the classic quest-myth centering on the orphan hero: Jim Hawkins is driven out of his daily round by extraordinary events, is admitted to a fantasy world by means of a secret map, acquires a powerful companion, and returns to bring a limitless source of wealth to his people. As soon as readers recognize this, however, they see that Stevenson is also doing other things, skillfully employing ironies and other literary devices that undercut the fairy-tale view of his story. These ironies have kept *Treasure Island* alive, while many other myth-adventures having a boy-hero protagonist have long been forgotten.

The first monster that confronts Jim in this tale is the seaman Billy Bones, the bully who terrorizes Jim's family at the Admiral Benbow Inn and seems to cause the death of Jim's father. Yet Jim never faces up to him and never overcomes him. Dr. Livesey subdues Billy, but Black Dog and Pew together, aided by liquor, summon the strokes that bring him down. Jim's heroism in this instance is limited. Later, Jim gains two powerful, paradoxical, and unlikely friends in succession, Long John Silver and Ben Gunn. Neither is satisfactory as a companion or father figure: Silver turns out to be the principal conspirator against the company, a villain all the more treacherous because he is disguised and one who shows no hesitation to murder to gain his ends, although he twice saves Jim's life.

Other relations and values prove equally enigmatic. Perhaps the most bewildering character of all is Squire Trelawney, the one who financed the far-flung and rather bizarre enterprise of journeying from England to an island in the Spanish Main based on a dead pirate's map. Trelawney is not a character of depth. His judgment in readily trusting Long John Silver and making him his agent is dubious. He likes to play the hale and hearty leader, but lets the doctor take over in the clinch. Captain Smollett proves a bulwark of strength and reliability, but he gets injured early and is inconsequential thereafter. The doctor is stable, but even he acts strangely at times, such as when he tempts Jim to turn on his word to Long John and escape. The most enduring relationship that Jim forms, finally, is with Long John Silver, who develops into a rather attractive villain. The man who is cruel enough to impale a reluctant mutineer with his wooden leg and kill him on the spot proves also to possess the capacity for pity, remorse, and generosity. He is a man who has reckoned the course of his life by means of a fiercely independent compass. Rather than seeing him as a powerless cripple, the reader incorporates the peg leg into the overall image of distinctiveness. The very treachery he reveals consistently—to the squire, to the captain, and to his men—is balanced by Jim's inexplicable trust in him, which he vindicates. Jim places the value of his word to Silver above the value of his own life, and Silver returns the trust in kind. Even after Jim has learned the full extent of Silver's treachery, Silver saves Jim's life, not once but twice. The novel pivots on the relationship of Jim and Long John Silver. Through the experience, Jim learns about and likes the role of the rogue-villain, but also appreciates the necessity of rejecting it in himself and others if he is to grow to become his own man.

Context

Treasure Island is generally regarded as the best of the adolescent narratives of Robert Louis Stevenson. It is probably the best-integrated composition of his entire career—the first of the series of romances on which his fame rests. Other works are *Prince Otto* (1885), *The Strange Case of Dr. Jekyll and Mr. Hyde* (1886), *Kidnapped* (1886), *The Black Arrow* (1888), *The Master of Ballantrae* (1889), and *David Balfour* (1893). *Weir of Herminston* (1896), which he had planned to be his masterpiece, was left unfinished at his death in 1894. To an extent, Stevenson first found his characteristic voice in *Treasure Island*. These books are all distinguished by a singular ease of style and happiness of expression, though none more so than *Treasure Island*. Henry James considered Stevenson the only English writer of his generation capable of crafting an honest sentence. In contrast to the styles of his predecessors in romantic fiction, Sir Walter Scott and Charles Dickens, for example, Stevenson's style seems natural and illuminating. Yet the most distinctive features of Stevenson's romances are irony and subtlety of moral vision. Unlike most adventure writers, Stevenson is fully aware of the ambiguity of evil.

James L. Livingston

A TREE GROWS IN BROOKLYN

Author: Betty Smith (1896-1972)
Type of plot: Domestic realism
Time of plot: 1912-1918
Locale: Brooklyn, New York
Principal themes: Coming-of-age, education, family, poverty, and sexual issues
First published: 1943
Recommended ages: 13-15

A girl grows up in an urban environment of poverty and ignorance in the early part of the twentieth century. Because of her love of reading and the strength of character she has inherited from her mother, she is able to achieve self-reliance and financial independence.

Principal characters:
FRANCIE NOLAN, a frail, sensitive girl whose main solace in her impoverished slum life is her love of reading
KATIE NOLAN, her mother, a strong and determined woman who is forced to work as a janitor because her husband is a poor provider
JOHNNY NOLAN, Francie's father, a handsome, lovable man but a drunkard who works odd jobs as a waiter
NEELEY NOLAN, Francie's younger brother, who shows promise of being another charming but ineffectual male like his father
SISSY, Francie's aunt (her mother's sister), a lusty, earthy woman who teaches Francie to be strong and self-reliant

The Story

This autobiographical novel is divided into five books. The first introduces Francie Nolan, who is eleven years old, plain-looking, and frail. The impecunious Nolans live in an impoverished Irish Catholic neighborhood in Brooklyn, New York, in the year 1912. Francie has certain traits that make her stand out in this blighted environment: She is intelligent, sensitive, observant, and imaginative. Her main pleasure and escape is reading. She discovered at an early age that books can provide a ladder by which an intelligent child can escape, both figuratively and literally, from an unpleasant environment.

Book 2 is a flashback that tells about Francie's mother and father before she was born. It becomes plain that Francie has acquired the best qualities of both her parents: her mother's strength and courage and her father's artistic sensitivity and love of life.

Book 3 is almost as long as all the other books put together. It is made up of unconnected events in the life of Francie Nolan, ranging from humorous to tragic and portraying life in Brooklyn in the period before World War I. The novel belongs to the school of naturalism, a style of fiction pioneered by the French writer Émile Zola and the Russian writer Ivan Turgenev. As such, it does not strive for dramatic peaks but depicts life as most people experience it: a series of uneventful and not very memorable days. Her father continues to deteriorate and eventually dies from pneumonia resulting from alcoholism. Shortly after his death, Francie's mother gives birth to a third child. Francie and Neeley are unable to go to high school, because they have to contribute to the family income.

In book 4, Francie goes into the working world at fourteen. Her first job is doing assembly work in a factory. Yet because of her brains, ambition, and self-education, she is able to obtain an office job across the river in Manhattan and begins to move into the middle-class world. She has to lie about her age, telling everyone she is sixteen. She begins meeting men, and this adds a whole new dimension to her life. Her mother remarries. Francie's affluent new stepfather offers to put her through college. Because of her intelligence and her years of reading and writing in a private journal, Francie is able to qualify for college without ever having gone to high school.

Book 5 is brief. Francie says good-bye to her old neighborhood. She has changed much over the years. Though only seventeen, she is remarkably poised and self-assured. She has become worldly-wise as a result of her exposure to this tough environment, yet she has managed to escape its limitations and can look forward to a life of achievement and prosperity.

Themes and Meanings

The theme of the novel is based on a single overarching metaphor: The struggle of Francie Nolan to survive in a slum neighborhood is like the struggle of a tree to grow in the same environment out of a cement sidewalk or a rubbish heap with barely any sunlight or water. That Francie, a sickly child who was not expected to live, manages not only to survive but also to succeed in life, is attributed to three things. One is the strength of character that, as the author makes clear, she has inherited from her mother. The second important element in her life is her love of reading. Though both her grandmother and mother were ignorant women, they fostered a love of literature in Francie. She learned that books are truly democratic: They offer friendship, comfort, and instruction to the poor as well as to the rich. Through the process of reading and writing—and the thinking that both activities naturally entail—she develops her mind to an exceptional degree. Because of a third very important element in her life, the fact that she lives in the United States, the land of opportunity, she is able to climb out of the ignorance and poverty that had stultified her mother and grandmother and all her ancestors in the Old World. At the end of the novel, Francie is able to look forward to a satisfying vocation, financial security, interesting friendships, and children who will enjoy even more of the good things of life.

All of this might sound like the Horatio Alger novels were it not for the fact that *A Tree Grows in Brooklyn* is strongly autobiographical in nature. Betty Smith grew up in just such an impoverished environment as she describes in her novel, and she became a successful novelist, playwright, actress, and teacher. In our time, the most important question raised by novels such as *A Tree Grows in Brooklyn* is whether it is enough for the exceptional individual to pull himself or herself out of an unsavory environment or whether people should recognize poverty, ignorance, crime, unemployment, welfare-dependency, disease, and general slum-bred misery as social problems that should be solved by government intervention. This is a question on which the whole world has been divided and may continue to be divided for centuries to come. In the meantime, however, the novel will continue to offer hope and inspiration to the lonely individual. Like Charles Dickens' highly influential novel *Oliver Twist* (1838), *A Tree Grows in Brooklyn* paints a vivid picture of social conditions that will stay in the reader's memory even though the young protagonist does manage to escape from them.

Context

A Tree Grows in Brooklyn is a coming-of-age novel. As such, it is in the tradition of novels such as Charles Dickens' *David Copperfield* (1850) and *Great Expectations* (1861), two of the greatest novels ever written. It is also related to such famous works as Hugh Walpole's *Fortitude* (1913), Jack London's *Martin Eden* (1909), Samuel Butler's *The Way of All Flesh* (1903), and Somerset Maugham's *Of Human Bondage* (1915). Coming-of-age novels generally follow a simple pattern similar to Hans Christian Andersen's tale "The Ugly Duckling": The protagonist feels like a despised nonentity until he undergoes a transformation upon reaching maturity and realizes that he is actually superior to those who despised him.

An important difference from most of the earlier coming-of-age novels is that in *A Tree Grows in Brooklyn* the viewpoint character is a girl rather than a boy. Francie Nolan is growing up in the early years of the twentieth century, a time when the Industrial Revolution was beginning to create some limited opportunities for women. For the first time in history, women were beginning to think of themselves as subjects rather than objects—as independent individuals capable of doing anything that males could do. William Dean Howells and Henry James had recognized this tendency of young women to leave their homes in large numbers, and Theodore Dreiser turned the spotlight on the phenomenon with the publication of his masterpiece, *Sister Carrie*, in 1900.

Prior to the great social upheavals of the twentieth century, it was generally believed that a young woman leaving her parental home for the big city was like a lamb going to slaughter: She would end up either in a house of prostitution or returning to burden and disgrace her aging parents with an illegitimate baby. Contemporary feminists believe that much of the protectionism displayed toward women has simply been exploitation in disguise.

The book was published in 1943, a time when the United States was deeply involved in World War II. The mechanized slaughter and atrocities being reported every day had desensitized Americans. They were turning from romanticism and escapism in popular entertainment to material that dealt with the darker side of life. *A Tree Grows in Brooklyn* was shocking in its time: It deals with such subjects as sexual perversion, juvenile sexual curiosity, and sexual promiscuity in a totally matter-of-fact way. The author's intention is not to titillate but to illustrate how Francie Nolan's exposure to the mean streets of Brooklyn make her sufficiently tough-minded to take care of herself on her own.

Bill Delaney

THE TROUBLE WITH DONOVAN CROFT

Author: Bernard Ashley (1935-   )
Type of plot: Psychological realism
Time of plot: The early 1970's
Locale: London, England, and surrounding suburbs
Principal themes: Emotions, family, and race and ethnicity
First published: 1974; illustrated
Recommended ages: 10-13

Donovan Croft, the son of Jamaican immigrants to England, becomes a foster child living with the Chapman family. The shock of the event leaves him unable to speak even though nothing is physically wrong with him.

> *Principal characters:*
> DONOVAN CROFT, a black foster child of Jamaican descent living with the Chapmans, a white family
> KEITH CHAPMAN, Donovan's friend, companion, and defender
> DOREEN CHAPMAN, Donovan's foster mother and Keith's natural mother
> TED CHAPMAN, Donovan's foster father and Keith's natural father
> MR. CROFT, Donovan's natural father, who is temporarily unable to take care of Donovan because of work obligations
> MR. HENRY, a teacher to Donovan and Keith at Transport Avenue Junior School
> MR. ROPER, the school's principal
> MRS. PARSONS, a heartless, loud-mouthed neighbor to the Crofts
> FLUFF, Keith's guinea pig and an object of affection for Donovan

The Story

The Trouble with Donovan Croft is essentially the story of a young boy who becomes an isolate through circumstances and not through any choice of his own. Donovan Croft's parents must temporarily separate because Mrs. Croft's father is sick, probably dying, and she chooses to return to Jamaica to be with him against the wishes of Donovan's father. The youth is further traumatized when his father, because of his work schedule, is unable to take care of Donovan with any regularity and so must place him in the hands of social workers who find a foster home for him with the Chapman family.

Donovan responds to these shocking changes in his life by not speaking: It is never clear whether he does not speak as a willful expression of his anger and revulsion or because he is physically unable to do so as a result of the psychological damage. In either case, this inability/refusal to communicate forms the basis for his psychological isolationism. Additionally, the matter is made more complex because

Donovan is black and an immigrant, living in what is basically a white society where he is something of an outsider.

The story is told from the point of view of the Chapman family, and, in particular, the events unfold as they are seen through the eyes of Keith Chapman. At the beginning, the family prepares for Donovan Croft's arrival in their home. The reader soon sees the anxiety that this occurrence creates in all members of the family. Despite the changes, all goes well except for problems that develop when Donovan does not speak. The Chapmans accept this silence and live around it, but Donovan's first day at school is a different matter.

Here, it becomes Keith's lot to explain, protect, and defend his foster brother's peculiar behavior. There occurs a ghastly episode when Mr. Henry, the boys' teacher, loses his control after Donovan fails to answer his name during roll call. Mr. Henry calls Donovan "a stupid black idiot" and strikes him. Donovan then runs away from school. The Chapmans are notified, and Mr. Roper (the principal) organizes a search with all the teachers and pupils at the school, seeking Donovan. They fail to find him and are ready to call the police when he is discovered hiding in a building behind the Chapmans' house.

Donovan's father writes a letter to him before a short visit. Mr. Croft has no explanation for Donovan's sudden inability to speak. Mr. Chapman decides that the boys and their fathers should go together to a soccer game near Donovan's home; he hopes that the excitement of the game and his father's influence and presence might entice him to speak. The plan, however, does not work; as they are leaving the game, Keith steps in front of a car, and Donovan, in the sense of the emergency, calls out to warn him. After that, he goes on to talk, thus ending the trouble with Donovan Croft.

Themes and Meanings

The major point of *The Trouble with Donovan Croft* is that love and compassion triumph over isolationism and adverse circumstances. Donovan is, to an extent, like all children and all humankind, a victim of circumstances far beyond his control. Too, he is not able to alter his inability to speak until he is shocked out of this state by an emergency, another circumstance beyond his control if he remains silent.

Donovan's isolation is defined by three matters: his separation from his parents, his race, and his immigrant status. All are severe matters that produce their own anxieties and damage him psychologically. He cannot understand his parents' separation from himself or from each other; moving in with the Chapman family—even though they provide a caring, compassionate family environment—is not enough to negate the loss of his own mother and father.

The racism depicted in the novel provides a second theme. His teacher has no qualms about calling Donovan a "stupid black idiot" and hitting him. Similarly, Mrs. Parsons, the Chapmans' neighbor, hurls racial insults at Donovan and the Chapman family without any concern for their damaging effect on all involved. The behavior of these racists, however, is more than counterbalanced by the actions of the Chapmans and Mr. Roper. The world is shown to be one where fairness and justice are stronger than bigotry and ignorance. Similarly, problems that occur because Donovan is an immigrant are also dismissed as these are overriden by reason and a sense of justice.

Context

Although this novel appeared in 1974, it is essentially a product of the cultural milieu of the 1960's in Europe. This is not to say that the novel can be accurately described as a "sixties timepiece"; it cannot. The concerns of the author are readily identifiable as those of the time in which he reached his prime as a writer. In his novels, he visits the world of children of the day, and in so doing, he takes the prevailing attitudes and convictions about life held by the society at large to explore their reality for an individual child.

Thus, such matters as alienation of the self, a lack of communication, deterioration of the family, and racial tensions are all set in the context of the society and its problems. At the same time, *The Trouble with Donovan Croft* is a children's novel; such problems, while realistically described, are all successfully dealt with at the end. As in all Ashley's novels, circumstances eventually work toward a positive end. The writer typically focuses on misunderstood children who do not fit into their immediate world; school life and home life are depicted in what is, on the one hand, thoroughly sanitized and, on the other, realistically focused on genuinely captivating events. The novel, like his others, studies the behavior and motivation of children in trouble through no fault of their own. The school setting and home life provide important and necessary backdrops in the resolution of conflict.

That Donovan Croft is unable to speak embodies problems of all young people growing up. An inability to communicate carried to this utmost extreme is both generational and nongenerational. That Donovan Croft is finally able to talk when it is required for the simple reason of doing what is right and necessary shows that such limitations in communication and emotions can and will eventually be overcome.

Carl Singleton

THE TRUMPETER OF KRAKOW

Author: Eric P. Kelly (1884-1960)
Type of plot: Historical fiction
Time of plot: The mid-fifteenth century
Locale: Krakow, Poland
Principal themes: Politics and law, religion, and family
First published: 1928; illustrated
Recommended ages: 10-13

In order to gain control of the Polish Ukraine, Ivan, the Russian czar, strikes an agreement with the Tartars: He will arrange the theft of the Great Tarnov Crystal; in return, the Tartars will attack the Polish Ukraine.

> *Principal characters:*
> ANDREW CHARNETSKI, whose family has guarded the Great Tarnov Crystal for centuries
> JOSEPH CHARNETSKI, the son of Andrew, a naïve country boy who finds Krakow dangerous
> PETER OF THE BUTTON FACE, or BOGDAN THE TERRIBLE, a cunning Tartar who disguises himself as Stephan Ostrovski
> JAN KANTY, a compassionate priest and scholar who helps the Charnetskis survive in Krakow
> NICHOLAS KREUTZ, a scholar and alchemist
> ELZBIETKA KREUTZ, his niece, who becomes Joseph's close friend
> JOHANN TRING, an evil student of Kreutz
> KING JAGIELLO, the ruler of the Polish kingdom

The Story

A Krakow legend from the 1200's tells of the Tartar invasion, in which a young trumpeter is struck down by an arrow when he sounds an ancient hymn, the "Heynal," from the cathedral steeple but is killed before finishing the tune. His martyrdom is revered by trumpeters who, since that event, end the hymn on a broken note.

The legend provides the backdrop for a dramatic plot set in fifteenth century Krakow. Accompanied by his wife and his son, Joseph, Andrew Charnetski flees the Tartar attack on his country home with the Great Tarnov Crystal hidden in a pumpkin on the cart behind him. They are stopped by Peter of the Button Face, masquerading as Stephan Ostrovski, a fellow Pole. Eluding the Tartar, the Charnetksi family head to Krakow.

Told primarily from fifteen-year-old Joseph's point of view, the story winds its way through medieval Krakow, carrying the reader along through street scenes, customs, and religious rituals of the time. Andrew attempts to deliver the crystal to the king, but the king is not in residence. The family seeks asylum with a cousin but finds that the cousin has been murdered. Joseph finds an apartment in a building shared by Nicholas Kreutz, an alchemist, and Elzbietka, his niece. Andrew is hired by Jan Kanty to play the "Heynal" from the cathedral. Joseph also learns to play trumpet for the night watch and becomes close friends with Elzbietka.

While Andrew is away on watch, a group of Tartars, led by Peter of the Button Face, sneaks into the Charnetskis' lodging to steal the crystal. Above them, Kreutz suspects an evil happening. He explodes powders and creates startling fireballs to frighten Peter and his men. Peter escapes without the crystal.

Peter believes that the Charnetskis still possess the crystal. Raiding the church, he subdues Joseph and his father in the steeple. Knowing the custom of the watch, Peter permits Joseph to play the hymn as usual, but, cleverly breaking tradition, Joseph finishes the tune. Aware that Joseph is playing the hymn differently, Elzbietka finds Jan Kanty, who summons rescuers for Joseph and his father. Peter again escapes, and the crystal is still missing.

Two weeks later in his loft, Kreutz is hypnotized by the evil Tring, and he reveals to Tring that he has the crystal. Under Tring's influence, Kreutz causes a terrible explosion that eventually sets the wooden section of Krakow on fire. Both Kreutz and Tring leave, with Kreutz hiding the crystal under his robe.

Peter of the Button Face is captured during the fire. Jan Kanty finds the dazed Kreutz with the crystal and takes him to the Charnetskis, who then gain an audience with the king. Now the captured Peter admits that he is Bogdan the Terrible and, in exchange for his life, tells of the plot to cause chaos in the Polish Ukraine in return for possession of the Great Tarnov Crystal. He is banished forever, while Andrew and his family are rewarded for their faithfulness.

The king turns to look deeply into the crystal, succumbing to its magic, but Kreutz grabs the crystal and, racing outside, throws it into the Vistula River. Aware of the misery and destruction that it has caused, King Jagiello leaves the crystal in the riverbed.

Themes and Meanings

The desire of Peter of the Button Face for the Great Tarnov Crystal signifies evil in *The Trumpeter of Krakow*. Since Peter is overcome and the Charnetski family is rewarded by King Jagiello, the main theme of good-versus-evil is easily recognized. Religion and political survival, however, serve as complicated subthemes.

Since the Tartars are non-Christian and the majority of Poles are Christian, the question of faith in Christianity and loyalty to the king becomes increasingly important in the story. Both Christianity and the kingdom appear in jeopardy because of the proximity of Ivan, the Russian czar. Ivan wants the Polish kingdom, and the pagan khan, ruler of the Tartars, wishes to possess the Great Tarnov Crystal. The greed for the supposed magic of the crystal stems from the alchemy and black magic that Christianity wishes to destroy, so Christians do double battle here, against the pagan Tartars from without and against those in their own population, such as Kreutz, who engage in alchemy and black magic.

Most of the characters, including Joseph, appear flat in that they are either all good or all evil, but Nicholas Kreutz is one who does show growth and development, for it is he who throws the crystal into the Vistula River. Elzbietka also appears courageous when, despite the danger of being on the street at night, she decides to seek aid alone. She is a strong person willing to assist Joseph, her close friend.

When Joseph plays the tune all the way through, he is a trumpeter breaking out of the legend, but he embodies the same Christian faith as the earlier trumpeter. By risking his life for the church and kingdom, he links Christianity and politics together. As trumpeter, Joseph is a symbol of the church reaching out to protect even in the dark night, and the reader finds Christianity finally triumphant when the Great Tarnov Crystal, a symbol of alchemy and black magic, disappears forever.

Context

As the first historical fiction about medieval Poland written in English, *The Trumpeter of Krakow* is a significant work. Best known of Eric P. Kelly's books for children and winner of the Newbery Medal in 1929, it presents a well-crafted plot in an episodic narrative structure.

Like Howard Pyle's *Otto of the Silver Hand* (1888), *The Trumpeter of Krakow* engages a young hero and his family in adventures in medieval times. In this novel of plot (rather than character), the wealth of detail of fifteenth century Krakow enriches the narrative description that surrounds the action of the characters.

In placing the Catholic church at the center of the busy Krakow city life, Kelly's story is similar to Victor Hugo's novel *Notre-Dame de Paris* (1831; *The Hunchback of Notre Dame*, 1833), in which the church is recognized as center of the political and social world of Paris. In *The Trumpeter of Krakow*, the symbolic nature of the Catholic church as center of the spiritual world as well as of the physical kingdom of the Polish people brings together themes of religion and politics.

Kelly melds the legend of the trumpeter and Polish history, creating a richly descriptive narrative that incorporates authentic Polish legend and accurate historic setting, thus offering the young reader a classic work of historical fiction.

Norma Sadler

TUCK EVERLASTING

Author: Natalie Babbitt (1932-   )
Type of plot: Fantasy
Time of plot: The late nineteenth century
Locale: Treegap
Principal themes: Coming-of-age, death, and family
First published: 1975
Recommended ages: 10-13

The forest, a place of mystery and magic, is entered for the first time by Winnie Foster, a lonely girl trying to establish her own identity. There, she finds the spring, a source of immortality, and is forced to make her own decisions and question those of the grown-ups in her life.

> *Principal characters:*
> WINNIE FOSTER, a curious girl who stumbles upon the spring and enters the Tucks' lives, forcing them to tell their story for the first time
> JESSE TUCK, a young, carefree boy whom Winnie meets in the forest and who has not aged for eighty-seven years
> MILES TUCK, elder brother of Jesse, who is dulled by the losses caused by his immortality
> MAE TUCK, their mother and the wife of Angus Tuck; she is a strong and loving woman who also cannot die
> ANGUS TUCK, or TUCK, husband of Mae and father to Miles and Jesse, a wise, kind, and immortal man
> MAN IN THE YELLOW SUIT, a malicious stranger to Treegap who wants to sell the spring water to the world

The Story

In its plot and setting, *Tuck Everlasting* has the attributes of a fairy tale, but the intensity of the emotions that the characters feel is very real. Winnie Foster is the only child in a family of oppressive pride. Her sole friend is a toad to whom she talks through the fence while her mother and grandmother pass the day watching Winnie through the living room window.

Winnie leaves the confines of her house and encounters several things that enable her to grow. She discovers the freedom of the forest. She discovers Jesse, reclining against the broad base of a tree, waiting for Miles and Mae as he does every ten years. She also discovers the water that she sees Jesse drink, the source of the Tucks' immortality. This forces her into the dynamic world outside her fence and into the intimate and compassionate world of the Tucks. With her, they share their story for the first time, competing with one another for her attention and making her feel special. Miles tells of how his wife and two children left him, sure that he had sold himself to the devil, because he had grown no older. Mae and Jesse speak of lost friends and neighbors. They talk of having to move often, so that no one becomes suspicious, and never really having a home. Even more, they talk of their isolation from other living things because they have fallen off the life cycle and are unable ever to return. For this, along with other pains they have endured, they tell Winnie the spring must be a secret. They explain that people would not know the mistake they had made until it was too late.

The man in the yellow suit, unbeknown to Winnie and the Tucks, has heard the entire story and returns to Winnie's home telling her family she has been kidnapped. After securing property rights to the forest from them, he proceeds again into the woods, with the constable following behind him. They go to the Tucks' home, also in the forest, where they have taken Winnie, both reluctantly and willingly. Before the constable arrives, the man in the yellow suit tells the Tucks of his intentions to sell the water and asks them to join him. They decline. He grabs Winnie's arm roughly and drags her outside. There, Mae confronts him with Tuck's forgotten shotgun, to stop him from using Winnie in his ploy and from giving out the secret. She swings the gun until the stock hits his skull with a resounding crack, just as the constable arrives at the house. He takes Winnie home and Mae to the jail.

Finally, Jesse creeps to Winnie's fence with a bottle of the spring water, asking her to keep it and drink it when she is seventeen, like him. Together they think of a successful plan to free Mae from the jail. It is imperative that they free her, for, though Mae is sentenced to the gallows, she cannot die.

Themes and Meanings

Starting in the restrictive world of fences and general society, Winnie enters into a world of mystery and freedom in the woods. While this freedom is necessary for Winnie's growth, there is also an element of danger: the spring. For this reason, Winnie needs the Tucks. In their static state, they are still able to offer her the safety of their warmth and their love. In it she blossoms: running, singing, and laughing through the woods, living in a disordered house for a day, and learning that some people are different from her parents. In the freedom of the woods and the safety of the Tucks' love, Winnie is able to develop into her own true self.

Mae represents the Great Mother. She has the wisdom to foresee the dangers of immortality. She also has enough warmth to nurture Winnie, Tuck, and her own children. Even more significant, perhaps, with these two qualities combined, Mae is the protector of all future children. She cares and is active in not stopping the human race and allowing people to evolve and develop and reach their full potential.

At a glance, the Tucks (before their story is known) do not seem extraordinary. Only after the reader feels the Tucks' warmth and tenderness through Winnie, in spite of their tremendous pains and losses, can one truly understand their strengths. The spirit of life blazes in Jesse, despite his absence from the life cycle. This is not an oversight or an error in Babbitt's writing, for her intelligence and details are too careful. Instead, they are examples of true human spirit, the spirit that all people have that is evident in those people who have been separated from society and are thus able to take risks and chances, living as their hearts truly desire.

Context

Natalie Babbitt, as a children's author, is known for imaginative nuances and twists of plot told with clarity in poetic language. This is true in her previous books, *The Search for Delicious* (1969), *Kneeknock Rise* (1970), *Goody Hall* (1971), and *The Devil's Storybook* (1974). Her stories include elements of otherworldliness, blended with real people to form a not-too-outrageous fantasy. Often, Babbitt's settings are places where magic and real people can exist. This is exemplified in *Tuck Everlasting*, in which Babbitt chooses a traditional setting of magic and mystery—the woods. Babbitt does not simply limit the possibilities of the woods to those conventional uses, though. She allows life to emerge. This life is full of strength and passion, not merely encompassing bare reality but also accepting magic and imagination to make it complete. It is a sophisticated integration of two powerful elements of childhood, an example of a very rich life that would simply be ordinary if either part were missing. It is also a powerful work, taking on components of the adult world while still addressing the world of children, serving as a concrete example of that transition and a hypothetical assimilation of the two.

Perhaps the greatest strength of the story is the wholeness and truth of the characters, especially Mae. There is tremendous love, nurturing, and compassion inside Mae, but there is also the harshest reality: death. Mae kills a man, in front of Winnie, Tuck, Miles, and Jesse. Even though the motivation is understandable and the justification behind such action is perhaps plain, the inevitable reality of the potential for violence inside her is inescapable. In Mae, opposite polarities of hate and love exist, each equally intense and true. More important, especially for a woman, especially in the context of a children's story, goodness as well as evil are assimilated in one character. Unlike traditional children's stories, the characters of *Tuck Everlasting* are amazingly complex and not simply limited to the confines of good and bad and traditional roles. They interact completely with their environment, with all facets of their personalities: feelings, intelligence, strength, fear, and pain. *Tuck Everlasting* contains the luxury of depth and richness that entitles it to its many acclaims.

Susan P. Hutton

TULKU

Author: Peter Dickinson (1927-   )
Type of plot: Historical fiction
Time of plot: During the Boxer Rebellion (1900)
Locale: China and Tibet
Principal themes: Coming-of-age, religion, and friendship
First published: 1979
Recommended ages: 15-18

Theodore Tewker barely escapes with his life during a raid on his father's mission at the time of the Boxer Rebellion. Alone, he joins amateur botanist Daisy Jones and her Chinese lover as they journey toward Tibet, where the woman's unborn child is hailed as the new Dalai Lama.

> *Principal characters:*
> THEODORE TEWKER, the adolescent son of a Christian missionary
> DAISY JONES, an amateur botanist whose free spirit Theodore
>   finds shocking
> LUNG, a Chinese guide who becomes Mrs. Jones's lover
> THE LAMA AMCHI, the religious leader of a lamasery, who is
>   searching for the reincarnated Dalai Lama

The Story

Theodore Tewker is awakened and hustled out of the mission run by his father. The wave of hostility toward foreigners that is sweeping China has not spared their small compound, which is now under attack. Although reluctant to leave, Theodore is not practiced in disobedience: He follows orders to retreat to at least temporary safety in the nearby woods.

The morning reveals that the settlement has been completely destroyed and the missionary and his followers killed. Numbed by his loss and fearful for his future, Theodore is surprised to hear the strident, blasphemous voice of an Englishwoman intrude on his thoughts. The youngster at first tries to disguise himself as a native, but when he notices some of the woman's porters preparing to attack her, he shouts a warning. Daisy Jones grabs her gun and aims it at the rebels, forcing them to depart without their hoped-for booty.

Now alone, with only her Chinese guide, Lung, she enlists Theodore's company. The boy is aghast at the woman's indecorous behavior and irreverent language, but, orphaned and clearly without options, he unenthusiastically agrees to join them.

The terrain they must traverse is treacherous; bands of brigands roam the countryside, certain to regard the unprotected trio as easy prey. Mrs. Jones, however, is fearless and canny; although seemingly indifferent to danger, she is neither naïve nor reckless. An ardent botanist, she will not be deterred from her search for flowers unknown in the West. Avoiding encounters with marauders as best they can, the weary travelers come across a valley filled with lovely blossoms, where they plan to rest and recover while Mrs. Jones adds the unusual specimens to her collection.

To his dismay, Theodore discovers that Mrs. Jones and Lung have become lovers. Her sinfulness initially seems intolerable, but the youngster finds it increasingly difficult to hold on to the condemning attitudes toward such behavior that he thinks he should have. Their idyllic interlude is interrupted by the realization that they are about to be attacked. The three race toward a bridge that they hope will lead to safety; their passage, however, is blocked by a party traveling in the opposite direction. At first indifferent to their plight, the strangers are joined by their leader, who shows a special interest in Theodore. The Lama Amchi, recognizing signs that suggest that this adolescent may be the reincarnated Dalai Lama, orders his men to drive off the bandits and escort the trio across the bridge and into Tibet.

After they arrive at the lamasery, the Lama Amchi realizes his error: It is not Theodore but Mrs. Jones's unborn child who will be the new Tulku. It is clear that the travelers will be detained, willingly or not. The woman agrees to be instructed in the knowledge and behavior proper for the mother of the future religious leader, while secretly planning their escape. Her demeanor and attitude change, however, under the Lama's guidance, and she decides to remain and allow her infant to assume his rightful mantle.

Lung, frantic at the loss of the woman he loves, plans to assassinate the one responsible for her defection. Theodore rightfully interprets his companion's strange behavior in time to prevent the Lama's death. Through Mrs. Jones's intercession, the two are escorted beyond the borders of Tibet.

The youngster returns to England and locates the man Mrs. Jones loved in her youth, to whom he tells the story of their adventures, presenting him with a lily collected by Daisy during their sojourn in the valley outside Tibet.

Themes and Meanings

Tulku is a highly unusual coming-of-age novel in which the protagonist is transformed from a protected, rigid, unimaginative, ethnocentric boy into a mature, sensitive, worldly man. Although living in a culture vastly different from his own, Theodore is sheltered from its influence by the force of his father's personality and the insular nature of their compound. He sees the world in absolutes: sinfulness versus righteousness, heathen practices versus true belief. His experiences are characterized by a continuing need to reconsider what he had always known to be unshakable verities.

Mrs. Jones, both his antagonist and his model, serves repeatedly as a catalyst for his growth. Their initial encounter is shocking. Not only does she sport a painted face, but her language is coarse and blasphemous. Worse yet, she seems oblivious to the outrageousness of her behavior.

Theodore has scarcely allowed himself to look beyond what he considers her grievous flaws, when she provokes him further. She makes no secret of her romantic liaison with Lung, a man many years her junior; although not actually flaunting their relationship, she seems totally devoid of shame. Theodore knows that he should respond with pity and horror, but his old habits of judging slip inexorably away.

When Theodore enters the lamasery, he is deeply troubled again. He is afraid to be among heathen idols and uneasy with religious practices he can neither accept nor find a way to challenge. He notes Mrs. Jones's increasing serenity as she is instructed by the Lama Amchi and must rethink his former precepts concerning holiness and the function and process of a religious life.

His return to England symbolizes his return to his origins—very much the same person, yet vastly changed.

Context

Peter Dickinson's versatility makes his work difficult to describe easily. He has written for an audience ranging from grade school children to adults; his stories may be speculative or realistic and are set in exotic as well as domestic locales. Typically his subjects transcend limited, personal issues, focusing instead on moral, philosophical, or social ones.

Dickinson is able to communicate a strong sense of place, whether the sixth century Byzantium of *The Dancing Bear* (1972), the feudal England of *The Weathermonger* (1968) and *Heartsease* (1969), or turn-of-the century China and Tibet in *Tulku*. Although setting is of critical importance in the latter novel, the strongest aspect of this work is the characterization of Daisy Jones.

She is vivid, unique, and memorable. Compelling from her first appearance, she commands the reader's attention. One of the author's most successful creations, Daisy Jones is also one of a rare breed of characters in young adult fiction, which nearly always gives center stage to an adolescent character. In the case of *Tulku*, the young Theodore has the more passive role, providing an initially familiar viewpoint which slowly evolves as he reacts to his experiences. Mrs. Jones is a wonderfully complex character: manipulative yet open, commanding, self-assured, fearless, astute, and adventurous. Theodore is perpetually surprised by her, but as he matures, he is able to accept, then respect the person who has forced him to reexamine his beliefs.

Tulku has not been as widely reviewed as other works by Dickinson, and critics have differed in their assessments. Although describing this work as "extraordinary and powerful," Marcus Crouch argued that it lacked unity, having two separate and distinct parts with the former one being more credible and interesting. *Horn Book* reviewer A. A. Flowers, however, described *Tulku* as a "tour de force" and found it compared favorably with James Hilton's *Lost Horizon* (1933). Others have stated that they thought the work demanding and predicted a limited readership. Some readers may indeed find the exotic elements and the descriptions of a seemingly arcane way of life too foreign for their comfort. Others may find the challenge to traditional values and the transformation of Theodore disquieting, but these same features, together with an original plot and the fascinating character of Daisy Jones, will form the major appeal for many.

Karen Harris

TUNES FOR A SMALL HARMONICA

Author: Barbara Wersba (1932-   )
Type of plot: Psychological realism
Time of plot: The mid-1960's
Locale: New York City
Principal themes: Emotions, friendship, and love and romance
First published: 1976
Recommended ages: 10-13

J. F. McAllister is in love with her poetry teacher, who she believes is a struggling scholar. She plays the harmonica as a street musician in order to fund his progress. When she discovers that he is married and wealthy, she must deal with her disappointment and reappraise herself.

> *Principal characters:*
> J. F. (JACQUELINE FRANCES) MCALLISTER, a sixteen-year-old girl
>   who lives with her affluent parents
> MARYLOU, her best friend, a girl whose parents are both
>   playwrights
> HAROLD MURTH, a thirty-year-old poetry teacher, who is mild-
>   mannered and pale
> DR. WAINGLOSS, an ineffectual analyst whom J. F. is obliged to
>   visit regularly

The Story

Tunes for a Small Harmonica is, at once, a novel of initiation and a story of one-sided romance. It centers on what happens to J. F. McAllister as she pursues a compelling infatuation with her poetry teacher. J. F. lives with her self-indulgent, insecure mother and her workaholic father in a fashionable New York apartment. Apathetic and remote from her parents, she feels out of place in her pink-and-blue bedroom, which has been decorated to resemble "the boudoir of an aging debutante." Actually, she is a chain-smoking tomboy whose wardrobe consists of Levis, sweatshirts, and windbreakers. Her real possessions—a ten-speed bicycle, racing skates, and hockey sticks—are kept in the basement of her building. J. F.'s disapproving mother claims that she looks and acts like a teenage cab driver and insists that her daughter seek help from an analyst, Dr. Waingloss. He proves to be inept and irritating. J. F. fictionalizes most of her answers to his questions.

Having received the gift of a harmonica from Marylou as incentive to stop smoking, J. F. teaches herself to play it well and delights in her new mode of expression. She remains concerned about the question of her sexual identity, and resolves the matter by first marching in a Gay Liberation parade and later kissing her girlfriend. Feeling nothing in either case, she rules out the possibility of being homosexual.

In her poetry class at Miss Howlett's School for Girls, J. F. initially finds her anemic teacher, Harold Murth, an impossible bore, who gazes over the heads of his students when he lectures. Yet one day, inexplicably, when he is bathed in sunlight slanting from a stained glass window, J. F. falls hopelessly in love with him. From this point on, she devotes herself to studying his habits, to sending him gifts, and to playing the harmonica on his behalf, earning enough money to send him abroad for one year so that he can complete his thesis on an obscure poet.

In one of the novel's most amusing scenes, J. F. is playing her harmonica outside a New York theater as Nelson, Marylou's younger brother, passes the hat and murmurs pathetically. Suddenly, at intermission, out march J. F.'s parents, Nelson's parents, Miss Howlett, and five teachers from her school. Caught in the act of impersonating a needy street musician, J. F. is thrust into the nearest cab by her horrified parents, who subsequently confiscate her harmonica and cut off her allowance.

Chancing to find Harold Murth's telephone bill with her own name doodled on it in his handwriting and thus convinced that he loves her but is too shy to act, J. F. resolves to seduce him. On Christmas Eve, dressed in black velvet and coiffed by Marylou, J. F. goes to Murth's apartment. Before she has either an opportunity to present the check that is in her pocket or to throw herself on him, however, he reveals that he is hardly the penniless bachelor she has perceived all along. Instead, he is the son of a wealthy hotel family and the husband of Margery Murth, a librarian in New Jersey.

Humiliated, J. F. decides to commit suicide on Christmas Day by jumping into the East River. First, however, she opens Marylou's present, another superlative harmonica, and takes a phone call from the same friend who announces that Melvin Babb, a director, wants to cast J. F. in a film. Arriving at his apartment, she basks momentarily in his pseudoadoration, but suddenly snaps to recognition: Babb wants only to exploit her as if she had the characteristics of a freak. She is incensed and refuses his offer.

As the novel ends, J. F. accepts that she must now cope with her own problems. She sits by the East River, playing her harmonica for assorted lonely people she knows and for herself, coming to terms with life as a mixed bag and with herself as a genuine original.

Themes and Meanings

Following its main character through a non-affair in which she will inevitably take a fall, *Tunes for a Small Harmonica* is a story of growth and self-discovery. The novel's central interest is how J. F. becomes inspired and focused when she falls in love. In the beginning, she admits to being spoiled and unappreciative. Yet, as she begins to devote herself to making Harold Murth happy, she changes: "I was turning into a different human being. I, who had never had a goal in my life, now had one." She becomes kinder and more considerate of everyone.

J. F.'s friendship with Marylou is also an important aspect of the book. The loyal and long-suffering Marylou stands by J. F. through the latter's breathless excesses and occasional lapses of judgment. She gives her friend superbly chosen gifts from the heart and never discounts or ridicules the powerful feelings that J. F. describes. In fact, much of the caring and self-sacrificing tendency in Marylou is transferred to J. F. as she nurses Harold Murth, ill with the flu, and tirelessly earns the one thousand dollars for his trip to England. The harmonica, not merely a means for raising money as a street musician, is a symbol of J. F.'s lyric and loving nature, catalyst for discovering her artistic abilities, and, in the end, solace to her broken heart.

Key to her character is J. F.'s willingness to take responsibility for her actions. She resolves by way of experiment that she is not gay. Without knowing the first thing about expressing her love for Harold Murth, she throws herself full force into the experience and then manages to bear her defeat and embarrassment with dignity when she learns that he is married. Reversing roles with Dr. Waingloss, near the end, when he is distraught over the impending departure of his own analyst, J. F. is strong and understanding. Most significantly, she sees through the phoniness of Melvin Babb and refuses to be used by him. Capable and prepared to take care of herself, she emerges at the end of the novel with an affirmation of her individuality and a healthy sense of reality.

Context

Among more than twenty children's and young adult novels she has written, *Tunes for a Small Harmonica* is one of Wersba's best-known and most amusing books. Unlike other titles such as *Run Softly, Go Fast* (1970), in which a young boy rages at life and the death of his father, or *The Country of the Heart* (1975), in which a young man becomes seriously involved with a woman in her forties who is both idealistic and bitter, award-winning *Tunes for a Small Harmonica* is of a lighter vein.

By showing a young girl who is indeed out of touch with reality at times and admittedly making a fool of herself, Wersba creates a sympathetic character from whom the reader learns. J. F.'s honest appraisal of friends and of her feelings makes for a candid and entertaining book. In fact, slapstick scenes and wry character sketches make the book memorable: Marylou's hippie parents, who write plays all night and sleep all day; Miss Howlett, a brisk and eccentric British Royal Air Force veteran; and the limp, but polite Harold Murth.

Sometimes bordering on farce and pathos, other books by Wersba feature characters trying to make sense of life. A trilogy composed of *Fat: A Love Story* (1987), *Love Is the Crooked Thing* (1987), and *Beautiful Losers* (1988) tells the story of quirky Rita Formica, a sixteen-year-old who weighs two hundred pounds, and the older man with whom she is intimately involved. Later titles include *The Farewill Kid* (1989) and *The Best Place to Live Is the Ceiling* (1990).

Regardless of her subject matter, Wersba can be expected to deal deftly with relationships, often between younger protagonists and older partners, and to show compassion for young people, especially teenagers.

Linda M. Morrow

THE TURBULENT TERM OF TYKE TILER

Author: Gene Kemp (1926-   )
Type of plot: Social realism
Time of plot: The late twentieth century
Locale: Cricklepit School, England
Principal themes: Gender roles, coming-of-age, friendship, education, and family
First published: 1977; illustrated
Recommended ages: 10-13

Tyke Tiler, an athlete and leader, and Danny Price, a slow learner from a disadvantaged home, are inseparable best friends in a British combined school. During their adventurous last term, they come of age: Tyke learns the value of family and honesty, and Danny learns to accept and value himself.

Principal characters:
> TYKE TILER, an energetic, independent, caring twelve-year-old
> DANNY PRICE, an insecure and impetuous boy, with an angelic face, a speech defect, and learning disabilities
> WILLIAM MERCHANT, a well-liked, creative teacher at Cricklepit School
> THE HEADMASTER, or "CHIEF SIR," a disciplinarian whom Tyke and Danny see often
> JENNY HONEYWELL, an attractive student teacher who believes in Danny
> EDWARD TILER, Tyke's father, who is running for a seat on the British Council
> MARY PHYLLIS TILER, Tyke's mother, a night nurse
> BERYL "BERRY" TILER, Tyke's older sister, a college student
> MARTIN KNEESHAW, Tyke's enemy, the son of her father's rival
> CRUMBLE, a lovable shaggy dog, Tyke's constant companion
> FATTY, a large piebald mouse, Danny's constant companion

The Story

When Danny, a self-confessed kleptomaniac, steals a ten-pound note from a teacher, Tyke climbs into the old school attic and hides it, thinking to return it later. The Headmaster finds the money and knows that Tyke put it there, for only Tyke can climb the high loft without a ladder. When Danny lets his pet mouse loose during morning opening, Tyke tries to catch it, but chaos results. When Danny convinces Tyke to go into the river to get a sheep's skeleton, Tyke barely escapes injury, and Danny gets "house points" at school. Repeatedly, both get warnings from the Headmaster and notes sent home, but Danny, with his sincere apology and sad eyes, is taken to tea and receives more "child guidance."

Sent to the Headmaster's office for giving Martin Kneeshaw a bloody nose, Tyke overhears the faculty discussing transferring Danny to a boarding school for slow learners. Spotting the Verbal Reasoning Tests on Chief Sir's desk, Tyke takes a copy of the questions. After Tyke's older sister, Beryl, helps work out the answers, Tyke spends hours tutoring Danny, hoping to ensure their attendance at the same school.

The turning point for Danny comes when Ms. Honeywell, while teaching a lesson about King Arthur, picks Danny to play Sir Galahad, who had the strength of ten because his heart was pure. Inspired by Sir Galahad, Danny, with new confidence, decides to live a pure and honorable life.

All is well until Danny and Tyke are separated. On the night of Mr. Tiler's political victory over Mr. Kneeshaw, Tyke comes down with influenza and must then miss many days of school. Martin Kneeshaw and friends steal a teacher's gold watch and place it in Danny's schoolbag. The police are called in, and Danny, innocent and frightened, spends a hungry night alone waiting for Tyke in their secret spot—an abandoned paper mill. Deciding to trust the Headmaster, Tyke convinces him that Danny was set up, and Danny is rescued.

As the term ends, Tyke finds that the test plan has backfired: Danny passes, but Tyke is recommended for a special school for the gifted. Nevertheless, to celebrate the last day, Tyke shinnies up the school's outside drainpipe to ring the old bell, last used during World War II. A teacher shouts to warn "Theodora"—revealing to the reader that Tyke is a girl. After a few brief rings, the roof collapses; Tyke and tiles fall to the courtyard. Luckily, Tyke receives only a broken arm, a concussion, and several bruises. She confesses the test episode to the understanding Mr. Merchant, who arranges for both Tyke and Danny to go to the comprehensive school. Through these experiences, Danny learns honesty, trust, and self-confidence; Tyke learns that she has some limitations, but many opportunities, and that her family and friends love her just as she is.

Themes and Meanings

Resembling Scout and Jim in Harper Lee's *To Kill a Mockingbird* (1960), Tyke Tiler and Danny Price in *The Turbulent Term of Tyke Tiler* learn much about life, except "maybe algebra." The various themes branch into those human verities of honesty, friendship, loyalty, responsibility, and respect but converge always in love and belief in oneself, one's friends, and one's family.

Danny Price's home life is in sharp contrast to Tyke's. Although busy, the Tiler family members clearly support one another, whereas Danny's father, whom he hardly knows, is in prison, his one brother is in another home, and his mother is too busy with her boyfriend to notice Danny. Tyke's steady friendship carries Danny through that difficult time when he needs someone to believe in him so that he can believe in himself. Tyke is Danny's counterpart. Together they function as one: male and female, yin and yang. Danny, Tyke, and their friendship are like the biblical threefold cord that is not easily broken.

In coming of age, they learn that adults can be trustworthy, that adults, too, have conflicts, and that life is not black and white. Mr. Merchant is an excellent friend, and the Headmaster, who has been amazingly patient, even merciful, actually does believe in Danny's innocence and transformation. Tyke's conflict with Martin is juxtaposed to Mr. Tiler's political and personal conflict with Martin's father. When Tyke and Danny admit that they put her father's posters all over Mr. Kneeshaw's house on the night of Mr. Tiler's victory, he does not get upset and even laughs at the prank. Mr. Merchant, though attracted to the beautiful new student teacher, decides to marry Ms. Bonfire, a fellow teacher and companion whom he truly loves. Although Tyke does steal the test questions, her long hours helping Danny study are productive for both of them, having become more collaboration and cooperative learning than cheating.

Context

Gene Kemp's depiction of the conflicts, the language, and the turf of preteens makes *The Turbulent Term of Tyke Tiler* one of his best-known works; it received the American Library Association's Carnegie Medal for an Outstanding Children's Book and the Children's Rights Workshop Other Award. Kemp's works are frequently set in schools. Like his *Gowie Corby Plays Chicken* (1979), *The Turbulent Term of Tyke Tiler* (1977) is a departure from his Tamworth Pig series (*The Prime of Tamworth Pig*, 1972; *Tamworth Pig Saves the Trees*, 1973; *Tamworth Pig and the Litter*, 1975; and *Christmas with Tamworth Pig*, 1977). *The Turbulent Term of Tyke Tiler* has much in common with the later *Gowie Corby Plays Chicken*, whose protagonist is an outsider whose only friends are animals led by Boris Karloff, a pet rat. Like Danny Price, Gowie is befriended by a girl, Rosie Angela Lee, a black American. Animals are essential characters in Kemp's stories: Gowie's pet rat, Danny's mouse, and Tyke's dog play significant roles.

Kemp's realism is evident especially in *The Turbulent Term of Tyke Tiler*. Mr. and Mrs. Tiler argue passionately and publicly over Tyke's possible entrance into a gifted school and Tyke's sister's upcoming marriage. It was common in the 1960's for young adult novels to pit adults against children and to portray the former as ogres. Kemp's adults, however, are fairly drawn: Mr. Merchant is a favorite, trusted teacher who clearly loves his students and commands their respect. The student teacher is sincere and learns from her mistakes. The Headmaster is remarkably fair, but Mrs. Somers, the deputy head, perhaps should find some other career.

In addition to the realism that was by the 1970's fairly common in young adult literature, *The Turbulent Term of Tyke Tiler* challenges typical gender roles. Some readers might be surprised to learn that the protagonist, Tyke, is female. Even with today's rapidly changing roles, often it is assumed that it is the male who is strong, athletic, and a leader. Although Tyke's mother pursues a typical female career, she does work outside the home, breaking the mold of the servant mother of the 1950's. Tyke's sister, Beryl, is active in politics, headed for a public service career, and it is Beryl, not Tyke's brother, Stanley, who is the mathematics whiz.

Realistic, innovative, humorous, *The Turbulent Term of Tyke Tiler* evokes the tenderness and the toughness of those trying years that usher in adolescence. Little wonder that Kemp says, *"Tyke Tiler* is my most interesting book."

Barbara Dickinson-Findley

THE TURN OF THE SCREW

Author: Henry James (1843-1916)
Type of plot: Thriller
Time of plot: The nineteenth century
Locale: Bly, an isolated English country house
Principal themes: Gender roles, sexual issues, social issues, and the supernatural
First published: 1898
Recommended ages: 15-18

A governess attempts to explain how it came about that one of two children placed in her charge died without an apparent physical cause. She believes that evil ghosts committed this crime, but she fears she may also be to blame.

Principal characters:
  THE GOVERNESS, an unnamed clergyman's daughter, whose first job is caring for a pair of young children at Bly
  MILES, an orphan about ten years old, who has come to his uncle in England after his parents and grandparents died in India
  FLORA, Miles's younger sister
  MRS. GROSE, the housekeeper at Bly and the governess' confidante
  MISS JESSEL, the former governess, now dead, whose ghost the governess believes haunts the children
  PETER QUINT, the uncle's deceased valet and Miss Jessel's former lover, whose ghost joins in Miss Jessel's evil acts
  DOUGLAS, an elderly gentleman who knew the governess when he was young and who reads her story to a group of friends

The Story

The Turn of the Screw is one of the very few ghost stories that literary critics consistently rate as a masterpiece of world literature. While the setting and plot are like those of gothic tales of terror, this short novel is set apart by its insistent ambiguity. Readers continue to disagree about whether the apparitions of Peter Quint and Miss Jessel are real ghosts or only figments of the governess' imagination. This ambiguity creates an intensity of terror matched by few other gothic tales.

The story's ambiguity arises mainly out of the way it is told. The novella opens with a narrator who tells about a Christmas gathering of leisure-class friends at a quiet country house. They find themselves telling ghosts stories, as has been traditional at that season at least since Charles Dickens published *A Christmas Carol* (1843). Douglas, a quiet gentleman, reveals that he has a true ghost story to tell, and then he sends to his home for a copy of a manuscript given him by the governess.

This account, as it turns out, is of her first job at Bly, written some time after the events themselves and after she told Douglas the story when she was in charge of his younger sister.

The governess' manuscript concerns a distant past. She herself is dead, and no corroborative witnesses are produced. Based on how she writes, what she says about herself, and a few impressions given by Douglas, the reader must decide how to accept her account of the horrible events at Bly. It is probably impossible finally to determine whether her account of events is to be accepted as completely true.

She explains how she took a job that frightened her because it was isolated and demanded great responsibility, and because she was young and inexperienced. She agrees to the position because the employer, the children's uncle, charms her. At first she does well and feels proud of herself, but gradually her charges, Miles and Flora, come to seem too good, and she wonders whether she is doing as well as she has thought. At the same time, she begins to see two strange people at Bly. It develops that no one else sees them, but when she describes them to Mrs. Grose, both become convinced that these are Quint and Jessel.

The governess is forbidden by strict social convention to speak of ghosts with the children, unless the children bring them up first. She becomes more and more convinced that the ghosts mean to harm the children and, even worse, that the children welcome contact with the ghosts. She is caught in a silent struggle, with a little support from Mrs. Grose, to separate the children from the ghosts and to drive the ghosts away. This struggle reaches a crisis in two confrontations. When the governess mentions Miss Jessel to Flora, the little girl seems to turn away from her would-be protector and to become like Miss Jessel. When the governess tries to get Miles to speak freely of what seems to be bothering him, he experiences extreme stress and quite suddenly dies, in the governess' arms. The governess' manuscript ends with the death of Miles and her expressed belief that when he died, he was no longer "possessed" by Quint. As many readers have pointed out, there is no way for her, however, to be sure this is true.

Themes and Meanings

The Turn of the Screw is too complex a work to allow an easy statement of themes. Central questions in the novella concern the tension between supernatural and psychological explanations of Miles's death and the degree to which gender and social class determine the characters' fates.

Literary critics have argued at great length for three main ways of looking at the problem of the supernatural. One way is simply to accept the governess' account; there really were two ghosts who tried to possess the two orphans, but she fought them off, giving Flora a chance to return to herself and at least freeing Miles's soul before he died. Another way is to examine the governess' psychological weaknesses in order to show how she might well have unconsciously invented the ghosts. Such a reading usually argues that she wanted to attract the uncle's attention because she had fallen in love with him. The ghosts were expressions of her sexual frustrations and were tools to attract his attention. The third way is perhaps the most complex. In this view, James is said to have written a story for which both explanations are possible but not quite adequate. The result of this deliberate and very complicated ambiguity would be that readers are unable ever to settle the question of whether the governess saved the children or unconsciously harmed them.

Gender and class themes subtly pervade the tale, affecting all the characters. The governess' position at Bly is difficult because she is a poor, young gentlewoman, who is required to play the role of father toward the children. The uncle remains in London and orders the governess not to bother him with the children's concerns. As difficulties develop, such as over Miles being expelled from his school, the governess feels she can turn to no one. Even when ghosts threaten the children, she cannot consult the uncle, for he would surely believe she was making up the ghosts to attract his attention—that is what a poor young woman would do. If she tells him what she believes, she can only succeed in abandoning the children to supernatural monsters. Gender and class repeatedly prove to be traps that isolate the governess and that may subvert her sanity.

Context

Henry James thought of himself as a writer for adults, and few of his tales are accessible to young readers. He wrote a number of ghost stories for popular magazines, however, most of which are collected in Leon Edel's edition, *Henry James: Stories of the Supernatural* (1970). Several of these stories—for example, "The Last of the Valerii" (1874) and "The Ghostly Rental" (1876)—will remind readers of the more popular supernatural stories of Edgar Allan Poe, Nathaniel Hawthorne, Robert Louis Stevenson, and Sir Arthur Conan Doyle. *The Turn of the Screw* is unique among James's supernatural stories in having achieved such fame and praise, though he wrote others nearly as puzzling and interesting, notably "The Jolly Corner" (1908).

In the history of gothic fiction, *The Turn of the Screw* shares the quality of unresolved ambiguity with the most celebrated tales, such as Poe's "The Fall of the House of Usher" (1839), E. T. A. Hoffmann's "Der Sandmann" (1816; "The Sand-Man," 1844), and Guy de Maupassant's "La Horla" (1887; "The Horla," 1890). A sometimes overlooked aspect of the context of James's novella is that it was published in the midst of a rich period in gothic fiction that has given the world several recognized classics: Stevenson's *The Strange Case of Dr. Jekyll and Mr. Hyde* (1886), Oscar Wilde's *The Picture of Dorian Gray* (1891), and Bram Stoker's *Dracula* (1897), as well as the chilling tales of Oliver Onions and Algernon Blackwood. Similar to the best of these, *The Turn of the Screw* continues to fascinate a large audience. The art by which James created such complete and yet absorbing ambiguity repeatedly earns the respect of readers of all ages throughout the world.

Terry Heller

TWENTY THOUSAND LEAGUES UNDER THE SEA

Author: Jules Verne (1828-1905)
Type of plot: Science fiction
Time of plot: 1867-1868
Locale: The oceans of the world
Principal themes: Science, travel, crime, death, and friendship
First published: Vingt Mille Lieues sous les mers, 1870 (English translation, 1873)
Recommended ages: 13-15

Kidnapped by Captain Nemo, master of the powerful submarine Nautilus, *Pierre Aronnax, a French professor, embarks on a fantastic sea voyage and disputes his host's hatred for a flawed humanity.*

Principal characters:
> PIERRE ARONNAX, the narrator, an adventurous forty-year-old French professor who, while hunting for a sea monster, is captured by Captain Nemo and forced to travel aboard his submarine *Nautilus*
> CAPTAIN NEMO, inventor and designer of the world's first electric submarine, consumed by his hatred for humanity, who vows to live at sea forever
> CONSEIL, the trusty servant of Aronnax, a Belgian of thirty who prides himself on his formality and undying loyalty
> NED LAND, a jolly Canadian harpooner, companion of Aronnax and Conseil aboard Nemo's sub, an avid hunter
> COMMANDER FARRAGUT, captain of the *Abraham Lincoln* and initial host to Aronnax; his ship is damaged by Nemo
> NEMO'S CREW, a multinational mix of Europeans who have invented a language of their own

The Story
The travels of the *Nautilus*, an incredibly advanced and powerful submarine, form the basic structuring device for the plot of Jules Verne's science-fiction novel *Twenty Thousand Leagues Under the Sea*. After many sightings of an uncannily destructive sea monster, the American government in 1867 launches an exploration by the *Abraham Lincoln* under Commander Farragut and with Professor Pierre Aronnax as resident naturalist. After they hunt down what they presume to be a large whale, Farragut's frigate is attacked and Aronnax swept overboard. Conseil follows his master and together they meet Ned Land, harpooner of the ship; all three come to rest on the metal planks of a man-made submarine.

Taking in the three shipwrecked men, Captain Nemo reveals himself as designer and master of the *Nautilus*, an electricity-driven submarine, far beyond the technological possibilities of Verne's time. The three men soon find themselves in opposition to the enigmatic Nemo, with Aronnax as the scientific mind and natural leader and the Canadian Protestant Ned Land standing in for "practical man," while Conseil serves as Aronnax's confidant and foil. Nemo himself is driven by a fanatical desire to sever all ties with humanity, which seems to have treated him badly, and vows to live in the oceans of the world forever. Because of his scientific genius and the commitment of his crew, the *Nautilus* is totally autonomous to the point of recharging its batteries in a process requiring not much more than seasalt.

The first human observer of a submarine landscape that has been off-limits to people so far, Nemo embarks in his *Nautilus* on a fantastic voyage across the oceans of the world. While occasionally exchanging ideas and opinions with the reclusive, dark captain, Aronnax uses every opportunity to learn more about this new world and dutifully records his amazing observations.

After touching Nemo's home base inside an extinguished volcano within the territory of the sunken Atlantis of Plato's fable, and after discovering a wildlife refuge at the South Pole, where no human has yet wrought destruction, *Twenty Thousand Leagues Under the Sea* turns increasingly to the conflict boiling in Nemo's soul. The taking of an underwater photo by Nemo for Aronnax—the only visible evidence of his adventure to remain with him—is the last crucial moment of harmony. Unwilling to let go of the men, who are witnesses to the existence of his ship, Nemo becomes their enemy. Consumed by his hatred for humanity, the captain finally attacks and sinks a hostile warship; his guests/prisoners watch with him in horror as all hands go down with their stricken ship.

Driven by guilt and a need to quench the fire of revenge burning up his character, Nemo is finally caught in the whirling waters of the maelstrom off the Norwegian coast, where the *Nautilus* is or maybe is not destroyed while Aronnax and his two friends escape in a dinghy. Waiting for passage home in a fisherman's hut, Aronnax composes his narrative and expresses hope that Nemo has survived and that "the contemplation of so many wonders" at sea may "extinguish in him the spirit of revenge."

Themes and Meanings

The scope and intensity of Captain Nemo's hatred for a flawed humanity, and the morality of this desire, are central topics of *Twenty Thousand Leagues Under the Sea*. Nemo's answer after experiencing injustice at the hands of men is to choose radical isolation and quite literally to flee the land of a despicable humanity. His vengeful contempt for Western society in particular is reinforced when his submarine voyage leads Nemo to more and more scenes of irreversible environmental destruction and merciless exploitation of South Sea pearl divers by a morally callous society. Further, the *Nautilus*, like its crew, is a multinational conglomerate with parts manufactured all over the Western world; this is a remarkably internationalist idea in an age when patriotism and even chauvinism ran rampant among the nations of Europe and America. Thus, it is with Nemo, his boat, and his crew that Verne's text embraces strikingly modern themes and, morally ahead of many contemporaries, anticipates issues of the next century.

Yet *Twenty Thousand Leagues Under the Sea* also explores the limits to which revenge and negation can be carried before the avenger himself sinks to the same level as his enemies. Nemo's final moral demise, which occurs with his brutal sinking of a clearly outclassed warship, is foreshadowed when his attack on carnivorous sperm whales becomes a bloody massacre. In both cases, Nemo's way is revealed to be morally reprehensible and to lead to nothing but guilt and self-destruction. Only if the deep-rooted instinct for revenge is overcome, Verne's text insists, can a person truly be human and benefit from the revelation of the natural wonders that technological ingenuity has enabled him to see.

Thus, it is no wonder that Professor Aronnax stands at the moral core of the narrative, which is in itself a celebration of the scientific method and field work of the naturalist, a profession that attained the height of its social prestige in Verne's time. The text spends a long time presenting Aronnax's punctilious recordings of direction and duration of the voyage and his almost instinctive immediate scientific classification—done with proper Latin names—of all the natural wonders he is allowed to see, be they strange maritime life-forms or a fantastic submarine passage below the Suez Canal.

Context

Although not written primarily with a young audience in mind, *Twenty Thousand Leagues Under the Sea* has become a favorite classic among young readers. Its intense description of fantastic undersea wonders, emphasis on exciting characters, prevailing sense of adventure and action, and clear narrative style that reverberates with the pure joy of telling an entertaining story overcome the occasionally burdensome use of Latin names for creatures and plants observed and have given Verne's work a timeless freshness and ability to endear itself to a young person.

The clear relation between *Twenty Thousand Leagues Under the Sea* and Herman Melville's much more literary and ambitious earlier novel, *Moby Dick* (1851), has been pointed out by many critics. Both works share the setting of a vast seascape against which the drama of one man's obsessive revenge for an earlier wrong is played out to its cataclysmic end: Nemo shares his fanatical hatred for humanity with Captain Ahab in his similarly fierce desire to hunt down the white whale who took his leg.

Verne's text itself is quite conscious of its literary ancestor and contains many important allusions to Melville's work. The final possible shipwreck of the *Nautilus* echoes the end of Ahab's whaler *Pequod*; with its reference to the historic attack by a sperm whale on the whaler *Essex*, *Twenty Thousand Leagues Under the Sea* quotes one of Melville's sources. Details such as Ned Land's occupation of harpooner, which he shares with Ishmael's exotic friend Quequeg, or the mirroring of Ahab's nailing of a gold doubloon to the mast of his ship by Commander Farragut's more prosaic prize of two thousand dollars for the first to spot the "monster," are too many to be anything but deliberate. In due time, Verne's own fiction became a classic of its own right and has influenced the direction of many later writers, especially in the genre of fantastic literature and science fiction.

Yet Verne's story does not only draw on fictional texts but also mirrors closely the real—and often no less fantastic—accounts of exotic adventures and strange findings, which intrepid European explorers and naturalists published in such magazines as the British *Nature* or *Edinburgh Review*.

As is the case with Verne's other works, such as the more probable sounding, but nevertheless similarly fantastic, *Le Tour du monde en quatre-vingts jours* (1873; *Around the World in Eighty Days*, 1873), *Twenty Thousand Leagues Under the Sea* leaves the reader with a craftily spun "tall tale" full of adventures that continue to fascinate even in the age of supersonic jets and atomic submarines hanging motionless beneath the ice of the North Pole.

R. C. Lutz

THE TWENTY-ONE BALLOONS

Author: William Pène du Bois (1916-   )
Type of plot: Adventure tale
Time of plot: 1883
Locale: San Francisco and Krakatoa, an island near Java in the South Pacific
Principal themes: Travel, science, and nature
First published: 1947; illustrated
Recommended ages: 10-13

William Waterman Sherman recounts how he chanced to land his balloon on the diamond-filled, volcanic island of Krakatoa, inhabited by twenty American families, and how he lived with them until the volcano erupted and destroyed the island.

Principal characters:
PROFESSOR WILLIAM WATERMAN SHERMAN, a teacher of mathematics in a San Francisco boys' school, who decides to travel around the world by balloon
MR. F., one of the Americans living on Krakatoa, who discovers Professor Sherman on the beach and becomes his friend and guide
MR. M., who discovered the volcanic island and its vast diamond mines, founded its society, and recruited the American families who live on Krakatoa

The Story

The Twenty-one Balloons, a travel adventure in the spirit of Jules Verne's *Le Tour du monde en quatre-vingts jours* (1873; *Around the World in Eighty Days*, 1873), opens with the surprising discovery of Professor William Waterman Sherman floating in the Atlantic Ocean among the wreckage of twenty deflated balloons. Since Professor Sherman had set off three weeks earlier from San Francisco in *one* balloon, intending to sail across the Pacific Ocean, his rescue causes enormous curiosity throughout the world.

Professor Sherman tells how he sets off in his balloon for a leisurely float across the Pacific. A few days into the trip, however, a seagull punctures his balloon and forces him to make a dangerous landing on an apparently deserted island. Exhausted by his ordeal, he falls asleep on the beach. When he awakes, he is astonished to find an American man, who introduces himself as Mr. F., kneeling beside him, dressed in spotless, white, formal attire. Mr. F. takes Professor Sherman through the jungle and shows him a most amazing sight: a huge mine chock-full of millions of diamonds. While they make their way across the island, their progress is interrupted several times by violent earthquakes, which Mr. F. explains are caused by volcanic action.

The next morning, Mr. F. shows Professor Sherman around the island's town, which consists of a variety of grand houses, each built in a distinct architectural style. Mr. F. tells him how the island was discovered by Mr. M., a San Franciscan, who returned to his native country and recruited nineteen other families to settle on Krakatoa and share in the fabulous wealth of the diamond mines. Together the families formed a Utopian society based on "Gourmet Government" organized around food. Each family runs a unique restaurant, offering food from a particular country, and each must feed the whole island's population on their specified day of Krakatoa's special twenty-day month. Hence, on "C" day the C. family serves Chinese food; on "D" day the D. family serves Dutch food.

The families on the island are nearly all scientific-minded and have invented a variety of strange and ingenious contraptions, from the M. family's automatic bed-maker, sheet-washer, and electrified living-room furniture to the amazing balloon "airy-go-round," a dazzling construction of boats and balloons that form a flying carousel. Everyone on the island cooperates fully and works in perfect concert. Even the smallest children patiently wait their turn for a ride in the balloon contraption and cheerfully help with the work on the island. The unique society of Krakatoa is as logical and scientific as its inhabitants.

Professor Sherman's stay on Krakatoa, which the Krakatoans firmly tell him must be a permanent one, is to be cut short. Soon after his arrival, the island's huge volcano begins to erupt. The people of Krakatoa have only enough time to launch their giant, balloon-lifted life raft before the volcano explodes, and, with it, nearly all the island. The Krakatoans are all unharmed, and their evacuation plan succeeds precisely as planned, with the one unfortunate exception that Professor Sherman has not had time to have his parachute made. The other families, one by one, parachute from the life raft as it passes over Asia and Europe, and Professor Sherman crash-lands the raft in the Atlantic Ocean.

Themes and Meanings

In *The Twenty-one Balloons*, elements of science fiction, fantasy, adventure, satire, and a certain playful irony are combined. On one level, *The Twenty-one Balloons* is a joyful celebration of technology and whimsical scientific invention. Both the author and his main character delight in the minute details of the various balloon contraptions and the other fantastic inventions of the Krakatoans. Throughout the story, William Pène du Bois and William Waterman Sherman show an exuberant faith in the power of technology to improve and enhance everyday life.

A related theme is that of a natural world, powerful and dangerous, that can be overcome with discipline and intelligence. Coping with the violent earthquakes on the island is simply a matter of getting accustomed to them and acquiring one's "mountain legs." The eruption of the volcano is escaped, with a minimum of inconvenience, via the combination of technical ingenuity, cooperation, and careful planning, which have gone into the balloon-life-raft evacuation system.

The society depicted on Krakatoa is as reasonable and efficient as the inventions of its citizens. The "Gourmet Government" is a scientific-minded and vaguely comical Utopia in which everyone acts with a cheerful, practical rationality. There are echoes of a kind of pilgrim sensibility in the way Krakatoans have founded a unique and idealistic new society in a rich, remote wilderness.

Context

The Twenty-one Balloons is probably the most popular of William Pène du Bois's numerous books, many of which also reflect his fascination with modes of transportation and incongruous inventions. Two of these are *The Forbidden Forest* (1979), in which a kangaroo stops World War I, and *Bear Party* (1951), about a group of quarreling bears' masquerade party. They exhibit the same absurdly logical treatment of fantastic situations as *The Twenty-one Balloons*.

In 1948, *The Twenty-one Balloons* was awarded the Newbery Medal, an annual award by the American Library Association for the most distinguished children's literature in the United States. William Pène du Bois is also a notable illustrator; in addition to producing the precise and graceful illustrations for his own books, he has illustrated numerous other children's books, such as Rebecca Caudill's *A Certain Small Shepherd* (1965) and George MacDonald's *The Light Princess* (1962).

The subject and themes of *The Twenty-one Balloons* connect it to many other currents in literature, juvenile and otherwise. As a work of science fiction it shares the same optimistic faith in technology as the works of Jules Verne, L. Frank Baum's *The Master Key* (1901), and Victor Appleton's Tom Swift stories. Underlying this cheerful confidence in humanity's scientific and mechanical inventions is an almost Enlightenment-like belief in the power of human rationality to produce not only fantastic and useful machines but also ideal and efficient societies. The enduring popularity of *The Twenty-one Balloons* is no doubt the result in good measure of the author's skill in couching his piquant, fabular examination of the contrast between the forces of nature and human ingenuity in a lively and imaginative adventure story.

Catherine Swanson

TWO YEARS BEFORE THE MAST

Author: Richard Henry Dana, Jr. (1815-1882)
Type of plot: Adventure tale
Time of plot: 1834-1836
Locale: Ships at sea and California
Principal themes: Coming-of-age, travel, and friendship
First published: 1840
Recommended ages: 15-18

When measles weaken his eyesight, Richard Henry Dana, Jr., interrupts his junior year at Harvard College and signs on as a common seaman on the brig Pilgrim *bound for California. After two years of adventure, he returns home, is graduated from Harvard, begins the practice of law, and resolves to write a true account of the life of a common seaman.*

> *Principal characters:*
> RICHARD HENRY DANA, JR., the narrator
> CAPTAIN FRANK THOMPSON, the master of the *Pilgrim* on the
>   outward bound voyage and of the *Alert* on the voyage home
> SAM, a seaman who is unjustly flogged
> JOHN THE SWEDE, the best seaman of the *Pilgrim*, who is also
>   flogged for standing up for Sam
> KANAKA HOPE, a Sandwich Islander whom Dana befriends in
>   California
> TOM HARRIS, an English sailor who is Dana's watchmate on the
>   *Alert*

The Story

This tale of shipboard adventure and camaraderie begins on an August day in 1834 as the narrator, Richard Henry Dana, Jr., boards the brig *Pilgrim* bound for California. Left behind on shore are the frock coat and kid gloves of a proper Bostonian; in their stead, he is wearing the loose duck trousers and checked shirt of the ordinary seaman. The first and shortest part of the book describes Dana's introduction to life at sea during the outward voyage to California. Very quickly, he is introduced to the hard work and constant danger that attend the life of a seaman aboard a sailing ship. The first storm leaves him so seasick that he cannot eat for three days; nevertheless, he is sent aloft to slush down the mainmast in a rolling sea. A few days out of Boston, a strange sail is sighted that proves to be a heavily armed black-hulled brig giving chase, but the *Pilgrim* is finally able to escape by setting every sail the ship can carry and wetting these down with water to increase speed. The most sobering experience, however, comes just after the *Pilgrim* rounds Cape Horn into the Pacific. Dana is aroused from a sound sleep by the cry of "man overboard." A young English sailor much liked by the crew has fallen from aloft and, being heavily dressed and unable to swim, he drowns. In an instant, a man with whom the rest of the crew had shared cramped quarters and ship's duties for more than two months is gone—his existence obliterated by the sea. The tragedy lingers with the crew for days as the *Pilgrim* sails north in the Pacific, but California, where trade will begin for hides to supply the Boston shoemakers with leather, is reached without further incident.

The second and by far the largest section of the book is devoted to Dana's experience in California. This structure is faithful to the journal style in which *Two Years Before the Mast* is written, for as numerous critics have pointed out, Dana spent considerably more of his time ashore in California than in either the *Pilgrim* or the *Alert*. California in 1835 was a part of Mexico, and the description of life there—the hide trade, the Sandwich Islanders who work in it, the customs of the Mexican inhabitants—is invaluable for those seeking information about the region on the eve of conquest by the United States. Although this part is perhaps less interesting to young readers than the passages relating to ships and the sea, the most celebrated incident in the book occurs on the California coast: the flogging of Sam and John the Swede. The incident had all the necessary ingredients to capture the attention of Dana's contemporaries: Captain Thompson in a fit of rage orders Sam, a slow-thinking sailor hesitant in speech, to be flogged; the crew sees the captain's action as harsh and unjust, and John the Swede attempts to intervene on Sam's behalf and is himself ordered flogged. This classic case of injustice leaves lingering bitterness among the crew, and the *Pilgrim* is not a happy ship. Not long thereafter, however, Dana is able to transfer to another ship, the *Alert*, owned by the same company that owns the *Pilgrim*, and, while Captain Thompson also transfers to the *Alert*, the new ship is a happier one. It is on the *Alert* that Dana for nine months shares the watch with Tom Harris, a seaman whom Dana declares to be the most remarkable man he has ever met.

The third and final part of *Two Years Before the Mast* deals with the return voyage and opens on a note of suspense. Captain Thompson, who has promised Dana that he may go home in the *Alert*, suddenly changes his mind and says that he must stay on the California coast in the *Pilgrim*. Only by offering an attractive sum of money to pay a man to stay in his place is Dana able to return home in the *Alert*. By now, Dana holds Captain Thompson in contempt, a view only confirmed by the captain's poor navigation, which endangers the ship in the dangerous waters off Cape Horn on the voyage home. Fortunately for Dana and the rest of the crew, the ship escapes destruction in the storm and ice off Cape Horn and, to the delight of all on board, slides alongside the wharf in Boston harbor as the bells of the city are ringing one o'clock in the afternoon.

Themes and Meanings

In the original preface to *Two Years Before the Mast*, Richard Henry Dana, Jr., writes that his purpose in publishing the book is to give an accurate account of the life of the common seaman since "a voice from the forecastle has hardly yet been heard."

(The forecastle—pronounced "fo'c'sle" by sailors—is in the bow of a ship and is where the seamen's living quarters are located. The term goes back to medieval times, when structures known as castles were erected on the bow and stern, fore and after, or aft, for archers to use in sea fights.) An accurate account is exactly what the reader gets; modern critics (of whom the best are James D. Hart, Robert F. Lucid, Samuel Shapiro, and Robert L. Gale) agree that Dana invests little or no symbolic or philosophical content in his story.

It is, by necessity, however, an account of a young man coming of age, in this case, a young man of upper-class background testing himself against the rigor of an unforgiving sea. On the outbound voyage during a fierce storm off Cape Horn, Dana springs past others of the crew who are holding back to go out on the bowsprit and help John the Swede furl the jib sail. After the task is completed and they are back safely on the deck, Dana is proud to hear John the Swede tell him that the bowsprit had been a dangerous place. By the time the *Pilgrim* has reached California, Dana has moved from the steerage into the forecastle with the rest of the seamen and can consider himself one of them. In fact, it is at Monterey that Dana volunteers to go aloft and send down a royal yard, and when it is done and the mate tells him "well done," Dana feels as satisfied as he would have felt on being praised for a Latin exercise at Harvard.

Context

Two Years Before the Mast enjoyed a success that was both immediate and lasting. Its popularity created an entirely new market for factual books about life at sea, ranging from *A Green Hand's First Cruise* (1841) by an anonymous author to James Fenimore Cooper's *Ned Myers: Or, A Life Before the Mast* (1843), and its influence on the works of Herman Melville has been amply documented. One misconception of the work showed up immediately in the reviews and has lingered into the twentieth century: the view that *Two Years Before the Mast* is social criticism. Dana himself made it clear that the book was not intended as an indictment of conditions at sea, but the two decades prior to the Civil War constituted a period of intense reform, and many critics saw the work as a call for maritime reform, especially the abolition of flogging. On the other hand, as a lawyer, Dana defended the rights of seamen in court as well as in articles and speeches, which has lent credence to the view of his book also being reform-oriented.

What has endeared *Two Years Before the Mast* to young readers over the years is its simple, straightforward style. Although it has remained in print and has been compared favorably with works of the same nature stretching from Francis Parkman's *Oregon Trail* (1849) to Ernest Hemingway's *Green Hills of Africa* (1935), Dana considered the book that made him famous as merely the product of a youthful episode in a life that was devoted to the law and politics. Dana, in fact, considered his life to have been a failure, for despite having made lasting contributions to the interpretation of maritime law, he never accomplished his goal of holding high public office. His other works, in particular *The Seaman's Friend* (1841) and *To Cuba and Back* (1859), were not expected to rival *Two Years Before the Mast*—and neither did. Nevertheless, the work that Dana sometimes resented is considered an early example of realism in American literature.

R. M. Day

UNCLE TOM'S CABIN
Or, Life Among the Lowly

Author: Harriet Beecher Stowe (1811-1896)
Type of plot: Moral tale
Time of plot: The mid-nineteenth century
Locale: The southern states of the United States; Ohio; and Canada
Principal themes: Race and ethnicity, and social issues
First published: 1851-1852, serial; 1852, book
Recommended ages: 13-18

This novel was to become the first very widely read fictional work on the moral injustice of slavery in the United States before the Civil War. It treats the sufferings of slave families who, because of their owners' legal rights over them, were separated by forced sale of wives and husbands, children and parents.

Principal characters:
> UNCLE TOM, a loyal slave who endures great injustice at the hands of his masters
> GEORGE SHELBY, the son of Tom's original master, who gives him the nickname Uncle Tom and tries to make it possible for Tom to return to his family
> AUGUSTINE ST. CLARE, Tom's second master, who begins to understand the value of human compassion for oppressed slaves but dies before being able to help Tom
> MARIE ST. CLARE, Augustine's wife, who cares little about the value of Tom's loyalty and sells him to raise money after her husband's death
> ELIZA, a runaway slave, the wife of slave George Harris
> EVA ST. CLARE, the daughter of wealthy Southerner Augustine St. Clare; Uncle Tom saves Eva's life during his transport to New Orleans, where he is to be sold
> SIMON LEGREE, Tom's third and last owner, who treats his slaves cruelly; when he suspects Tom of aiding other slaves to escape, Legree has him fatally beaten

The Story

At the outset of this novel, the reader meets Mr. Shelby, a Kentucky plantation owner. Because of his debts, Shelby is forced to sell Tom, his most trusted hand, and Harry, the son of Eliza, to a slave trader. Tom has always enjoyed a favored position with the Shelbys. He has spent many hours with Shelby's son George, who refers to the slave as "Uncle Tom."

Tom's wife wants him to flee, but he refuses, saying he cannot betray Shelby's trust. At first Eliza, too, resists her husband George's insistence that the only way to escape slavery is to go to Canada. When she learns that her son Harry is to be sold, however, she flees with him across the Ohio River. After several difficult experiences, Eliza is finally able to rejoin George in Indiana.

Uncle Tom, meanwhile, is carried off in chains by a slave trader who travels down the Ohio River, purchasing other slaves along the way. Among the boat's regular white passengers is Eva St. Clare, a child whom Tom saves from drowning. Recognizing that he owes him a debt, Eva's father, Augustine, decides to purchase Tom, who becomes the family's carriage driver. As confidence in him rises, Tom not only handles market shopping and cares for the fatally ill Eva; he chides his master for his excessive drinking and failure to observe Christian ways. Augustine St. Clare is clearly overcome with feelings of guilt toward Tom specifically and toward slavery in general. By the time he begins planning for Tom's emancipation, however, he is killed senselessly while trying to end a drunken brawl.

Meanwhile, Tom's former owners, the Shelbys, encourage his wife and children to believe that means will eventually be found to repurchase Tom and bring him back to his family. Tom's new mistress, Marie St. Clare, shares none of these humanitarian hopes. To raise money, she sells Tom to the infamous Simon Legree. Legree assures the loyalty of slaves by terrorizing them. He has trained two black overseers, Sambo and Quimbo, to use brutal means to ensure order on the plantation.

When Tom tries secretly to help his fellow slaves, he is caught and beaten. Cassy, Legree's preferred mulatto mistress up to this point, tries to convince Legree that his brutal methods against his slaves will not work. When her efforts fail, Cassy approaches Tom with a plan to kill Legree. Tom's intense Christian faith makes him recoil at the idea of murder; resignation to the Lord's will, even if it means his own death, remains first in his mind.

Cassy and a fifteen-year-old slave, Emmeline, decide to flee, with the eventual hope of freedom. Insane with anger at their flight, Legree has Tom flogged for complicity, but, once again, Tom's Christian admonitions prevail: Both Sambo and Quimbo repent and at long last prove they have a conscience by offering the miserable slave comfort as he lies dying.

George Shelby, son of Tom's earlier master, now arrives prepared to buy Tom back. Tom is close to death but refuses to let Shelby denounce Legree's barbarity; instead, he insists that Legree has worked the way of the Lord by opening the gates of heaven for his final escape from misery.

After Tom's death, Shelby returns home by riverboat and discovers that Cassy and Emmeline, in disguise, are on board. News is exchanged concerning the other slave couple who had fled from the Shelby estate. Cassy discovers that George's wife Eliza is none other than her own daughter, taken from her by her master years before and sold.

The novel ends after the family of slave fugitives is rejoined in Canada. Their lives are totally transformed when George and Eliza, Cassy, and Emmeline all move to France, where George succeeds in obtaining a university education and makes plans to take his family to Liberia, a haven for former slaves that had recently been established in Africa.

Themes and Meanings

The main themes of Stowe's work involve the brutal injustices of slavery and the moral forces within individuals that can combat them. A considerable amount of attention is given by the author to the personal psychological makeup of the protagonists. Such psychological traits help explain the actions that weave the story's plot. The most obvious example of this is Uncle Tom himself, but other figures, especially Legree, reveal dimensions of human psychology that can be tied to base urges of exploitation.

Diverse human reactions to injustice make up a set of complementary themes. Some of these are easily grasped in terms of simple human decency. The reader thus encounters a series of benevolent white people in the story—even slaveowners who see that the exercise of humanitarian concern can ease the burden of responsibility for the forces of fate that have made some masters and others slaves.

Probably the most controversial theme in this novel, however, is to be found in Beecher's depiction of Uncle Tom himself. Tom's steadfast belief that individual resignation to suffering will be rewarded after death ("final liberation") has attracted critics' attention ever since the book's appearance. The religious psychology of the need to confront injustice (for "higher moral victory" in the hereafter) presented a profound and perplexing issue during Stowe's time—one that has remained unsolved long after the disappearance of slavery.

Context

The assumption that the author of *Uncle Tom* was consciously devoted to the cause of the antislavery movement continued to be the object of controversy into the twentieth century. A well-known example of twentieth century criticism marking the beginning of a new militant attitude toward Black civil rights was James Baldwin's essay, "Everybody's Protest Novel," published in the *Partisan Review*, in 1949.

If one places the career of Mrs. Stowe in its original historical context, however, the book's underlying characteristics are easier to understand. The author was the daughter, sister, and wife of New England Congregational ministers. The ethical attitudes of such descendants of the original Pilgrims involved an evangelical commitment to social reform.

Harriet Beecher Stowe presents an image of slavery as part of a "providential" force. Her purpose may not have been to take a political position on slavery, but rather to moralize on the theory of salvation. In this moral literary context, Tom's identity is to be seen less in political terms than in a role as a black Christ or a black representative of Protestant virtue.

One should contrast possible original motivating forces behind Stowe's unprecedented novel with what may be called the radical political press of the era. A clear antislavery abolitionist cause had already taken root in America by the 1850's, represented most notably by activists such as publisher William Lloyd Garrison with his *The Liberator* and John Brown, a radical leader of the Underground Railroad. Although Stowe's original intention may not have been to aid the abolitionist cause, public reception of the story did more to help it than anything the members themselves had done.

Harriet Beecher Stowe's emergence as a controversial literary figure helped earn for her favorable reviews in such prestigious publications as *The Times* of London; on the European continent, she was heralded in 1854 as a spokesperson of the moral and political outrage that was widely held there against the evil institution of slavery. *Uncle Tom's Cabin* represents a historic milestone in America's perception of itself. The essence of its themes formed the core of causes of the great Civil Rights movement of the 1950's and 1960's. The influence of this book upon the course of a nation cannot be overestimated; the book belongs to the ages.

Byron D. Cannon

UNLEAVING

Author: Jill Paton Walsh (1937-   )
Type of plot: Psychological realism
Time of plot: The late twentieth century
Locale: Cornwall, England
Principal themes: Coming-of-age, death, family, friendship, and love and romance
First published: 1976
Recommended ages: 15-18

Madge Fielding rents the seaside house she inherited from her grandmother to a university reading party. During the summer, Madge witnesses the excitements and the perils of intellect. Through Patrick Tregeagle, whose professorial father leads the group, she struggles to understand the nature of life, death, and love.

Principal characters:
>MADGE FIELDING (GRAN), a curious, caring young woman and, sixty years later, a spirited, loving grandmother
>PROFESSOR TREGEAGLE, one of the Oxford professors of philosophy leading the summer reading party
>PATRICK TREGEAGLE, the professor's son, a brooding young man who feels deeply
>MOLLY TREGEAGLE, Patrick's retarded sister
>PAUL FIELDING, Madge's brother

The Story

The novel is set during a summer visit at the house Madge Fielding inherits from her cherished grandmother. The house in Cornwall, England, sits close to treacherous cliffs and welcoming ocean beaches. Jill Paton Walsh employs a narrative shape that shifts between Gran's calm, reflective point of view and Madge Fielding's involved, passionate perspective. Slowly, the two distinct voices merge into one story as the reader recognizes Madge and Gran as the same person.

When Miss Higgins, Madge's schoolmistress, encourages her to rent the house to a reading party of undergraduates from Oxford, Madge hesitates. She still mourns her grandmother's death and is unsure she wants to disturb her grandmother's presence in the house. Still, the idea tempts Madge, and she allows herself to be persuaded. Feeling only somewhat invaded, she welcomes the two professors, their families, and eight university students. She also invites her brother Paul to join her.

The group fascinates Madge, who is preparing for entering college. Their philosophical discussions intrigue and challenge her intellectually and emotionally. Not one who has studied the philosophical foundations structuring the students' debates, Madge initially only eavesdrops. As the summer progresses, she befriends various members of the group, especially Matthew Brown and Andrew Henderson. Soon, she dares to enter their heated intellectual discussions about life, death, and God.

To Paul's surprise and concern, Madge shows particular attraction to the dark, complicated, and moody Patrick Tregeagle. Feeling peripheral, uninvolved, and unwanted, Patrick rejects the philosophical discussions. He spends most of his time playing the piano, with characteristic intensity, and caring for his mongoloid sister Molly. Slowly, he begins to share himself and his feelings of ambivalence about his family with Madge. During the summer, Madge and Patrick spend much time together and develop a strong bond.

One afternoon Molly is discovered missing. Her parents fear she has wandered off and fallen into an abandoned mine shaft. Luckily, she is found and is safe. This occurrence foreshadows the tragic incident that drives the narrative. Later, Madge and Paul seek Patrick, who has taken Molly for a walk. In a brief, tense scene, Madge and Paul see Molly fall from a cliff to her death. This first death leads to another. In an unlikely but committed attempt to rescue Molly, a native boatman, and beloved friend of Madge and Paul, drowns.

At Molly's fall, Paul and Madge see Patrick. Despite Paul's conviction to the contrary, Madge questions what she saw. Did Patrick reach out to save Molly or did Patrick push his sister? These questions, and their potentially disturbing answers, haunt Madge and Patrick not only for the remainder of the summer but also throughout their lives. Even as a mother and grandmother, Madge reflects on the events of this summer and searches her memory, her mind, and her heart for the elusive answers.

Themes and Meanings

Gerard Manley Hopkins' poem "Spring and Fall to a Young Child" serves as touchstone for both *Goldengrove* (1972) and its sequel *Unleaving*. Both titles are taken directly from the lines of the poem. They succinctly reveal these books as coming-of-age novels.

High cliffs provide an apt setting for this story of a man's descent into the darkness within himself. The ocean, a constant force that both gives life and takes it, conveys the author's vision of the human condition: It is a burdensome responsibility to possess the ability to nurture and extinguish life.

Not only does the novel's setting recall Virginia Woolf's *To the Lighthouse* (1927) but also Jill Paton Walsh's prose style and thematic concerns echo Woolf's work. They both focus on the essential importance of "the moment" to alter the direction of a life. Both authors write about a woman's concern with life and death and the tension between emotion and intellect. Paton Walsh's writing style here is fluid and lucid.

Patrick Tregeagle has particular thematic resonance. Madge's research reveals the mythic significance of the name Tregeagle in Cornish folklore. Evil, dead or alive, Tregeagle's voice can be heard howling in the night, keeping all awake and troubled. His reputation closely follows Patrick's characterization. Patrick's subconscious desire to be free of Molly causes his brooding outlook. After her death, Patrick's guilt, real or implied, torments him and those who love him. He chooses to see the darkest side of himself and cannot escape his own human capacity for evil.

The novel's provocative narrative shape, Paton Walsh's graceful, imagery-rich prose, and the intricate philosophical debates may challenge readers. Yet they also form a unifying foundation for the novel's thematic concerns. The discussions themselves articulate the questions Madge asks as she strives to understand Patrick's role in his sister's death. Is knowledge innate? What is the nature of existence? Can ends justify means? Does God exist? As Gran, surrounded by two generations of her loving family, recalls the heated philosophical discussions she overheard as young Madge, the reader recognizes the personal struggle between emotion and intellect. The terse title, *Unleaving*, captures the resonance of these questions for Madge. The novel's structure allows readers to know Madge during her adolescence, at the moment these questions arise. It also presents Madge as an adult, demonstrating her resolution of these issues. She rejects pure intellect and pure emotion for a precarious but healthy balance of the two extremes.

Context

Unleaving is Paton Walsh's most critically acclaimed novel for young adults. Contemporary setting and creation of a realistic world make it different from her other works of historical fiction, such as *The Emperor's Winding Sheet* (1974), *Fireweed* (1969), and *A Parcel of Patterns* (1983), or futuristic fiction, including *Torch* (1988). Featuring the same characters as its predecessor *Goldengrove*, this novel leaves the safe world of childhood comfort and protection and ventures into the complexities of adolescence. Where *Goldengrove* explored Madge's physical and emotional entry into adolescence, in *Unleaving* one discovers that coming-of-age is never a completed process but an ongoing one. As Gran searches her past, giving it shape and force, the past gives insight and meaning to her present life.

The novel employs an original psychological realism. These young characters, on the precipice of adulthood, are not sentimentalized. They are intelligent, insightful, and talented. Energetic and feisty, they also feel deeply. These characters are not simply good or undeniably evil; they are both simultaneously. Patrick and Madge especially demonstrate man's natural, inherent capacity for both good and evil. In Jungian terms, their real triumph, their real coming-of-age, stems from their ability to acknowledge this capacity, to recognize and incorporate their "shadow-selves."

In *Unleaving*, Paton Walsh breaks with the traditional structure of the novel. Rather than telling the story chronologically, or framing it by memory, or using a flashback technique, Paton Walsh creates two parallel but distinct voices from two fully realized perspectives. Both stories are told in the third-person. They do not alternate predictably from Gran to Madge; instead, the two weave in and out of each other. The tenuous thread of memory connects them. Memories spiral, building upon one another as past and present merge into a cohesive, tightly controlled whole.

While Paton Walsh returns to a more traditional format in later novels, *Unleaving* remains an original achievement. The narrative sophistication may prove demanding to young readers, but the reward will be a rich, memorable reading experience.

Cathryn M. Mercier

UP A ROAD SLOWLY

Author: Irene Hunt (1907-   )
Type of plot: Psychological realism
Time of plot: The 1930's
Locale: A small Midwestern community
Principal themes: Coming-of-age, family, friendship, and love and romance
First published: 1966
Recommended ages: 13-15

Following the death of her mother, Julie Trelling is sent to live with a maiden aunt. Under the care of her stern but loving Aunt Cordelia, Julie grows from a bewildered seven-year-old to a bright and confident seventeen-year-old.

Principal characters:
JULIE TRELLING, a talented young girl who is reared by a maiden aunt
AUNT CORDELIA, her schoolteacher aunt, who is stern but compassionate
UNCLE HASKELL, Cordelia's brother, an alcoholic recluse who aspires to be a writer
ADAM TRELLING, Julie's father, a pleasant man who is a professor at a local college
ALICIA TRELLING, Julie's wise stepmother and her high school English teacher
BRETT KINGSMAN, Julie's first boyfriend, a brash, shallow young man
CHRIS and
DANNY TREVORT, neighbor boys

The Story

The title of *Up a Road Slowly* aptly portrays the life of its main character, Julie Trelling. At seven, Julie finds it difficult to understand all the commotion surrounding her mother's death and funeral, and she is even more bewildered when she awakens one morning at Aunt Cordelia's, where she had been taken after being given a sedative. Her first morning, Julie hides in a closet. When Cordelia climbs in with her, holding the trembling child and sharing her tears, Julie warms to her caring gesture. Reality sets in and Julie recognizes that she and her brother Chris, who is nine, will live with Cordelia and go to school while her seventeen-year-old sister stays in town with their father to finish her senior year.

School begins, and Aunt Cordelia is the teacher in the one-room country schoolhouse. She is a stern, rigid teacher who, Julie laments, likes the boys, especially her neighbors Chris and Danny Trevort, better than the girls. Aunt Cordelia persists in calling Julie "Julia," because that is the proper pronunciation and spelling of the name. Julie learns quickly to accept Aunt Cordelia's eccentricities and takes them in stride.

For amusement, Julie, Chris, and often Danny, spy on Uncle Haskell, who lives in a carriage house behind the main house. In the evening, Uncle Haskell goes into the woods carrying a golf bag. The children discover its contents buried in shallow graves: Uncle Haskell is disposing of liquor bottles. This episode prompts Adam Trelling to put Chris in a boarding school, leaving Julie alone with Aunt Cordelia.

When Julie is ten, her sister Laura marries. Even the prospect of spending a summer vacation with Laura and Bill does not ease Julie's sense of loss. When the vacation is over, however, she realizes that Laura can love both Bill and her sister. Julie is happy for Laura and at the prospect of becoming an aunt.

Julie begins eighth grade with the realization that this will be her last year with Aunt Cordelia. The death of a classmate, Aggie Kilpin, gives Julie more insight into her generous, kindly aunt, while the return to town of Jonathan Eltwing with his wife, Katy, provides her a glimpse into Aunt Cordelia's past, for Jonathan was once Cordelia's sweetheart. Finally, the marriage of Adam Trelling and Alicia is a significant turning point. Although Julie likes Alicia because she is more carefree than Aunt Cordelia, the changes Alicia makes in the Trelling home make Julie uncomfortable. Preferring the comfort of the familiar, she decides to remain at Aunt Cordelia's for her high school years.

Julie tackles the challenges of high school with normal adolescent anxieties. Academically, Julie is a very good student; English is her favorite subject, because she likes to write. Socially, life is slow until Brett Kingsman enters her life. Julie is overwhelmed by Brett's good looks, while Brett takes advantage of Julie's academic talent. Recognizing Julie's style and ideas in Brett's work, Alicia issues a firm warning that helps to end this unhealthy relationship. Aunt Cordelia's warmth and care help Julie recuperate.

Julie's focus now shifts to her writing. Under the tutelage of Uncle Haskell, a stern taskmaster, she rewrites and polishes her short stories while trying to keep up with her schoolwork. Her reward is getting a piece published in a literary magazine, a surprise to Julie, who did not know that Uncle Haskell had submitted it. Her exuberance is dimmed by Uncle Haskell's untimely death from a liver disease.

During her senior year, Julie's friendship with Danny Trevort blossoms into romance. She is the class valedictorian and plans to attend a state university, while Danny will go to a school several hundred miles east. Julie and Danny will be separated as Aunt Cordelia and Jonathan Eltwing were many years ago, completing the cycle of parallels between the life of Julie Trelling and that of Aunt Cordelia.

Themes and Meanings

Up a Road Slowly opens in early autumn and ends in springtime, taking the reader through the many seasons of Julie Trelling's young life. The theme is the development and maturation of a girl whose life is shaped by many diverse characters, especially the strong, though often inflexible, Aunt Cordelia. From this role model,

Julie learns discipline, propriety, the value of integrity, and, most of all, kindness and compassion.

Other family members contribute to Julie's growth in a variety of ways. Through Uncle Haskell she learns that self-centered people can be selfless sometimes and that substance abuse is deadly. Her father and stepmother enhance her self-esteem by their pride in her achievements and by providing her with a relaxed environment to encourage flexibility and fun. From her sister, Laura, she understands the pangs of jealousy and the pleasures of love, both familial and marital.

Julie's character is further molded by her young friends. She is inspired to be tolerant of and compassionate to the less fortunate by Aggie Kilpin. Dating Brett Kingsman is a lesson in the pain of misguided young love. From Carlotta Berry she understands that people must suffer the consequences of their actions. Most of all, from Danny Trevort she learns the rewards of loyalty and friendship.

Context

Praised as a significant contribution to children's fiction, *Up a Road Slowly* was awarded the American Library Association's Newbery Medal in 1967. It was Irene Hunt's second novel. Her first work, *Across Five Aprils* (1964), a historical piece, was a Newbery runner-up in 1965. As a contributor to the emerging genre of young adult fiction, Hunt was quickly recognized as a first-rank writer who could deal with adult issues that face young readers without being sentimental or patronizing.

As the young adult novel moved into the 1960's, writers understood the need to deal with knotty problems facing adolescents. Writing about the impact on young lives of such issues as death, alcoholism, and sex became common. Ann Head's *Mr. and Mrs. Bo Jo Jones*, also published in 1966, is set in the 1960's and focuses on the consequences of premarital sex. Though Hunt's work is set in the 1930's, Julie also faces these consequences—vicariously, through her friend Carlotta. After Julie escapes the sexually aggressive clutches of Brett Kingsman, Carlotta and Brett begin to date. Soon, however, Carlotta is sent away to live with an aunt—a typical means for dealing with teenage pregnancy in this era.

In her Newbery Medal acceptance address, Hunt stated her conviction that from books, children learn about life. Her works reflect this philosophy, for her subsequent novels expand on many of the poignant issues she raises in *Up a Road Slowly*. In *No Promises in the Wind* (1970), Josh develops and matures through the many people he meets, gaining a better understanding of himself and his alcoholic father and accepting life's tragedies when a friend dies. George in *The Lottery Rose* (1976) is victimized by an alcoholic mother and subjected to abuse. George finds solace in kindly neighbors, especially a retarded child, and the beauty of a rosebush he has won. Julie, Josh, and George are emerging adults whose characters are shaped by a heterogeneous cast of family and friends with whom they interact while coping with life's adversities and relishing its triumphs. There is no better way to teach children about life. That is life.

Dorothy Trusock

THE VIRGINIAN
A Horseman of the Plains

Author: Owen Wister (1860-1938)
Type of plot: Historical fiction
Time of plot: The late nineteenth century
Locale: Wyoming
Principal themes: Love and romance, social issues, and gender roles
First published: 1902; illustrated
Recommended ages: 13-18

Against a backdrop of late 1870's Wyoming, an unschooled cowboy of superior character excels at every test—physical, emotional, and spiritual—and wins the educated Eastern woman whom he loves.

Principal characters:

THE VIRGINIAN, the hero, a young cowboy of impressive bearing who works at Sunk Creek Ranch

MISS MOLLY STARK WOOD, a spirited, intelligent young woman from Bennington, Vermont, who comes to Wyoming to teach school at Bear Creek

THE NARRATOR, an Eastern gentleman visiting Judge Henry who is first entrusted to the Virginian's care and later becomes his friend

JUDGE HENRY, the owner of Sunk Creek Ranch and the recognized leader of the area

TRAMPAS, the villain, a cowboy whom the Virginian bests several times and whose deep resentment erupts in a final challenge to fight

The Story

The Virginian is introduced through the eyes of an Eastern gentleman who is the narrator of the story. The cowboy has been sent by Judge Henry to meet this tenderfoot's train in Medicine Bow; through incidents there, the Virginian (he is not more specifically named) shows himself to be a man of playfulness and wit, as well as honor and courage.

Miss Molly Stark Wood is an independent young woman from a good family in Bennington, Vermont, that has fallen upon hard times. She secures a position as the first schoolmistress in Bear Creek, Wyoming, and, during a stagecoach mishap, is rescued by the Virginian. He is instantly smitten and, although Molly ostensibly spurns his attentions, he begins to ride to Bear Creek to see her. Borrowing her volumes of Shakespeare, Sir Walter Scott, Dickens, and others, the Virginian sets out to educate himself.

Although young, the Virginian is respected by his employer and the other cowboys. The exception is the sullen villain Trampas, who also comes to work for Judge Henry; they confront each other several times during the narrative, mostly verbally. The Virginian is made foreman of Sunk Creek Ranch. In all his beliefs and actions, for example his dealings with a rancher who mistreats horses, the Virginian exemplifies the code of the West. The principles of the cowboy hero are further revealed throughout his determined courtship. It culminates when Molly, confused by her growing feelings, decides to leave Bear Creek before the Virginian can return and speak his mind to her. In an agitated state, she races off on her horse and unexpectedly comes upon him, seriously wounded. Despite his insistence that she leave and save herself from the Indians still nearby, Molly brings the Virginian to safety. With a neighbor's help, she nurses him back to health and, at the end of his long convalescence, they become engaged.

The Virginian then returns to Sunk Creek and finds that cattle and horse thieves have been at work. Through an incident in which the narrator unexpectedly comes upon the Virginian leading a posse that is hanging rustlers, the reader learns about the Virginian's character and about the Western code of justice. The experience is terrible for the Virginian because he has to hang a former friend, but his belief in the principles and customs of the West nevertheless remains staunch. Molly becomes upset by this vigilante justice and decides to call off the engagement. Through a discussion with Judge Henry, however, in which he reconciles the Western code of justice with institutionalized law, she finally comes to accept the Virginian's actions, and the two make plans to wed.

The day before the wedding, Trampas issues a public challenge that the Virginian cannot ignore. Molly cannot understand why he must fight, and they part, estranged. In a dramatic encounter, almost everyone in Medicine Bow—except Molly—watches the prototype of what has become the standard Western shootout. Trampas and the Virginian meet, Trampas shoots first and misses, and the Virginian shoots him dead. The Virginian then returns to Molly, who greets him with open arms, and they are married. The couple spend an idyllic month in the mountains and then go East to meet her family. The novel concludes with an epilogue explaining that the Virginian becomes Judge Henry's partner upon his return to Sunk Creek. Over the years, his business ventures become very successful, and his family grows and prospers.

Themes and Meanings

In *The Virginian*, Wister presents the conflict between Eastern and Western values through his characters Molly and the Virginian, respectively. Molly is a young schoolteacher from a good family in Vermont who goes West; the Virginian is a self-sufficient cowboy, the idealized hero of the old frontier. Wister resolves the East/West dichotomy through their romance and marriage, which forms the major theme of the work. The marriage reconciles perspectives on male/female roles, the individual versus society, and differing views of social justice that are presented in opposition through much of the narrative. As a result of their union, the Virginian moves toward greater interaction with society and increased prosperity through his business dealings with the expanding railroad, yet he loses none of his integrity and honor. As the Virginian embraces his inevitable role in the industrialization of the nation, Wister suggests that he becomes more, not less, of a man.

The novel is structured with subplots, which intersect the main thread of the romance: principally, the interactions between the Virginian and Trampas, which develop the theme of good triumphing over evil, and a series of incidents that show the evolution of the Virginian's character. Many of these incidents also involve the education of the unnamed narrator, who comes to display some of the self-sufficiency and honor of the cowboy and loses his Eastern vulnerability, showing the contribution that the West can make to more "civilized" society.

Wister was fascinated and regenerated by the frontier, but he was still born and bred an Easterner. Some critics have suggested that he was caught between romantic and realistic views of the West, and the novel has been read as a reflection of Wister's own ambivalence and its resolution. The Virginian is depicted as the superior man of action, the honorable hero, yet Wister places him realistically in a frontier that calls forth violence even from the best of men, a country that could be both physically and culturally barren.

In addition to representing the ideal hero of the old West, the Virginian has been interpreted as symbolic of the basic tenets of the United States: democracy and individualism. From this perspective, the West is viewed not as antagonistic to civilized society but as the final frontier within which the ideals of Western civilization can be examined and reenlivened. The Virginian represents a new kind of natural aristocracy—the superior man who is needed to provide political leadership for the United States. In Molly's acceptance of his code of honor, the aristocracy of inheritance (represented by her family status) is replaced by the natural aristocracy of the individual, based on a man's inner integrity and the actions he takes. Wister considered this true aristocracy to be the real basis for the democracy of the United States.

Context

The Virginian is recognized as a landmark in the history of American literature, representing the transition between the dime novels of the West and the modern literary Western. It established the legend of the idealized American cowboy hero in the national imagination and is also credited with developing, almost single-handedly, the structure within which most stories of the West have been told throughout the twentieth century. This is despite the fact that this rather quiet narrative is notable as much for what it leaves out as what it puts in, choosing to detail scenes of rescue and the telling of tall tales rather than the violence and other antisocial behaviors that have come to be associated with life in the old West.

The novel, which was an instant and immense success, offered the public a fictional account of the frontier myth that was compatible with Theodore Roosevelt's political actions at the turn of the century. Wister, in fact, dedicated the novel to Roosevelt, whom he called "the greatest benefactor we people have known since

Lincoln." The novel also reflected the cultural tensions of its time and has been interpreted as an expression of the duality of the progressive mind, looking backward with sentimental attachment to rugged individualism and, at the same time, forward toward a more integrated society.

Wister's personal experience of the West formed the basis for his literature. Although some critics believe that several short stories are better written, *The Virginian* is Wister's best-known and most popular work, and its publication in 1902 marked the high point of his career. Within four months, it sold fifty thousand copies and was reprinted fifteen times within seven months. In 1904 it was made into a play, in 1914 into a silent film, and in 1929, Gary Cooper played the Virginian in a talking film that launched his career.

Wister has been credited with inventing the cowboy as a literary hero, yet critics generally consider him to be a mid-level writer in the genre of Western American fiction. Although he wrote more realistically and has been recognized as a better craftsman than some of his contemporaries, Wister is not usually classed with such superior Western novelists as John Steinbeck, Willa Cather, and Wallace Stegner. Nevertheless, *The Virginian* is considered a great American Western classic. It is perhaps the most popular Western ever written and, in its many versions on stage, television, and film, has become a part of American folklore. Reading *The Virginian* offers young adults an opportunity to investigate the prototypical Western, the novel that established character types and plot devices that have come to be expected as basic ingredients of the genre.

Jean C. Fulton

VISITORS FROM LONDON

Author: Kitty Barne (Marion Catherine Barne, 1883-1957)
Type of plot: Adventure tale/psychological realism/social realism
Time of plot: Summer, 1939
Locale: Steadings, a rural manor and farm near Poleham, Sussex, England
Principal themes: Family, coming-of-age, and war
First published: 1940; illustrated
Recommended ages: 10-13

The peaceful summer vacation of the Farrar children and their aunt is disrupted but enriched by the arrival at Steadings of early World War II evacuees from London.

> *Principal characters:*
> MYRA FARRAR, the Farrar children's aunt, cool, efficient, yet sympathetic and attuned to children, especially her red-headed nieces and nephews
> GERDA FARRAR, fifteen, steady and fond of her family, especially her brother David
> DAVID FARRAR, thirteen, mature for his age, practical, efficient and authoritative, but likable
> JIMMY FARRAR, eleven plus, dynamic, inventive, helpful, and a mechanical whiz
> SALLY FARRAR, ten, unruly, fond of small children but given to tantrums
> LILY TIPPING, twelve, an indomitable Cockney evacuee, acting cheerfully as "mother" to her small siblings
> FRED FELL, thirteen, a surly, undernourished London urchin transformed by the joyous discovery of the shepherd's blood in his veins
> STEVE FELL, eleven, Fred's brother, sly and streetwise, an accomplished and confirmed petty crook

The Story

The Farrar children are reunited for the summer holidays at Poleham, Sussex, to stay with their aunt, Myra. (Their stay with her at Poleham village the previous Christmas is the subject of *Family Footlights*, 1939.) They are eagerly anticipating this stay at Huggetts, a farmhouse attached to ancient Steadings, all that is left of a huge estate now owned by the ailing "Mus" Bloss and presently leased to Roly Martingale, a London writer, a largely offstage but romantic presence and benefactor in the Farrars' lives. The middle-aged Huggetts farm the Steadings lands; the Farrar children enjoy the farm animals, chores, and the freedom of the Sussex countryside. After three weeks, however, a telegram arrives from Roly, telling them that he has lent

Steadings to the Women's Voluntary Service for the sheltering of children evacuated from London to escape the threatened bombing raids marking the outset of World War II. The Farrars are to prepare Steadings and supervise the evacuees. From then on, the holiday peace is shattered.

The Farrars undertake frantic preparations, at first with reluctance but soon with increasing ingenuity, a sense of adventure, and the help of new friends from the village. When the evacuees arrive unceremoniously, they are not only the expected children but mothers with their families. These visitors from London are an exhausted and nervous group, confirmed city dwellers plucked from their working-class lives and deposited in a rural setting as alien to them as the moon. Once settled into their fancifully named Steadings bedrooms, the evacuees quickly sort themselves into those who can and those who cannot cope.

There are the Tipping children, headed by shrewd, practical twelve-year-old Lily, who despite her tough manner cares with fierce love for her small siblings, proving more efficient than some of the actual mothers. Mrs. Fell, a grim older woman, rules her family of six with liberal slaps and never reconciles herself to her stay at Steadings. Her sullen son Fred, however, falls in love with the Sussex downs and discovers that he was born to be a shepherd; with the tutelage and love of Old and Young Tolhurst, colorful local shepherds, Fred finds his niche and fills out to become a sturdy, tow-headed, serene country boy, never to return to gang life in squalid London. Yet brother Steve, already permanently shifty and unloving, earns everyone's dislike with his underhandedness and a series of petty thefts he undertakes to acquire betting money. Young Mrs. Thompson is pitiful; disabled by fear of her husband, the threat of bombings, and the alien countryside, and exhausted by recent childbirth, she is a near-invalid. She shuts herself in her room, imprisoning her children with her, until they are finally coaxed out by the cajoling and ingenuity of Jimmy Farrar. This small family's growing, if timid, confidence is quickly scotched by the aggrieved, authoritarian husband who arrives to sweep his weeping family back to London. The Jacobsons fare the best overall; sustained by her solid marriage, kindly, hardworking Mrs. Jacobson devotes herself to her three sons and proves invaluable in the Steadings kitchen. When her husband joins the army, she arranges work in the village and assures the continuing education of her children, especially her eldest son Joe. The Jacobsons are the family, Myra observes, who seem "always to get such a grip of things."

Noisy, mostly harmonious coexistence punctuated by quarrels, rivalries, outings, and tangles with farm pets form most of the novel's plot. Memorable highlights are a profitable seashore prawning picnic and a sojourn at the local fair; the idyllic aspects of both events, however, are spoiled by the nasty scheming of young Steve Fell. An uproarious nocturnal encounter with a zealous local air warden underscores the seriousness of the war that has otherwise come to seem so far away.

On the third Sunday of the evacuees' sojourn, the London husbands, Roly Martingale, and the autumn arrive simultaneously at Steadings. The Farrars throw a party; at its conclusion, the evacuees head, more or less enthusiastically, back to London, or scatter to take up their new lives around Sussex. The Farrar children prepare to return to school, enriched by their encounter with their visitors from London and better prepared for the shifting fortunes of wartime.

Themes and Meanings

Visitors from London is primarily a novel of character, and the character lovingly portrayed is quintessentially British. The novel's central theme is making the best of things. Conflict of many types drives the story; conflict is met and resolved one way or another through the actions and reactions of the varied, lively troupe of children and adults that peoples the novel. The London evacuees—lower-class, superficially worldly, suspicious, bewildered, and thoroughly urban—are thrust unwillingly into the upper-middle-class Farrars' rural idyll; the resulting clash of values is developed throughout the twenty-eight-chapter novel in a series of incidents that are usually lighthearted and entertaining but sometimes serious. Whatever the prevailing mood at Steadings, the outbreak of World War II creates an undercurrent of uneasiness and incipient catastrophe that makes the necessity for the characters to adapt and cope more urgent.

Though the children's activities and viewpoints dominate the novel, it is often through the adult characters that the novel's serious purpose is expressed, and Barne's adeptness at creating realistic people is most clear. Nita "Billy" Williams, the young secretary in the Women's Voluntary Service (a service in which Barne herself served during World War II), must cope with the bureaucratic details of supplying Steadings with the government necessities and allowances allotted to the evacuees; she handles the many administrative foul-ups with unfailing optimism, if some bemusement. The kind, hardworking Huggetts and Tolhursts depict a simplicity, serenity of spirit, and clarity of purpose that can be seen as typical of ancient British rural virtues, long blighted in many of the evacuees but rediscovered by young Fred Fell. In this novel, then, a certain type of sturdy, practical Briton is celebrated through both its child and adult characters.

Context

Though *Visitors from London* is a children's novel, and much of its gaiety and entertainment is expressed through the children, it has a serious intent for its young readers as well: to portray realistically ordinary people forced to react to the special tensions introduced by wartime, in addition to the other pressures affecting their daily lives. Author Geoffrey Trease noted that "the outbreak of war in 1939 gave [Barne] inspiration and immediately enlarged opportunities. No one could any longer pretend that young readers could or should be protected from reality." For example, this novel and its predecessor *Family Footlights* portray a family that, despite the elements in the stories of the "holiday adventures" familiar to readers of other British children's authors such as Enid Blyton, leads a life containing certain less positive aspects of British upper-middle-class life. Like Mary Lennox's in Frances Hodgson Burnett's *The Secret Garden* (1911), the Farrars' parents are civil servants in the

Indian colonial service, and so the Farrar children rarely see them; the children are also separated from one another during the school terms. The outbreak of war is likely to prolong these separations; however, the Farrar children, like many of the lower-class, disadvantaged evacuee children they house, are independent and adaptable, showing to young readers Barne's faith in the innate strength of young people.

The novel's adults are credible because they are vulnerable. Behind Myra Farrar's even-tempered good humor, the alert reader can detect loneliness; Mrs. Fell's chronic grimness masks her sense of helplessness in the face of the social pressures on her and her large family; young, pathetic Mrs. Thompson is simply overwhelmed, unloading on seven-year-old Ernest the responsibilities she cannot take.

Author Barne's central purpose is both to entertain and educate her young readers without condescending to them. Certainly the charm and appeal of rural life are vividly depicted; the antics of The Monarch, the imperious Steadings gander, and George, Lily's lovingly tended runt pig, provide much comedy; yet the reader also understands through the kindly but preoccupied Huggetts and the ailing Mister Bloss that a farmer's life consists largely of hard work. Perhaps the Tolhursts are the characters who best embody Barne's dual purpose. Readers can enjoy Old Tolhurst's colorful stories and shepherd's lore, and simultaneously learn about the idiosyncrasies of sheep and the nature of the Sussex countryside. At the Sussex seaside, as well, they can enjoy the London children's at first dubious, then joyous, encounter with the "real" sea and also learn about the rich marine life in the tidal pools. *Visitors from London* is a novel in which children take the spotlight and children are the foremost intended readers. Though the English rural life depicted has probably largely disappeared, the appeal of the novel's characters alone recommends it to young readers.

Jill Rollins

THE VOYAGES OF DOCTOR DOLITTLE

Author: Hugh Lofting (1886-1947)
Type of plot: Adventure tale
Time of plot: The late 1800's
Locale: Puddleby-on-the-Marsh, England
Principal themes: Animals, travel, and friendship
First published: 1922; illustrated
Recommended ages: 10-13

A young boy and an amazing doctor are able to talk to and care for animals, which leads them to journey and discover new places and new friends.

Principal characters:
DR. JOHN DOLITTLE, a naturalist, animal doctor, and speaker of animal languages, known for his top hat and little black bag
TOMMY STUBBINS, the cobbler's son, who becomes the doctor's assistant
POLYNESIA, a two-hundred-year-old parrot with an excellent memory, who always has an opinion
MIRANDA, the Purple Bird of Paradise, who is the guide on voyages
LONG ARROW, a great Indian naturalist and hermit
PRINCE BUMPO, the Crown Prince of Jolliginki and good friend to the doctor

The Story

The Voyages of Doctor Dolittle, in its fablelike and biographical manner, presents an imaginative and exciting tale of an eccentric doctor who cares for animals and who can speak animal languages. This tale is told by the cobbler's son, Tommy Stubbins, who became the doctor's assistant because of his interest in becoming a naturalist. Tommy is enchanted by the doctor's house, with its wonderful garden. Here, there are many birds and a private zoo in which the animals have locks on their own stone houses (and not cages) to be able to get away from annoyances of other animals and people. Many kinds of animals live in the doctor's zoo, including the Pushmi-pullyu, a two-headed creature from Africa. Tommy becomes interested in learning animal languages so that he, too, can help the animals. Polynesia the Parrot agrees to help Tommy; she advises him to be patient and to become a "good noticer" of animals and their languages. Tommy's job on the ship will be to help and learn from the doctor and to keep the ship's log on its journey to the island.

By opening up an atlas with their eyes closed and pointing at the page with a pencil, Doctor Dolittle and Tommy decide upon Spidermonkey Island, a floating island off the coast of Brazil, as the destination of their first journey of discovery together. Their voyage to the island, which coincidentally is the place where Long Arrow, the hermit naturalist, has last been seen, is fraught with troubles, including stowaways and lost provisions. Their travels take them to a Spanish island, where the doctor enlists the bulls in his successful plan of banning bullfighting from the island. A storm nearly devastates the crew and the ship, but the doctor's ingenuity and friendship with the dolphins secure their rescue, and the doctor and his friends finally reach Spidermonkey Island.

Tracking the lost Long Arrow proves to be quite a task for the doctor and the crew, but with the help of an extraordinary Jabizri beetle and picture language, Long Arrow is found in a mountain cave. The doctor never has a dull moment, as he then helps the island's natives, the Popsipetel, in a battle against another tribe, teaches them about fire, and helps return warm temperatures to the floating island with the help of whales, who push it northward. The tribe crowns the doctor "King Jong Thinkalot," and the doctor continues to help the tribe to learn new things.

Finally and luckily for the doctor, the very rare seventy-thousand-year-old Great Glass Sea Snail appears; with the help of Polynesia's discreet plotting, the doctor realizes his goal of learning the language of shellfish. The sea snail, who has been nursed back to health by the doctor, offers to take Doctor Dolittle and his friends back to Puddleby-on-the-Marsh, where the animals anxiously await the return of the kind and lovable doctor.

Themes and Meanings

The major theme of *The Voyages of Doctor Dolittle* is that goodness and kindness can be found in all people and in all animals. It is a gentle tale, with brief, fast-paced chapters that move the reader through encounters with various people and animals, weaving a spell of enchantment that shows how everyone can work together all over the world.

Young readers can identify with the character of Doctor Dolittle, as he is kind, understanding, and finds animals much easier to relate to than people. Doctor Dolittle brings out the natural curiosity and wanderlust in the reader through his amazing adventures all over the globe. One gets a sense that the world is a place of many discoveries yet that people miss so much by not being able to understand and communicate with the animal kingdom. The characters of the numerous animals that live with Doctor Dolittle depict the diversity of personalities often found in people.

The simple life-style of the doctor seems to enhance the essentials of life: having good friends with whom to share your dreams and being able to dream about new places to learn about and visit. Doctor Dolittle seems to find himself in the strangest of places and predicaments, which is intriguing to the reader. The doctor utilizes good problem-solving techniques, which always seem to hinge on his understanding of animals and places. The "magic" the doctor possesses is his mind and his kindly manner with animals, along with his willingness to help at any time or in any place; the doctor most often is an "unsung hero." In his successful adventures, one learns about oneself as well as about other people and animals.

Context

The Voyages of Doctor Dolittle, a "classic" recognized for its originality and awarded the 1923 Newbery Medal, is the second book of a series of adventure stories written and illustrated by Hugh Lofting, who dedicated them to "all children—children in years and children in heart. . . . " Hugh Lofting aimed to create in Doctor Dolittle a new and gentle hero for children, who would show them an international view and an understanding of the goodness of all people. The characters in the stories were originally created for Hugh Lofting's children, Elizabeth and Colin, to whom he would write during his service in the British army in World War I. Lofting got the idea for his tales as he observed how animals were treated during the war. He saw that they were not given the same attention and treatment as the human wounded, and so he created an eccentric physician to administer to their needs.

The Voyages of Doctor Dolittle is a literary classic, for its characters, as well as its theme of a hero following the golden rule of treating others with kindness and understanding, are timeless. Hugh Lofting's friend, Sir Hugh Walpole, claimed the book "a work of genius—the first real classic since *Alice*" and predicted that Doctor Dolittle would exist through the centuries "as a kind of Pied Piper with thousands of children at his heels." E. H. Colwell in *The Junior Bookshelf* commented, "Whatever the danger, Doctor Dolittle remains calm and however awkward the situation he always retains his top hat and little bag." The stories about the doctor have been translated into nine languages, and many of his adventures were created from suggestions by children who wrote letters to Hugh Lofting about the doctor.

In recent years, the characterization of Bumpo has been found to be racist, even though the doctor treats Bumpo as an equal and acknowledges his wisdom throughout the voyage. Polynesia the Parrot uses the term "Nigger" in the original printings, surely not intended to be controversial. The term, however, has been deleted in recent prints. Despite this problem with the text, the overall message of kindness toward all prevails as the central philosophy of Hugh Lofting's writings. Lofting believed that a good story should be good for a reader of any age, and *The Voyages of Doctor Dolittle* is just that.

Other books by Hugh Lofting include *The Story of Mrs. Tubbs*, written in 1923, and *Gub Gub's Book: An Encyclopedia of Food*, published in 1932. In 1967, Twentieth Century-Fox made a film about Doctor Dolittle as an adaptation of *The Voyages of Doctor Dolittle*. Other books about the doctor's adventures include *Doctor Dolittle's Post Office* (1923), *Doctor Dolittle's Circus* (1924), *Doctor Dolittle's Zoo* (1925), *Doctor Dolittle's Caravan* (1926), *Doctor Dolittle's Garden* (1927), *Doctor Dolittle in the Moon* (1928), *Doctor Dolittle's Return* (1933), *Doctor Dolittle and the Secret Lake* (1948), *Doctor Dolittle and Green Canary* (1950), and *Doctor Dolittle's Puddleby Adventures* (1952).

Dennise M. Bartelo

WALK A MILE AND GET NOWHERE

Author: Ivan Southall (1921-   )
Type of plot: Psychological realism
Time of plot: The late twentieth century
Locale: Deakin Beach, Australia
Principal themes: Coming-of-age and emotions
First published: 1970; published simultaneously in the United Kingdom under the title *Bread and Honey*
Recommended ages: 10-13

Michael Cameron, age thirteen, wonders why he should not be naked in his yard, why the neighbor lady complained, and why Anzak Day is important. A girl named Margaret helps answer all three questions.

> *Principal characters:*
> MICHAEL CAMERON (MICK), a thirteen-year-old Australian boy who frets at what he considers meaningless conventions
> DAD (DR. G. D. CAMERON), a completely rational scientist with no sense of poetry or religion
> GRANDMA, who lives with Michael and his father (her son); she is emotional, religious, and inclined to superstition
> JILLIAN FARLOW, the eleven-year-old neighbor girl who likes Michael
> RAY FARLOW, Jillian's brother
> MR. FARLOW, Jillian and Ray's father; he is a good citizen, a war hero who marches in the Anzak Day parade
> MRS. FARLOW, Jillian and Ray's mother, a former Red Cross nurse in war; she does not like Michael
> BRUCE (BULLY BOY) MACBAREN, a big fifteen-year-old who likes to harass and occasionally punch Michael
> WARREN (FLACKIE) FLACK, Bully Boy's sidekick; he is smaller, unpopular, not too smart, and feels important around Bully Boy
> MARGARET HAMWORTH, a little girl who tags along after Michael

The Story

Thirteen-year-old Michael Cameron wakes up thinking he has missed the school bus. He lives with his grandmother and father, who is on a business trip. Then he remembers that it is Anzak Day (Australian War Memorial Day), a holiday. Standing nude and looking out at the rain, Mick wants to run out and roll in the grass, but when he did it before, Mrs. Farlow complained because Jillian saw him through a hole in the fence. His father is a scientist who has no interest in religion or poetry;

Gran takes an interest in nothing but religion and poetry. They both agree that he need not worry about running out once that way, but that it would not be good to do it again. Mick runs out naked and rolls on the wet lawn anyway. Coming in, he gets dressed and thinks he may be crazy and wonders about Anzak Day, which he does not understand.

The Farlow family gets ready for the parade. Mrs. Farlow wears her Red Cross uniform. She does not like Mick. Mick fixes breakfast, remembering his mother doing it. He thinks of his father, a defense adviser who hates war and thinks Anzak Day foolish. Grandma loves Anzak Day and all living things except poisonous mice. Things are never simple.

While Grandma sleeps, Michael walks to the parade and to amuse himself plays God by crushing some snails and not others. As with soldiers in battle, their life is a matter of chance. He walks down 198 steps to Deakin Beach. His mother fell from the eleventh step and was killed. Grandma said she went to heaven, but Dad doubted there was a heaven. Running into the road, Mick nearly gets hit by the Farlow's car. They give him a ride, but Mrs. Farlow's perfume makes him sneeze. She says that he is spreading germs and they put him out at the War Memorial.

Bully Boy MacBaren harasses Michael to tears. A little girl named Margaret comes up, babbles about her magic ring, and tags along. Ray watches his father lead the parade and remembers how his father shot thirteen men with a machine gun during the war "because he didn't like bullies."

Margaret chatters about being kidnapped, turns into a mouse, and pretends to escape. Mick starts home and she follows for a while, but then walks right into the sea. Mick swims after her, yelling at her to stop. Suddenly his hair is grabbed and she "rescues" him; he is annoyed. When she takes off her outer clothes, he is shocked and tells her to get dressed. She urges him to undress. Instead, he lectures her as his father did him. Carrying her wet clothes, she disappears ahead, falls on a reef, and cuts her head.

He finds her apparently dead. Frightened, he wonders what to do, and then she revives. They see Bully Boy, Flackie, and Ray. Mick is afraid that Margaret might say he hurt her. The boys taunt them, so Mick takes her and they swim close together. Feeling fiercely protective, he orders her to put on her clothes. Her dress tangles in her hair and he helps her. The boys watch and yell "take it off." After the dress gets untangled they run off, pursued by the boys. Margaret gets a stitch and falls. Mick feels that he has failed her, just as soldiers shot in war have failed in a sense. He fights Flackie, Ray runs off, and Margaret leaves with Bully Boy. Ray follows Mick admiringly and invites him to his house. "Maybe later," Mick responds, and goes home to Grandma, who is sad about missing the parade. Mick says he will put on his suit and that they will go lay a wreath at the War Memorial.

Themes and Meanings

Michael Cameron, the thirteen-year-old protagonist of *Walk a Mile and Get Nowhere*, matures considerably during Anzak Day (Australian War Memorial Day).

The larger theme concerns the relationship between rational or intellectual thought symbolized by his father and the intuitive, imaginative, and emotional side of human nature, represented by the grandmother. The two disagree frequently, but concerning Mick's nudity in the yard they agree completely.

This theme expands from the abstract into the particulars of Mick's life. The story chronicles the gaining of awareness and responsibility as the characters make the transitions that allow them to mature.

At the beginning of the day, Mick is not aware of the sexually provocative power of the nude human body, nor of the personal or social problems that might result from this provocation. Through his contact with an even younger, more innocent child of the opposite sex, Margaret, he experiences a revelation of the possible dangers of this behavior which his father was not able to impart through rational, intellectual explanation.

Margaret is a delightfully annoying, imaginative child with a tenuous contact with reality; she is the catalyst for Mick's insight and maturation. Through his fondness and protectiveness toward her free-floating, creative spirit and the individual person that she is, he is emboldened to be much more courageous. He even risks his personal safety by fighting a larger boy in her defense. In doing this, Mick is led, once again, to an emotional or gut-level knowledge of how millions of men might become aroused by protectiveness and possessiveness toward their homeland and the people they love to go to war and take the risk of "getting their heads blown off," as his father says. That the meaning of Anzak Day has become clearer to Mick is beautifully symbolized at the end by his offer to put on his best suit and take his grandmother to lay a wreath on the War Memorial.

Context

Ivan Southall is Australia's best-known and most highly awarded writer of children's literature. He received the Australian Children's Book of the Year Award for four of his books *Ash Road* (1966), *To the Wild Sky* (1971), *Bread and Honey* (published in the United States as *Walk a Mile and Get Nowhere*, 1970), and *Fly West* (1976). He also received the American Library Association award for Notable Book for *Walk a Mile and Get Nowhere* in 1970.

The subject of Anzak Day (the Australian War Memorial Day) in *Walk a Mile and Get Nowhere* has deep personal meaning for Southall, who received the Distinguished Flying Cross as a Royal Australian Air Force pilot during World War II.

Danger and stress are common features of his work, and he is noted for novels portraying groups of children facing disastrous situations, as in *Hills End* (1962), *Ash Road* (1965), and *To the Wild Sky* (1967), which require of them great courage and intelligence even to survive. Geoffrey Fox remarks that Southall "offers his readers a criticism of life which is often excruciating . . . in its insistence upon the pain, disillusionment and embarrassed failures which are integral to adolescence. . . . He writes of loss and consequent grief; the loss of parents, the loss of home, self-awareness. . . ." In a statement that applies to many of Southall's books, A

Times Literary Supplement review of *To the Wild Sky* remarks that it "is a book in which children will recognize themselves, but one in which adults may find it disconcerting to recognize their children."

Southall has also been accused of concocting "contrived," incredible plots, long on lyricism, short on clarity and "riddled with defects," but it is generally agreed that he tells a gripping, suspenseful tale. One otherwise critical reviewer finally notes that each of his books carefully explores some new situation.

The themes of loss and struggle have roots in Southall's own life. He says, "As a lad, the death of my father cut my education short, and professionally, for good or bad, I am self-trained," and this certainly seems evident in the recurrent theme in Southall's books, "that we survive not through external circumstances but because of whatever qualities we can dredge out of ourselves." *Walk a Mile and Get Nowhere* bears this message of the importance of strength of personal character.

Kay Haugaard

WALK LIKE A MORTAL

Author: Dan Wickenden (1913-   )
Type of plot: Domestic realism
Time of plot: The late 1920's
Locale: New York
Principal themes: Family and coming-of-age
First published: 1940
Recommended ages: 15-18

Gabriel Mackenzie, a popular high school senior in a small town in New York in the late 1920's, experiences extreme tensions simultaneously growing up and accepting his parents' divorce subsequent to his mother's affair with an artist.

Principal characters:

> GABRIEL (GABE) MACKENZIE, a highly popular high school senior, the main character of the novel
> JAMES MACKENZIE, Gabriel's father, an underwear salesman who has trouble communicating with his son, whom he loves dearly
> MARGARET SPEARE MACKENZIE, Gabriel's mother; mentally a teenager herself, she has an irresponsible affair with an artist and ends her twenty-year marriage to James
> CHARLIE COBDEN, an artist and Margaret's companion in adultery
> JULIA MACKENZIE SMITH, Gabriel's elder sister who is married and pregnant, living away from home
> HENRY and MAY MACKENZIE, James Mackenzie's brother and sister-in-law
> LUCY MACKENZIE, Gabriel's seventy-three-year-old paternal grandmother
> FRANCIS and NEIL MACKENZIE, Gabriel's cousins, the sons of Henry and May Mackenzie
> LOUISE CARPENTER, Gabriel's girlfriend
> CHRIS STEVENSON, Gabriel's best friend
> VERITY RICHARDSON, neighbor to the Mackenzie family

The Story

Set in the American 1920's, *Walk like a Mortal* is one of the earliest novels to deal with the effects of divorce upon the child. Even as such, Gabriel Mackenzie, who has his eighteenth birthday during these events, is nearly an adult and so the implications for him are ostensibly lessened. The narrative covers the time from the beginning of summer after Gabriel's junior year in high school until his graduation from high school some fifteen months later.

Gabriel Mackenzie is not characterized as a typical, normal teenager. Rather, he is the most popular boy at school, president of the general organization (today, this would be called the student council), a champion tennis player, and a winning orator. He is strong, handsome, responsible, level-headed, and well-liked by all. What should be the best year of his life, then, turns into a psychological cobweb when his mother loses interest in her marriage to his father. At the beginning of the book, Gabriel and his mother are spending their usual summer at a lake in upstate New York, where they are having a customarily good vacation, but are somewhat bored. Margaret Mackenzie, Gabriel's mother, happens to meet Charlie Cobden, an old friend, while shopping at the supermarket. Immediately, they begin to spend time with each other, and, when James Mackenzie, Gabriel's father, comes to the lake near the end of the summer, Margaret is with Charlie and does not even bother to meet James at the train station. This first section of the book ("At the Lake") ends with the realization by all the main characters that the marriage is over; the cottage at the lake will be sold, and Gabriel has had the last summer of his childhood.

The middle section of the work is entitled "At Home." "Home," here, means two things: school and not-home. Gabriel's school life proceeds in a predictably successful way, despite the troubled relationships he has with his parents. When it exists at all, his home life does not thrive well; after taking a job, his mother is absent most of the time, and, when present, unable to talk to Gabriel in any meaningful way. The same unfortunate circumstances are true of his father. Gabriel's life proceeds as well as can be expected: He dates, plays tennis, and attends football games with friends. Charlie Cobden, last seen at the lake departing for New Mexico, appears to visit Margaret. Gabriel finds his father drunk on their doorstep, unable to enter the apartment to confront Charlie and Margaret, who leaves home.

Gabriel's father, given his wife's absence, determines that he and Gabe will move into his brother Henry's house, which provides the setting for the rest of the novel, "At Uncle Henry's." Gabriel does not want to move there, but once he is relocated all goes well: He adjusts quickly and even begins to like the change. He feels guilty and overburdened, though, when a letter from his mother invites him to visit her on his eighteenth birthday. He decides at the last minute to do so, but he is out of place with his mother's friends and leaves his party abruptly and rudely. In school, he wins an oratorical contest and is otherwise occupied with choosing a college. His mother disappears for a few weeks and, upon returning, wants to start over again with her husband and son. They delay their answer, during which time she changes her mind about staying. The novel is concluded when Gabriel turns down his mother's invitation to go to Europe with her for a year, rather than to go to college. It is clear, though, that Gabriel's rejection of his mother's proposition represents more than his not accepting an invitation. It is also a permanent separation from her, and probably from his father, as he enters the adult world in a state of emotional independence from them.

Themes and Meanings

Walk like a Mortal is primarily concerned with depicting the impact of divorce upon a young man who otherwise is and has everything. Gabriel Mackenzie, like all offspring in such circumstances, muddles his way through life unable to understand even though he can functionally cope. He is never overwrought with trauma, yet the psychological pain, slow and relentless, defines his existence as a mild but incurable ache.

Even so, the divorce itself is of less importance than the fact that Gabriel is growing up. These two matters are basically inseparable; yet it is the divorce that must be overcome and left behind if the young man is to have success as an adult. The main theme, then, is that to grow up—to cross the line from childhood to adulthood— one must leave behind the immortal feelings, passions, ideals, and experiences of youth to assume the problems, troubles, and realities of mortality: Young people run, adults walk.

The author does an excellent job of showing human nature to be a mixture of good and evil. None of the characters reveals himself to be unrealistically entrapped in either extreme. Gabriel's father, as victim of an adulterous wife, is to be admired for the way he accepts the situation and handles it; yet he is culpable for being too emotionally immobile. Similarly, his mother is a likely candidate for the role of chief villain; yet she is undeserving of such characterization despite her immaturity and irresponsibility. Gabriel, too, must become such a person by learning to walk like a mortal. Gabriel learns that he cannot and should not define his parents' relationship either to each other or to himself. Gabriel is too clean and wholesome throughout the novel because the institutions of family and education have acted to protect him, thus far, from any truly negative events. Such wholesomeness, however, is artificial and childish; hence, it cannot survive any more than Gabriel's innocence or his parents' marriage.

Context

Walk like a Mortal must be read with some understanding of the time of the action. In the late 1920's, Prohibition was the law in the United States, running boards and crankshafts were features on automobiles, people traveled by train, smoking cigarettes was more rampant than in later years, the United States was drug-free though not alcohol-free, and talking films were becoming available and popular. It was a world in which divorce, for the most part, did not happen; it particularly did not happen as a result of infidelity on the part of the wife-mother.

Part of the author's intention is to desanctify some of the underlying premises holding the society together in its artificial wholesomeness. Thus Lucy Mackenzie, Gabriel's grandmother, calls his mother a "slut." Gabriel himself coughs when socially entrapped into smoking a cigarette; on one occasion, he swears by saying "damn." His girlfriend, though, can be scared away from him by a singular kiss given too forcefully. These and other such events function to neutralize the impossible, feigned sanitation that so many pretended was real and operative in society. Operative it was, but hypocritically so.

Despite the social milieu, Gabriel controls his own destiny in such a way as to become a survivor of both divorce and childhood, not victims of these two circumstances. To do so, he must effectually reject, not his mother or her love, but her control over and influence upon his own life and being. Such is the case, finally, for all children.

Carl Singleton

WALK THE WORLD'S RIM

Author: Betty Baker (1928-1987)
Type of plot: Historical fiction
Time of plot: The second quarter of the sixteenth century
Locale: New Spain (now Texas, New Mexico, Arizona, and Mexico)
Principal themes: Coming-of-age, death, friendship, race and ethnicity, and travel
First published: 1965; illustrated
Recommended ages: 10-13

Chakoh, a fourteen-year-old Avavare Indian, learns from Esteban the true meanings of honor, courage, and loyalty and that a person can be a slave without being owned.

Principal characters:
ESTEBAN, a loyal, courageous, honorable African slave
CHAKOH, a fourteen-year-old Avavare Indian who goes to Mexico to learn how to help his people
ÁLVAR NÚÑEZ CABEZA DE VACA, a Spaniard and the highest-ranking member of the four survivors of Pánfilo de Narváez's Florida expedition of 1527
ANDRÉS DORANTES, one of the Spanish survivors, who is the owner of Esteban
ALONSO DEL CASTILLO MALDONADO, another Spanish survivor, often weak and ill
FRAY MARCOS DE NIZA, a high-ranking churchman in Mexico (now Mexico City)

The Story

Walk the World's Rim is historical fiction based in part on fact. The three Spaniards Álvar Núñez Cabeza de Vaca, Alonso del Castillo Maldonado, and Andrés Dorantes, along with Dorantes' African slave Esteban, are the only survivors of Pánfilo de Narvaez's ill-fated expedition of 1527 to Florida. They arrive in the village of the Avavare Indians in what is now Texas in 1534 and spend the winter. Fourteen-year-old Chakoh, the headman's son, learns to admire and respect Esteban. Chakoh and his people abhor slaves, however, believing that all slaves are shameless cowards without honor. Chakoh does not know that Esteban is a slave even though Esteban tries to tell him that he is. Realizing how Chakoh feels about slaves, and because he likes Chakoh, Esteban does not attempt to tell him again.

Because they want to get to Mexico and are afraid of the coastal Indians, the survivors plan to travel northwestward through what is now New Mexico and Arizona before turning south. Chakoh goes with the men so that he perhaps can learn from the Spaniards and return to his people to make life better for them. The journey to Mexico is long and difficult, and the five travelers encounter trouble in some camps and villages. Esteban always smooths their way, resolves the difficulties, learns the languages of the various tribes, and leads the group to Mexico. From the Pima Indians, the men hear about the fabled city of Cíbola, and the three Spaniards hope that they will be able to return with an expedition to find the city.

Mexico brings disappointment to all. When the Spaniards tell the viceroy about Cíbola, he does not let them return. Dorantes does not give Esteban his freedom as he had promised but rents him to the viceroy to work in his stables. Under the care of churchmen, Chakoh learns the Spaniards' religion and wears European clothing, but he does not realize that he is becoming a slave to the easy life, good food, and warm bed of the abbey. Eventually, the viceroy sends a small expedition to search for Cíbola under Fray Marcos de Niza with Chakoh and Esteban as guides. Learning that Esteban is a slave, Chakoh no longer respects him. Unkind words pass between them; finally, Chakoh sees that Esteban is not like slaves he has known but is rather a man of great trust, honor, courage, and loyalty.

Esteban arrives at Cíbola ahead of Fray Marcos, and the Cíbolans attack him and the Indians who have come with him. Esteban dies, and Chakoh is wounded and returns to Mexico with Fray Marcos in a fevered, delirious state. When he gets better, he decides to go back to his people. As he leaves Mexico, Chakoh burns Esteban's most cherished possession in the center of the plaza to free his spirit so that it can return to Africa, the land of Esteban's people.

Themes and Meanings

Walk the World's Rim has several central concerns, but the chief one is that social rank or standing—slave, peasant, aristocrat, or king—does not reveal what people truly are. What is important is how people behave toward other human beings, how they demonstrate honor, courage, loyalty, friendship, and other virtues. Chakoh and his people passionately abhor slaves. To them, all slaves have been taken in war; therefore, they are cowards with no virtuous traits whatsoever. Slaves are merely humans to be scorned and ridiculed.

When Chakoh learns in Mexico that Esteban is a slave, he feels that Esteban has somehow betrayed him. He cannot see that knowledge of Esteban's being a slave blinds him to Esteban's many virtues. Esteban has been more than loyal to his friends and to his unkind and unappreciative master, Dorantes. When a group of Indians are ready to attack Chakoh because they think he has poisoned their tea, Esteban saves him. Time and again, Esteban demonstrates his honor, courage, and friendship. Even when he has a chance to abandon Fray Marcos, he goes on to Cíbola, where he dies because he has faithfully and honorably kept his word.

Another central concern of *Walk the World's Rim* is that a person can be a slave without being enslaved by another. A person can be a slave to anything: work, play, creature comforts. In Mexico, Chakoh becomes a slave to the good life that the churchmen offer him. Esteban's pointing out to Chakoh his entrapment makes Chakoh realize that he is a slave to the good life by his own choice, while Esteban became a slave to keep his brothers and sisters from starving. Chakoh leaves Mexico to return to his people wiser and more mature for having known Esteban.

Context

Esteban was a real person and was relatively unknown until Betty Baker wrote *Walk the World's Rim*; he is one of the unsung heroes in the history of the New World. Without him, the Spaniards with whom he traveled could hardly have survived their ten-year ordeal among sometimes hostile Indians, some of whom kept them prisoners because they seemed to be able to heal successfully many of their sick. Because of Esteban, the authorities in New and Old Spain learned the outcome of the expedition to Florida and discovered more about the unexplored parts of the New World through which Esteban and the Spaniards passed.

Walk the World's Rim not only reveals the heroic virtues of a historical person, but also was one of the first novels for young readers to show the injustice and cruelty of the conquering Europeans. The Cíbolans attack Esteban and his companions because they are afraid the Spaniards are coming to enslave and exploit them as they had the Aztecs and the Incas; the killing done by them is an act of desperation to save themselves from slavery and to preserve their way of life. With the exception of a few earlier historical novels, such as Carol Ryrie Brink's *Caddie Woodlawn* (1935) and Scott O'Dell's *Island of the Blue Dolphins* (1960), Baker's *Walk the World's Rim* shows customs and beliefs of Native Americans in a new light, demonstrating that they were not totally barbaric savages, as fiction for young readers and adults have usually portrayed them. Being among the first books to tell the Indians' side of the story of the Europeans' conquest makes *Walk the World's Rim* a landmark book in historical fiction for young readers.

Malcolm Usrey

THE WAR OF THE WORLDS

Author: H. G. Wells (1866-1946)
Type of plot: Science fiction
Time of plot: The early twentieth century
Locale: London, England, and surrounding counties
Principal themes: War, science, and emotions
First published: 1897, serial; 1898, book
Recommended ages: 13-15

Seeking an alternative habitat to their dying planet, Martians invade Earth. Military efforts to repel the technologically superior aliens fail, and London and the surrounding countryside are ravaged. Eventually, the Martians are destroyed by bacteria, and human survivors return to rebuild.

Principal characters:
THE NARRATOR, an unnamed philosophical writer who observed
    the course of the Martian invasion at close quarters
HIS BROTHER, a practical young man living in London when the
    Martians reached it
THE CURATE, a weak, hysterical man and temporarily the
    narrator's unwelcome companion
THE ARTILLERYMAN, an uneducated and ineffectual dreamer whose
    survival plans temporarily inspire the narrator

The Story

The plot of *The War of the Worlds* is set in motion when a cylinder containing Martians lands near the narrator's home in a county not far from London. The first response by scientific and political authorities and by local inhabitants is benign curiosity, but when a delegation attempting to communicate with the aliens is destroyed, panic ensues. Military efforts against the first Martian cylinder and against a second that lands the following day result in mass destruction of the area. Surviving inhabitants—the narrator's wife among them—flee. The narrator, however, remains.

Ten cylinders fall in quick succession, and the Martians construct enormous war machines with which they ravage the countryside, using heat rays and poison gas. Within days, the counties southwest of London are smoldering graveyards. The Martians are technologically far superior to humans, and earthly weapons cannot stop them.

The reactions of refugees range from senseless looting, to brutal self-interest, to (less frequently) compassion for other victims. People die in stampedes and fight for places on wagons and for food. Through a series of accidents and deliberations, the narrator falls well behind the general exodus. He meets a curate, with whom he becomes trapped in a house partly buried by the impact of the fifth cylinder. Immediate proximity to the Martians prevents escape, and for several days, the two humans observe technological wonders, the peculiarities of the invaders' physical forms, and their efficient but gruesome means of nourishment—direct self-injection of blood taken from living humans.

The curate proves hysterical and selfish, and he is unable to glean any hope from his religion. His lack of self-control in pragmatic matters such as food rationing and concealment results in conflicts with the narrator. Eventually, a disagreement comes to blows, which leave the curate unconscious and lead a Martian to investigate the disturbance. The narrator narrowly escapes, while the curate is hauled away as food.

Meanwhile, the narrator's younger brother observes similar destruction and panic in London. Escaping by ship with two women he has befriended, he observes a warship destroy a Martian. Retaliation, however, is swift, and the warship is destroyed along with numerous passenger boats. London, too, lies in ruins.

Once again on the move, the narrator makes for the capital, scavenging for food along the way. He encounters an artilleryman with whom he had briefly traveled after the first vain offensive against the Martians. The artilleryman outlines his vision of an organized resistance force living in the sewers and observing the invaders until humans acquire the scientific knowledge to defeat them. In his exhausted and depressed state, the narrator finds hope in these plans and joins in. Shortly, however, he realizes that his companion's vision is not supported by action, and he leaves this "strange undisciplined dreamer of great things to his drink and his gluttony." He strikes out for London.

The ruined capital is occupied by Martians. After a night, the narrator despairs and deliberately seeks his own destruction. He finds, however, that the Martians are dead, their bodies ravaged by dogs and birds. They have succumbed to terrestrial bacteria to which they had no resistance. Refugees, aided by foreign nations, return home to rebuild. In time, humankind learns much from the Martian invasion, both in scientific development and in understanding their own moral responsibilities to one another.

Themes and Meanings

In his account of the Martian invasion, the narrator of *The War of the Worlds* frequently speculates on the scientific pursuits of the late nineteenth century. Charles Darwin's evolutionary theories are the primary focus, as H. G. Wells presents the Martians as a species evolved into essentially a huge brain, devoid of emotional or sensual reactions. The implications for his time, one gripped by a passion for scientific advance, are clear. Also Darwinian are the comparisons of humanity to animals of lower orders when viewed next to the Martians, as well as the primal survival instincts in both races. The Martians' destruction by earthly bacteria absent from the planet on which they had evolved highlights the concept of a species' adaptation to their particular environment. Wells also presents a variety of technological visions, including space travel, flying machines, and heat rays, and includes a number of observations on various species of animals and insects on earth.

All the scientific data in *The War of the Worlds*, however, ultimately is brought to bear on human society and moral behavior. Repeatedly comparing the Martians' coldhearted extermination of humankind and occupation of English territory to the conquest and subsequent treatment of less technologically developed peoples by Europeans, Wells implies the inhumanity of such colonization practices. Furthermore, he examines how fear and the survival instinct, those most primitive of human emotions, lead to the destruction of oneself and others through panic and lack of forethought. Neither the pure intellect of the Martians nor the animalistic instinct of some refugees is attractive or successful. Only those characters, notably the narrator and his brother, who temper fear with reason and the survival instinct with compassion not only survive but also learn from the Martian invasion.

That Wells's moral and philosophical messages concerned him most is evident in the way in which *The War of the Worlds* is related. The narrator is a philosophical writer who has composed both moral and anthropological treatises, and he freely comments on the Martians' treatment of humans and on humans' treatment of one another. Even the lack of proper names for the story's characters emphasizes the basic equality of people. The narrator concludes that only when prejudices are dropped, as when nations band together to help rebuild England, is social progress possible.

Context

Although in his later years Wells turned to writing documentary and historical material, he is best remembered as the first writer of true science fiction. *The War of the Worlds* lies in the middle of his canon—between *The Time Machine* (1895), *The Island of Dr. Moreau* (1896), and *The Invisible Man* (1897), on the one hand, and *The First Men in the Moon* (1901) and *The War in the Air* (1908), on the other.

Wells's fascination with technology and evolution is evident in all of his novels, and his descriptions are filled with scientific details and hypotheses. His enduring interest, however, appears to have been with the effect of scientific progress on humankind itself. In *The Time Machine*, he explores the evolutionary possibilities of humans operating within a caste system in which one class is given completely to pleasure and the other to perpetual labor. Both, of course, are unattractive failures. In *The Island of Dr. Moreau*, genetic experimentation results in a race of grotesque monsters who ultimately destroy their maker. It is in *The War of the Worlds*, the first story ever to posit extraterrestrial life, that Wells arrives at the conclusion that pure intellect (and, by implication, pure scientific pursuit) and pure emotion (resulting in the indulgence of animal appetites or destructive fear and jealousy) are equally dangerous. Humankind, it seems, must maintain a balance between the two in order to survive as a species and to live in harmony. Ultimately, Wells's work stands as a criticism of inhumane colonization practices and of the racial and national prejudices of his time.

Although certain technical details presented in *The War of the Worlds* are now dated, general questions (such as those of space travel, intelligent extraterrestrial life, and germ warfare) have become even more pertinent. Wells's book thus remains popular with science fiction enthusiasts of all ages and particularly so with young adults, who are exploring scientific facts and theories for the first time both in and outside the classroom. More important for the younger reader, however, are the novel's underlying themes addressing human nature and moral and social responsibilities. In the early teens, these issues arise as major ones for the first time, and one's depth of thought about them at that age in large part contributes to the convictions held for the remainder of one's life.

Gwendolyn Morgan

THE WARDEN'S NIECE

Author: Gillian Avery (1926-   )
Type of plot: Historical fiction
Time of plot: Spring and summer, 1875
Locale: Oxford, England
Principal themes: Education and gender roles
First published: 1957
Recommended ages: 10-13

When Maria, a timid orphan, surprises herself by running away from a girls' boarding school to her uncle's care at Oxford, she learns that education can bring satisfaction and embarrassment as she discovers the identity of a boy in a seventeenth century drawing.

Principal characters:
> MARIA HENNIKER-HADDEN, an eleven-year-old orphan who daydreams about becoming a Professor of Greek at Oxford University
> THE REVEREND HENRY HENNIKER-HADDEN, Warden of Canterbury College, Oxford, her great-uncle, an unworldly scholar
> MRS. CLOMPER, the Warden's housekeeper and guardian of respectability
> THOMAS SMITH, thirteen, the oldest son of the Wykeham Professor of Ancient History, aloof and superior
> JOSHUA SMITH, eleven, the considerate one
> JAMES SMITH, eight, a redheaded pest and mischief-maker
> THE REVEREND FRANCIS COPPLESTONE, a substitute tutor for the Smiths and Maria

The Story

In the beginning of *The Warden's Niece*, Maria, whose parents died when she was too young to remember them, is singled out by her teacher as the most ignorant and untidy girl in the class. To escape the humiliation of wearing the label "slut" for the rest of the week, Maria leaves school. The train to Bath—where her great-aunt lives—has left, so she goes to Oxford, where her great-uncle is the warden of Canterbury College.

This "escape" sets a pattern that is repeated throughout the book: Maria, a Victorian girl whose life has been carefully supervised by elderly relatives, does not seek or even desire adventure. The combination of her fear of embarrassment, her desire for meaningful knowledge, and coincidence leads her into adventurous actions. She hopes that her great-uncle will help her get to Aunt Lucia's. At the end of the first chapter, however, her great-aunt has died; her great-uncle believes that she can learn more under a tutor at Oxford than in a school for young ladies.

The house next to the warden's lodgings is occupied by Professor Smith, whose three sons—Thomas, Joshua, and James—are being taught at home in preparation for Rugby School. Maria is at first frightened of the three boys, but she gradually becomes accustomed to them. Thomas seems knowing and superior and James is the quintessential little brother, always greedy for attention and sweets. Joshua, Maria's age, is the most like her in temperament; he thinks of consequences while the others plunge ahead.

On their own, the Smith boys pursue minor adventures, but coincidence brings Mr. Copplestone to replace their regular tutor. Mr. Copplestone is tall, eccentric, and agreeably disorganized in his teaching methods. On a river excursion to Jerusalem House, Maria's interest is aroused by a drawing entitled *An Unknown Boy*. A further, unauthorized visit with Thomas uncovers an inscription dated 1654 on a stone in the garden. In trouble, Maria decides to impress her great-uncle with what James calls "original research," to find out whether the boy in the picture carved the inscription. Her research involves more embarrassments: She gets into the Bodleian Library only after Mrs. Clomper has fainted on the stairs, Mr. Copplestone takes her back to Jerusalem House outside visiting hours, and she has to return a stolen letter to the scholar who owns it. She does learn, however, that the boy, Stephen Fitzackerley, carved the inscription as he escaped from Cromwell's soldiers.

One more coincidence completes Maria's research. On holiday with her great-uncle in Kent, she discovers Stephen Fitzackerley's grave. Maria is able to explain to Uncle Hadden who the boy was and how he came there, and he offers her the chance to explain it to the Kentish Historical Association. Still not eager for physical adventure, Maria is learning to appreciate the scholar's adventures of the mind.

Themes and Meanings

Throughout *The Warden's Niece*, education—especially education for women— is a primary concern. Maria's experiences introduce the reader to some of the possibilities for a Victorian child, from Miss Simpson's school, where grammar, arithmetic, needlework, geography, and history are taught with an emphasis on neatness and conformity, to the near-anarchy of Mr. Copplestone's tutorials that combine Greek and Latin with demonstrations of bullfighting. It is made clear that while the ideal is somewhere between the two extremes, an educational method that encourages curiosity and independent thought is preferable to one that stifles both. The conflict within the Victorian establishment concerning the education of women is conveyed through the adult characters: Uncle Hadden and Professor Smith actively encourage women as students; the librarian at the Bodleian is decidedly opposed to the idea.

The book also reflects a love of Oxford, university and town. Maria arrives in a drizzling rain and is frightened by unfamiliar people and half-remembered buildings but is reassured by the sound of bells. Other features of the Oxford setting—the river, the busts on Broad Street, Duke Humphrey's library, even the oath that must be read aloud and signed before one is allowed to read in the Bodleian—provide a sense of tradition.

This sense of tradition and a fascination with history are another central concern of *The Warden's Niece*. Maria becomes aware of what a twentieth century child can also observe, that England is a country of tombstones, old houses, inscriptions, and old pictures that are often mysterious. Further, her difficulty in finding out about the life of a boy who died at the age of fourteen reminds the reader that children are not always included in written histories. The book conveys that the pleasures of scholarship—of gaining information not only from libraries but also from the environment—are available to those with even fairly ordinary abilities.

Context

The Warden's Niece is Gillian Avery's first novel for children. Maria and the Smith boys appear again in other books, including *The Elephant War* (1960), which emphasizes more strongly the restraints placed on girls when the children try to involve themselves in a cause. In *The Italian Spring* (1964), Maria's background makes it almost impossible for her to enjoy the extravagant landscape and art of Italy. In the two Maria books, her orphan status prevents a detailed portrayal of family relationships, but family expectations are central to *The Greatest Gresham* (1962) and to *A Likely Lad* (1971), the latter of which has a boy as its central character. All the novels reflect the knowledge of children in history that informs Avery's *Childhood's Pattern: A Study of the Heroes and Heroines of Children's Fiction, 1770-1950* (1975) and other contributions to the history of children's literature.

The Warden's Niece could be classified as domestic realism because it makes no reference to historical events of the Victorian era; the critic John Rowe Townsend discusses it as realistic fiction in his *Written for Children* (revised edition, 1983). The novel emphasizes the influence of the past by combining Oxford landmarks with a nineteenth century main character who traces the life of a seventeenth century boy. Many historical novels express nostalgia for the past; *The Warden's Niece* presents a realistic view of the rules and constraints of Victorian society upon middle-class children. At the same time, however, the humorous escapades provoked by James or Mr. Copplestone lighten the serious theme. If young people are uninterested in history, they should nevertheless be attracted to Avery's fiction by the ability of characters such as Maria to progress toward their goals in spite of their fears of embarrassment or failure; once attracted, perhaps those young people will discover that history can be interesting.

Andelys Wood

WATERSHIP DOWN

Author: Richard Adams (1920-   )
Type of plot: Adventure tale
Time of plot: The late twentieth century
Locale: The Downs near Newbury in Berkshire, England
Principal themes: Animals, family, friendship, and nature
First published: 1972; illustrated with maps
Recommended ages: 15-18

When their warren is suddenly destroyed by the development of a housing estate or subdivision, a group of young buck rabbits seek to establish a new home far from humans and their other enemies.

Principal characters:
HAZEL, the leader, or chief rabbit, of the homeless bucks who establish a new warren on Watership Down
FIVER, the brother of Hazel, who possesses second sight
THAYLI, or BIGWIG, the biggest and strongest of the Watership Down rabbits
GENERAL WOUNDWORT, the tyrannical rabbit who rules the warren at Efrafa and seeks to destroy the Watership Down Warren
KEHAAR, a wounded gull whom the rabbits of Watership Down befriend
HYZENTHLAY, a doe from Efrafa, who runs away with nine other does to join the rabbits of Watership Down

The Story

On the simplest level of interpretation, *Watership Down* is an adventure story, and the fact that the majority of the characters are animals only adds to the fascination that captures the reader from the opening line. The anthropomorphic premise of the work is so natural, so skillfully done that the reader instantly identifies with one or more of the principal rabbits and thus is quickly drawn into the story.

In a vision, Fiver sees the destruction of the warren in which he was born. He persuades his brother, Hazel, to convey his apprehensions to their chief rabbit, who rejects the dream as nonsense. The brothers, however, resolve to leave, and they take several friends with them, including Bigwig, a large and belligerent fellow; Blackberry, an intellectual; Dandelion, a master storyteller; and Pipkin, a small and timid rabbit.

After a series of adventures, the refugees are welcomed into a warren where the rabbits are sleek, large, and indolent. Almost too late they discover that Fiver's premonitions about the warren are true. The inhabitants are fed by a man who snares them for their meat and pelts. Saving Bigwig from one of the traps, Hazel and his companions flee toward the Downs and safety. Once on Watership Down, they dig a splendid warren which they call the Honeycomb. They also discover a sea gull with an injured wing whom they befriend and nurse back to health. Kehaar becomes a valuable member of the community as a scout and airborne warrior.

A warren with no does, or females, is doomed to extinction, and the rabbits decide to try to free some caged rabbits at the nearby Nuthanger Farm and persuade them to join the new warren. Although they succeed in this mission, two does are not enough. Hazel thus sends an embassy to the great warren at Efrafa to secure more does, unaware that it is ruled by a dictator named General Woundwort. His ambassadors are barely able to escape with their lives, but Hazel is undaunted and is determined to secure does from Efrafa through a trick.

Because of his size and bravado, Bigwig easily infiltrates the Owslafa, or Council Police of Efrafa, which keeps the rabbits of that vast warren in complete subjection. Then he meets the doe Hyzenthlay, and together they plan a daring escape with a number of discontented female rabbits. Guided by Kehaar, they rendezvous with Hazel and his companions. When cornered by the general and his crack troops, however, they make good their departure from Efrafa aboard a small boat, which they set adrift on a trout stream not far from the general's warren.

An enraged Woundwort follows the Watership Down rabbits to their warren and lays siege to it. When the invaders from Efrafa breach the outer defenses, Hazel, accompanied by Dandelion and Blackberry, seeks help from an unlikely source. They free the dog at Nuthanger Farm and lure him to the Downs, where he scatters the invaders and attacks Woundwort. The general vanishes, and no trace of him is ever found. The rabbits from Efrafa, who do not flee, however, surrender and eventually are absorbed peacefully into the warren on Watership Down. In time, a new settlement is established halfway between Watership Down and Efrafa by rabbits from both warrens. All three groups prosper, learning to live with one another in peace and harmony. The book ends with the death of Hazel, old and honored by countless generations of rabbits.

Themes and Meanings

Watership Down is a very original recasting of the quest story, a favorite device which has enriched literature since ancient times. Like Aeneas, the hero of Vergil's epic poem, the *Aeneid* (c. 29-19 B.C.), who fled the destruction wrought by the Greeks and their Trojan horse, the rabbits of the doomed Sandleford warren flee the poison gas of the men who would raise their own monument on the ruins of the vanquished, be it Troy or a rabbit warren. As Richard Adams traces the journey of his heroes from their ruined home to the safety of the Berkshire Downs and beyond that refuge to the gates of Efrafa, he draws parallels to other quests, ranging from that of Odysseus to the seizure of the Sabine women and to the journey of the hero of H. G. Wells's *The Time Machine* (1895).

Cast in yet another mode, *Watership Down* may be treated as an allegory. Thus, the trials and triumphs of Hazel and his comrades mirror the timeless struggles between tyranny and freedom, reason and blind emotion, and the individual and the corporate state. Similarly, each rabbit combines in his or her personality many of the virtues and vices that make humans so complex—and interesting. Despite the almost constant tension that permeates the book, *Watership Down* reaffirms the positive evolution of human society, and at its conclusion, right predictably triumphs over might.

Context

Watership Down was Richard Adams' first, and certainly his most popular, novel. That success surely results in part from his descriptions of the area surrounding Newbury, which are gleaned from his own memories. Originally conceived to amuse his two daughters, *Watership Down* was first marketed in England as juvenile fiction, while the first American edition was aimed at a more general reading public. Because of its several levels of interpretation, it has enjoyed a wide audience and has received almost universal praise from critics.

Adams' concern for nature is also evident in his second and third novels. Published in 1974, *Shardik* explores the reasons why and how human beings choose their deities. In this case, it is a giant bear who shares none of the benevolent qualities of Frith, the god invoked so often by the rabbits in *Watership Down*. In his third novel, *The Plague Dogs*, published in 1977, Adams deals with the controversial practice of using animals for scientific experiments. A fourth novel, *The Girl in a Swing*, published in 1980, departs from Adams' usual subject matter and deals with human relationships as well as the supernatural. While his later works have been well received by the critics and the public alike, they have not enjoyed the same attention accorded *Watership Down*.

Watership Down is an unusual work for a number of reasons, not the least being the fact that the characters are real rabbits, not merely animals in human dress. While the themes that bind the novel together are universal ones, the situations are immediate and concern only the rabbits. Life moves in its daily pattern, the seasons change, and the people in the novel are totally oblivious to the drama of life and death that is occurring all around them. The real value of *Watership Down* is that the reader is allowed to view this spectacle not on human terms but on those of the kingdom of Lapine.

Clifton W. Potter, Jr.

WAYAH OF THE REAL PEOPLE

Author: William O. Steele (1917-1979)
Type of plot: Historical fiction
Time of plot: 1752-1753
Locale: Williamsburg, Virginia
Principal themes: Education, and race and ethnicity
First published: 1964; illustrated
Recommended ages: 10-13

Wayah leaves his Cherokee home in the Appalachians to study with Christian whites and other Indians at a Williamsburg, Virginia, school for one year. He learns how to help his people understand the white culture while preserving his own heritage.

Principal characters:
  WAYAH, Cherokee of the Chotas who, at eleven, leaves everything familiar to him to study in Williamsburg
  THE REVEREND THOMAS DAWSON, a white teacher who kindly helps Wayah understand some of the strange customs
  DUNCAN, a wealthy white student who befriends Wayah and takes him to the family plantation for a holiday

The Story

Because the young Wayah, in *Wayah of the Real People*, has learned several English words from a wounded trader recovering in his Chota Cherokee village, he is chosen for a one-year Christian education at Brafferton Hall in Williamsburg, Virginia. On his arrival, he feels very inadequate, but the schoolmaster, the Reverend Thomas Dawson, reassures him. Wayah's impressions when entering Brafferton Hall, the first multiple-story building he has ever seen, include viewing the "series of little wooden shelves, one above the other." He has never seen steps. Then he reaches to touch the tree just outside his room, and when something stops his hand (glass), he is amazed to be able to touch something he cannot see. He has heard of books, and so when he sees one in class he listens for the "talking marks" (letters) but hears nothing. The bell seems like the "voice of a powerful god," but he cannot understand its request. The clothes constrict, and the noisy and uncomfortable shoes hurt his feet.

Soon after his arrival, the college president announces that a valuable garnet is missing from his ring. Wayah has no idea what a garnet is. A week later, when a boy pushes him into a bush, his hand lands on a beautiful red stone. Delighted to have a lucky amulet, he expects it to help him survive the year. He hides it in his trunk, but one day, the Shawnee student and quasi-enemy, William Squirrel, almost catches him looking at it. Wayah rushes outside and hides the stone behind a loose brick. In the late spring, men come to repair the bricks and find the stone. No one confesses to hiding the stone, and not until Wayah sees it does he realize that they blame him. Master Dawson suddenly understands that Wayah thought the stone valuable only to himself.

During the year, two interesting opportunities occur. Duncan befriends Wayah. He takes Wayah to see the town's shops and to his plantation home. The mounds of food surprise Wayah, but he enjoys the games with Duncan's family. He even teaches Duncan's father to shoot his bow and arrow. He only tolerates Duncan's mother's playing on the "black box" with a "huge row of fiercely grinning white teeth" (piano), never adjusting to the music.

The second opportunity is the Emperor of Cherokees' visit to the school. Since this man belongs to the Great Tellico Cherokees, he is a Chota enemy. Master Dawson, equating all Cherokees, enlists the unwilling Wayah to translate. Wayah even attends William Shakespeare's *Othello* with them, riding in a carriage. Unable to understand the performance, Wayah sleeps.

During the Williamsburg year, Wayah learns to read and begins to comprehend number relationships; however, Uncle Two Sticks' arrival at the end of the year relieves him. He knows that he will miss Duncan and Master Dawson, but he longs for his family and his friends.

At home, he defuses an argument between a brave and a trader. The Cherokee pays three skins for an axe and the trader wants four. Wayah listens to the trader and translates that three skins in Virginia is reasonable but that the trader wants an extra skin for traveling to the village. The brave understands and acquiesces. Afterward, Wayah's paternal grandfather, Otonee, once opposed to Wayah's year in Williamsburg, admits that Wayah will help keep peace with the Virginians.

Themes and Meanings

Wayah of the Real People as a *Bildungsroman* adds the twist of a protagonist undergoing maturity in not one, but two, cultures. Wayah's experience at Brafferton introduces him to a world in which he must change his name to Adam Wolf. He believes that men sell scalps in shops rather than collect them as trophies until his friend explains about wigs. To Wayah, people ride in rooms (carriages), wear too many clothes, build unnecessarily large houses, sleep on uncomfortably soft pads, and eat bland food not when hungry but when a bell rings. Wayah endures these customs without adopting them. He reminds himself that he comes from the Real People and must not complain. That he actually likes most of the white people regardless of their culture surprises him.

Steele frames Wayah's Williamsburg experience with a symbol. Otonee, Wayah's paternal grandfather, disapproves of Wayah's journey, believing that Wayah will be like a split tree with neither shoot producing; as half Indian and half white, he will be worth nothing. Otonee has no power in the family because only the mother's side makes the important decisions, but Otonee has preserved the old ways and taught Wayah to hunt and to keep his values. Since he cannot keep Wayah at home, he prays to the river god, Long Human Person, to protect Wayah on his journey.

During his long life, Otonee has seen whites with guns and drink negatively influence the tribe by helping the people forget the values of their past. In the white man's world, however, Wayah has difficulty understanding why Otonee is so hostile when the axe and gun are clearly superior to stones or bows and arrows. Wayah sees a contrast between Otonee's stories and the one in the Bible in which a chief was killed on a piece of wood. Wayah recognizes the nobility of the death but cannot see how this chief could prove his bravery if he did not believe in enemies and go to war.

Yet, after Wayah returns and solves the argument between the Cherokee brave and the trader, Otonee tells Wayah that he has seen a split tree with the two halves healed, each side growing strongly. Wayah proves that he can speak for Indian and white without sacrificing his own beliefs. Wayah's great respect for his grandfather continues when Otonee finally acknowledges the value of understanding even when not accepting the customs of others.

What Wayah really gains from this year-long trial is inner strength, when he comprehends that his magic amulet had nothing to do with his survival. His skills of hunting and stalking have prepared him to draw conclusions from faint footprints or broken twigs in the forest. He reflects that he has always "heard" with his eyes, even though he could not, at first, "hear" the "talking marks" in a book. Thus his grandfather's training proves to be adaptable. By going into the "world," and surviving, even thriving, Wayah returns home mature, ready to help his people.

Context

During William O. Steele's youth and adulthood in Tennessee, stories about the strength of the prerevolutionary pioneers and the historic Cherokees continued to engage his imagination. In many of his thirty-nine books, he presents the viewpoint of the white pioneers, their blood cooling at the startling fierceness of Indian war whoops. *Wayah of the Real People*, however, reveals Steele's ability to take the Indian's point of view, amazed at the white man's magic and uncertain in the white man's world, yet content and competent in his own. Some of Steele's critics have complained that all of his stories show pioneers wanting to kill the Indians; to a pioneer, as Steele reiterated, "the best Indian was a dead Indian." These same critics could not have read *Wayah of the Real People*. In this story as well as in *The Man with the Silver Eyes* (1976), the reader begins to empathize with the Indian and to comprehend the difficulties that Indians would have understanding the motivations of the white man.

Most important, Steele illustrates that the term "Indian" is generic. He emphasizes the battle between the Chotas and the Great Tellicoes for control of the Cherokee tribe. Additionally, Steele chooses to have Indian boys from four different tribes at Brafferton. Their differences reveal that the contemporary name for Indian, Native American, more accurately reveals diversity.

Wayah of the Real People, as the first quality work published for young people presenting the continental Native American point of view, has led the way for insightful interpretations such as Scott O'Dell's *Sing Down the Moon* (1970) and Elizabeth George Speare's *The Sign of the Beaver* (1983). Wayah's appraisals of the white culture help the reader cast a more objective eye on the time—not only to identify excess but also to appreciate achievement.

Lynda G. Adamson

THE WESTING GAME

Author: Ellen Raskin (1928-1984)
Type of plot: Mystery
Time of plot: The late twentieth century
Locale: Westingtown, on the shores of Lake Michigan
Principal themes: Crime and friendship
First published: 1978
Recommended ages: 10-13

Sixteen unlikely heirs puzzle over mysterious clues in the will of millionaire Samuel Westing to discover which of them is Westing's murderer. The first to solve the mystery wins the bulk of Westing's fortune, but the life of each heir is forever changed by playing the Westing game.

Principal characters:

SAMUEL W. WESTING, a reclusive millionaire who directs the investigation of his own death

TURTLE WEXLER, a thirteen-year-old who plays the stock market and terrorizes fellow heirs by kicking shins when she is angry

FLORA BAUMBACH, a lonely old dressmaker selected by Westing as Turtle's partner in the Westing game

ANGELA WEXLER, Turtle's pampered elder sister who is bored with her sheltered life

SYDELLE PULASKI, a hypochondriac middle-aged secretary who becomes Angela's partner

GRACE WINDKLOPPEL WEXLER, Turtle and Angela's mother, who wants to seem more important than she is

JAMES SHIN HOO, a restaurant owner and one-time inventor who is Grace Wexler's partner

SUN LIN HOO, the second wife of James Hoo, isolated by her limited English and homesick for her native China

JAKE WEXLER, Grace's podiatrist husband (and a bookie), who becomes Mrs. Hoo's partner

DOUG HOO, a high school track star pushed to excel by his proud father

THEO THEODORAKIS, a high school senior who works in his family's coffee shop, selected as Doug's partner

CHRIS THEODORAKIS, Theo's wheelchair-bound younger brother with halting speech, who hides his intelligence

DR. DENTON DEERE, a medical intern in plastic surgery engaged to Angela Wexler, made Chris's partner

JUDGE J. J. FORD, daughter of a Westing servant and the first black
    woman elected judge in the state
SANDY McSOUTHERS, a likable old doorman at Westing's Sunset
    Towers apartment house and partner to Judge Ford
BERTHE ERICA CROW, an aging cleaning woman at Sunset Towers
    whose volunteer work at the Good Salvation Soup Kitchen
    helps soothe the guilt in her religious soul
OTIS AMBER, a sixty-two-year-old deliveryman with a mental
    handicap who is Crow's partner

The Story

The Westing game begins when news of Samuel W. Westing's death brings together sixteen carefully selected heirs for the reading of Westing's last will and testa-
ment. A man with a dramatic flair for elaborate games, he presents his unlikely
assortment of heirs with a challenge from beyond the grave. Westing's will pairs the
heirs, providing each team with ten thousand dollars and a few mysterious clues to
the identity of his murderer. The bulk of his multi-million-dollar estate will go to
the one who names the heir responsible for taking Westing's life.

With no two sets of clues alike, the heirs struggle to make sense of their own
closely guarded clues while they conspire to discover others. A blizzard imprisons
them in Westing's Sunset Towers apartment house, increasing the tension as teams
compete to win the fortune. The Westing game players employ a variety of strat-
egies. Turtle talks Flora Baumbach into investing their ten thousand dollars in the
stock market, convinced that Westing will reward a good return on his investment.
Sydelle Pulaski puts her secretarial training to use by taking shorthand notes on the
unfolding events. Judge Ford draws on her legal talents to gather evidence about fellow heirs' past connections to Westing.

Ford and her partner, Sandy McSouthers, discover some startling links between
Westing and his heirs. James Hoo once accused Westing of stealing an invention.
Flora Baumbach made a wedding dress years before for Westing's daughter, another
reluctant bride with a striking resemblance to Angela. Chris and Theo's father was
once in love with Westing's now-dead daughter.

The key to the clues is discovered by another pair of heirs. Sydelle and Angela
ponder their collection of clues, suddenly realizing that the clues spell out most of
the lyrics to "America the Beautiful." They recover from their injuries in time to
join the other heirs as each team is called upon to unravel Westing's puzzle.

In Westing's mansion, events unfold at an alarming rate. Messages from the dead
Westing reject the answers offered by each team and challenge any individual to
name the murderer. Judge Ford suddenly recognizes her old mentor Westing, alive
and well, disguised as Sandy McSouthers. Sydelle and Angela reveal the meaning
hidden in the clues, the missing parts of which spell out the name of Berthe Erica
Crow. Suddenly Sandy drops to the floor with an unseeing stare. Amidst a stunned
silence, Crow names herself the murderer to obtain Westing's prize for her beloved

soup kitchen and for her favorite Angela. Following Crow's arrest, the heirs learn that she was once Westing's wife, that Westing has been masquerading as the door- man, and that Crow thus cannot be held for a murder that never took place.

Meanwhile Turtle slips quietly away to collect the big prize, for only she has deduced Westing's latest disguise. Samuel Westing, born Windy Windkloppel, has become Sandy McSouthers, and sometimes his mysterious agent Barney Northrup. The clues West, South, and North lead Turtle to East—Julian R. Eastman, present chairman of the board of Westing Paper Products. Westing/Eastman becomes Tur- tle's mentor and friend as he grooms her to inherit his industrial empire.

Themes and Meanings

Hardly anyone in *The Westing Game* is exactly who he or she seems to be. No one is the same after playing the Westing game. Turtle grows with Westing's guidance into a successful corporate lawyer. The lovely but rather useless Angela postpones her marriage to Dr. Deere and becomes an orthopedic surgeon. Insecure Mrs. Wex- ler stops trying to appear important and becomes a confident and successful restau- rateur. The unsuccessful restaurateur Shin Hoo turns back to what he loves best, being an inventor.

Maneuvering the heirs like pieces in the chess game that forms a motif throughout the story, Westing throws together his odd assortment of players in unlikely com- binations that invariably complement one another. Turtle blossoms under the loving care of Flora Baumbach, and Flora, having lost one daughter, blooms in her role as Turtle's "Baba." Chris Theodorakis overcomes his physical handicap to become a successful ornithologist with the medical help of Dr. Deere, who switches from plas- tic surgery to neurological medicine, and the financial help of Judge Ford, who by helping Chris repays the debt she owes her own mentor Westing.

While crimes, clues, and solutions abound in Raskin's book, it is in many ways first a novel of relationships and then a mystery. As they are caught up in Westing's game, Raskin's characters change and grow because of their interactions with one another. The lonely find friends. The bored are challenged. The handicapped are freed. Connections are woven: Turtle, who becomes known as T. R., marries Theo, loves her Baba, and worships Westing. Angela and Denton Deere make their belated trip to the altar, and it is their daughter, Alice, who later becomes Turtle's protégée. Mrs. Hoo learns enough English to communicate with those around her. Theo makes it into publication, Doug makes it to the Olympics, the former Josie-Jo Ford makes it to the U.S. Supreme Court, and, at last, Samuel W. Westing, his work accom- plished, makes it to the grave.

Context

Far from the typical whodunit, *The Westing Game* draws the reader into the search for a solution. Described by its author as a "puzzle-mystery," the book piles detail upon detail with such abundance that the reader is constantly evaluating and re- evaluating which is significant and which is not. Clues are revealed in a carefully orchestrated manner that lets the reader piece them together like one of Westing's heirs.

Raskin's story grew, literally, from a puzzle. She began writing it in 1976 by typing out the words to "America the Beautiful" and cutting them apart. In honor of the bicentennial celebration, her characters represent the ethnic melting pot that is the United States: Black, Chinese, German, Greek, Jewish, Polish. A rags-to-riches tribute to U.S. capitalism, the story begins and ends on the Fourth of July.

Raskin began her career as an illustrator and author of picture books for younger children. She is well known for authoring and illustrating *Nothing Ever Happens on My Block* (1966), *Spectacles* (1968), *Who, Said Sue, Said Whoo?* (1973), and nearly a dozen other picture books. While her picture books reflect the same imagination that characterizes *The Westing Game*, it is Raskin's longer books, all of which are mysteries, that overflow with inventiveness. Her first novel, *The Mysterious Disappearance of Leon (I Mean Noel)* (1971), is full of games and puzzles like *The Westing Game. Figg & Phantoms* (1974) and *The Tattooed Potato and Other Clues* (1975) are also filled with outrageous characters, improbable events, and rich wordplay.

It is *The Westing Game*, however, that emerges from Raskin's body of work as the most successful. As proof of the critical acclaim that has greeted this demandingly complex novel for children, the American Library Association in 1979 presented Ellen Raskin the prestigious Newbery Medal for excellence in books for children.

Diane L. Chapman

THE WESTMARK TRILOGY

Author: Lloyd Alexander (1924-   )
Type of plot: Adventure tale
Time of plot: The seventeenth or eighteenth century
Locale: The fictitious country of Westmark
Principal themes: Social issues, war, death, and friendship
First published: Westmark, 1981; *The Kestrel*, 1982; *The Beggar Queen*, 1984; with
    map
Recommended ages: 13-15

The street waif Mickle ascends the throne of Westmark after it is determined she is the missing heiress. To remain on the throne, however, becomes a matter of considerable adventure.

Principal characters:
THEO, a youth of Westmark, who falls in love with Mickle and
    assists her in defending the kingdom
MICKLE, a street urchin, who becomes the Beggar Queen of
    Westmark
COUNT LAS BOMBAS, a good-natured mountebank, who befriends
    Theo and Mickle
CABBARUS, a tyrant, who commits dastardly deeds in his struggles
    to become ruler of Westmark
FLORIAN, a charismatic leader, who controls a band of
    revolutionaries
JUSTIN, a young zealot, who seeks to abolish the monarchy
DR. TORRENS, the court physician, who becomes chief minister
KING CONSTANTINE, the king of Regia, who attacks Westmark

The Story

The Westmark trilogy is an intricate tale of adventure, intrigue, and suspense that swirls throughout the kingdom of Westmark, revealing a motley cast of characters that would do credit to Charles Dickens. It is also a tale of introspection that wrestles with important issues. Westmark, a mythical kingdom, has an impotent king on the throne and a dangerous tyrant named Cabbarus as chief minister. The king's only heir, Princess Augusta, is believed dead, and the king spends much time attempting to contact her through spiritualists. Theo, a printer's apprentice, becomes a fugitive from the law and is befriended by an itinerant showman, Count Las Bombas. Las Bombas makes his living in various guises, all relying on fakery for success. Theo and the count are joined by Mickle, a waif who smokes cigars, curses vehemently, and needs a bath but who is clever and talented. Mickle and Theo develop a close rapport, but he is unhappy about the deviousness of Las Bombas and runs away.

Theo meets Florian and joins his group of revolutionaries. Florian, for reasons of his own, agrees to help Theo rescue Las Bombas and Mickle from the jail at Nier-keeping. Theo is assigned to accompany Justin, one of Florian's lieutenants. During the raid, Theo is unable to kill an officer who is threatening Justin's life, an incident which haunts Theo and Justin throughout their relationship. After the raid, Mickle, Las Bombas, and Theo are brought to the palace by Cabbarus, who has learned of their chicanery. Cabbarus intends to force them to "raise" the missing princess and trick the king into enlarging Cabbarus' power. Once at the palace, Mickle's memory of her childhood returns, and it is determined that she is the missing princess whom Cabbarus had tried to murder. Cabbarus escapes to Regia, a neighboring kingdom.

Mickle is installed in the palace as the future queen, and Theo is sent on a tour of the kingdom to prepare him for his role as consort. Mickle, however, wearies of the long absence from Theo and beguiles Count Bombas into taking her in search of Theo. While she is away from the palace, the king dies, and Mickle becomes Queen Augusta, known to her subjects as the Beggar Queen. The King of Regia, aided by treasonous elements within Westmark, sees this as an advantageous moment to in-vade, and he moves his army within Westmark's boundaries. The army of Westmark is betrayed by its commanding general and retreats in disarray. Florian agrees to aid Mickle on condition there will be changes in the government at the end of the war.

Theo, who has joined Florian's army, is sickened by the slaughter he witnesses but gradually becomes hardened to the war. He takes the name "Kestrel" and becomes known for his vicious raids on the enemy. The war is brought to an honorable con-clusion for both sides when Mickle and the young King Constantine of Regia meet privately and arrange a settlement. Back in the capital city of Marianstat, Mickle di-lutes the powers of the monarchy and installs Florian, Justin, and Theo as her direc-tors.

Not all the subjects of Westmark are pleased with the populist reforms begun by Mickle, and Cabbarus uses the unrest among the courtiers and military to engineer a coup. Mickle eludes arrest as she and Theo go underground to organize forces to defeat Cabbarus. Florian is wounded and must recover before he can rally his fol-lowers, and Justin's hatred for the monarchy and his distrust of Theo lead him to betray his promise to help. It seems the rebellion against Cabbarus will fail when help comes unexpectedly from the citizens of Marianstat, who unite to attack the palace and oust the usurpers. Mickle insists that the people of Westmark have earned the right to rule themselves and abolishes the monarchy. She realizes that she must go into exile if unrest in Westmark is to end. Accompanied by the faithful Las Bom-bas, she and Theo board a ship for a new adventure, a new life.

Themes and Meanings

The Westmark trilogy tells a picaresque tale of dashing, romantic adventure, but it is also a story with moral overtones. Its theme in its simplest form concerns the conflict of good with evil, but the issues involved are complex. They include the struggle to determine what is good and what is evil when the perimeters are not so clearly defined; of the sometimes battle between good and good; and of the moral dilemma of doing evil to ensure good.

To aid the development of the theme, Alexander peoples his trilogy with myriad characters reflective of society: heroes, villains, visionaries, rogues, scholars, and comics. They are rarely one-dimensional stereotypes, the evil Cabbarus being a notable exception, but multifaceted creatures who are marked by ambiguities: Kings who should be noble are weak and ignoble while ordinary peasants act with uncommon valor; a scoundrel who deals in fakery and sham proves to be a trusted and loyal friend; a street waif who washes irregularly is, indeed, a princess; and a hero motivated by high ideals falls miserably short of his goals.

The theme advances primarily through young Theo, an idealist striving to be upright and honorable. Resolutions to dilemmas, however, are not easily reached. The exigencies of war bring Theo to the agonizing discovery that one can do terrible things for noble reasons. Assuming the role of Alma, leader of the revolution against Cabbarus, he dispassionately sacrifices the lives of his followers. So great is his anguish at falling short of his ideals that he is prepared to offer his life as a means of setting things right. Fortunately, author Lloyd Alexander provides healing. Theo remains a worthy hero because of the inner battles he wins. Unlike Justin, whose devotion to an ideal dehumanizes him, Theo accepts the realities of his humanity, with its multiplicity of possibilities for doing right and wrong. When he plunges with Mickle into the well in the Old Juliana and the water closes over his head, he symbolically leaves behind Kestrel and Alma and all that he has been and comes ashore to be something better. As they leave Westmark, he and Mickle have the remainder of the world as their arena for growth and fulfillment.

A secondary theme developed in this trilogy is the ideological argument between rule by monarchy and the right of a people to rule themselves. There is an offering of hope for society as the people of Marianstat ignore arguments of ideologues and move to effect their own fate. Justin would have given them freedom; it is significant that they demanded it for themselves.

Context

The Westmark trilogy is a departure for Alexander from the writing of fantasy which characterizes his previous work. The trilogy, however, has much in common with the Prydain chronicles (1964-1968), which relate the adventures of Taran, who, like Theo, is struggling to be a worthy hero but does not find the path always clearly marked. In the Westmark trilogy, Alexander explores universal questions, and it is this questioning that lends grandeur to his work. As the occupants of Westmark struggle with the issues of power and greed, war and inhumanity, and self-aggrandizement and debasement, the reader must struggle with them also. One must deal with the question of Kestrel, who fights nobly but relishes his acts of vengeance; of Florian, who wants to be one of the common people but clings to his aristocratic lineage because of the adoration it engenders; of Constantine, who believes death suitable punishment for treason—even for an uncle.

Alexander states in his American Book Award Acceptance for *Westmark*, "We must not be intimidated or, worse, intimidate ourselves into telling less than we know. Above all, we cannot be afraid to tell what we do *not* know or have been unable to learn. We owe it to our young people." It is a windfall for the reader that Alexander does his telling so well, with verve, excitement, and suspense. Once having entered the Kingdom of Westmark, one leaves reluctantly.

Mary Jo Clegg

WHAT IT'S ALL ABOUT

Author: Vadim Frolov (1913-   )
Type of plot: Domestic realism
Time of plot: The mid-1960's
Locale: Leningrad
Principal themes: Coming-of-age, love, family, and emotions
First published: Chto k chemu, 1966 (English translation, 1968)
Recommended ages: 13-15

A fourteen-year-old is bewildered by his parents' separation. Unwilling to accept it and hurt by his father's silence, he searches for his mother, but when he finds her, he realizes that she is happier with her friend than she has ever been with his father.

Principal characters:
> ALEXANDER SASHA LARIONOV, a fourteen-year-old high school
> student
> NIKOLAI LARIONOV, his father, a navy man working in a scientific
> research institute
> VERA, his mother, a theater actress
> NYUROCHKA, his three-year-old sister
> YURA LIVANSKY, his uncle
> LYUKA, his aunt
> YURKA PANTYUKHIN and
> OLGA, his high school friends
> DOLINSKY, a friend of his mother

The Story

What It's All About treats an age-old subject: the impact of a divorce upon children and their finding the way to deal with the devastating experience. The family Larionov of Leningrad is going through a crisis: Sasha's mother, an actress, has left home with her colleague Dolinsky, ostensibly on a theater tour. Sasha and his three-year-old sister, Nyurochka, are puzzled by her long absence, but their father is strangely silent about it. A sensitive child, Sasha suspects that something is very wrong when everybody is reluctant to answer his questions about his mother's whereabouts. He is deeply troubled by his father's refusal to deal with him honestly, pretending that nothing is wrong while withdrawing into himself and seeking solace in drinking. Sasha is further bothered by his father's insistence that a boy is not worth half a kopeck if he cannot work out his own problems. The boy believes, however, that if the grown-ups would only explain things to children more often and more honestly, perhaps they would not do so many stupid things.

Sasha gets a similar response from his uncle and aunt, who love him dearly but treat him as a small boy; in effect, they refuse to do his father's job for him. Sasha finds the only solace in his school friends, especially in Yurka Pantyukhin, who himself is caught up in a similar predicament at home: His father is absent, his mother is unable to cope, and his sister is on the verge of becoming a prostitute. Sasha is well liked by his schoolmates, especially by girls, for in their eyes he is good, honest, and brave, one who stands up for his convictions. That does not, however, solve his main problem. He is becoming increasingly frustrated with his relatives, with his friends, and with school. The intolerable situation comes to a head when a schoolmate tells him maliciously what everybody else knows—that his mother has run away with an actor and abandoned him and his family. Sasha beats him savagely and is expelled from school. He now feels an urge to run away from home, and he and Yurka plan to go to a village, where they would work and make a living. Yurka's absent father, an inveterate drunkard, shows up, however, and Yurka decides that he must stay at home to take care of him.

Sasha is still determined to go away. Olga, who turns out to be his most sincere friend, understands his predicament and helps him with his plans. Instead of going to a village, however, he goes to Irkutsk in search of his mother. When he finally finds her and sees her on the street with her friend Dolinsky, he realizes that she has never kissed and looked at his father the way she kisses and looks at Dolinsky. Without talking to his mother, Sasha returns home, thinking that he has begun to understand what it is all about, although he may never understand it completely, nor will anybody else.

Themes and Meanings

The central theme of *What It's All About* is divorce and its impact on everybody concerned, especially children. Not only are the children often ill-equipped to deal with this experience by themselves, but they also often get very little help from their parents and, in this case, from anyone else. The reader surmises that Sasha would have been able to cope with the situation had he been told the truth right away. His father's expectations that a boy of his age should be able to figure it out by himself do not take into account the fact that Sasha has not been told anything about his mother's relationship with his father. For example, when Sasha's little sister constantly asks him about their mother, rather than playing the adults' game of lying and concealing, he simply does not have anything to say. It remains an unanswered question, however, whether Sasha's knowing the true nature of his mother's behavior would have indeed assuaged his feelings about her betrayal or loss. Also questionable is whether a father could muster enough strength and wisdom to explain rationally to a fourteen-year-old what is happening emotionally between the adults, a situation that the father cannot explain even to himself. The fact remains, however, that Sasha is badly hurt—as much by his father's lack of courage to tell him the truth as he is from his mother's seeming failure to return her children's love and affection.

Thus, the impact of divorce is coupled with the age-old question of rearing children. Time and again, Sasha blames his parents, especially his father, for not dealing openly with him, for lacking the courage to do so, and for not being able to keep their own affairs in order. This hypocrisy, as perceived by Sasha, makes it almost impossible for parents to teach their children what is right and what is wrong. Sasha goes a step further by calling the grown-ups cowards and scoundrels; they do not deserve pity since they do not, for their part, feel sorry for children.

Sasha learns soon, however, how difficult it is to tell the truth at all times, because sometimes the truth hurts more than it helps. When he is called to reveal the reason for his brutal beating of his schoolmate, he remains silent because he does not want to tell the world what is really troubling him. When he finally locates his mother, he lacks the courage to tell her that she should return to her family. Sasha begins to learn that the truth is not so simple and that often telling the truth is not enough or even possible.

This learning of "what it's all about" helps Sasha understand life better, giving him strength to cope with misfortunes and disappointments. His sorrow leads not to destruction but to the process of growing up. It also enables him to understand that children should be less harsh in judging their parents, since life is not made up of black and white but of complex shades of various colors. The theme of growing up thus acquires a sad but no less poignant meaning. Finally, the bitter experience confuses Sasha in his own budding feelings about the opposite sex, leaving him with a void and even repulsion in dealing with such sincere friends as Olga.

Context

What It's All About, the first of several works by Vadim Frolov, is also his best. Even though he continues to write books for juveniles, he has not yet duplicated the success of his first novel. What makes this novel successful is its delicate treatment of a psychological interplay of human emotions and relationships. Frolov shows a remarkable understanding of the complexity of emotions and their potentially destructive force. He downplays the sensationalistic possibilities of the situation, guarding against slick and melodramatic posturing. Following the long-standing tradition of a psychological novel in Russian literature, he shows that he has learned well from his illustrious masters, such as Aleksandr Turgenev, Fyodor Dostoevski, and Leo Tolstoy. While it is true that, possessing a far lesser talent he never reaches their level, he accomplishes his task in his own way.

Frolov succeeds in avoiding a pitfall that has plagued Soviet writers, many of whom have succumbed to, or have been coerced to follow, the utilitarian and pedagogical approach to literature. The subject matter of *What It's All About* can easily be misused as an educational, even preaching tool. Frolov avoids that trap by addressing the problems forthrightly, allowing the reader a glimpse into the real problems Soviet adolescents are facing, which are not much different from those in the rest of the world. In this sense, he is in line with a more objective approach to literature, which has been increasingly evident in the Soviet Union since the 1960's.

Vasa D. Mihailovich

WHAT KATY DID

Author: Susan Coolidge (Sarah Chauncy Woolsey, 1835-1905)
Type of plot: Domestic realism
Time of plot: The mid-nineteenth century
Locale: Burnet, a small U.S. town
Principal themes: Coming-of-age, family, friendship, and health and illness
First published: 1872
Recommended ages: 10-13

Impetuous, carefree twelve-year-old Katy Carr, the eldest of six children, sustains a crippling injury from a fall but ultimately learns gentleness, consideration, and familial responsibility.

> *Principal characters:*
> KATY CARR, an irresponsible, fun-loving, and untidy tomboy, who
>   is the oldest of her five siblings
> DR. CARR, Katy's levelheaded and kind father
> AUNT IZZIE, Dr. Carr's sister, who comes to manage the Carr
>   household and children after their mother dies
> COUSIN HELEN, an invalid for life by an early injury, who is ever
>   cheerful

The Story
What Katy Did is almost plot-free, and, indeed, the first half of the novel has no plot at all. Rather, the beginning is a series of episodes meant to show young readers how blissful and delightful life for the Carr children has been. True, the children's mother has died, and Aunt Izzie, who seems fussy and stern, has come to care for them. Also, Katy, the eldest, who had been admonished at her mother's death to care for her five younger siblings, has not been living up to her mother's wish but is instead always getting herself and her brothers and sisters into trouble at school and at home with Aunt Izzie because of her untidiness and careless behavior. In these early chapters, the author paints a wonderful portrait of how the six carefree children, totally self-sustaining, entertain themselves in a small town in the mid-nineteenth century, just as the author did with her four brothers and sisters in Cleveland, Ohio.

The plot begins when Helen comes to visit on her way to a health spa. Beautiful, neat, and tidy, generous and well dressed despite her illness, Helen, disabled for life from an accident, instantly becomes the children's great friend. After she leaves, however, Katy, angry at one of her sisters, spitefully disobeys her aunt, plays on a swing that has not been secured well, falls, and becomes lame from some mysterious spinal "disease." In pain and unable to frolic with her brothers and sisters or even go to school, Katy becomes listless and sullen and more untidy than ever—not a pleasant person to be near. This state of affairs is remedied only by another visit from Helen, who explains to Katy that she must use this time to good advantage. From misfortune, good can come; by going to what Helen calls "the School of Pain," Katy can learn to be patient, cheerful, and hopeful, and not to be selfish or mean to her brothers and sisters. Furthermore, by cleaning up her room and making herself look more attractive, Katy will begin to feel better about herself and others. She is able to put this advice into practice almost immediately when Aunt Izzie suddenly dies, and Katy, at age fourteen, must take on the role of housekeeper and surrogate mother from the confines of her bedroom.

In the end, after four difficult but ultimately rewarding years, Katy regains her ability to walk and, when she walks downstairs for the first time, Helen, whom the children have invited as a celebration surprise, is there to share not only Katy's physical triumph over her illness but also her more important psychological triumph over her emotions.

Themes and Meanings

Although *What Katy Did* has been classified as domestic realism, it is also a moral tale—a typical nineteenth century cautionary tale—that focuses on the transformation of the protagonist from a rude, irrational, peevish child (who selfishly yearns to do good and be famous) to a considerate, loving, thoughtful, and helpful young woman. A "rite of passage" book, it reinforces typical Victorian attitudes about the place of women in the family, community, and society. This theme is echoed by the fact that the guiding force in Katy's reformation is a lame, selfless woman, that is, a stereotype of the Victorian woman as invalid. The "cautionary" message of the story is simply that those who get angry and disobey will get hurt (a typical message of early Victorian children's novels); the moral message is that one will be happier, more productive, in command, and even healthier (Katy is not able to walk until she has become a better, kinder person) only if one can use misfortunes to mature from being a self-absorbed and carefree child to a wise, thoughtful, and caring young adult.

Context

What Katy Did was the first of five books in the "Katy series" (followed by *What Katy Did at School*, 1874; *What Katy Did Next*, 1886; *Clover*, 1888; and *In the High Valley*, 1891). Sarah Woolsey (who wrote under the pseudonym Susan Coolidge), though born in Cleveland, Ohio, moved to New England when she was twenty, and she lived and wrote there all of her life. Her work can best be understood in context when it is compared to the work of three other important, contemporary New England women writers of domestic children's fiction: Susan Bogert Warner's *The Wide, Wide World* (1850), written under the pseudonym Elizbeth Wetherell; Martha Farquharson Finley's *Elsie Dinsmore* (1867); and Louisa May Alcott's *Little Women* (1868-1869).

Elsie Dinsmore and *The Wide, Wide World* are both in the tradition of what is called the "lachrymose" novels, books in which the heroines are extremely religious, highly moralistic, and thoroughly good. These novels are termed "lachry-mose" because the heroines are often in tears. Louisa May Alcott's *Little Women* differs and, in fact, is a landmark book in the history of children's literature; though subtly didactic, its aim was not to preach but to portray a happy family in its New England setting, its members living a rather routine existence.

Although the heroine in *What Katy Did* does, in fact, shed copious tears (mostly of remorse), the novel is more in the tradition of *Little Women* than the other two books. The main character and her sisters and brothers (all of whom are skillfully portrayed as distinct human beings) are depicted as imperfect, somewhat flawed (until they "grow up"), and happily engaged in childlike games, pranks, and mischief. This (what one critic in 1872 called) "fidelity to average child-life," the portrayal of six children at play and enjoying one another, makes *What Katy Did* historically significant and also continues to keep it readable.

Sarah Woolsey's book is in part informed by the period and place in which she wrote it, by the New England Puritan ethic which cherished hard work, selflessness, and responsibility. Nevertheless, despite the currently unpopular reformatory message of the book, reflecting those values, which says in effect that Katy has to slough off her tomboy ways to be happy and fulfilled, *What Katy Did* is noteworthy and still readable as a fresh, unsentimental, and sometimes humorous, detailed study of a "real" family in small-town, mid-nineteenth century America.

Susan Steinfirst

WHEN THE LEGENDS DIE

Author: Hal Borland (1900-1978)
Type of plot: Moral tale
Time of plot: The early twentieth century
Locale: Southern Colorado and northern New Mexico
Principal themes: Family, nature, and race and ethnicity
First published: 1963
Recommended ages: 13-18

Thomas Black Bull, who lived as a young boy in the forest of Colorado, where he learned to live in harmony with nature, is forced after his parents' deaths to live in the reservation school dormitory. He becomes a bronc rider who rides horses to death until a serious injury sends him back to his roots in search of self.

Principal characters:
THOMAS BLACK BULL, or BEARS' BROTHER, a Ute Indian, who becomes a bronc rider
BLACK BULL and
BESSIE, his parents, who live in the old way in a lodge on the mountain
BLUE ELK, an old greedy Ute who betrays his people for white man's money
THATCHER, a trading post owner, who cares about Indians
RED DILLON, a onetime bronc rider, who takes Thomas to New Mexico, trains him, and uses him
MEO, a Mexican cook and once a rider, who lives with Red and Thomas in New Mexico
MARY REDMOND, a nurse who tries to befriend Tom in the hospital

The Story
    When the Legends Die opens about 1920, when Native Americans are suffering the shock of giving up a free life to live as white men determine. Thomas Black Bull, or Bears' Brother, lives his early years in an Indian lodge hidden among the trees on a mountain in Colorado. His family is of the Ute tribe and have escaped from the reservation, where his father was accused of murder. Thomas' only friend after his father is killed in a snow slide and his mother dies the next year is an orphaned grizzly bear cub, which he found and took to his lodge. He gives himself the name "Bears' Brother." When Blue Elk finds him and takes him to the reservation, he is forced to send the bear back to the forest. The teachers and administrators at the school try to get Thomas interested in learning a trade, but he shows no

motivation. Finally, though he does not like the job, he spends two years with a sheepherder on the reservation.

It is while with the sheepherder that Thomas learns to ride horses. Red Dillon sees him ride and obtains a permit from the reservation for Thomas to go with him to New Mexico. Red and Meo, an old Mexican who was crippled from having had so many bones broken from riding broncs, live in an old ranch shack. Difficult riding lessons begin for Thomas. Learning to endure pain, Thomas becomes expert, and Red takes him on the rodeo circuit, where he makes Thomas lose some contests to increase betting on the finals. Thomas takes his hate for Red and the others who have mistreated him out on the horses and, in several instances, rides them to death. He has no friends.

Thomas Black Bull finally stands up to Red Dillon and rides to win in competitions all across the United States. He suffers broken bones several times. When he returns to the ranch in New Mexico to recover from a fall, Red rides into town and dies as a result of many years of drinking. Later, when Thomas again returns to New Mexico after traveling a winning circuit, he finds that Meo has died. In all the years of riding, Meo was the closest thing to a friend that Thomas had. Thomas ends this phase of his life by packing his things and burning the barn and shack they had called home.

After the death of Red and Meo, Thomas continues to make the circuit, living in hotels, until one final ride when he is severely injured. He recovers long before expected, but, still unable to work, he returns to the small town where he started in Colorado. To complete his recuperation in solitude, he takes a job as a sheepherder and goes to the pastures on the same mountain where he had lived with his parents. Alone in the mountains, he remembers the old ways. He faces a grizzly, and strange feelings of brotherhood battle with fear as he refuses to shoot the bear. He has faced his hates and fears and found a healing peace at last.

Themes and Meanings

The culture in which one is reared becomes an integral part of the individual. Bears' Brother was a part of a world of legends and harmony with nature that made him akin to the birds, chipmunks, deer, and bears. Bears were sacred to the Utes; killing a bear was like killing a brother. Thomas names himself "Bears' Brother" and refuses to accept his baptismal name until forced to do so.

When he is forced to live without the friends of the forest, to forget the loves of his childhood, he finds it impossible to form other relationships, especially since few offer him sincere friendship. The forced change leaves him without self-knowledge and without the ability to accept love and concern from those who would have extended it, as Mary Redmond would have taken him to her home and nursed him after his last serious injury from riding. He shuts her words of kindness out of his mind because he does not trust her but thinks that she, too, would deprive him of his freedom.

To Thomas, the broncs are symbolic of the people he has hated. To survive, he endures their mistreatment. Not until his return to the mountains, where he trails a grizzly and confronts again the legend of brotherhood, does he begin to understand his thirst for revenge and his need for friends. At that time, he begins to sing the old chants, feel the rhythm of nature, and find peace within.

Context

When the Legends Die was selected by Reader's Digest Book Club and has had nine foreign editions. It vividly depicts the difficulty of leaving one culture and adopting another. Hal Borland lived in Colorado and knew the country and the people about which he wrote. He was awarded the Meeman Award for conservation writing, 1966, and the John Burroughs Medal for distinguished nature writing, 1968.

In writing a book that shows character-in-the-making through influences by man and nature, Hal Borland has painted a bold picture. Many of the characters in *When the Legends Die* are rough and crude but true to life. Renewal comes not with winning rodeos or with money but with going back to one's roots, hearing in one's mind the old chants and meanings, recognizing one's hate and anger.

When the Legends Die gives insight and understanding of Native Americans. It pictures a culture beautiful but lost in time. Borland wrote many books and articles about nature, including his autobiography *High, Wide, and Lonesome* (1956). His knowledge of life in the mountains of Colorado and mesas of New Mexico makes *When the Legends Die* a valuable addition to literature about the Ute Indian culture.

Mary Joe Clendenin

WHEN THE PHONE RANG

Author: Harry Mazer (1925-   )
Type of plot: Adventure tale
Time of plot: The present
Locale: A city in Massachusetts
Principal themes: Coming-of-age, death, and family
First published: 1985
Recommended ages: 13-15

The phone rings and Billy learns that his mother and father have been killed in a plane crash. Now, Billy, his older brother Kevin, and their younger sister Lori must cope with growing up alone.

Principal characters:
> BILLY KELLER, a sixteen-year-old boy, who tells the story of his family's survival after the death of his parents
> LORI KELLER, his twelve-year-old sister
> KEVIN KELLER, his twenty-one-year-old brother, who comes home from college
> MILO MILLER, a Children's Services agent
> UNCLE PAUL and AUNT JOAN, relatives who wish to sell the household goods and have the children live with them

The Story

A normal family comes to an abrupt end when the phone rings one afternoon. Billy, the younger of the two boys, learns from the airline that his parents have been killed in a plane crash. What follows is the struggle of these young people: Lori, twelve; Billy, sixteen; and Kevin, twenty-one, who is away at college.

Uncle Paul, Aunt Joan, and Grandmother arrive soon after news of the plane crash. Kevin, too, is called home from school. The group discusses what should happen to these three young people. Billy soon realizes that Uncle Paul, Aunt Joan, and Kevin are talking in terms of selling the house, packing up the household belongings, and separating the family: Billy will live with his aunt and uncle, Lori will go with Grandmother, and Kevin is old enough to be on his own. Billy cannot accept this arrangement and approaches Kevin with a plan: He wants what is left of the family to stay together. Kevin agrees, even though it means that he must drop out of school. The children agree that they want to stay together and convince their relatives that they should be allowed to try to make it on their own.

The family begins to function again: Kevin gets a job as an ambulance paramedic, Billy returns to school, and Lori finds a new friend. Soon Mr. Miller, an agent from the local Children's Services, arrives to interview the family. The reader anticipates that this may be the end of this living arrangement, but that is not the case. Miller talks to Billy and Lori and leaves. He returns in a few days to talk to Kevin but fails to see him. When Miller does meet Kevin, in the grocery store, they exchange telephone numbers and Miller leaves.

The struggles of family living get worse. Kevin and Billy continue to argue, Kevin spends long weekends in Boston to be with his girlfriend, and Lori spends more and more time with Maryanne, her new friend of questionable reputation. Billy is left to fend for himself. Kevin loses his job as a result of spending too much time in Boston. The lack of money forces Kevin to sell the Mercedes, the last connection between Billy and his father, which causes the family conflicts to escalate. At the same time, Billy realizes that Lori is getting the attention she needs from Maryanne and that both girls are shoplifting at the local store. When Billy confronts Lori, she goes to the rooftop and threatens to commit suicide.

Each of the three realizes that while all were committed to staying together the family was disintegrating because each was thinking of him- or herself, and not giving one another the attention and support necessary for the family's survival.

The novel ends on a positive note. All accept the tragedy and begin to work together as a team. Lori is about to visit her grandmother for a month, Kevin is going to school, and Billy is going to work part-time at the CYO, an athletic club, to earn some extra money and to be near his newfound girlfriend.

Themes and Meanings

The reactions of the young people from the time they take the phone call to their final acceptance of the death of their parents reveal the stages through which humans pass when faced with this tragedy. Throughout the novel, the reader is exposed to the emotions of denial, anger, depression, and acceptance experienced by the characters.

At first, all three young adults deny what has happened: Billy and Lori carry on with their activities after the phone call. It is after they see the report on television that they begin to sense what has happened. Billy, however, goes out and plays basketball. Kevin, upon his return from school, shows no emotion toward Lori and Billy; he simply carries on with things around the house. Even though there is an attempt to continue life as a family, conflicts take place among them; they become quite angry at one another as well as angry at their parents for causing this to happen. They begin to make pacts with one another. They transfer their commitments in other ways, too. Kevin finds new strength in his work and his girlfriend in Boston, and Lori gives total attention to Maryanne. Lori finally falls to the depths of depression after the shoplifting incident and contemplates suicide. When all three finally hit bottom, they still have enough strength to analyze the situation and decide what must be done if their family is to survive. It is at the end of the novel that the three are able to accept the deaths of their parents and the needs of one another. Billy acknowledges, "You don't lose the grief. You live with the loss, but gradually— you're hardly aware it's happening—something new grows."

Another theme that runs through the novel is the struggle for survival. Can they survive as a family when there appears to be nothing left to keep them together? The reader experiences the disintegration of the family primarily through Billy. It is Billy who exerts enough pressure to have the family stay together and it is Billy who forces Kevin and Lori to evaluate their behavior in terms of family survival.

Context

When the Phone Rang is one of many young adult novels that Harry Mazer has written. Others include *The Girl of His Dreams* (1987), *Hey Kid! Does She Love Me?* (1986), and *City Light* (1988). The strength in these works lies in the consistency with the general characteristics of literature written for young adults.

The characters are believable. Billy, the main character, faces the struggle of survival with death as any sixteen-year-old would. His sense of family unity is to be admired. His struggle with death exemplifies the struggles that everyone has when a loved one is lost. Lori, not getting the attention that she needs at home, turns elsewhere. She is vulnerable, and succumbs to the negative influence of Maryanne. Kevin, however, thinks of himself—he does not want to quit school or give up his girlfriend in Boston.

In young adult literature, adult characters are frequently portrayed in a negative fashion. Mazer seems to follow this: Uncle Paul, Aunt Joan, and Milo Miller seem superficial. They do not seem to consider the welfare of the young people a primary concern. The exception is Grandmother, who is a positive influence in the novel.

Some would argue that the plot is the weakest element in the novel. The events could happen, but would they? Readers will need to make their own decisions in this regard. That the authorities allow the three young people, two of whom are under-age, to live alone seems a bit unbelievable. The fact that a young married couple lives in the apartment below them and an older couple lives above them may offer some support for this arrangement.

It would seem that Mazer has accomplished a creditable goal. He has taken a devastating subject and given it a sensitive treatment, combined with humor, detail, and enough credible teenage action to create a positive experience for the young adult reader.

John H. Bushman

WHEN THUNDERS SPOKE

Author: Virginia Driving Hawk Sneve (1933-   )
Type of plot: Social realism
Time of plot: The early 1970's
Locale: An Indian reservation in South Dakota
Principal themes: Race and ethnicity, and coming-of-age
First published: 1974; illustrated
Recommended ages: 13-15

While climbing the Butte of Thunders in observance of an ancient rite of manhood, Norman Two Bull, a young Indian boy, discovers a relic that brings good luck to him and his family. He refuses to sell it to tourists who make him a good offer and later buries it where he found it in affirmation of his Sioux heritage.

Principal characters:
  NORMAN TWO BULL, a fifteen-year-old Indian who becomes a
    man while torn between two cultures
  SARAH TWO BULL, his mother, a Christian convert who wants to
    leave behind the "heathen" ways of her Indian past
  JOHN TWO BULL, his father, a hardworking man who is
    ambivalent about his Indian heritage yet defends it
  MATT TWO BULL, his grandfather, one of the last of the old
    Indians, who not only remembers the old ways but also lives
    them as much as possible
  MR. BRANNON, the local storekeeper and trader, who buys agate
    rocks from Norman
  THE REVEREND PARKS, a local minister who does not understand
    or appreciate Indian ideas

The Story

When Thunders Spoke is essentially the story of a person and family torn between two cultures. That the Indian way of life must die—indeed, is dead—is an assumption made by this story in several ways. The Two Bull family lives as Indians, but not the way Indians of previous generations did. Their language and culture have virtually disappeared. They know only a little of past rituals, beliefs, and language. Being an Indian means not being a white, yet it does not mean existence with much connection to history or heritage.

At the beginning of the story, young Norman Two Bull resolves to go to the western slopes of the Butte of Thunders, a nearly inaccessible place that is holy to the Sioux Indians. Ostensibly, he goes there to find pieces of agate to trade to Mr. Brannon at the local store; yet it is clear that his real reason for going is to reenact a traditional rite of passage for young boys becoming men. Norman successfully makes the trip, during which he finds an ancient "coup" stick that is buried at the Butte. ("Counting coup" was an ancient Indian tradition that required a young brave to touch an enemy of an opposing tribe with a sacred stick. Similar in some respects to modern war games, in which participants shoot pellets of dye rather than real bullets, it was sometimes used as a substitute for battle and was an important part of the rites of passage from boy to warrior.) Norman takes the stick home with him but immediately regrets having done so, because it causes an incredible argument between his parents: His father wants to hang the stick in their living room; the mother objects to the pagan relic.

Norman's father prevails, and the family immediately experiences good luck: Norman is able to make a much better deal selling the agate rocks, and his father receives a promotion to foreman at his place of work. Simultaneously, each member of the household notices changes in the stick itself as the elements of deterioration begin to disappear.

A white tourist visits the Two Bulls with his family, attempting to buy agates without the local storekeeper, Mr. Brannon, serving as middleman. The tourist also tries to buy the coup stick, offering fifty dollars, then seventy. Sarah Two Bull is ready to accept the money, primarily because she truly wants the house rid of the object. John Two Bull is eager to sell it simply for the money and the help seventy dollars would give to the family budget. Norman declines the offer, however, determining that he will not sell the coup, which, to him, would be selling his heritage, his people, and himself. The parents abide by his decision. The white tourist leaves, whereupon John and Norman take the stick, once again showing its age, back to the base of the Butte of Thunders, where they rebury it near the creek.

Themes and Meanings

When Thunders Spoke is more than a coming-of-age story; it is something of a lament for the past and a bittersweet acceptance of the future. The Two Bull family is trapped between two cultures, unable to function in either and remain at peace with themselves. They cannot be Indians because Indians, in any traditional sense of the word, no longer exist: Indians are a thing of the past. At the same time, they cannot become white—not by accepting the white man's religion or by attending his schools or by living in his kind and style of house. They are left to find some similitude of peace and identity within themselves while divorced from the Indian past and the white present.

The book explores for young readers what it means to be an Indian in the modern age. Norman's trip to the mountain functions on several levels in this respect. He goes there seeking agate rocks to sell to the local white trader so he can make money, which will assure his survival in the white world. He goes there to fulfill a basic requirement of manhood made by the Sioux and told to him by his grandfather. He goes there to establish his own identity and independence and to brood about his place in the world. Norman serves as a representative of his race and time. The "new Indian" man is in a period that is like a sociological adolescence. He is forced to function in the white man's world, yet he is not recognized as an equal by white society, and Indian culture is no longer accessible or relevant.

All of these matters reach culmination at the end of the story when Norman and his father symbolically bury the coup stick. Appropriately, the stick itself is a product of Norman's heritage, yet it is explained that the stick and its use in war had actually been introduced by the French. The burial of the stick means the interment not only of a relic of the Indian past, but of a white past that had resulted in the ravaging changes of the nineteenth century. The burial is something of an attempt to embrace the past—a "farewell hug"—while negating the effects of the present; returning the relic to the ground assures that it will never become a tourist's souvenir.

Context

The context of *When Thunders Spoke* is defined by its setting and characters. Like all literature, the novel is encompassed by the boundaries of a certain cultural vantage, which is especially noticeable because of its contrast to that of the dominant society.

Lightning often hits the top of the Butte of Thunders, accounting for the mountain's name and providing an explanation for the legend that claims that the gods are speaking in this holy place. Norman Two Bull travels here to discover the message from these lost gods. They give him no direct answer, and yet he is provided with the coup stick. Norman Two Bull experiences the pressures and anxieties of any young man, and finds meaning and direction in his life as a result of finding the relic. These are uniquely determined by the reservation, its geography and history, and by the closeness of his family and Indian society.

When Thunders Spoke is the product of a white society. The author, who spent her childhood on the Rosebud Sioux Reservation in South Dakota, realizes the hopelessness of trying to keep up most of the old ways. Accordingly, she writes about those who struggle with the death of civilization while being assimilated, rather than integrated, into a new and different way of thinking and living. Norman Two Bull will not attend the white man's college; he will not move to the white man's city with its crime, traffic, and pollution; he will not seek to become a stockbroker. He will, however, live peacefully in his heart in ways that only an Indian can know and understand.

Carl Singleton

WHERE THE LILIES BLOOM

Authors: Vera Cleaver (1919-   ) and Bill Cleaver (1920-1981)
Type of plot: Domestic realism
Time of plot: The mid-twentieth century
Locale: Trial Valley in the Smoky Mountains of North Carolina
Principal themes: Family, gender roles, death, nature, and poverty
First published: 1969
Recommended ages: 10-13

With courage, humor, and resourcefulness, fourteen-year-old Mary Call vows to keep her orphaned family together and to keep her older sister from marrying their despised landlord, Kiser Pease.

Principal characters:

ROY LUTHER, a mountain "wildcrafter" who is terminally ill and ultimately dies, leaving his four children orphaned

MARY CALL LUTHER, a fourteen-year-old who assumes the role of head of the family upon her father's death

DEVOLA LUTHER, her seventeen-year-old "cloudy-headed" sister

ROMEY LUTHER, her ten-year-old brother

IMA DEAN, the youngest Luther child

KISER PEASE, the Luthers' landlord, who wants to marry Devola

The Story

Fourteen-year-old Mary Call Luther tells the story of the proud, impoverished Luther family, who eke out an existence on land owned by their neighbor, Kiser Pease. Roy Luther has exacted promises from Mary Call while on his deathbed: that he will be buried in the grave he dug himself high up in the Smokey Mountains; that the family will stay together and take pride in the Luther name; that they will never accept charity; and that pretty, dreamy Devola will not marry the villainous Kiser Pease. Though it angers her that Roy Luther has allowed himself to be beaten down by the inhospitable land, a greedy landlord, and poverty, Mary Call intends to carry out her promises.

After their father's death, she and ten-year-old Romey pull his body in a wagon up to the burial place. Keeping his death a secret from nosy neighbors who would have the children sent to the county charity home becomes a difficult and sometimes hilarious challenge. No less challenging is keeping the family in food and clothing. It takes hard labor and some browbeating by the indomitable Mary Call for the children to supplement their meager income by "wildcrafting," the gathering of medicinal herbs from the mountainsides. It is dreary work to the rebellious Romey, in spite of the breathtaking beauty of their surroundings. As for Kiser Pease, his relationship with the Luthers becomes much more complex than Mary Call had imagined when she made her promise to Roy Luther.

When Mary Call and Romey discover Kiser Pease deathly ill of pneumonia, they use the folk medicine onion cure, and in exchange for saving his life, Mary Call persuades him to sign the house and land they live on over to the Luthers. That strategy works only until Pease's sister reveals that the land they live on belongs to her, not to her brother. At one point, Mary Call even proposes to Kiser Pease herself. After all, she had promised her father only that she would not allow Kiser to marry Devola; she did not promise that she would not marry him herself. If the family could somehow be provided for, they would not have to spend their days in the mountains wildcrafting; best of all, she could concentrate on what she wants so much: an education to "correct her ignorance," as she puts it.

When the parlor roof caves in from snow and a hungry fox peers in at their only chicken, Mary Call is almost ready to give up. Eventually, however, she realizes that positive changes are taking place. Devola is no longer the dreamy, childlike person that she had been when her father was alive. Closer contacts with Kiser Pease reveal that he is not the villain Mary Call had thought him to be. Thus, when spring comes and the valley is reborn in beauty, a new life begins for the Luthers. Devola and Kiser are married, and the rest of the Luthers have their own home as well as land. Mary Call and Romey can pursue their school studies and their various money-making projects with new energy and zest. Perseverance and courage have conquered a hostile environment, and Mary Call can look out in peace at what a traveler once called "the fair land."

Themes and Meanings

Family, poverty, and death are inextricably interwoven in *Where the Lilies Bloom*, which takes its title from an old hymn about a land "where the lilies bloom so fair." It is the theme of family, however, that comes through especially strongly. The father, Roy Luther, exhorts Mary Call to inculcate family pride in the Luther children. He thinks of family when he digs his own grave high up in the mountains to save the expense of a funeral. He considers the welfare of his "cloudy-headed" daughter, Devola, when exacting a promise from Mary Call that she will always care for her sister and specifically not allow her to marry Kiser Pease. He knows that Devola is easily persuaded, and the need to protect her weighs heavily on his mind.

The theme of a strong, courageous female is carried out in the character of Mary Call. She has inherited the Luther family pride, the same sense of dignity that led her father to tell her never to accept charity. Family is an all-consuming passion. As head of the household, she courageously plans, plots, and conspires to keep the family together and shows utmost ingenuity in seeking ways to provide for her siblings. When Romey or Ima Dean asks how she intends to accomplish some especially difficult task, she responds, "I haven't figured that out yet," but the implication is clear: In time, a plan will emerge. Thus, Mary Call is a strong role model of her gender: enterprising, resourceful, independent, and proud.

Also implicit in the story is the theme of death: its impact on the fortunes and misfortunes of those whose physical and emotional welfare had been dependent upon the departed. Roy Luther probably has as great an influence on Mary Call after his death as before. She remembers his pride and perseverance; she recalls the death-bed promises, possibly longer than it is legitimate to do so. Yet the reader learns another truth about death: Its impact may moderate and change over time. Roy Luther's requests to Mary Call were made in the same good faith in which she promised to carry them out. Yet times and circumstances change, and in the broader interest, even deathbed promises may need to be rethought.

Nature as friend and adversary is another theme in *Where the Lilies Bloom*. Descriptions of birds, trees, flowers, and herbs paint a picture of a bright and binding loveliness in the region of Trial Valley. Yet this land is basically hostile to even a modest livelihood, as evidenced in the slow, tedious work entailed in the primitive job of wildcrafting. The poverty of the Appalachian people is seen not only in the struggles of the Luthers but also in the image created by Mary Call as she tells about the valley and its inhabitants. This land is mesmerizing, but it offers little in resources for a livelihood. Thus, the name Trial Valley stands in marked contrast to the idyllic descriptions and serves as an emblem of the hardships of Appalachia.

Context

Vera and Bill Cleaver's books deal with reality that is often grim, whether it is the suicide of the mother and the alienation of the father in *Grover* (1970), the social ills depicted in *The Mimosa Tree* (1970), or the impact of mental retardation on family members in *Me Too* (1973). There is often sadness and poignancy, but the books are not somber. One critic commented on the Cleavers' "whole-grain" characters and their absorbing imagery. The struggles of the characters with themselves and their environment are handled not only with dignity and depth but often with wry humor as well.

Where the Lilies Bloom is perhaps the Cleavers' most successful book in its demonstration of the qualities of good fiction. Such qualities were identified by Bill Cleaver himself when he commented on the importance of holding incident and characters together and of seeking answers to questions of what, why, where are we going, and what is on the other side. It is this combination of incident, characters, and answer-seeking that is likely to engage and inspire juvenile readers.

The authors have created a setting that leads to an understanding and respect for Appalachia and its people. Romey and Ima Dean complain about the arduous task of gathering pollen for medicinal purposes while wildcrafting, but they also notice the fragrant air and majestic mountain peaks. Still, there are wild animals, rattlesnakes, and bottomless chasms, and the promise of a harsh winter when all lies dormant. The love-hate relationships that develop within families and among neighbors are mirrored here in the relationship between people and the setting in which they find themselves.

The credibility of the story, however, lies in the penetrating characterization of

Mary Call. Her courage and determination in dealing with death, poverty, and an unforgiving environment make for something more than a realistic "problems" novel. One critic compared her with Mattie Ross of Charles Portis' *True Grit* (1968), suggesting that the courage of the frontier did not disappear with the pioneers. Yet the other Luthers grow, too. Romey becomes increasingly assertive, often in response to a demanding, impatient Mary Call. Devola, outwardly sweet and pliable, quietly asserts her independence; she intends to marry Kiser Pease and finds ways to be with him. Moreover, while the resolution of the family's problems might seem a bit pat, within the context of setting, story, and characters it is entirely believable and memorable.

Inga Kromann-Kelly

WHERE THE RED FERN GROWS

Author: Wilson Rawls (1913-1984)
Type of plot: Adventure tale
Time of plot: The early twentieth century, c. 1920
Locale: The Oklahoma Ozarks
Principal themes: Animals, family, and coming-of-age
First published: 1961
Recommended ages: 10-13

Billy Coleman works and saves for two years to buy the pair of coon hounds for which he longs. With old Dan and Little Ann he finds exciting adventure and enduring love, but he also finds heartbreak, which pushes him toward growing up.

Principal characters:
>BILLY COLEMAN, a young boy, who trains his two coon hounds to be the best hunting dogs in the Ozarks
>OLD DAN, his male hound, which is noted for his strength and tenacity
>LITTLE ANN, his female hound, which is noted for her comeliness and intelligence
>GRANDPA, his doting grandfather, who is his accomplice in many of his adventures
>PAPA, his father, who encourages him in training and hunting the dogs
>MAMA, his mother, who is lenient and kind, and allows Billy freedom to roam at will

The Story

Billy Coleman is a boy growing up in the Oklahoma Ozarks—wild, sparsely settled country, a hunter's paradise. His father works hard at farming to provide for the family, and his mother diligently cares for Billy and his three younger sisters, but neither does much supervision of Billy. He spends his days roaming the out-of-doors, exploring hills and river bottoms, and longing for a pair of coonhounds with which to hunt. The family is too poor to buy the dogs, but so strong is Billy's passion that he vows to earn the money himself. It takes him two years of hustling, but eventually he acquires the pups.

Billy names his dogs Old Dan and Little Ann, and begins teaching them all the lore he has learned from his years in the woods and any additional information he can pick up from the coon hunters who congregate at Grandpa's store. As the three spend their nights in search of ringtails, an extraordinary bond of trust and devotion develops among them. The dogs learn to hunt as a team, a beautiful pair of hounds working in precision, and Billy learns to anticipate their movements, to know instinctively what they will do. More important, they learn that they can rely on one another, even to the point of risking death when necessary.

It is inevitable that Billy's halcyon days cannot last forever, and trouble does come. It is the growing reputation of his dogs' prowess that precipitates the trouble. Grandpa and Billy are pushed into making a bet with two bullies, Rubin and Rainie Pritchard, that Old Dan and Little Ann can tree a ghost coon. During the subsequent hunt, Rubin is tragically killed. Billy is greatly affected by the death but gains maturity as he gropes with the pain and eventually is able to comfort Grandpa.

The dogs are entered in a championship coon hunt. Billy grooms Little Ann with Grandpa's dresser set and homemade butter, and she wins a silver cup for best-looking hound at the hunt. Later she and Old Dan tree sufficient coons to win the gold cup and the money that goes with the championship.

The commitment that has grown consistently stronger between Billy and the dogs is ultimately tested when Old Dan is attacked by a mountain lion. Billy and Little Ann rush unhesitatingly to his aid. The lion is killed, but Old Dan is fatally wounded. Little Ann's wounds are superficial, but she loses her will to live and also dies. Billy is bowed in grief, but his sorrow is mitigated when a red fern springs up between the dogs' graves, and he recalls the legend that only an angel can plant the seeds of a red fern. That spot where it is planted becomes sacred.

Soon after, the family uses the championship money and the money saved from Billy's hunting to move out of the Ozarks into town, where the children can attend school. Thus, Old Dan and Little Ann give the family a chance for a new life with broadened opportunities.

Themes and Meanings

The plot of *Where the Red Fern Grows* follows the classic animal genre wherein a protagonist develops a deep attachment to an animal, thus making himself vulnerable to great pain when the animal is lost to him. Fred Gipson's *Old Yeller* (1956), Marjorie Kinnan Rawlings' *The Yearling* (1938), James Otis' *Toby Tyler* (1881), and James Street's *Good-bye My Lady* (1954) are other examples. The love that develops between Billy and his dogs, the dogs' eventual death, and his subsequent reaction to that death comprise the central theme of the book. Inherent within the theme is the ageless question posed by all romantic tragedies: Is the joy that comes from such a commitment worth the risk it engenders? Billy, whose only siblings are younger sisters and who has no school friends or close companions, invests much of his emotional self in Old Dan and Little Ann. The reader watches as their relationship progresses from its ebullient beginnings, when Billy would love any dog—as long as it is a coonhound—to his devotion to these particular dogs. The love that the three share becomes the warp and woof of their existence: in the end, each risks death for the safety of the others.

Although the death of the dogs is foreshadowed by the death of Rubin Pritchard, Billy is unprepared for the intensity of his sorrow. His grief leads him to question the values espoused by his parents and to an initial estrangement from God. Spiritual balm comes in the form of the red fern, and Billy is able to move on to new plans, a new future.

A secondary theme of the book is family life and its role in shaping the person one becomes. Billy is an extraordinarily independent, self-reliant boy, a Robinson Crusoe figure with his feet firmly planted on the Ozark river bottoms. Much of his self-sufficiency is the result of the laissez-faire attitude of his family. There is never any question of devotion. Mama and Papa empathize with Billy's feelings, whether he is moping for hounds that they have no money to buy, celebrating winning a championship, or grieving over his dogs' deaths. Grandpa is always there to be his confidant. Billy, however, is allowed to roam without stricture, devote long hours to private pursuits, and find his own solutions to problems. Billy does not grow strong fighting for independence; he grows strong celebrating independence.

Context

Rawls published one other book, *Summer of the Monkeys* (1976). It, too, is set in the Oklahoma Ozarks and contains much that is similar in plot and characterization to *Where the Red Fern Grows*. In choosing the Ozarks for the setting of his books, Rawls states that he is writing about his own boyhood. It is the picture he creates of rural life in the early part of the twentieth century that gives Rawls's work an importance beyond the telling of a good tale. He preserves something of the indigenous flavor of life in that time, at that place.

Through the eyes of Billy Coleman, the reader is permitted a look at the mores, value systems, and social customs that exist within his community. One is made aware of the topography of the land, its still virginal state, the loneliness spawned by sparse settlements, and the lack of social institutions such as schools and churches. Rawls records an obedience to the work ethic so ingrained that Papa is reluctant to leave his work for even a few days to attend the championship coon hunt. Recorded also are the patched overalls, the reverence for one's dogs, the home-canned huckleberries made into a cobbler, the superstition of the screech owl, the need to go to a hair-cutting to keep one's hair groomed, and the legend of the red fern.

Perhaps one of the most striking comments on rural life of that day is made by Rawls in the freedom that he gives both his protagonists to roam freely about their woods and river bottoms without undue fear for safety. During hunting season, a period of several months, Billy is permitted to stay out all night, every night. Of interest also to the social scientist is the lack of compunction that Billy feels on cutting a giant, stately tree because his dogs have treed a raccoon among its branches, as well as the glee he and other hunters experience in the repeated slaughter of raccoons.

When Billy makes his first trip to Tahlequah, he is stared at, laughed over, and called a hillbilly, but he cannot imagine why. After all, he is not that different from everyone he knows. The significance of Rawls's work is not only in how Billy differs from his contemporaries but also in the extent to which Billy's life contrasts with the reader's. That the reader can have some sense of the breadth of change is a measure of Rawls's achievement.

Luther Bryan Clegg

WHICH WAY FREEDOM? and OUT FROM THIS PLACE

Author: Joyce Hansen (1942-   )
Type of plot: Historical fiction
Time of plot: 1861-1866
Locale: South Carolina and Tennessee
Principal themes: Race and ethnicity, and social issues
First published: Which Way Freedom?, 1986; *Out from This Place*, 1988
Recommended ages: 13-15

In the first of these novels, three slaves run away from slavery and plantation life in the early years of the Civil War. Obi, a young man, joins the Union forces, while Easter, his female companion, and Jason, an orphan for whom the two of them care, escape to the Sea Islands off the South Carolina coast. In the second book, Easter and Jason struggle to be reunited with Obi during the early days of freedom and Reconstruction.

Principal characters:
  OBADIAH (OBI) BOOKER, a slave on the Jennings' plantation in
      South Carolina who runs away from slavery to join the Union
      army
  EASTER, a young teenage black girl, companion to Obi and
      functional mother of Jason, who also runs away
  JASON, a child and the third of the slaves to escape
  BUKA, an elderly slave on the Jennings' plantation who helps the
      three escape
  ROSE, a woman slave on the Phillips' plantation who becomes
      Easter's friend and confidante after the escape
  MISS GRANTLEY, a Northern, white missionary teacher who
      encourages Easter to go to the North to school so that she can
      return to teach the freed slaves
  JOHN JENNINGS, owner of the plantation and master to the three
      runaways
  MARTHA JENNINGS, John's wife, a good woman who believes that
      someday whites will pay God for the sin of slavery
  WILSON JENNINGS, John's cruel elder brother
  RAYFORD, a proud and arrogant slave on the adjacent plantation
      who escapes with Buka and others
  THOMAS, a Northern black who serves in the same regiment as
      Obi and who becomes a close friend to him

The Story
    These two companion novels are excellent works of historical fiction. Set during

and shortly after the American Civil War and peopled mainly with characters who are slaves, *Which Way Freedom?* and *Out from This Place* serve mainly as novels of intrigue written to reveal the problems, evils, and intricacies of the institution of slavery; to emphasize the role that blacks played in fighting in that war; and to dramatize the difficulties facing the newly freed people after the fighting stopped and slavery was abolished. Joyce Hansen is able to re-create these turmoils and social upheavals realistically and make them readable for young audiences without resorting to sanitizing the violence of this human conflict.

The primary action of *Which Way Freedom?* is composed of two unfolding events: the determination of the slaves to escape and Obi's experiences in the Union army. At the beginning of the novel, the slaves are rightfully desirous of their freedom. Even so, they act out of some sense of loyalty to their master, John Jennings, and do not actively seek their freedom by means of escape. Yet when an official from the Confederate army comes to the plantation to determine that Obi will be conscripted into the Southern military since Jennings himself is too old to fight, Obi believes that he has no choice and must run. At the same time, when Jennings decides to sell Easter and Jason, they feel forced to run away with Obi.

Joyce Hansen uses these events to reveal the evils of slavery as an American institution. The brief glimpses of life on the plantation show that black slaves had no family or experience with family structure—even mother and child are separated in this greatest violation of human compassion and decency. Hansen reveals the evils of the auction block as the slaves are sold and traded like cattle. She writes of their endless hard labors, poor living conditions, and lack of food and medical attention. Similarly, the degradation suffered from the illegality of slaves' becoming literate is portrayed.

Having decided to escape, the first real problem is to decide where to go. The obvious choice is to the Union forces or, at least, to Union-controlled land. This alternative is nearly ruled out when they learn that Union forces are, more or less, returning runaway slaves to their masters by refusing to take them in and become responsible for them—thus the title *Which Way Freedom?* The slaves have no freedom in the South or in the North. Under the leadership of the elderly slave Buka (now freed because of his old age and uselessness for plantation work), they decide to escape to the Sea Islands, where they will be under Union control and yet will be in charge of their own lives.

The three do, in fact, make it to the islands, where they live in a colony with other escaped slaves. Soon afterward, Obi, not permitted to join a white Yankee regiment, enlists in a newly formed black one and goes to fight in the Fort Pillow Massacre at Fort Pillow, Tennessee, where hundreds of blacks were killed. At the end of the novel, he is left still searching for his mother, from whom he has been separated since early childhood. Now, however, he is also lost from the only two persons in the world about whom he truly cares: Easter and Jason.

Out from This Place picks up the narrative at this point, but the point of view generally shifts from that of Obi to that of Easter. Accordingly, she, rather than Obi, is the main character in the second novel. She struggles not to become a field hand in the cotton crops by working out a plan under which she will take care of the children of those women who do work there. She struggles with Jason, who has become spoiled, unloving, and removed from reality while living with the slave owners during a period of separation from Easter. She must decide whether to marry another freed slave, as Rose did, or to await the return of Obi from the war. Her biggest and hardest decision, however, is whether to give in to Miss Grantley, her Northern white teacher, who pressures her to go North to school so that she herself can return to teach other newly freed slaves to read and write.

None of these problems is actually resolved until the end. Easter does decide to go to school to become a teacher; Jason's behavior slowly returns to normal as he becomes loving, hardworking, and realistic; and, finally, the reader learns at the end of the novel that Obi is returning to the Sea Islands to find Easter, presumably to marry her. Thus the ending is vaguely duplicitous, since Hansen does not make it clear that Obi will find Easter, now studying in the North; nor does she indicate that the two will remain permanently and hopelessly separated.

Themes and Meanings

In both of these novels Joyce Hansen depicts problems that confronted American blacks during this historical period. Her works provide an understanding to young readers about the evils of slave auction blocks, incessant hard labor, hunger, and poverty. Most pervasive of themes in these novels and in many ways the only central theme, alienation and separation control the writer's purpose and intent. That the evils of slavery were vile indeed is not the main point here, though to be sure Hansen does create events that expose the horrors that constituted the system.

To begin with, all the slaves are separated from other members of their families. So-called "slave marriages" were not legal and so owners could and did routinely sell slaves apart from other members of their families. Obi's main objective is to find his mother, from whom he had been separated in this way. Similarly, Easter and Jason have lost their own parents and siblings. Obi must make a choice between leaving Easter and Jason in order to search for his mother or staying with them and building what can be a family of his own. Easter's dilemma in the second novel is just as severe: Should she go to the North for study, thereby taking a chance that she will miss Obi if he returns for her, or should she stay, waiting patiently but hopelessly, not even knowing if he is alive?

Separation is an omnipresent fact in these people's lives, so much so that it becomes even more basic as a drive and objective than the search for freedom itself. Obi, Easter, and Jason cannot be "free," despite the Emancipation Proclamation and the end of the Civil War, until they come to terms in their own hearts with their own choices, which these two events did make them free to make. Obi chooses to return to Easter without finding his mother, and Easter chooses to go to the North without him. Hansen rightfully recognizes that being free means only being free to make choices—it does not mean being free from misery.

Context

Both novels are overwhelmed by two contexts. First of these is the historical back-drop provided by slavery, the Civil War and the role of blacks in it, and the era of Reconstruction. Characterization, structuring, and plotting are all subservient to the author's purpose of describing what it meant to be alive and to be black at this time. Hansen writes a fictional story set in history in such a way as to make it unfold in a believable manner, without tampering with the facts of two actual events: the escape of plantation blacks to the Sea Islands and the Fort Pillow Massacre in Tennessee.

The other context is social and racial. The author embeds her characters in real-ities of the day, compassionately speculating about their feelings, fears, and motiva-tions. There is a certain air of struggle, suffering, and endurance in her depiction of occurrences in the daily lives of these people, which assures accuracy in understand-ing their turmoils and triumphs. There is little contemporaneous coloration of the characters and the events, which would serve only to make the novels social com-mentary rather than works of literature.

The greatest attraction to these stories is their accomplishment in accuracy—not in terms of historical correctness but in their fidelity to expressing the oppression of the people. The novels, because of their subject matter, are of interest to young black readers; however, their success is not limited merely to this audience. Persons of any race, and particularly anyone concerned about the Civil War, will want to read these award-winning works. Hansen has captivated the excitement of the era in this fic-tional re-creation of history.

Carl Singleton

THE WHIPPING BOY

Author: Sid Fleischman (1920-   )
Type of plot: Adventure tale
Time of plot: An undefined time in the past
Locale: A castle, woods, and sewers in an unspecified European country
Principal themes: Coming-of-age and friendship
First published: 1986; illustrated
Recommended ages: 10-13

A bratty prince and his whipping boy have many adventures when they inadvertently trade places after becoming involved with dangerous outlaws

> *Principal characters:*
> PRINCE HORACE (BRAT), the mischievous, spoiled, arrogant heir to
>   the throne
> JEMMY, a resourceful boy of the streets and sewers who serves as
>   the whipping boy
> HOLD-YOUR-NOSE BILLY and
> CUTWATER, two cutthroats who capture Prince Brat and Jemmy
> BETSY, a girl who rescues the boys
> PETUNIA, Betsy's trained bear
> MR. NIPS, a stagecoach driver and hot-potato man

The Story

Set in an undefined time and place, this fictitious tale of a whipping boy and a prince is based on a surprising historical fact: Some royal households in past centuries actually kept boys to suffer the punishments due a misbehaving prince, because it was forbidden to punish royalty.

Jemmy, the son of a rat catcher who had lived in the streets and sewers, is the whipping boy for Prince Horace, who has amply earned the nickname "Prince Brat." Prince Brat is mischievous and lazy. His pranks and failure to listen to his tutor cause Jemmy to suffer frequent and severe lashings. Jemmy bears the beatings without flinching, a fact that the prince perceives as a taunt to him.

The boys feel only dislike and contempt for each other. Though Jemmy likes his new palace life-style, he decides that the price he pays is too high and makes plans to run away. Meanwhile, he absorbs the education the prince refuses to accept. Learning to read, write, and do sums, he seizes opportunities that the prince evades.

The prince becomes bored with his life in the castle and forces Jemmy to run away with him in the dead of night. Jemmy secretly determines to desert the prince. As they travel, the two boys are grabbed by a pair of cutthroats, Hold-your-nose Billy and Cutwater. The two illiterate and inept kidnappers are perfect foils for the haughty prince and the streetwise urchin.

The prince's arrogant nature surfaces, and he demands to be released, identifying himself as a prince. Jemmy desperately denies this, realizing the danger in which it puts them. He almost convinces the terrorists to release them, but again the prince's arrogance gets them in trouble, and the boys are held in a cave for ransom.

Neither terrorist can write, and neither can the prince, only Jemmy. The outlaws believe that the educated boy is the prince. This misconception fits Jemmy's plans perfectly. Jemmy is trying to save the prince more because he fears the beatings he will get if he does not than because he really cares what happens to Prince Brat. After tricking the kidnappers into letting the horse deliver the ransom note, Jemmy attempts to escape but is betrayed by the prince. The boys' mutual contempt and distrust deepens.

Finally, both Jemmy and the prince escape, going in different directions. Jemmy is badly frightened by a huge bear. When the two boys meet again, the prince, now dirty and ragged, refuses a chance to return safely to the castle. He is assuming some of Jemmy's characteristics of independence and autonomy. When the prince starts doing his share of scrounging for scrap to sell, he takes another step toward maturity. Jemmy's intense dislike weakens slightly.

The fast pace of the story continues as the boys hitch a ride with Captain Nips. Two firsts occur here: Jemmy calls the prince his friend, and the prince smiles.

The boys are recaptured by the thugs, who are so infuriated at being tricked that they whip the prince, thinking that he is the whipping boy. Bearing the lashes without a whimper, Horace wins Jemmy's respect completely. They are rescued again, by Betsy and her bear, but found once more by the kidnappers. The climactic chase through rat-infested sewers will hold the most reluctant reader.

By tale's end, the metamorphosis is virtually complete. Each young man has assumed some of the better qualities of the other. They return to the castle as equals, while the villains are suitably dispatched.

Themes and Meanings

This fast-paced adventure tale takes place over a time span of only a few days, but its major themes of the triumph of good over evil, the coming of age of the two young men, the bonding of friendship and trust, and the importance of education will not be lost on its readers. The swift action and witty dialogue hold attention while not so subtly delivering the story's messages.

Both Jemmy and Horace grow and develop in the story. Jemmy is symbolic of wit and endurance overcoming adversity. He seizes each opportunity for growth. The scene in which he persuades the kidnappers to deliver the ransom note, which only he can write, dramatically emphasizes the value of education.

It is the prince, however, who changes most. He grows from an immature, selfish boy into a young man who will someday be fit to rule. The scene in which he takes Jemmy's place and endures the beating without flinching marks his coming of age. He proves to himself that he is as much a man as Jemmy and thus no longer feels threatened by him. He is free now to mature at his own pace. When the prince inadvertently learns that his subjects dread the time he becomes king, he reacts with humility rather than arrogance, as he would have before his experiences with Jemmy and the kidnappers.

Jemmy and Horace may be likened to Damon and Pythias, the central characters in a Roman myth about two young men who have become symbolic of strong friendship. Pythias is sentenced to death for speaking against a cruel king. Damon takes his friend's place in prison so his friend may see his family once more before he dies. The stipulation is that Damon will die if Pythias does not return. Damon stakes his life on his friend's word. In *The Whipping Boy*, Jemmy tries to take Horace's place several times when he is in jeopardy to spare him, and Horace repays the debt when he takes Jemmy's beating.

Context

The Whipping Boy was approximately number forty on Sid Fleischman's list of children's books and stories at the time of its publication in 1986. This prolific writer authored the highly successful and entertaining McBroom and Mr. Mysterious series and numerous others. Yet *The Whipping Boy*, though it has some fairy-tale characteristics, contains more depth than Fleischman's former works. Beneath the banter and quick-witted repartee lies a story of ignorance and arrogance overcome, of trust and respect earned, and of maturity evolving.

The story has an English flavor from its characters' language and accents and its monarchical government. Its tone is somewhat similar to Mark Twain's *The Prince and the Pauper* (1881), in which there is also an exchange of identities. The switch there, however, has its basis in the striking physical resemblance between Edward VI and Tom Cantry. Some critics have discerned a further English influence on Fleischman going as far back as Charles Dickens' *A Tale of Two Cities* (1859), in which Charles Darnay's voluntary substitution for Sidney Carton ends in his trip to the guillotine.

The Whipping Boy was awarded the 1987 Newbery Medal and was the 1988 winner of the Charlie May Simon Award. It seems destined to become a children's literary classic.

Billie Taylor

THE WHISTLING BOY

Author: Ruth M. Arthur (1905-1979)
Type of plot: Domestic realism
Time of plot: The late 1950's to early 1960's
Locale: Sussex and Norfolk, England
Principal themes: Coming-of-age, emotions, family, friendship, and the supernatural
First published: 1969; illustrated
Recommended ages: 10-13

Kirsty Newton becomes emotionally isolated from her family. When she distances herself from the home situation, her self-centered problems resolve themselves.

Principal characters:

CHRISTINA "KIRSTY" NEWTON, the narrator, who cannot adjust to the sudden death of her mother and the marriage of her father to a woman twenty years his junior

JAKE MERYON, Kirsty's friend at Norfolk, who provides the mystery and love interest in the story

LOIS NEWTON, the young stepmother, who has insecurities that will eventually allow Kirsty to accept her

GERRY NEWTON, Kirsty's father, a reserved man who is so caught up in the love of his new wife that he is blinded to the needs of his young daughter

DINAH PURDY, the new girl in Kirsty's form at school, who has problems at home with which she is unable to cope

JANET WOODWARD, the "daily" in the Newton household, who helps Kirsty find the distance the teenager needs to cope with her changing home and life situations

JOEL CORPUSTY (OLD CORPUSTY), who resisted the call of the whistling ghost years before and helps to unlock the mystery that haunts Jake

The Story

The Whistling Boy has two main conflicts that are woven together in this first-person narrative: Kirsty must adjust to a new home situation and wishes to solve the problems of both Dinah and Jake.

At a school concert, Lois is taken for Kirsty's sister rather than the father's new wife; this realization comes as a shock to the young girl. As Kirsty begins to experience panic attacks over her feelings about Lois, her home situation deteriorates and she feels more and more alienated. Kirsty's emotional self-indulgence prevents her from trying to get Dinah, her friend, to seek the help she needs in her debilitating home situation.

Finally, Kirsty turns to Janet, the "daily," who helps her obtain a summer fruit-picking job in Norfolk. During her first night at the Dillions', Janet's relatives, Kirsty hears a hauntingly familiar tune coming from a vacant room next to her bedroom. As Kirsty explores the old village, she discovers that the sea is encroaching on the land and that it is only a matter of time before the Dillions' farmhouse will be reclaimed by the sea.

On the way to the Dillions' home after her first day at work, Kirsty sees Old Corpusty. Jake Meryon, whom Kirsty had first seen at the village, warns her to stay away from Old Corpusty, who is a hermit and keeps rats for company. As the two teenagers become friends, Kirsty discovers that Jake suffers from a memory loss, which he sustained while staying at the Dillions', and appears to go into a "different world" on occasion. He also whistles the same haunting tune that she hears at night. As the stresses of her home situation begin to recede, Kirsty begins to reach out to Jake. She later sees a figure moving toward the sea that could be Jake, were it not for his ragged and old-fashioned clothing. As Kirsty watches, the boy begins to play Jake's tune on a wooden whistle, and the Whistling Boy dissolves into the sea.

When Janet calls to tell Kirsty that Dinah was caught shoplifting, Kirsty is determined not to fail Jake as she did Dinah. Jake enables her to realize that what Dinah did was a cry for help, and he discovers that he, like Dinah, must confront the "dangerous magic" that would destroy him. In the Dillions' vacant room, Kirsty finds a slim, wooden whistle with the carved letters "JACQUES MERINEAU 1686." At last, Kirsty understands the connection between Jake's memory loss and the legendary Whistling Boy.

Kirsty hears the legend of the Whistling Boy from Old Corpusty. When urged by the apparition to follow him into the sea, Old Corpusty stayed to care for a blind sister, but he never forgave her for his lost chance. She also learns that the Whistling Boy appears only when there is going to be a surge from the sea.

Kirsty again reaches outside herself when Marcus, her favorite brother, is involved in an accident. Reassured by her father that Marcus did not need her or his twin, Kirsty realizes that her father has never been able to understand the emotional needs of his children. A call from Lois helps Kirsty decide that she must return temporarily to help Marcus face his fears.

In Sussex, Kirsty learns that Lois is going to have a baby; instead of being outraged, she has newfound sympathy for her stepmother. A call from Jake's parents that a flood has come to Norfolk and that Jake is missing sends Kirsty scurrying back to the village. She realizes that Jake must be in Old Corpusty's cottage and that Jake had sounded the old church bell to warn the people of the impending flood.

Themes and Meanings

The Whistling Boy is a first-person narrative in which the protagonist, Kirsty, reaches a significant emotional milestone in her growth toward maturity. The audience of the novel, adolescent girls, will identify closely with the central character as she laments her inability to control her self-centered feelings. Kirsty's character is dynamically developed, growing as she moves toward caring and helping others. The primary theme of learning to care for the well-being of others is illustrated by the changes that take place within Kirsty. She did not help Dinah; however, she is determined to save Jake and help her sensitive younger brother face his fears. Once she overcomes her negative feelings, she reaches beyond her self-centered problems toward her young stepmother. The author has established a "grown-up" problem that is realistic for someone Kirsty's age, and she has presented it in a way that is understandable to the young adolescent.

Although Gerry Newton, the father, provides some conflict, he is not the foil against which Kirsty's character development is contrasted. This is an "enemy within-thyself" or self-against-self novel in which the reader experiences Kirsty's developing maturity through inner monologues, as Kirsty berates herself for not accepting Lois in a maternal role or helping Dinah in her desperate home situation.

Jake serves as the romantic interest for Kirsty and is the catalyst who provides opportunity for her to mature. Old Corpusty's character is at first presented negatively; however, he becomes a more sympathetic figure as his history is revealed, and he provides some valuable clues for Kirsty in her quest to help Jake. Dinah's character of the disadvantaged teenager, envious of the Newton's family situation, contrasts with the middle-class English background of Kirsty.

Context

The setting of *The Whistling Boy* is a small town close to the sea, similar to those of the author's other novels. Ruth M. Arthur's major characters are often young adolescent girls who face and solve adult problems. For example, the plot of *After Candlemas* (1974) is similar to that of *The Whistling Boy:* The major character, Harriet, is also isolated from her family, the story contains elements of the supernatural, and there is a young boy who is rescued by the main character.

In the mid to late 1960's, juvenile characters became more realistic. They were depicted as rebelling against adult authority and as having a life of their own outside the family. Girls were viewed as more capable of taking charge. Ruth Arthur's female protagonists solve mysteries and help others. In doing so, they mature emotionally and socially. *The Whistling Boy* reflects these trends.

Nell Powers Braswell

WHOSE TOWN?

Author: Lorenz Bell Graham (1902-   )
Type of plot: Social realism
Time of plot: The 1960's
Locale: North Town, a fictional city in the Northeastern United States
Principal themes: Social issues, race and ethnicity, and coming-of-age
First published: 1969
Recommended ages: 13-15

David Williams, a black high school senior, and his family and friends must deal with bigotry after a violent confrontation between blacks and whites brings about the death of one of David's best friends. The answers to racial problems are not easily settled as citizens of North Town attempt to calm conflicting emotions that arise in the community.

Principal characters:
 DAVID WILLIAMS, a black high school senior who must learn to deal with conflicting ideas about racial problems
 MR. WILLIAMS, his father, a mechanic who has brought his family north in an attempt to give them a better life
 MRS. WILLIAMS, his mother, who must go out to work when his father is laid off
 SAM SILVERMAN, a hardware-store owner who hires him to work part-time
 JOHN BOWMAN, his friend and coworker, who tries to convince him that it is time for black people to fight back
 JEANETTE LENOIR, his girlfriend, a college freshman
 BETTY JANE WILLIAMS, his sister

The Story
 Whose Town? is a contemporary novel that sets forth in simple, readable language the story of its young protagonist, David Williams, as he confronts the growing-up problems of a black teenager in a predominantly white Northern community.
 After leaving a party, David and a group of friends stop at the Plantation Drive-in for hamburgers, and David is jumped by a group of white boys. His friends, Jimmy Hicks and Lonnie Webster, come to his aid, but the police arrive on the scene, and the white boys accuse David of jumping them. The group of young blacks, including their girlfriends, are taken to the police station, but they are later released to Sergeant Reed, the father of one of the girls.
 When they return to Jimmy's car, which was left parked at a service station, they find that all the glass in the car has been broken, and the attendant denies seeing anyone doing the damage. Later David, Jimmy, and Lonnie return to the service

station to try to get the man to give them more information, but instead he orders them away, pulls a gun, and kills Lonnie. David is arrested because the attendant testifies that the three young blacks were attacking him and that he fired only in self-defense.

A normal return to high school life and his part-time job at Sam Silverman's hardware store seems impossible for David. He questions himself about whose town this is. He finds himself confronted with racial prejudice in the local newspaper and among the white students and faculty. The principal warns him that he may not be allowed to graduate even though he has excellent academic and sports records. Only Coach Henderson, his football coach, seems interested in his side of the story, and even he does not understand that David has feelings of often wanting to join with the blacks who fight back. David tries to explain that he is a victim of race prejudice and hatred, but not even the coach is sympathetic.

David's father and mother attempt to help him in every way possible, but his father has been laid off from his job at the Foundation Iron and Machine Works, and his mother must return to doing housework for white people. David's trouble brings more legal and financial problems to their already depleted income.

At the inquest into Lonnie's death, the jury finds that the action of the attendant was justifiable homicide, but the district attorney does not bring charges against David.

David is graduated, but his thoughts about the incidents of the past year and the problems his parents and other blacks are having continue to make him question himself about many issues. The drowning death of a young black boy, which is believed to have been caused by white teenagers, brings rioting to the neighborhood. The ugly question of whose town it is arises once more in David's mind. His co worker John Bowman urges him to go to a meeting called by the Reverend Moshombo, who David believes is spreading hatred, while his parents encourage him to attend church, where the Reverend Hayes attempts to calm the people with the message that all white people are not in opposition to the rights of others. David decides that he should choose the message of the Reverend Hayes.

David joins with his boss, Sam, and other workers who begin to rebuild what fire has damaged during the riot. He attempts to understand and sincerely believe that not giving up is a form of success.

Themes and Meanings

Beginning with the title, *Whose Town?*, Lorenz Graham asks the reader to confront an important question: How can the many racial problems that confront the communities of the United States be solved? The teenage black protagonist's search for the answer to this question is always foremost in the novel.

In the first chapter, young David Williams tells his father, "You got to listen to every side, and then make up your own mind. That's what you've always said."

David does try to listen to both sides as he goes to the meetings of the Reverend Moshombo, where he hears the white man described as one who is still unwilling to recognize the God-given rights of the black man, and as he attends his church, where the minister, the Reverend Hayes, tells his congregation, "We must realize that white people also are people, no better and at the same time no worse than colored people. And that within the body of the white race there are many—nay, millions—of people who are on the side of right."

In simple, straightforward language, Graham presents David's thoughts as he struggles between these two strongly opposing beliefs and tries to find for himself a road to adulthood that is not marred by hate, bigotry, and violence. When David begins to realize that his own feelings are more in tune with the Christian ideals of the Reverend Hayes, he then tries to think of ways to help stop the hatred. The novel cannot reach a settlement of all his questions, as many of the questions of the 1960's remain unanswered, but it does keep alive a hope for the time when all races can live together more harmoniously.

Context

Whose Town? is the third volume of a series of four novels by Lorenz Graham which deal with fifteen years in the life of David Williams, a young black man who must confront racial problems as he comes of age in the 1950's and 1960's. The series begins with *South Town* (1958), in which the Williams family, confronted with bigotry and violence, decide that they must leave their home in the South to try to make a better life for themselves. The second and third volumes, *North Town* (1967) and *Whose Town?*, continue their story, as they find a better financial way of life but unhappily realize that there is no way of escaping racial conflicts. The last of the series, *Return to South Town* (1976), relates David's return to the small town the family left and the problems he encounters as he attempts to establish his medical practice as the first black doctor in the town.

In the series, Graham makes the reader aware of the strong social message he is delivering: Prejudice arises from the lack of understanding of both blacks and whites for the other group. He always creates key characters who attempt to calm disturbing situations and to bring the two sides together. Each book ends with a hopeful look toward a time when race relations will be better.

Graham, the son of a minister, began to write Bible stories for young people after serving as a missionary in Liberia. His strong Christian values are evident throughout the series about the Williams family. Most of the principal characters have a strong belief in God and in the settling of racial problems without resorting to violence.

Graham's books were among the first to present the problems of young black people for adolescent readers. Through the viewpoint of David Williams, they offer young readers of both races insight into the conflicts young black people must face.

Joan Parker Posey

THE WIND IN THE WILLOWS

Author: Kenneth Grahame (1859-1932)
Type of plot: Adventure tale
Time of plot: The early twentieth century
Locale: Toad Hall and its environs in the English countryside
Principal themes: Animals, friendship, and nature
First published: 1908; illustrated
Recommended ages: 10-13

Five animal friends of very different temperaments live along the bank of a river or in the nearby wildwood and share in one another's advantures, maintaining their fellowship through many trying episodes.

Principal characters:
> TOAD, a wealthy, overindulged, and egotistical reprobate, who constantly seeks new experiences
> MOLE, a somewhat impetuous but industrious character, both provident and faithful to his friends
> RAT, an excellent oarsman, a kind, sympathetic, and contented inhabitant of the riverbank
> BADGER, the patriarch of the wildwood, an older, more thoughtful and experienced member of the group, a philosopher
> WAYFARER RAT, a transient, who beguiles Rat with tales of adventure in distant lands
> OTTER, knowledgeable about the byways and paths of the wildwood, who acts as its policeman and supervisor

The Story

Ostensibly a children's story in the form of a fable, *The Wind in the Willows* has always been popular with adult readers as well, because the principal characters have the traits of humans and their behavior, values, and actions offer valuable insights into human motivations and relationships. The riverbank and the wildwood are, in fact, a microcosm of human society, and the inhabitants offer a typical cross section of real-life persons, with their ambitions, weaknesses, strengths, and needs— among which is companionship.

The story opens with a memorable domestic scene: Mole is whitewashing and spring-cleaning his house. Like everyone else, however, he soon tires of these chores and decides to picnic in the inviting outdoors, where he meets the other inhabitants of the area and, ever impetuous, tries to row Rat's boat but soon falls overboard. Rat and Mole visit the celebrated Toad, whose mansion, Toad Hall, is renowned throughout the region. Rat, somewhat too generous in his evaluation of others, describes Toad as "always good-tempered, always glad to see you, always sorry when you go!" He then adds, however (by way of second thought), "Perhaps he's not very clever—we can't all be geniuses; and it may be that he is both boastful and conceited. But he has got some great qualities, has Toady." This characterization of Toad reveals Rat's own character well: He is inclined to overlook weaknesses in friends, to be forgiving, charitable. This generosity is sometimes taken advantage of by others.

The three friends set off in Toad's latest passion, his Gipsy caravan, but it is soon wrecked. As winter arrives, Rat and Mole visit Badger, who is a perfect host and entertains them admirably, even recounting Toad's seven car accidents with some disdain for his frivolous life-style. After being entertained by caroling fieldmice, Mole reflects on his life and concludes that the simple life, dull and boring when compared to the world beyond, is nevertheless to be valued highly: Home has a value that cannot be measured by anyone else. "He saw clearly how plain and simple—how narrow, even—it all was; but clearly, too, how much it all meant to him." Otter arrives, announcing the concern of the inhabitants of the riverbank over Rat's absence; he leads Rat home but soon requires his friends' assistance in finding Portly, a young otter who has wandered off.

Throughout the story all the other characters, including the Wayfarer Rat (who tells Rat about the wonders of Constantinople, Venice, Marseilles, and other fabled cities), come to the conclusion that while the world beyond their narrow confines has a temporary attraction and charm, even the simplest, dullest home has greater satisfaction to offer. This viewpoint is captured in the chapter entitled "Dulce Domum" (home sweet home). Toad, always irrepressible, is the last to accept this: He plans to buy a new red sports car but is discouraged by Badger; however, he escapes from his friends, steals a high-powered car parked outside the Red Lion inn, and is sentenced to twenty years in jail. He escapes in disguise (as a washerwoman), persuades a train driver to give him a free ride, is pursued and then manages to get a ride on a canal boat before stealing the horse and selling it to a Gipsy. On the highway again, he is given a ride by the owners of the car, inveigles the owner into letting him drive, and crashes into a pond.

On his return to the riverbank, Toad learns that Toad Hall has been taken over by stoats and weasels. Badger, who knows of a secret passage into the house, plans an attack during a banquet and recovers the house for Toad, who is forced by him to celebrate with a great banquet for the neighborhood friends. To the very end, however, Toad exhibits his vanity: He wants to make several speeches; to recount his great adventures in order to suggest his cunning, skill, bravery, and sophistication; and to sing several songs of his own composition. Badger, however, forbids this and orders a simple celebration. He makes Toad reimburse those whom he had defrauded during his adventures. The result is a chastened Toad, an animal of greater worldly wealth than his companions but one who has come to appreciate the sterling qualities of his friends who are content with a simpler, less flamboyant life-style.

Themes and Meanings

The Wind in the Willows is constructed in the traditional epic form of twelve books, the final one of which is entitled "The Return of Ulysses," thus drawing attention to the character of Toad as a sort of hero whose multifarious adventures and narrow escapes keep the reader's attention. Against Toad are contrasted the more sedate, conventional characters who hold the world of the riverbank and the wildwood together—and who are ultimately responsible for Toad's safety, salvation, and rehabilitation. That is, the story can be seen as an allegory of life (as indeed fables are intended to be).

Furthermore, the events of the story transpire over two years, beginning in the spring (when the reader is introduced to the denizens of the riverbank) and concluding in the late fall of the following year (when Toad Hall is recaptured). Each season's mood is beautifully captured in the descriptive passages, and the contrast between the frenzied activities of summer and the somnolence of fall and winter is carefully manipulated. Toad's high jinks are typically summer activities; Badger's quiet, philosophical nature is best seen during the autumnal and winter days, which he spends in his house. As he observes, "People come—they stay for a while, they flourish, they build—and they go. It is their way. But we remain." His is the voice of serenity, of contentment, of endurance, as when he comments, "We are an enduring lot, and we may move out for a time, but we wait, and are patient, and back we come. And so it will ever be." Between these extremes (Toad the hedonist, Badger the stoic) are Mole and Rat. Though Mole had managed to own a rather beautiful and well-appointed home (a windfall from an aunt), he made it over to his standards by "laborious savings and a certain amount of going without"; that is, he represents, in a manner, the Protestant ethic, the middle-of-the-road individual. Yet he comes to realize that friends and a modest existence are preferable to wealth and loneliness. Rat, similarly, is admirable: He is a congenial companion though not overly gregarious; he is not envious or proud; he is frugal yet a good entertainer; he is skilled in many arts and crafts, and a stalwart, reliable friend who understands the value of "mere silent companionship." He is a perfect foil to Toad: He is dignified, while his friend has "a strong sense of his own dignity."

Context

Kenneth Grahame's first book was *The Golden Age* (1895), a collection of stories in an English country setting; this was followed by *Dream Days* (1898), a sequel, which comprised eight additional stories in the same manner. *The Wind in the Willows*, notwithstanding the critical and popular success of these two predecessors, was initially rejected by a publisher who considered that the form of the story was "most unexpected." In this it might be said to have shared the initial fate of George Orwell's *Animal Farm* (1945): Since the eighteenth century, fables have not always been popular. *The Wind in the Willows*, however, has none of the trenchant social criticism of *Animal Farm*, and it lacks the political message that Orwell was intent on conveying: It is a rather straightforward, simple story of animals who act, feel, think like humans—and mix with them without being seen by humans as animals. That is, the animal and the human individuals and societies are presented as interchangeable, so that the reader can draw conclusions from the depiction of the animals of the wildwood and riverbank and easily make them applicable to analogous individuals. Perhaps for this reason the book has remained popular with adults and children.

Marian B. McLeod

WINNIE-THE-POOH and THE HOUSE AT POOH CORNER

Author: A. A. Milne (1882-1956)
Type of plot: Fantasy
Time of plot: The 1920's
Locale: 100 AKER WOOD, and Pooh Corner, England
Principal themes: Friendship and animals
First published: Winnie-the-Pooh, 1926; *The House at Pooh Corner*, 1928; published together as *The World of Pooh*, 1957, 1958; all illustrated
Recommended ages: 10-13

Personified stuffed animals show human characteristics as they explore the 100 AKER WOOD and Pooh Corner. Christopher Robin, their human owner, is the loving caretaker of his friends.

> Principal characters:
> WINNIE-THE-POOH, a humble bear, who is often told he has very little brain
> EEYORE, a pessimistic donkey, whose doleful comments provide much humor
> RABBIT, a self-centered hare
> PIGLET, a small, timid pig
> CHRISTOPHER ROBIN, the only human character, who helps his stuffed friends find solutions to problems

The Story

The World of Pooh is a story of childhood fantasy and fears. The setting is the English countryside outside Christopher Robin's home, specifically the make-believe 100 AKER WOOD. The characters have adventures that interweave nonsense and good sense in a way which appeals to children; because of the books' effective use of satire, they also have meaning for the more mature reader.

Author A. A. Milne, serving as narrator, begins the story by telling it to Christopher Robin. The animals take on the personality traits of humans, to an exaggerated degree. For example, Winnie-the-Pooh has a strong need for approval. One episode finds Pooh stuck in Rabbit's doorway because he ate too much honey. Another time, he teaches his friends the game of Poohsticks. This game is instrumental in saving Eeyore, the pessimistic donkey, from floating down the river. As Pooh acts, his many friends give him advice. Eeyore, dripping wet, comes up out of the river and tells everyone that he dived to avoid being hit by a stone that Pooh dropped to save him. Thus, Pooh the hero becomes Pooh the bear with very little brain. Eeyore demonstrates his caustic personality, while Piglet, the shy pig, tries to make Pooh feel better.

Another incident involves Rabbit, who considers himself very important and seems always to be busy. He tells the animals to search for Small but forgets to say who Small is. The animals hypothesize that it must be one of Rabbit's relatives, since he has so many. Piglet, fearful as he searches alone, falls into a pit. Pooh, hearing his name called by Piglet, also falls into the pit. He discovers that Piglet has found Small.

Other adventures include searching for the North Pole, being in a flood, and hunting for Huffalumps. If the animals get stranded or cannot solve a problem, one of them, on behalf of all, will search out Christopher Robin for help. Each episode is full of humor and goodwill that, however, sometimes goes awry.

When school becomes important in Christopher Robin's life, he has less time to spend with his stuffed friends. Thus, childhood is ending for Christopher Robin, but his friends do not change even though they try to learn the alphabet and to write. Their examples of invented spelling add humor for the reader.

The final episode finds Eeyore, not Pooh, writing a poem for Christopher Robin; the animals are all gathered as the poem is presented to Christopher Robin. They know that the time for farewells has come. Only Pooh stays while Christopher Robin reads the poem, after which the two of them go to the enchanted place. Since it is enchanted, Pooh is granted knighthood before the two friends say good-bye. The enchanted place will always be there when they want to return in memory.

Themes and Meanings

A. A. Milne, in his children's stories, portrays the dual characteristics of childlike egotism and innocence in his animal characters. In his *Autobiography* (1939), he states, "A pen-picture of a child which showed it as loving, grateful and full of thought for others would be false to the truth; but equally false would be a picture which insisted on the brutal egotism of the child." Fussy Kanga worries about the well-being of everyone; boisterous Tigger acts without thinking.

The story changes when the animals begin to wonder what letters are and how they are made; Christopher Robin is seldom home, because he has to learn about numbers and the alphabet. Time changes Christopher Robin's life, but his friends cannot change as their minds are made of sawdust. At the end of *The House at Pooh Corner*, Christopher Robin can still return to the time of Pooh—but only in his memory.

Context

Milne was a British author of plays, nonfiction, essays, poetry, and novels. He began his literary career as an assistant editor for *Punch*. Writing for children developed from watching his son, Christopher Robin, grow and play. His first book for children was *When We Were Very Young* (1924); it was written in poetic form and shows humor, charm, and an understanding of the child's mind. In 1927, his second book of children's poetry, *Now We Are Six*, was published.

Winnie-the-Pooh (1926) became Milne's first juvenile fiction. Although criticized for the use of invented spelling, it immediately became popular. Both children and adults love the characters. When *The House at Pooh Corner* (1928) was published, it too became standard reading for children. Soon the two were combined into one volume entitled *The World of Pooh* (1957, 1958). *The House at Pooh Corner* leads the reader to the farewell scene between Christopher Robin and Pooh. Although Milne returned to adult writing, he is best known for his children's books, which have become classics. Few other authors have so captured the pure innocence of childhood.

Milne's work characterizes British life in the 1920's. His characters mirror the manners and customs of a middle-class family in rural England at that time. The gentle nature and humanness of the culture can be seen reflected in them. These characters come to life with the exquisite illustrations produced by Ernest H. Shepard. Shepard's illustrations help endow the storybook animals with life and personality.

Marilyn Wikstrom

THE WITCH OF BLACKBIRD POND

Author: Elizabeth George Speare (1908-   )
Type of plot: Historical fiction
Time of plot: The late seventeenth century
Locale: Wethersfield in Connecticut Colony
Principal themes: Friendship, love and romance, religion, and family
First published: 1958
Recommended ages: 13-15

Kit Tyler finds Puritan life in Connecticut Colony radically different from life in Barbados. Difficulty in conforming eventually causes her to be tried as a witch, but a handsome seaman comes to her rescue.

> *Principal characters:*
> KIT TYLER, a headstrong, impetuous sixteen-year-old who arrives unannounced from Barbados to live with her aunt
> NATHANIEL EATON, the handsome son of the ship's captain
> RACHEL WOOD, Kit's aunt; a kind, loving woman who warmly welcomes her
> MATTHEW WOOD, Rachel's husband, a stern man; a leader in the church and in the colony
> JUDITH WOOD, the beautiful, self-centered elder daughter of Rachel
> MERCY WOOD, the handicapped younger daughter of Rachel; she has an air of gentleness and goodness
> WIDOW HANNAH TUPPER, a poor widow who has been labeled a witch and banished from the colony because she is a Quaker
> PRUDENCE CRUFF, the timid, abused daughter of Goodwife Cruff
> GOODWIFE CRUFF, a cold domineering woman who leads the movement to have Kit tried as a witch

The Story

Orphaned Kit Tyler grew up on the island of Barbados in the luxurious house of her loving grandfather. When he dies, circumstances force her to seek sanctuary in the home of her aunt. The story begins with sixteen-year-old Kit on a ship going from Barbados to Connecticut Colony. During the course of the trip, she discovers many ways in which her background differs from those of the people in this new place. The simple act of swimming to rescue a young girl's doll brings dire warnings that Puritans believe that only witches fail to sink when in deep water.

Upon her arrival in Connecticut, Kit is shocked by the restricting attitudes of the Puritans and the austere environment. Life is harsh in this new land, and there are no servants to do the work. Her aunt is delighted that she has come, and Judith and Mercy, her cousins, share in their mother's joy to some degree but are shocked at

Kit's lack of work skills. Her uncle is shamed by the quantity of her possessions. The family strives to make the best of it and to get along, but Kit finds it extremely difficult to conform to such rigid standards and rules. All too often her independence and impetuosity cause serious problems.

The cast of characters in the story unfolds quickly: Nathaniel Eaton, a striking figure, the first mate on the ship, and the son of the captain; John Holbrook, a young clergyman, also a passenger on the ship, going to Wethersfield to study; William Ashby, considered by many to be the most eligible bachelor in the settlement because of his wealth, who soon asks permission to call on Kit as a suitor much to the dismay of Judith, who has been seeking his attentions.

Kit first meets Goodwife Cruff on the ship and is accused by her of being a witch, because Goodwife does not approve of Kit's clothing or the fact that she went into the water to retrieve a doll. Prudence is the young, abused daughter of Goodwife.

A place called The Meadows, beside Blackbird Pond, reminds Kit of the freedoms of Barbados. The Meadows is where she meets the Widow Hannah, who lives alone in a small shack there with only her cats for company. Hannah has been accused by some of the townspeople of being a witch. A strong bond of friendship develops between Kit and Hannah, who has also been befriended by Nat.

Kit learns a painful lesson as she discovers the bigotry that exists in the community. She is accused of being a witch herself and is imprisoned. Nat comes to her rescue along with Prudence, who finds the courage to defy her mother and testify on behalf of Kit. Love and romance are an important part of this story, as Kit and her two cousins find the perfect mates and fall in love. Kit eventually decides that Wethersfield is home. She realizes that there is a place for her independence even in the Puritan community.

Themes and Meanings

Speare has created a story that depicts the lives of several young people who are in the midst of seeking to know themselves and to find their places in life. The story centers on the struggles of Kit Tyler. She is a high-spirited young woman, who is not afraid to think for herself but desires to fit into the life of the new community, where she finds herself after the death of her grandfather. *The Witch of Blackbird Pond* is a story of contrasts. Kit comes from Barbados, where the climate is warm and the environment is rich in color and refinement. She leaves the home of her grandfather, where she has been a highly favored only child living in affluence, encouraged to be free in spirit and thought, to go to the home of her aunt and uncle. She finds Connecticut Colony to be cold and barren. Survival is itself a major challenge. Servants did the work in Barbados, and in Connecticut there is grueling work that demands the efforts of every member of the household from morning until night.

Kit's two cousins, while close as sisters, are very different. Judith is a beautiful young woman, who delights in appearances and things. She puts concern for her own needs and desires before those of anyone else. Her sister, Mercy, on the other hand, seems to have an instinct for discerning the needs and feelings of others and consistently puts her own desires behind those of others. Although she is hand-icapped, she finds fewer things about which to complain than does Judith.

Kit is befriended by two young men who provide another contrast. Nat is the son of the ship's captain. He must work hard to earn all that he has and has little regard of what others will think of him. He has befriended the Widow Hannah in spite of the fact that the townspeople have called her a witch. William Ashby is the son of wealthy parents and is busy building the most beautiful house in the settlement, even before he has chosen his bride. Prestige and recognition are very important to him, and he could not be happy with a bride who did not take such things seriously.

Kit finds the people of the colony to be greatly concerned with the teachings of the Bible but only as it is interpreted by a few leaders. At times, they display little of the compassion and love taught therein.

Context

Speare has written five books of historical fiction, four of them for upper-grade readers and one for those in the middle grades. *The Witch of Blackbird Pond* is the most popular and, in 1959, was her first to receive the Newbery Medal. In 1960, it was added to the International Board on Books for Young Children. Her book *The Bronze Bow* (1961) won the Newbery Medal in 1962, and a third book, *The Sign of the Beaver* (1983), was a Newbery Honor Book in 1984 in addition to being the first recipient of the Scott O'Dell Award for Historical Fiction in 1983.

Speare's first novel, *The Calico Captive* (1957), was an expansion of an actual diary of a young woman who, along with her family, was captured by Indians and forced to march to Canada. Thorough research enabled her to portray the back-ground and setting of the story in a spellbinding manner, which enables the reader to become a part of that time period of history.

Speare's research abilities were again evidenced in the one piece of nonfiction that she did, *Life in Colonial America* (1963). Without presenting an overwhelming amount of material, she was able to depict the essence of life in the southern, cen-tral, and New England colonies through careful selection of artifacts and illustra-tions. Speare has been admired for her ability to develop strong, lifelike characters who are fully human. Many similarities may be found in Daniel of *The Bronze Bow* and Kit of *The Witch of Blackbird Pond*. Both are intense young people with strong feelings about life. Through the course of the respective stories, both change and mature, coming to terms with themselves and those around them. In the process, each acquires a deeper understanding of the meaning of love and justice and the personal need for balance between independence and cooperation. *The Witch of Blackbird Pond* is an outstanding example of Speare's skill in characterization. A wide variety of characters are presented, but all are fully developed and eerily viewed as real people. This book has effectively demonstrated the power of histor-ical fiction to make history come alive for the reader, even one who may not have a love for history as an area of study.

Beverly Taylor Simpson

THE WITCHES OF WORM

Author: Zilpha Keatley Snyder (1927-   )
Type of plot: Psychological realism
Time of plot: The 1970's
Locale: San Francisco
Principal themes: Emotions, family, and health and illness
First published: 1972; illustrated
Recommended ages: 10-13

Often neglected by her attractive young mother, Jessica Porter evidences strange behavior as she imagines her cat to be possessed by demons.

> *Principal characters:*
> JESSICA PORTER, a twelve-year-old only child living with her mother in an apartment
> JOY PORTER, an attractive, young, self-centered single parent who works as a secretary
> BRANDON DOYLE, a neighbor and former playmate of Jessica, who plays the trumpet
> MRS. FORTUNE, an elderly woman who owns the apartment building, has several cats, and befriends Jessica
> MRS. POST, a former baby-sitter for Jessica
> WORM, the newborn, orphan kitten that Jessica adopts

The Story

The Witches of Worm is a contemporary realistic fiction novel that deals with the concerns of Jessica Porter, a disturbed, lonely child from a single-parent home. San Francisco, with its suddenly changing weather of chilling wind, poisonous fog, and rolling clouds, forms the backdrop for this story of emotional turmoil. The Regency Apartment House has been Jessica's home for as long as she can remember, but during the last year, her neighborhood friendships and her relationship with her mother have deteriorated. Jessica, an avid reader and imaginative twelve-year-old, increasingly turns her emotions inward as the perceived rejection by her best friend, Brandon Doyle, and neglect by her attractive young mother, Joy, intensify.

To escape the unusual weather and oppressive loneliness of her apartment, Jessica climbs to Blackberry Heights, a flat hilltop overlooking the city. On the heights in a cave where Jessica once played pretend games with Brandon, she discovers a strangely colored newborn kitten. Although Jessica does not like cats, she takes the abandoned kitten to elderly Mrs. Fortune, owner of several cats and the Regency Apartment House. When the friendship between Brandon and Jessica was strong, they used to visit Mrs. Fortune to hear her strange tales of magic. Mrs. Fortune refuses to take the kitten but advises Jessica of its needs. Under Jessica's care, the kitten, which she names Worm, thrives, but his behavior and appearance seem increasingly strange as Jessica's relationship with the cat becomes more and more complex. She begins avoiding Worm as her loneliness, anger, and malicious deeds increase. Jessica hears voices that she attributes to Worm, telling her to lie and commit destructive acts. She believes Worm to be possessed.

Mrs. Post, her former sitter, catches Jessica in deceitful behavior and reports it to Joy, who arranges for Jessica to see the school psychologist, Mr. Weaver. Jessica believes that she has succeeded in fooling Mr. Weaver, but the howling demon voice still is not gone. Jessica decides to destroy Worm. Through the intervention of Mrs. Fortune, an exorcism is attempted, but Worm escapes from the apartment into a fierce storm. Brandon comes to Jessica's assistance in finding the almost drowned Worm. Jessica, wet from the storm and in a highly emotional state, arrives home with Worm. Her mother calls a physician. Jessica later realizes that she must tell the truth about her deeds and is relieved to learn that she can cry and is therefore not a witch. She is glad, too, that Worm is not dead.

Themes and Meanings

The major theme in *The Witches of Worm* concerns the nature of the emotional relationship between parent and child. Jessica, perceiving malice and deception in personal relationships, increasingly retreats emotionally into herself and into fantasies of revenge. In this suggestible state, her imagination is stirred further by her reading about witches. At this point of vulnerability, Jessica discovers the abandoned kitten with which she can identify. As the kitten grows, so do Jessica's disturbance, her spiteful acts, and her belief that Worm is controlling her. Joy's parental concern for her daughter's behavior mounts, until she takes responsible action and seeks help for her daughter's well-being.

The characterization and events are carefully drawn to maintain a sense of mystery. Whether the exorcism rite ends the demon's control over Jessica or Jessica is emotionally disturbed and helped by the school psychologist is left unexplained. At the conclusion, Jessica is able to express emotions, she has reestablished her friendship with Brandon, and her relationship with her mother is improved. Worm will be rehabilitated with the help of Brandon.

Context

The Witches of Worm was published in the early 1970's at a time when a number of children's novels were being written that described single-parent families and adult failings. The Civil Rights movement and social freedoms of the 1960's came to be reflected in children's novels of the following decade, when taboos restricting topics were swept away. The traditional approach of children's literature, with its carefree view of childhood, was replaced by novels highlighting the problems of youth. Adults were shown as fallible; divorce and single-parent-family novels began to increase in number to reflect social reality.

Few stories, however, were published that dealt with the emotionally disturbed child. *The Planet of Junior Brown* (1971) by Virginia Hamilton, which appeared about the same time, does have some parallels to *The Witches of Worm*. An interesting aspect of the novel is the careful balance of evidence regarding the cause of Jessica's emotional pain. How much of the problem may be the product of a lonely, intelligent, and imaginative child, and how much may be caused by parental neglect? Could Jessica have been under a demon's control or did a psychologist recognize her problem and successfully intervene? Zilpha Snyder has left these questions for the reader to decide, just as was done in her earlier work, *The Headless Cupid* (1971), which also involves the occult.

Emilie P. Sullivan

THE WIZARD OF OZ

Author: L. Frank Baum (1856-1919)
Type of plot: Adventure tale
Time of plot: The late nineteenth century
Locale: The Kansas plains and the fictional land of Oz
Principal themes: Friendship and the supernatural
First published: 1900, as *The Wonderful Wizard of Oz*; retitled, 1902
Recommended ages: 10-13

Dorothy, a young girl living in Kansas with her aunt and uncle, is caught in a tornado that sweeps her, her dog Toto, and her house to the strange land of Oz. They begin a journey that leads them across many lands and introduces them to all sorts of odd animals and people.

Principal characters:
DOROTHY, a sweet girl, living with her Aunt Em and Uncle Henry on the plains of Kansas, whose wish, as soon as she gets to Oz, is to go home
TOTO, her little black dog
THE SCARECROW, a walking, talking scarecrow who becomes Dorothy's first companion and goes with her to the Emerald City in search of a brain
THE TIN WOODMAN, Dorothy's second companion, a man made of tin who is looking for a heart
THE COWARDLY LION, Dorothy's third companion, who plans to ask the Great Wizard of Oz for courage
THE WIZARD OF OZ, ruler of the Emerald City, who will grant the wishes of the four travelers only if they kill the Wicked Witch of the West
THE WICKED WITCH OF THE WEST, a cruel old hag, slave master of the Winkies, who wants Dorothy's silver shoes, for they are magical

The Story

The Wizard of Oz is, in the words of its author, a "wonder tale" about a young Kansas girl who makes a journey into the land of Oz—a world peopled by unfamiliar beings, both good and evil, and from which she seeks to find her way home. Dorothy finds her way to this land when, one day in Kansas, where she lives with her Aunt Em and Uncle Henry, a tornado suddenly whisks their house away.

From the gray plains of Kansas, Dorothy and Toto, her small dog, are carried by tornado to Oz, a strange and uncivilized land. When they fall into Munchkinland, Dorothy's house crushes the Wicked Witch of the East.

The Munchkins, a small but friendly people, have never heard of Kansas. When the Good Witch of the North appears, she directs Dorothy to the Emerald City, home to the great and terrible Wizard of Oz. Before she leaves on the yellow brick road, Dorothy puts on the silver shoes of the wicked witch. She does not know their magic power. Along the yellow brick road, Dorothy and Toto meet the three characters who will be their companions for the rest of the journey. The Scarecrow, Tin Woodman, and Cowardly Lion agree to go with her in the hope that the Wizard can provide what they are lacking: brains for the Scarecrow, a heart for the Tin Woodman, and courage for the Cowardly Lion.

The journey is long and arduous, and they meet many obstacles. They cross ravines with jagged rocks below. They are chased by Kalidahs, fierce animals with the heads of tigers and bodies of bears. They fall asleep in the heart of a poppy field; and just when it seems as if they will sleep forever, they are rescued by thousands of mice.

When they reach the Emerald City, they are brought, one by one, to see the Wizard. He appears in a different form to each. To Dorothy, he appears as a big head. To the Scarecrow, he looks like a beautiful woman. To the Tin Woodman, he is a terrible beast. To the Cowardly Lion, he becomes a ball of fire.

His message to all is the same, however: Kill the Wicked Witch of the West, and he will grant them whatever they wish. So, worried and fearful, they set off to destroy the wicked witch. The witch sees them coming and tries to kill them three times: once with deadly wolves, once with crows, and finally with killer bees. Each time the heroes survive, only to be taken to the castle by winged monkeys.

At the castle, Dorothy is made a slave, and Cowardly Lion is put in a cage. Scarecrow's straw stuffing is flung away and he is left a rag on a treetop. Tin Woodman is battered against rocks and left helpless. When the wicked witch tries to steal the silver shoes, Dorothy becomes so angry that she douses her with water. The witch melts into a pile of black ashes, "liquidated."

When the winged monkeys, now under Dorothy's control, fly the restored heroes back to the Emerald City, there is a terrible surprise awaiting them. The Wizard is a fake, a humbug. He tells them how he came to Oz, carried away from a circus in Omaha in a hot-air balloon. He tells them that he has no magical powers.

They insist, however, that he help them as he promised, so he stuffs Scarecrow's head with pins and needles, convincing him that he now has brains. He gives the Tin Woodman a silk heart, which he puts into the hollow tin chest. He makes Cowardly Lion swallow a green liquid that the Wizard claims is courage. The three companions now have what they want.

To help Dorothy, the Wizard repairs his hot-air balloon, but just as all are ready to go, Toto disappears. The Wizard must leave without the dog—and Dorothy. Dorothy is forlorn, but the others vow to stay with her until she gets back to Kansas.

They begin another journey which takes them across forests, valleys of china, and hills of Quadlings—strange creatures with heads on springs. In the end they meet Glinda, the Good Witch of the South, who tells Dorothy about the power of her silver shoes. After saying farewell to her friends, Dorothy takes three steps and, flying through the sky, is soon home in Kansas.

Themes and Meanings

The Wizard of Oz is an adventure story about the triumph of good over evil. The way the book is structured, with each chapter offering a new obstacle to overcome, keeps the reader interested. With magic, talking animals, and vivid colors, in contrast to the gray plains of reality, or Kansas, *The Wizard of Oz* is an adventure fantasy for children.

The book, however, is much more. First, there is the theme of friendship, recounted again and again. Any time there is danger, some character puts his life on the line for his friends. When the killer bees attack, Tin Woodman stands alone against them. When Cowardly Lion is caged and starved, Dorothy feeds and comforts him.

This bond continues to grow stronger, culminating in her three companions' refusal to abandon Dorothy, even though they have obtained what they wanted. Their loyalty for one another is unbreakable; their love, unquestioned. They will part only when she gets what she wants: to go home.

The theme that runs strongest through the book is self-reliance. While all the characters look for something outside themselves, they discover that they have been looking in the wrong direction, for the exact qualities they desire are within themselves. When a situation takes brains to analyze, it is always Scarecrow who does so. When courage is needed to fight an enemy, it is Cowardly Lion who has plenty of it. Tin Woodman is forever in danger of rusting himself because he is always on the verge of tears, thanks to his big heart.

Even Dorothy finds she has the power, with the silver shoes, to bring herself back home. Like the others, she has never looked within herself. What she wanted was there all the time. This is probably the strongest message *The Wizard of Oz* bears, a message as old as Plato: Know thyself.

Context

The Wizard of Oz is the first of fourteen Oz books that L. Frank Baum wrote about that now-famous imaginary land. Immediately successful, they created what Baum calls a "wonder tale"—a story, he writes in the foreword, "in which the stereotyped genie, dwarf and fairy are eliminated, together with all the horrible and blood-curdling incidents devised by their authors to point a fearsome moral." The book, Baum explained, was to be a modern-day fairy tale in which joy and wonder were retained and fear and horror left out. This is obvious from the text, where evil is conquered by the end of each chapter, and goodness reigns supreme over the land.

This is quite a departure from previous children's books, such as the work of the brothers Grimm, who based their fairy tales on local folklore. It is even quite different from Lewis Carroll's *Alice's Adventures in Wonderland* (1865), which has a dreamy and unfocused presence as opposed to the straightforward and fast-paced vision of Baum. The Oz series stands well beside later works such as C. S. Lewis' *The Chronicles of Narnia* (7 vols., 1950-1956) and J. R. R. Tolkien's *The Hobbit* (1937). That the book is a landmark in children's fiction is beyond doubt. By 1938, more than one million copies of it were in print. Several motion pictures— including two silent films and the Metro-Goldwyn-Mayer extravaganza, starring Judy Garland as Dorothy—were based on it. With more than a billion people having seen the film, *The Wizard of Oz* is probably the most famous children's story of the twentieth century.

Michael Verdon

THE WOLVES OF WILLOUGHBY CHASE

Author: Joan Aiken (1924-   )
Type of plot: Adventure tale/thriller
Time of plot: The late nineteenth century
Locale: Willoughby Chase estate and London, England
Principal themes: Crime, family, friendship, and social issues
First published: 1962
Recommended ages: 10-13

Two young cousins, Bonnie and Sylvia Green, are left in the care of a distant relative, Miss Slighcarp, and find themselves in great danger when she proves to be cruel and dishonest.

Principal characters:
> BONNIE GREEN, the high-spirited daughter of a wealthy nobleman
> SYLVIA, her frail, orphaned cousin from London
> MISS SLIGHCARP, a distant relative hired to act as Bonnie and Sylvia's governess and guardian
> SIMON, a young boy who raises geese and lives in a cave near Willoughby Chase
> PATTERN, Bonnie's devoted maid
> AUNT JANE, Bonnie and Sylvia's impoverished aunt
> MR. GRIMSHAW, a mysterious traveler
> JAMES, a loyal footman at Willoughby Chase

The Story

The Wolves of Willoughby Chase is a gothic-style thriller that pits two young girls against their evil governess and her plans to seize control of the family estate and fortune. The Willoughby Chase of the title is the estate in question, a grand house in the English countryside where Bonnie Green lives with her parents, Sir Willoughby and Lady Sophia Green. As the story opens, Sir Willoughby is taking his wife abroad to restore her health and has arranged for Bonnie's orphaned cousin, Sylvia, to live at the house as her companion. He has also sent for a distant relative, Miss Slighcarp, to act as the girls' governess and to manage the estate in his absence.

Sylvia's departure from London is a sad one; she is leaving behind her elderly, impoverished Aunt Jane. On the train trip to Willoughby Chase, she shares a carriage with Mr. Grimshaw, a man who saves her from a wolf attack and is injured by a falling suitcase when the train arrives. He is taken, unconscious, to the estate along with Sylvia. The two young girls quickly become fast friends, and Bonnie introduces her cousin to Simon, a young boy who raises geese and lives in a cave on the estate.

Bonnie's parents depart and the girls soon learn, to their dismay, the true nature of Miss Slighcarp's intentions toward them as she fires Sir Willoughby's longtime servants, dons his wife's fine clothes, and begins selling off items from the estate. The girls also discover that Mr. Grimshaw is in reality a cohort of Miss Slighcarp, who faked his injury to gain entrance to the house. Only Bonnie's maid, the devoted Pattern, who has hidden herself in the house, and a loyal footman named James remain to help the cousins, smuggling food to them in the nursery by means of a secret passage. The girls use the passage to spy on Miss Slighcarp and Mr. Grimshaw, and see them destroying Sir Willoughby's will and substituting a forged one of their own devising. The reason for this becomes apparent when the governess tells Bonnie that her parents' ship has sunk and she is now an orphan like her cousin.

When Bonnie devises a plan to send for help, Miss Slighcarp finds her message and the girls are sent to live at an orphans' charity school run by another of the governess' friends, the tyrannical Mrs. Brisket. The school is a damp, dismal place where the students work night and day, sewing and laundering clothes, receiving only meager meals, and suffering cruel punishment for any disobedience. Simon locates the pair, however, and engineers their escape, and the girls travel with him to London on his annual trip to market his geese.

Arriving in the city, the children seek out Aunt Jane and find her perilously close to starvation. They are assisted by a kind doctor, who also helps them subdue Mr. Grimshaw when he attempts to break in. At the police station the following day, Grimshaw confesses to plotting with Miss Slighcarp to take over Willoughby Chase, and the children accompany the police back to the estate, which Miss Slighcarp and Mrs. Brisket have turned into a school. The two women are arrested with the help of James and the secret passage. To Bonnie's delight, her parents return home, very much alive, having survived the shipwreck in a small boat. Sir Willoughby decides to bring Aunt Jane to the estate and establish her as the head of a small school for the orphans left homeless by Miss Slighcarp and Mrs. Brisket's arrests, and Bonnie and Sylvia are sent to bed to dream of their recent adventures.

Themes and Meanings

The Wolves of Willoughby Chase is for the most part a straightforward children's adventure story without very much underlying symbolic meaning. Its central theme is the courage and resourcefulness shown by its young protagonists in the face of the dangers they encounter. Bonnie is forthright and brave from the story's outset, but Sylvia begins the book as a frail and timid girl. Her adventures cause her to grow and develop as she withstands Miss Slighcarp's cruelty and the horrors of the orphans' school. Indeed, the very nature of the children's reactions, left to rely on their own resources in a world of untrustworthy and powerful adults, offers a model for young readers of characters who respond in a responsible and intelligent manner to their problems.

The book is also adroit at capturing those details that hold a special fascination for children. The character of Simon, who lives on his own in a cave in the forest, growing up on a diet of chestnuts and goose eggs and surviving without the interference of parents or schooling, is an image as carefree and appealing as that of

Huckleberry Finn drifting down the Mississippi on a raft. Woods beset by wolves, a house with hidden passages, and the terrifying prospect of losing one's parents and becoming an orphan all play a part in the story's strong appeal to a juvenile audience.

Perhaps the true message contained in the book's rousing story is the very real dangers children face when they are at the mercy of an uncaring adult world. The harrowing plight of the orphans in Mrs. Brisket's charity school is a reminder of an age when there were few laws to protect minors, but even in contemporary times, children remain among the most powerless and mistreated of minorities.

Context

The Wolves of Willoughby Chase is an exciting thriller that combines the elements of a children's story with those of a gothic novel. Its setting, its story line, and its characters are all cast in the gothic tradition, while many of its touches draw on ideas and events that appeal particularly to a young imagination. Willoughby Chase is a mansion with many gothic overtones—an isolated location, hidden passages, priest holes, and a dungeon—yet it is also described as a warm and cheerful place, as befits the home of a much-loved heroine. The same is true of the novel's plot, which places its young characters in great peril yet also offers them the grand adventure of traveling the countryside in disguise—and without adult supervision.

The novel that the book most closely resembles is Charlotte Brontë's *Jane Eyre* (1847), with its early scenes of Jane's stay in the dismal boarding school and its later intrigues in Mr. Rochester's mansion. *The Wolves of Willoughby Chase*, however, stops short of any of the real horrors that unfold in *Jane Eyre*, opting instead for a world in which wrongs are always righted and no one comes to any serious harm. The book also owes a debt to Charles Dickens, with many of its characterizations and character names—Miss Slighcarp, Pattern, Mr. Gripe—possessing a distinctly Dickensian ring.

Joan Aiken is a writer who has moved with ease between the worlds of adult and juvenile novels, and critics often comment on the energy and spirit that she brings to all of her works. These qualities are certainly present in *The Wolves of Willoughby Chase*; it is a lively, entertaining tale that offers enough mystery and danger to please young readers with a taste for suspense.

Janet E. Lorenz

THE WONDERFUL ADVENTURES OF NILS

Author: Selma Lagerlöf (1858-1940)
Type of plot: Adventure tale
Time of plot: The early twentieth century
Locale: Sweden
Principal themes: Nature, animals, and friendship
First published: Nils Holgerssons underbara resa genom Sverige, 1906 (English translation, 1907)
Recommended ages: 10-13

After being transformed into an elf, Nils Holgersson learns about his native Sweden when he rides around the country on the back of a gander. More important, his life among the birds and animals teaches him to respect all creatures.

Principal characters:
> NILS HOLGERSSON, called TUMMETOTT, a fourteen-year-old boy whose laziness and cruelty have made him a disappointment to his parents
> MORTEN GANDER, a tame gander on whose back Nils rides
> AKKA FROM KEBNEKAISE, the ancient leader of the flock of wild geese
> MR. SMIRRE FOX, the persistent foe of Nils and the geese
> HERR ERMENRICH, a stork at Glimminge Castle
> OSA THE GOOSE GIRL, a child who, like Nils, tended geese in the summer
> LITTLE MATS, Osa's small brother

The Story

The Wonderful Adventures of Nils contains all the components of a good adventure tale: travel, danger, discovery, and a certain element of magic. The son of Holger Nilsson, a poor farmer in West Vemmenhög, Nils is a totally disagreeable lad. His hardworking parents despair over his self-indulgence and mean temper. Left alone while they go to church, Nils captures an elf who retaliates by shrinking Nils to his own small size. Nils's shock at his new form is accompanied by the realization that he can no longer bully the barnyard creatures but is now at their mercy. Nils searches the farm for the elf in hopes of being changed back into a regular boy. When some wild geese pass overhead, he grabs the neck of his father's gander just as it flies away to join them. Thus Nils's adventures begin.

It does not take long for Nils and the gander, both out of their natural element, to realize that they must depend on each other. In forcing the gander to drink at the end of the day's long flight, Nils performs his first act of kindness. It is not long before he is trying to help the wild geese as well, although in his first attempt, the geese end up having to rescue him. They spend the night on the ice, usually a place safe from predators. However, movement of the ice toward the shore of Vomb Lake enables Mr. Smirre Fox to attack one of the geese. Forgetting his size, Nils runs after what he thinks is a dog. He succeeds in diverting attention from the goose long enough for it to escape, but in so doing, he must take refuge in a small beech tree. In the morning, he sees the geese fly overhead and assumes he has been forgotten. Instead, the geese come back one by one, flying so low that the fox exhausts himself in trying to catch them, and Nils is able to escape.

Nils's personality does not change overnight. At the beginning, his motivation for staying with the geese is purely selfish: He longs for excitement, and he hates the thought of facing his parents. Behind many of his conciliatory acts is the fear of being sent home. On the advice of Akka of Kebnekaise, he tries to protect himself from wild beasts by getting on good terms with the birds and small animals. Unfortunately, they are aware of his former cruelty and refuse to help him. His part in reuniting Sirle Squirrel's wife with her babies is less an act of atonement than one of appeasement. He saves Herr Ermenrich's Glimminge Castle from the gray rats for the same reason that he has rescued the goose: to vindicate himself and prove that being small and human does not make him inferior. Slowly, as he receives gratitude for his kind acts, he begins to want to do them for themselves.

The plot of *The Wonderful Adventure of Nils* is episodic. The migration of the geese takes Nils and the gander to every part of Sweden, and in every place they alight, a new experience waits. At first, Nils revels in his new life. He sleeps tucked under the gander's wing at night and explores his new surroundings by day. Only gradually does he begin to miss human contact. He remembers companions with whom he shared goose-tending duties the past summer. At that time, he cared little for Osa the goose girl and Mats, as he cared for no one. Nevertheless, when he encounters them again, he runs to them eagerly and is ashamed and grieved when his size terrifies them. In hearing the story of an old peasant woman who has died far from her children, Nils thinks of his own parents. No longer is he afraid to return to them; now he hopes to make reparations. Once he heard an owl say that if the boy brought the gander home safely, he might be restored to human form. That seems to be the hope that sustains him as the story ends.

Themes and Meanings

The Wonderful Adventures of Nils uses as thematic material the natural world Nils shares with the animals. From his vantage point on the gander's back, Nils looks down on the patchwork of fields, the islands, the lakes, the bustling ports, the desolate fjords of Sweden. When the geese come to rest, he is able to see the physical features of the land at close hand. From Ronneby River made violent by melting snow to the Lake Tåkern marshland threatened by man's greed, nature is seen from Nils's and thus the animals' point of view.

Although the birds and animals are given human characteristics, their actions reveal Selma Lagerlöf's insight into animal behavior. The repeated speech of the geese echoes the wild goose call. The goose-play to trick Mr. Smirre Fox is an established ploy in the animal world to lure a predator from an intended victim. The great crane dance at Kullaberg, the arrogant behavior of the swans, the thievery of the crows, all bear witness to a close observation of nature.

The theme of friendship is also developed within the world of nature. Nils has been compared to Mowgli in Rudyard Kipling's *The Jungle Book* (1894), but there are some pertinent differences. Rather than growing up among the animals, Nils moves into their world as an adolescent with a history of mistreating them. Only when he becomes part of their world does he begin to understand and appreciate them, while the animals, both domestic and wild, must look beyond his past performance before they accept him. As Nils's responsibility develops, his relationship with the creatures changes from wary sparring to mutual concern.

Context

Although Selma Lagerlöf's short stories are still anthologized and her adult novels are still read, it is *The Wonderful Adventures of Nils* which has retained universal appeal. A contemporary of August Strindberg, Lagerlöf inevitably faced comparison of her work with that of her countryman. Judged by Strindberg's standards of naturalism, Lagerlöf was dismissed by many turn-of-the-century critics as an obsolete romantic. She is a romantic, although such a classification has hardly discouraged her readers.

Lagerlöf draws on a strong sense of place: the home in Mårbacka where she grew up had been in her family for hundreds of years. In the rural areas of Sweden, entertainment was of the homemade variety—reading, recitation, music, and storytelling. When the child Selma grew to adulthood, she would recall many of the stories, both true and supernatural, and weave them into her novels.

In none of her works does the blend of the real and the unreal work better than in *The Wonderful Adventures of Nils*. When the National Teachers' Association asked Lagerlöf to write a book to teach children the geography of Sweden, she spent three years studying the material she wanted to include. By using a boy changed into a Tummetott, or Tom Thumb, with an aerial view, she devised an ideal way to present not only the geography of Sweden but the history, myth, and natural science as well. When she finally began to write, her native storytelling ability and the imaginative setting she had invented combined effectively to get across the information.

For her service to the Swedish schools, Lagerlöf was awarded an honorary doctorate from the University of Uppsala in 1907. The next year, the entire nation honored her on her fiftieth birthday. Then, in 1909, she became the first woman and the first Swede to receive the Nobel Prize in Literature. In presenting the award, the president of the Swedish Academy praised her "wealth of imagination, idealism in conception, and fascinating presentation."

The Wonderful Adventures of Nils has been translated into many languages and is read by children everywhere. In writing her geographical reader for Swedish students, Selma Lagerlöf has introduced Sweden to the world.

Marcia J. Songer

WORDS BY HEART

Author: Ouida Sebestyen (1924-   )
Type of plot: Historical fiction
Time of plot: The second quarter of the twentieth century
Locale: The cotton-growing country of Texas
Principal themes: Coming-of-age, family, and religion
First published: 1979
Recommended ages: 13-15

Through the example and eventual death of her father, Lena Sills comes to under-
stand the nature of love and forgiveness. She also learns what it means to grow up in
a black family that takes its strength from its religious convictions, its past tradi-
tions, and its own unity and love.

> *Principal characters:*
> LENA SILLS, the oldest daughter of the Sills family
> BEN SILLS, Lena's father and the thematic hero of the novel
> CLAUDIE SILLS, Lena's stepmother, who carries the fear of the past
>> with her
> HENRY HANEY, the father of the shiftless Haney clan
> TATER HANEY, the oldest son of the Haney clan, who is anxious to
>> prove his own worth
> SAMMY HANEY, a younger son who is persecuted by his
>> schoolmates
> MISS CHISM, a wealthy widow who is Ben Sills's employer
> WINSLOW STARNES, a schoolmate of Lena who is able to overcome
>> the prejudice shown by those around him
> JAYBIRD KELSEY, a prominent inhabitant of the town

The Story

Before the action of the novel begins, Ben Sills has taken his family and followed
his father's dream: He heads west, leaving Scattercreek, a Southern black community. They settle in a town in which they are the only black family and find both
acceptance and prejudice. When Lena defeats Winslow Starnes at a memorization
contest, she feels that she has asserted her own worth and individuality. When,
however, she receives the prize for her victory, a boy's bow tie, she rejects it and
feels cheated. Arriving home, the family finds more disturbing evidence of how the
town—or at least the Haneys—feel about their presence: A butcher knife has been
struck through a loaf of bread, and their dog, Bullet, has been killed.

Lena is angry and confused; Claudie is angry and frightened. She fears a repeti-
tion of her own past, when white riders had destroyed her home and murdered her
neighbors. Yet Ben will not be mastered by fear, nor will he allow someone else to

define who he is or how he should act. His major struggle, as Claudie explains to Lena, is his inability to reconcile the words of Scripture—"Do good to those who persecute you"—with his recognition that he might have to act violently in order to protect his family. Little by little, Lena comes to understand his struggle and his courage. He works out in his own life a very Christian approach to living, manifested by a true desire to understand others rather than to hate or fear. As Lena puts it, Ben looks to the inside of things.

Ben has been working for Miss Chism, a rather crabby wealthy woman whom the town seems to ignore. When Miss Chism asks for Lena's help in preparing for a major dinner party, Ben agrees and Lena must miss some days of school; she accedes only grudgingly. The very next day, she begins her work, and while cleaning the attic she finds a box of books: poetry, atlases, and novels. She longs for them, as she longs for anything that she might read. Miss Chism, however, sternly directs her to put them under the eaves. Lena cannot abide the temptation and takes an atlas. That night, she tells her family that Miss Chism has lent her the book, and they all examine it with delight.

The next day, Lena returns the book and takes another, this time a collection of poetry. During her work, she brings Miss Chism's dying bird to Jaybird Kelsey, hoping that he can find some remedy. He cannot, and for the first time Lena glimpses some of the pain that fills Miss Chism's life as she sees this connection to her dead husband severed. Lena, however, is too busy to comfort Miss Chism, as she is directed to clean the bathroom—the first one she has ever seen—and helps to unload crates of merchandise which Miss Chism has bought in an attempt to use her money before she dies and before it goes to her children.

That night, Lena and Ben pore over the book of poetry, and Lena writes down many of Walt Whitman's poems. By morning, however, an accident has ruined the book, and Ben finds that Lena has been taking the books without permission. Despite her realization that the books mean little to Miss Chism, Lena comes to accept that she must confess to Miss Chism. Ben accompanies her, and on the way they stop at the Haneys to retrieve some wire and fence posts that Miss Chism had bought. She had intended for Mr. Haney to mend fences on some property, but he has delayed too long and now she has given the job to Ben. Angry at losing the job, Mr. Haney has already sold the wire and posts. When he rides away, ostensibly going to talk with Miss Chism, Ben tries to look inside the barn and is attacked by Tater Haney. Lena comes to his defense, swinging the bag containing the blighted book, but Ben stops her, wishing to show her that she must try to understand why Tater attacked him, but also recognizing what it might mean if a black man in this community attacked a white boy.

Miss Chism is quite angry over the book, but when she hears Ben agree to mend the fences (a job entailing some days' absence from his family), she becomes willing to lend the books to Lena. Lena is overjoyed and is especially happy when Winslow becomes increasingly friendly during the next few days. They are not happy days for Miss Chism, however, who finds that no one comes to her dinner party. She recognizes that, except for the Sills family, no one really cares for her.

When Ben leaves to ride the fences, Lena's life becomes more complicated. Winslow's father tells him to avoid Lena, and Mr. Haney comes to threaten the family, appearing at night while Lena is alone with the young children. When Ben does not come home at his appointed time, Lena steals out of the house to find him. She travels for a full day, finally coming upon the wagon and, eventually, her own father. He has been shot by Tater, who has been dragged by his horse and who also lies dying. Ben has tried to help him, but he is too weak. He lays a terrible burden on Lena: to help the one who shot her father. He sends her away to find Tater's horse, though she knows that he is really sending her away so that she might not see him die. When she returns, she has made her decision; his life has been an example to her. She covers her father after placing him on the wagon and then lifts Tater in beside him. They drive back to the Haney home, she leaves the boy, and then she makes the difficult journey to her own house.

Lena never tells what happened in that field. She never implicates Tater, though she is pressured to do so. Her father's forgiveness becomes hers. Her inner struggle, however, is not without fruit. At the close of the novel, she looks across the fields and sees Mr. Haney, bent against the weight of his sack, picking their cotton for them.

Themes and Meanings

The character who carries most of the thematic meaning of the novel is Ben. Faced with an enormous struggle, he must decide if the scriptural truths by which he lives can actually be practiced in the very dangerous situation in which his family lives. He resolves the struggle by showing Lena that indeed they can be. His forgiveness of Tater is a final emblem, a final act that shows Lena the implications of a radical life-style and one that is based upon love. For Ben, and eventually for Lena, the most important thing one can do is to understand another person—to get inside people and recognize why they act as they do. With this recognition will come love.

Lena grows into this knowledge slowly and reluctantly. She has lived in a sheltered world and now comes to see the potential violence and hatred that fill it. Her response is not, however, that of her stepmother, to withdraw and to hide from the world. Her response is that of her father: She recognizes that she is somebody, that she defines who she is, and that she must not let others define her roles and her limitations.

The world of the novel is an ambiguous one. There are images of a very strong family, that of the Sills. Their strength comes from their mutual love, their hard work, their willingness to support one another, and their desire to understand one another. They are set against other families that do not have this kind of love and that in fact are breaking apart. Miss Chism finds that all of her wealth cannot buy the love of her sons; the Haneys find that as they live without dignity and respect for one another, others have little respect for them.

The final image of the book, Mr. Haney picking cotton, draws all these themes together, as he comes to recognize the strength of the Sills family and their ability to give so much out of this strength. It is something that he does not have. It is something that Lena has grown into.

Context

Words by Heart is the best known of Ouida Sebestyen's four novels for young adults, the others being *Far from Home* (1980), *IOU's* (1982), and *On Fire* (1985). *On Fire* is set in Colorado and follows the further adventures of the Haney family. The story focuses on Sammy, and Tater eventually comes to recognize that he has killed a better man than he. *Far from Home* is set in Texas, *IOU's* in Colorado. All the novels are based on Sebestyen's own experience and store of remembered stories.

In writing about a strong black family that must face the prejudice of a white community and in writing her story as historical fiction, Sebestyen inevitably invites comparison with Mildred Taylor, particularly her *Roll of Thunder, Hear My Cry* (1976) and *Let the Circle Be Unbroken* (1981). Each of those works also tells of a strong black family in the South. A significant difference is Sebestyen's insistence in *Words by Heart* on focusing not so much on the horrors of prejudice as on the religious themes that give meaning to Ben Sills's life.

In the end, a deep religious consciousness informs this novel, as well as Sebestyen's other novels. This is not to say that the novels are didactic or moralistic; rather, they lead a reader to see the importance of faith in one's life and to recognize the small miracles—and the big miracles—to which strong faith can lead.

Gary D. Schmidt

A WRINKLE IN TIME

Author: Madeleine L'Engle (Madeleine Camp, 1918-   )
Type of plot: Fantasy/moral tale/science fiction
Time of plot: The mid-twentieth century
Locale: The Eastern United States and the planets Uriel, Camazotz, and Ixchel
Principal themes: Coming-of-age, emotions, family, science, and the supernatural
First published: 1962
Recommended ages: 10-13

A young girl and her little brother are transported to a distant planet, where they must confront their own fears and self-doubts as they fight to save their father from the forces of darkness.

Principal characters:
    MEG MURRY, an awkward adolescent girl, unsure of her own self-
        worth
    CHARLES WALLACE MURRY, Meg's strangely precocious five-year-
        old brother
    CALVIN O'KEEFE, a bright, good-natured fourteen-year-old, lost
        among his eleven siblings
    MRS. MURRY, Meg and Charles Wallace's mother, a scientist who
        misses her long-absent husband
    MR. MURRY, a scientist whose work on a top-secret project led to
        his capture by IT
    MRS. WHATSIT, a cheerful, mysterious figure with strange powers
        who befriends the children
    MRS. WHO, a friend of Mrs. Whatsit's who speaks only in literary
        quotations
    MRS. WHICH, the third and most powerful member of the odd
        trio, who never fully materializes
    IT, the central power behind the forces of darkness in the
        universe

The Story

Meg Murry is an awkward, unhappy young girl caught in the throes of adolescence. The daughter of two highly intelligent scientists, she deeply misses her father, who left home several years earlier to work on a top-secret government project. Meg is fiercely protective of her adored, misunderstood brother, Charles Wallace, an alarmingly precocious five-year-old with an uncanny ability to understand Meg's thoughts and feelings.

In the middle of a stormy night, the Murrys are visited by a strange woman named Mrs. Whatsit. She and her two friends, Mrs. Who and Mrs. Which, are in reality former stars (of the astral variety) who lost their lives in the struggle against a terrible darkness that is spreading throughout the universe. They have come to Earth to take Meg and Charles to their father, who is a prisoner of the darkness on the planet Camazotz. Gifted with special powers, the three travel by means of something called a "tesseract"—a wrinkle in space and time that brings two points together.

Meg and Charles, along with their friend Calvin O'Keefe, are transported by the trio first to the planet Uriel and then to a planet in Orion's belt. In both places, the three women show the children signs of the growing darkness that threatens the universe—including Earth itself. Although they are frightened by what they have seen, the children know that they must face this force of pure evil if they are to help their father.

Mrs. Whatsit, Mrs. Who, and Mrs. Which leave the children on Camazotz, a planet of chilling conformity, run according to rigid schedules and painful "re-education" sessions for those who fail to comply. Even play is regulated, as the three visitors learn when they see children up and down the residential streets all bouncing their balls exactly in unison. Meg, Charles Wallace, and Calvin make their way into the heart of the city to CENTRAL Central Intelligence, where they first encounter the power of IT. IT is the source and ruling intelligence behind the darkness, and IT wants Charles Wallace. Hoping that he can use his intuitive abilities to learn about IT and overcome its power, the little boy unwittingly permits the dark force to gain control of him. Transformed before Meg's horrified eyes into a small automaton who possesses her brother's body but speaks and behaves like IT, Charles Wallace leads Meg and Calvin to a room where they find Mr. Murry imprisoned inside a transparent column.

Meg uses a pair of magical glasses given to her by Mrs. Who to free her father from the column, and they are led by Charles Wallace to meet IT—a pulsing brain lying on a pedestal. As the brain begins to exert its deadly power over them, Mr. Murry saves Meg and Calvin by performing his own inexpert tesseract to the plant Ixchel. Meg has suffered greatly during the journey and is nursed back to health by one of the planet's wise, blind inhabitants, whom she calls Aunt Beast. When she has recovered, they are joined by Mrs. Whatsit, Mrs. Who, and Mrs. Which, who tell Meg that only she can save Charles Wallace from the grip of IT.

Although she is frightened, Meg returns to Camazotz, armed only with Mrs. Which's parting words that she has something that IT does not. Barely able once again to resist IT's evil pull, Meg is close to losing her will to the dark forces when she realizes that the special power she possesses is love. Focusing all her love on her small brother, she is able to free him from IT's terrible grip, and the three children and Mr. Murry find themselves transported instantly back to Earth, where the Murry family is reunited.

Themes and Meanings

The central theme of *A Wrinkle in Time* is the struggle between good and evil, the power of love in the face of hatred and deception. The book offers a vivid portrait of evil made visible in the form of spreading darkness and a pulsing, disembodied brain, setting up a confrontation between this monstrous force and an insecure young girl who must discover her own strengths in order to save her father and brother from its clutches. The terrible IT that Meg, Calvin, and Charles Wallace must battle— and that Mr. Murry has fought for years—symbolizes the very real evil and cruelty that exist in the world, and the children's adventure represents the moral choices that each individual must make throughout his or her life.

An important part of the story is Meg's coming of age as she learns to face her fears, explore her strengths and weaknesses, and confront problems on her own. In the novel's opening chapters, Meg believes that her problems will be solved if her father returns. After she is reunited with him on Camazotz, however, she learns that she can no longer look to her parents for everything; she must learn to rely more on herself and to draw on her own inner resources in times of trouble.

The book presents an accurate portrait of the difficulties of adolescence. Meg is a bright, sensitive girl who finds herself an outsider among her peers and longs to become more like them. During the course of her adventures, she learns to value herself as an individual and to reject mindless conformity when she sees its devastating results on the planet Camazotz. Author Madeleine L'Engle's social—and perhaps political—message is clear: One must listen to one's heart, think for oneself, and learn to value one's own distinctive qualities.

Context

A Wrinkle in Time is Madeleine L'Engle's best-known book. It was enthusiastically reviewed at the time of its publication in 1962 and entered almost immediately into the ranks of literary classics for children, receiving the prestigious Newbery Medal. Yet it was not until eleven years later that L'Engle wrote a sequel to the novel, entitled *A Wind in the Door* (1973), in which she picks up the story of Meg and Charles Wallace as they once again confront the dark forces threatening the universe. Their saga is continued in *A Swiftly Tilting Planet* (1978), which finds Meg now grown and married and a teenage Charles Wallace attempting to stop the destruction of the world at the hands of a mad dictator.

In her story of the Murry children and their confrontation with the terrible powers of evil, L'Engle offers a blend of fantasy and science fiction that transcends both genres with its firm grounding in the reality of human emotions. Although its scientific speculations and episodes of space travel give the book a contemporary tone, the story's deeper concerns and its message of the worth of human individuality are timeless. The society the children encounter on Camazotz has parallels with both Ray Bradbury's chilling portrait of the future in *Farenheit 451* (1953) and George Orwell's *Nineteen Eighty-Four* (1949), while the book's coming-of-age theme has been a familiar element in classic literature from Mark Twain's *The Adventures of Huckleberry Finn* (1884) to the novels of S. E. Hinton.

L'Engle is a writer who knows how to capture the imagination while also reaching the emotions, and *A Wrinkle in Time* offers young readers a chance to contemplate issues as vast as the conflict between good and evil while still identifying with its characters and their everyday concerns.

Janet E. Lorenz

WUTHERING HEIGHTS

Author: Emily Brontë (1818-1848)
Type of plot: Psychological realism
Time of plot: 1771-1802
Locale: The West Riding of Yorkshire, England
Principal themes: Nature, emotions, death, and love and romance
First published: 1847
Recommended ages: 15-18

> *Mr. Earnshaw brings a mysterious child to live with his family at Wuthering Heights, an isolated Yorkshire farm. The child is given the name Heathcliff. Ultimately he succeeds in destroying the Earnshaw family. Heathcliff's love for Catherine Earnshaw, even after her death, is his solitary passion and torment.*

Principal characters:
MR. EARNSHAW, the owner of Wuthering Heights
HINDLEY EARNSHAW, his son, who loses Wuthering Heights to
    Heathcliff
CATHERINE EARNSHAW, his daughter, who is Heathcliff's
    childhood friend and confidante
HEATHCLIFF, a waif, who is brought to Wuthering Heights by
    Mr. Earnshaw
HARETON EARNSHAW, Hindley's son, who is reared by Heathcliff
    in poverty and ignorance
CATHY LINTON, the daughter of Catherine and Edgar Linton
ELLEN "NELLY" DEAN, the servant, who tells the story to
    Mr. Lockwood, the new tenant of Thrushcross Grange

The Story

In 1801 Mr. Lockwood, the new tenant of Thrushcross Grange, comes to pay his respects to his landlord, Mr. Heathcliff. Lockwood is forced to spend the night at Wuthering Heights during a snowstorm. That night, a little voice pleads to be let in at the window; it is the ghost of Catherine Earnshaw.

Lockwood returns to the Grange and asks his housekeeper, Ellen Dean, to tell him the tragic story of the Earnshaw and Linton families. She relates a story of almost unrelenting passion and hatred, which began when Mr. Earnshaw brought home a starving waif from the slums of Liverpool. The child was given only one name: Heathcliff.

The novel traces Heathcliff's rise to master of Wuthering Heights and the elegant neighboring estate, Thrushcross Grange. After the death of his father, Hindley Earnshaw treats Heathcliff worse than a servant, but Heathcliff stays because of his love for Catherine. She, however, finds the life-style of Edgar Linton and his sister,

Isabella, very attractive. Heathcliff believes Catherine despises him, and leaves Yorkshire.

Hindley marries the consumptive Frances, who gives him a son, Hareton. Hindley's decline into drunkenness is accelerated by his wife's death. Catherine marries Edgar and takes Ellen Dean with her to Thrushcross Grange. Heathcliff reappears, but his behavior is more refined. He has acquired an education and wealth. He secretly buys up Hindley's debts. He moves into the Heights. Edgar grows jealous of Heathcliff, who continues to meet Catherine. Isabella Linton falls madly in love with Heathcliff and finally elopes with him. She becomes pregnant and dies soon after giving birth to a sickly boy, Linton Heathcliff.

Hindley dies, and the rightful heir of Wuthering Heights, his son Hareton, is badly treated by Heathcliff. The cuckoo in the nest has dispossessed the legitimate heir. Heathcliff's revenge is almost complete. His next step is to engineer a marriage between his son and Cathy, thus adding Thrushcross Grange to his usurped properties. When Edgar Linton dies without changing his will, the plan succeeds.

The date is now 1801—Lockwood knows all the events prior to his fateful visit. He leaves soon after, but returns the following year. Heathcliff is dead, having starved himself to death so he could be reunited with his beloved Catherine. The plot has almost come full circle. Young Cathy is educating Hareton, and the future may well see a marriage restoring the two houses to their rightful families.

Themes and Meanings

Few books have been scrutinized as closely as *Wuthering Heights*. It has been analyzed from every psychological perspective; it has been described as a spiritual or religious novel. Broadly speaking, it is the story of an antihero, Heathcliff, and his attempt to steal Wuthering Heights from its rightful owners, Catherine and Hindley Earnshaw. Thus, in this complex story of fierce passions, Heathcliff is portrayed as a cuckoo, who succeeds in dispossessing the legitimate heirs to Wuthering Heights. His revenge is the driving force behind the plot, though he betrays occasional glimpses of affection for Hareton, the young man whom he has ruined.

"Wuthering" is a dialect word descriptive of the fierceness of the Yorkshire climate, with its "atmospheric tumult." The title of the novel refers not only to the farm house and its inhabitants but also to the effect that Heathcliff's desire for Cathy has on him and those around him. As the story progresses, his nature becomes successively warped, and he loses Cathy. After Heathcliff returns from a self-imposed exile—educated and wealthy—the meetings with Cathy further lacerate his soul and bring ruin to all those around him. Heathcliff's ultimate revenge is to make Hareton, Hindley's son, suffer as he did. "Wuthering," "tumult," and "stunted growth" apply equally to nature and humans in this novel. Yet no hatred as powerful as Heathcliff's can sustain itself; it burns too fiercely. When his desire for vengeance has run its course, Heathcliff achieves his greatest wish—to be united with his beloved Catherine. This reunion can take place only in the grave and the spirit world beyond it.

During Heathcliff's life, Wuthering Heights was a hell; it will never become a heaven, but as the second generation of Earnshaw and Linton children grow up free of Heathcliff's corrupting influence, Emily Brontë suggests, a spiritual rebirth is possible. Optimism peeps through her dark vision.

Context

Emily Brontë was a solitary person. She stayed in the village of Haworth virtually all of her short life. She and her three siblings had to amuse themselves, as their mother was dead and their father was somewhat solitary in his habits. Their highly charged imaginations found release in writing stories—an activity that began in earnest when their father Patrick (himself a minor literary figure) gave Branwell Brontë a box of wooden soldiers. Their juvenilia led to a book in 1846, *Poems*, by the three sisters under the pen names Currer, Ellis, and Acton Bell. Its total sale was two copies, but this failure did not deter them from attempting novels that were published the following year.

Wuthering Heights is one of three books originally intended to be published as a set. The others are *The Professor* (1857) by Charlotte Brontë and *Agnes Grey* (1847) by their sister, Anne. Charlotte's book was rejected and was not published in her lifetime. While their father was in Manchester, recovering from an eye operation, Charlotte began *Jane Eyre* (1847), and this book was published before her sisters' were.

Because Emily lived such a solitary life, what became important was not the world around her but that within. She imagined a world of solitude and elemental forces. Her few short adventures beyond the village of Haworth made her miserable and convinced her of the preeminent importance of the imaginative over the real world. Thus, in a time of growing social criticism—Charles Dickens' novels led the way—Emily Brontë remained absolutely unmoved. Elizabeth Gaskell, writing in the next county, wrote *Mary Barton* (1848), which attacked the injustice of poverty. Such matters Emily Brontë considered to be of more temporal concern than those found in *Wuthering Heights*.

Though not written for children, the novel has always been popular with young adults. Its brutal side is counterbalanced by one of the most famous love stories in the English language. It has been considered too "adult" by some, but this opinion ignores the strict morality and essential optimism of the conclusion. What is remembered is the love of Catherine and Heathcliff, not the cruelty.

Wuthering Heights is a unique creation. There are some sources that Brontë may have read before writing her novel, such as a short story by E. T. A. Hoffmann, "Das Majorat" ("The Entail"). There are obvious influences from Lord Byron, Sir Walter Scott, and less well-known Gothic writers, but their contribution is minor. In essence, there was nothing like *Wuthering Heights* before and nothing after.

Gilbert B. Cross

THE YEARLING

Author: Marjorie Kinnan Rawlings (1896-1953)
Type of plot: Domestic realism
Time of plot: The late nineteenth century (specifically, 1870-1871)
Locale: The swamp/scrub country of Florida, south-southwest of Saint Augustine
Principal themes: Family, gender roles, nature, poverty, and coming-of-age
First published: 1938; illustrated
Recommended ages: 13-15

An orphaned deer (its mother was killed to save Jody's father from death by snake-bite) is raised as the brother Jody never had. They grow up together, and the boy learns about death, loyalty, poverty, and responsibility, and that choices are often painful but survivable.

Principal characters:
JODY BAXTER, a boy of twelve or so who loves to play
FLAG, his playmate, a male fawn that fills in for brother and friend to Jody but that becomes a recurring problem to the family
PENNY BAXTER, Jody's father, small and physically weak, but a hard worker, who wishes Jody could have a play-filled childhood
ORA BAXTER, Jody's mother; practical and worn down by life, she has trouble expressing her motherly love; the young deer is simply a pest to her
THE FORRESTERS, a clan of huge, rough, but generally good-hearted neighbors (except for Lem, who carries grudges)
FODDER-WING FORRESTER, twisted of body, Jody's friend, who loves animals and has a vivid imagination
GRANDMA HUTTO, Penny's friend from the past
OLIVER HUTTO, her sailor son and Jody's idol
TWINK WEATHERBY, Oliver's girl
OLD SLEWFOOT, an enormous bear with a missing toe, the villain and mortal enemy of the Baxter family

The Story

The Baxters live on a pine "island" in the Florida scrub, surrounded by deer and other animals that threaten their livestock. Jody Baxter, a boy playing with flutter-mills turned by running water, enjoys the beauty of nature around him and the joy of April, but not hoeing grass out of the corn.

When Old Slewfoot kills the brood sow, Penny Baxter goes after him, Jody tagging along. Penny's gun misfires and the bear escapes. Penny has to have a gun that works, and so the two go to visit the Forresters, Penny carrying a worthless dog that ran from the bear; the care he gives the dog makes the Forresters think the dog is special, even though Penny assures them that the dog is no good. Lem Forrester— the black-hearted member of the family—will not let Penny refuse a trade, a fine new gun for the dog. Penny gives in but makes Lem promise not to kill him after he hunts the dog. While the grown-ups talk, Jody plays with Fodder-wing Forrester, so named because he once tied some fluffy fodder to his arms to help him fly off the barn; he fell, breaking bones and becoming even more "crookedy," as his mother describes him.

On a hunting-trading trip to nearby Volusia on St. John's River, Jody kills a deer (with help from Penny) and they skin it, to take hide and venison to town for trading; the blood of the deer and its glazed eyes affect Jody powerfully. In town, Jody has an unfriendly meeting with a storekeeper's daughter (he hates girls); after his display of bad manners, they go to visit Grandma Hutto, an older lady who still has life and charm, a strong contrast to Jody's mother. Jody hears that Oliver Hutto is courting Twink Weatherby; when Oliver comes home from the sea, Jody tells him that Lem Forrester considers Twink to be his girl, and the stage is set for trouble. Twink is a threat to the world as Jody knows it. There is a fight between Oliver and three of the Forresters—Lem especially. Seeing the mismatched fight, Penny gets into the battle, despite his size. Jody hates Twink for causing it all, but he eventually jumps in to help Penny and Oliver, and winds up unconscious. Jody knows the fight will cut off relations between the Baxters and the Forresters, but hopes that he can still visit Fodder-wing.

Looking for missing hogs led toward the Forresters' place by a trail of shelled corn, Penny is bitten by a snake. He kills a doe, splits the liver open, and lays it on the bite to draw out some of the poison. Penny sends Jody to ask the Forresters to go for the doctor. As Jody starts, he notices that the doe had a fawn. Buck Forrester comes to carry Penny home; when Jody begs to have the orphaned fawn for a pet, Penny tells Ma Baxter that the fawn is to be part of the family. Jody finds the fawn and brings it home. The doctor and Penny's determination bring him through the battle with the rattlesnake poison, and Buck stays to work the crops until Penny recovers.

Jody looks after the fawn, which repeatedly gets in Ma's way. He longs to visit Fodder-wing, to show him the fawn. When there is finally time for a visit, Jody discovers that Fodder-wing has died. Jody "sits up" most of the night with Fodder-wing's body, as custom demands. Penny comes looking for him, stays for the funeral, and is asked to say a few words, since he has had "Christian raising."

As time passes, a torrential rainstorm destroys most of the Baxter crops and brings a plague that kills many of the wild creatures. While playing with his fawn, which he names Flag, and getting him out of trouble at home, Jody fears the plague or a bear will get his "brother." Both boy and deer are growing, and Jody wonders when Flag will be a yearling. One day, Penny sadly tells Jody, "You're a pair o' yearlin's."

The idea is exciting to Jody, but then real trouble begins: Flag pulls up the shoots of corn they have planted for food. After Jody works hard to replant the corn, Flag pulls it up again. Penny has been hurt, but Jody works manfully to build a fence around the crops. Flag jumps the fence at its highest point, and again the corn is destroyed. The Baxter food supply is vital; Penny and Ma agree that Flag has to be killed. Jody plots to run away and tries to give Flag to the Forresters—anything but what he has been ordered to do. Finally Ma, who is no hand with a gun, has to shoot Flag, only wounding him.

Jody has to put his playmate out of his misery. Afterward, he runs away from home, hoping somehow to get to Boston, where Oliver has gone with his mother and Twink, his wife. Several days of hunger, drifting on the river in a leaky dugout, and feverish dreaming bring Jody to the realization the Penny has not "gone back on him." Picked up by a riverboat crew and fed, Jody finally makes his way toward home, stopping to build a flutter-mill, as he had done only a year before, but he realizes it is a toy and tears it down. When he reaches home, he finds Penny sick and weak and his mother gone to the Forresters to trade for seed corn. Jody tells Penny where he has been, and they make plans together for the family's future.

Themes and Meanings

The Yearling deals with a year in the maturation of a boy—from April to April. The time of year, when nature is coming to life after a winter of rest, sets the stage for beginnings, growth, and joy from being alive. A year later, however, the scene is less lighthearted: The boy has "lived" more than merely a year.

The setting, in a wilderness little touched by the hand of man, is filled with opportunities to share the love of nature that the author has within her. For example, another writer might say there were many flowers, but Rawlings describes in detail the multitude of flowers of all sorts and colors.

She is not only being descriptive; the beauties of nature, flowers, birds, animals, streams, and trees are a part of Jody's own nature. Once, coming home from fishing (for food, not sport), Jody and Penny are caught up in the wonders of nature when they see whooping cranes dancing, as if in a minuet. Another time they find twin bear cubs amazing: One of Jody's proudest moments is recalling the two bears dancing in a clearing. At times, Jody becomes almost drunk on the beauty around him. Nature is also a source of food for the Baxter family. The beautiful deer, with their soft eyes, provide food and leather, although Jody is sickened by the death of such animals. Nature is also filled with dangers. A crippled wolf that comes at night to play with the Baxter dogs, out of loneliness for its own kind, is a sad survivor of a pack of wolves that earlier destroyed livestock in the neighborhood. For all its excitement, the hunting of Old Slewfoot is "mighty fearsome."

Fodder-wing's love for taming animals—he has a regular menagerie of coons, birds, and others—is contrasted with his knowledge that, in cages, his animals would not breed. He also knows that some animals can never be tamed, preparing the reader for Flag's "uncivilized" behavior. It is the death of deer especially that makes Jody sick, although other creatures cause him—and Penny—to regret that animals must die so that people may eat. At no time, however, do the Baxters kill for fun (although the Forresters do).

Ma Baxter is an example of what life sometimes does to people. Penny tells Jody that a man must get up again when he is knocked down. Yet what is one to say about the little Baxter graveyard, which is filled with tiny graves—the buried hopes of a woman who has most of the tenderness stripped out of her by her losses? Rawlings says of her that Ma Baxter became almost alive, forcing the author to soften her original intent of presenting a typical nagging wife; it became apparent that Ma Baxter's losses caused her to have a sharp tongue, which she used to cover up her hurting.

The Yearling is a realistic picture of life, including the beauties and terrors that fill it. Its ending is uplifting, even though Jody has learned the bitter lesson that life can turn its back on a person. He is growing up and knows that flutter-mills have their place, but only for a time.

Context

Florida is the land to which Marjorie Kinnan Rawlings moved in 1928, opening her heart to its mysterious swamps and beautiful wilderness. It is the setting for many of her works, but in few of them is her appreciation for the wonders of nature so clearly presented as in *The Yearling*. The Florida flowers and creatures are different from what is to be found in other parts of the United States, making them especially appealing, even magical, to the reader. Yet Rawlings also saw the daily battle for existence that the scrub-dwellers endured; she lived among them and saw them face life with courage and hope, as Penny Baxter did, even when Old Slewfoot destroyed the meat for the winter or the rainstorm ruined the crops.

Her other writings, *South Moon Under* (1933), especially, and her short stories in *When the Whipporwill—* (1940), attract readers of many ages. *Golden Apples* (1935), for more mature readers, shows her tenderness toward people and their unhappinesses. Her stories, long or short, are always realistic, never denying facts of life such as death and separation, and generally ending on a peaceful note, if not a happy one.

The Yearling won a Pulitzer Prize, was a national best-seller, and with Gregory Peck playing Penny, Jane Wyman as Ma, and Claude Jarman, Jr., as Jody, it became a popular success as a feature Metro-Goldwyn-Mayer film (1946) that is remarkably true to both the plot and spirit of the novel. The film received several Oscar nominations and won in four categories, including one for Jarman as outstanding child actor.

John Oliver West

A YELLOW RAFT IN BLUE WATER

Author: Michael Dorris (1945-   )
Type of plot: Domestic realism
Time of plot: The 1970's and the 1980's, with flashbacks covering forty years
Locale: The Pacific Northwest, primarily a reservation in Montana
Principal themes: Race and ethnicity, family, and friendship
First published: 1987
Recommended ages: 15-18

*A Native American grandmother, her daughter, and her fifteen-year-old grand-
daughter share important personal and family events that span a forty-year period.*

> *Principal characters:*
> RAYONA, the fifteen-year-old daughter of Christine and Elgin
> (a black postal employee), narrator of the first section of the
> book
> CHRISTINE, Rayona's Indian mother, who narrates the second part
> of the book
> IDA, the maternal "grandmother," who narrates the last section of
> the book and reveals the family secret: Christine is really the
> daughter of Ida's father and Ida's aunt

The Story

A Yellow Raft in Blue Water has three different narrators who represent three
different generations. The book spans forty years and tells the story of a family on a
Montana reservation.

Rayona, named for rayon material, tells her story first about the hospitalization for
alcoholism of her mother, Christine, and of the departure of her father, Elgin, to be
with another woman. Rayona describes Christine's attempted suicide and return to
the Montana reservation where she grew up. Rayona feels abandoned when her
mother leaves her with Ida, and she has intercourse with a priest on a yellow raft in
the blue water. Later she says of the raft, "Somewhere in my mind I've decided if I
stare at it hard enough it will launch me out of my present trouble." When the priest
does not rescue her, Rayona runs away. She finds a home with Evelyn, the girlfriend
of a young man whom she meets at a service station. Rayona builds a fantasy world,
which she presents to Evelyn as real. When Rayona at last tells the truth, Evelyn says
quite frankly, "Your poor aunt is probably worried to death, that damn priest should
have his ass kicked, and your mother is off sick somewhere." Evelyn resolves that
"Norman and me are driving you home." Through Evelyn's efforts, Rayona is at last
reunited with Christine and Ida.

Christine, in the second section, tells of the only person she truly loved—her
brother Lee. She describes his entry into the service and her feelings at his death.

She describes her love for Elgin and the birth of Rayona. Ironically, Christine is cared for during her illness by Dayton, Lee's suspected lover, toward whom Christine had once felt competitive. It is Dayton who manages to reunite Christine with Rayona.

Ida, the last narrator to speak, tells of her bedridden mother who brings her sister Clara to care for her. Clara, however, becomes pregnant by Ida's father. To spare the family the shame of such an occurrence, Ida leaves with her Aunt Clara and, when she returns, pretends that the baby Christine is her own child. Christine is even taught to call Ida "Aunt Ida" to continue the falsehood.

Through narration, the characters reveal themselves and others to the reader. The characters often use denotation to say exactly what they mean. Their "earthy" language is evident throughout the book. For example, when Rayona, instead of her cousin, wins a contest, Christine says, "Just seeing her crap on my lousy cousin should count for something."

The characters at times use connotation. For example, Ida, in the last lines in the book, compares the blending of their three lives to the braiding of hair:

> As a man with cut hair, he did not identify the rhythm of three strands, the whispers of coming and going, of twisting and tying and blending, of catching and of letting go, of braiding.

Modern-day dialect is evident in the characters' speech at times. At one point Christine says, "To hell with that noise." When Christine tells Rayona that she is going to kill herself, Rayona says, "Go for it!"

The denouement is closed. Aunt Ida leaves the reader with the feeling that the women's lives will continue in a union only they can know. The reader believes that the characters will be separate strands but will achieve greater strength against any adversity in their unity.

Themes and Meanings

A Yellow Raft in Blue Water is a family tale of a child with a dual heritage. The separate but interrelated lives of two women and a girl and the friendship among them are vital to the plot. The reader realizes that, despite outside forces, the bonds of family, race, and friendship that bind these three Native Americans will remain strong. The bonds, however, are tested by tensions that are timeless (unfaithfulness, illegitimacy, homosexuality) and tensions that result when the life-style on the reservation comes into conflict with the outside world with its additional pressures upon each new generation. When traditional sources of support (such as the white male priest and the father) fail them, the solidarity and support of the three women for one another become their web of safety (yellow raft) in troubled times (blue water). The reader observes some cultural and individual differences in the lives of these characters but realizes that many problems that they face are in fact universal.

There is an implicit moral of service to others throughout *A Yellow Raft in Blue Water*. Those who serve (Ida, by rearing the illegitimate Christine; Rayona, by helping her ill mother; Lee, who plans to lead his tribe; Dayton, who assists Lee in his rodeo career and later aids the critically ill Christine) find meaning for their lives; those who serve their own desires (the husband, who sires Christine under his own roof while his wife lies terminally ill and knowledgeable about his actions; Christine's husband who finally leaves with another woman; the priest who rapes the teenage Rayona) fade into oblivion as if swallowed by the blue waters surrounding them.

A Yellow Raft in Blue Water could be a depressing tale, but an element of hope is ever present. This hope leaves the reader believing that, despite fortune, distance, and outside influences, the bonds of these three women will remain strong and their desire to serve one another and others will give meaning to their existence. Many readers (both male and female) will be aware of the implicit didactic message of service to others that is present in *A Yellow Raft in Blue Water.*

Context

A Yellow Raft in Blue Water is part of a growing tradition of novels for young adults that feature Native American characters. Among these are the Caldecott winner *Island of the Blue Dolphins* (1960), by Scott O'Dell; *The Friendly Wolf* (1975) and *The Girl Who Loved Wild Horses* (1978), by Paul Goble; and the children's book most suggestive of *A Yellow Raft in Blue Water*, Virginia Hamilton's *Arilla Sun Down* (1976). This work is also about a young girl of mixed heritage. Each member of her family is unique and, in the end, Arilla find her own uniqueness.

A Yellow Raft in Blue Water (1987) is Michael Dorris' first novel. Through Dorris' first fictional work, young adults of all colors can learn about the culture of the Native American. Dorris' writings may also appeal to adults. He has written *The Broken Cord* (1989) and *Native Americans: Five Hundred Years After* (1975), co-written *Racism in the Textbook* (1976) and *Separatist Movements* (1979), and contributed to professional journals. Dorris, who was born in 1945 in Dayton, Washington, is a member of the Moduc Tribe and is involved in such organizations as National Indian Education Association and National Indian Youth Council. His personal involvement in his heritage allows for a more in-depth portrayal of the Native American situation.

Anita P. Davis

YOU NEVER KNEW HER AS I DID!

Author: Mollie Hunter (1922-   )
Type of plot: Historical fiction
Time of plot: The mid-sixteenth century
Locale: Lochleven Castle, Scotland
Principal themes: Coming-of-age, politics and law, and love and romance
First published: 1981
Recommended ages: 13-15

Mary, Queen of Scots, is held prisoner in Lochleven Castle while Will Douglas tries to show his devotion to her by devising a scheme of escape.

> *Principal characters:*
> WILL DOUGLAS, the illegitimate son of the lord of Lockleven Castle
> MARY, QUEEN OF SCOTS, the deposed queen
> SIR WILLIAM DOUGLAS, the lord of the castle
> SIR GEORGE DOUGLAS, Sir William's younger brother
> LADY MARGARET DOUGLAS, the mother of Sir William and Sir George
> MINNY, the laundry maid and mother of Will Douglas

The Story

A romance plot is used by Mollie Hunter to tell the story of Will Douglas, the sixteen-year-old illegitimate son of Sir William Douglas, lord of Lochleven Castle. The story begins with the musing of a middle-aged Will: "News of her has come at last from England; and it is the worst I ever dreaded to hear." A courier has just delivered the message of Mary's death, and at this point Will begins to remember the year at Lochleven Castle when he first fell in love with Mary, Queen of Scots.

The queen has been arrested and is brought to this island castle to be interned during the Protestant Reformation in sixteenth century Scotland. Upon meeting Will, the queen immediately recalls him from his younger years and even uses the pet name she coined for him then. Will becomes infatuated with this attractive, congenial, and articulate lady. He is not alone, as Mary has captured the hearts of many men; Sir George Douglas is one of them. It is through the guidance and leadership of Sir George that Will becomes a part of the scheme to free the queen.

Quite soon after Mary's capture and internment at Lochleven, she is forced, in fear of her life, to sign a deed of abdication. Will is horrified to realize that men of rank could treat their queen so harshly, and he vows to be her defender. The queen refuses to accept her fate, and through her gracious ways she manages to mold the

Lochleven community into her own royal court, winning most of the castle inhabitants to her side. By doing this she succeeds in helping Will and Sir George in their plans for her escape. Sir George's love for the queen is discovered, and he is banished from the castle, leaving Will to execute the plan of escape that has been devised.

When this escape plan is foiled, Will responds with self-pity. The well-thought-out plan failed, as Will states, because of bad luck; yet he still feels guilt for taking too lightly his encounter with his half-sister, Ellen, who is spying on the queen. His ability to stifle his urge to gamble with the gold given him by the queen also alerted the guards. The discovery of his part in the escape attempt leads to Will's being banished from the castle, the only home he has ever known.

Sir William's love for his offspring is so strong that Will is eventually reinstated to his former place, and this event sets the stage for the second and successful escape. As was the first attempt, this plan is thought out by Will, but this time he is more cautious and more willing to accept advice and assistance from the older supporters of the queen.

Throughout the story, Will matures from a frivolous teenager to a young man willing to fight for a cause he considers worthy. The story of Mary, Queen of Scots, ends with the successful escape, but Hunter brings the middle-aged Will back briefly to explain what has taken place in the span of time between the year at Lochleven and when Mary is beheaded.

Themes and Meanings

Will, the hero, takes a symbolic journey of emotional growth from a frivolous teenager to the maturity of an adult in his thoughts and actions. Will's growth is directly related to the time and setting of the story. A year can be an extremely long interval for a sixteen-year-old, especially when he is confronted with as many changes as those faced by Will. The setting is an island in the Scottish Highlands. This is double isolation, because the island community is removed both from social and political happenings of the cities to the south and from the small local village that can only be reached by a boat trip to the mainland.

The isolation is ended for both Will and the castle community with the arrival of the queen. Throughout the year, Will is forced to look beyond himself and his own pleasures as he becomes more involved with the plots to free the queen. His exposure to men and women of rank who are interested only in furthering their self-interests help Will realize that not everyone is as gentle and kindhearted as Sir William.

Working with those who wish to free the queen and give her back the throne makes Will aware of the necessity of thorough planning and caution. This realization is in direct contrast to the impetuousness he has shown previously.

War is a secondary theme to Will's coming of age but still one that needs to be discussed. The Scotland of Will's day was in constant turmoil. The Protestant Reformation and the constant skirmishes among the clans kept war in the forefront. In his

isolated environment, however, Will has not been overtly exposed to war. His naïveté is quite obvious in his willingness to become involved with the escape attempt:
He sees war as something to relieve the boredom of his isolated castle existence. Not
until almost a year later does Will realize that war divides families and can cause
feelings of guilt and despair.

The theme of love and romance takes two forms: romantic love and familial love.
In the beginning Will is infatuated with Mary. By the end of the story he is devoted
to her and probably loves her, but the reader is led to believe that it is a love of
admiration for a strong-willed and brilliant person rather than physical love. The
second form of love is that of a family. Will is rather blasé about his lack of a known
mother. The young Will is quite content to use Minny and her love for him for his
own gratification. He also views Sir William, Lady Margaret, other members of the
family, and girls from the village as people to be used for his own pleasure and
profit. Not until he is banished from this family community does he begin to understand his need for this type of love and support.

A year of physical, mental, and emotional hardships, along with the broadening
of his island community, proves to be what makes Will Douglas come of age.

Context

In the genre of historical fiction there are certain eras, locales, and characters that
get the majority of the attention from writers. Mollie Hunter has broken these barriers with her adolescent novel about the Protestant Reformation in Scotland and
Mary, Queen of Scots. The story as told by the sixteen-year-old Will gives a perspective on these mid-sixteenth century happenings that would not be gained by
reading a nonfiction text by a historical researcher. Hunter, who has written numerous books about Scottish folklore and the supernatural creatures said to frequent
the countryside, glens, and lakes of Scotland, uses her storytelling ability to chronicle what life may have been like at Lochleven Castle. Historically, the events in *You
Never Knew Her As I Did!* are accurate. In the foreword to the book Hunter explains
that she has thoroughly researched this one episode in the life of the controversial
queen. Hunter's use of her storytelling ability and the first-person point of view
helps the reader gain a better understanding of this monarch who was both loved
and hated by her subjects.

By showing the devotion of Will, Sir George, John Beaton, and others, Hunter
presents an aspect of the battle for the Scottish throne that is often ignored by other
writers on the subject. It is obvious to the reader that Mary's followers had as many
motives for her reinstatement to the throne as her enemies did for keeping her captive. Will's infatuation and blind devotion are in sharp contrast to the feelings of
James Douglas, Earl of Moray, Mary's half-brother, who wants to control the throne
for his own benefit.

Works of historical fiction that break new ground are needed to keep the genre
viable. Backing an interesting story line with researched fact keeps the genre pure.
As a Scot writing about a controversial fellow Scot, Mollie Hunter has blended both.

The life of Mary, Queen of Scots, will continue to be debated. *You Never Knew Her As I Did!* presents a fresh point of view in this debate.

Rosemary Oliphant Ingham

YOUNG FU OF THE UPPER YANGTZE

Author: Elizabeth Foreman Lewis (1892-1958)
Type of plot: Moral tale/adventure tale
Time of plot: The 1920's
Locale: Chungking, China
Principal themes: Coming-of-age, family, friendship, and jobs and work
First published: 1932; illustrated
Recommended ages: 13-15

Young Fu, a Chinese boy in his early teens, comes from the country with his widowed mother and is apprenticed to the coppersmith Tang. While learning this trade he has a variety of exciting adventures, makes new friends who change his life, and grows up into a responsible young man.

> *Principal characters:*
> YOUNG FU, an enterprising boy from the country, who has come to Chungking to learn the trade of coppersmith
> FU BE BE, his mother, who accompanies him and worries about his adventurous spirit
> WANG, the old scholar who teaches Fu to read and write
> TANG, young Fu's employer, who befriends as well as instructs his apprentice
> THE FOREIGN WOMAN, an administrator at the foreign hospital in Chungking
> DEN, another apprentice, hostile to young Fu

The Story

Thirteen-year-old Fu Yuin-Fah's experiences in the ancient and turbulent city of Chungking begin the same evening that he and his widowed mother arrive and move into their one-room apartment in a poor quarter of the city. On this last evening of leisure before he officially becomes an apprentice, young Fu meets Wang, an aged teacher who lives in the same tenement. This association will in time prove mutually beneficial: Wang Scholar will instruct Fu, and when Wang becomes ill, he will be cared for by his young friend and the boy's mother, Fu Be Be.

Fu is one of several apprentices being trained by Tang the coppersmith. He quickly befriends one named Li and is generally successful in his dealings with Tang, his assistants, and the journeymen, but from the very first day he encounters open hostility from Den, another apprentice, who mocks him because he is country-bred. Den blames Fu, although he does not say so at first, because one of his cousins failed to be accepted as an apprentice, even though Tang had already made that decision before young Fu's arrival.

During the period of approximately five years covered in the narrative, Fu grows physically and emotionally; he learns his craft and moves to various levels of responsibility. Yet his path is not without difficulties. On more than one occasion he makes errors of judgment or must pay a price for a hasty or thoughtless action. Quickwitted and curious by nature, he tends to seek out new experiences, and in the process he encounters such scourges of early twentieth century Chinese society as gangs of professional beggars, murderous soldiers, and opium smugglers.

His courage and resourcefulness are tested when he assists Tang in hiding money from bandits encountered on a business trip to Hochow, and again when he climbs onto the roof of the foreign hospital in Chungking to help extinguish a fire. Through this latter action he meets the "foreign woman" (her name is not given), who becomes a friend and helps Li when he is ill; both she and Fu assist an elderly couple made homeless by the flooding of the Yangtze River.

Young Fu's successes are a result in part of his disregard of tradition, such as the taboos against associating with a foreigner; luck, too, plays a part. At the same time, his good fortune is enhanced by the efforts of the important people in his life: his mother Fu Be Be, a shrewd, devout peasant woman, whose caustic remarks only partially hide her concern for her only child; Wang Scholar, who opens up new worlds to the boy by teaching him to read and write; and his master Tang, who recognizes Fu's potential, corrects him, rewards him with increased duties, and eventually decides, since he has no family, to adopt Fu as his son and ultimately his heir. On this note of optimism the story ends.

Themes and Meanings

Young Fu of the Upper Yangtze is a moral tale set within the framework of an exotic locale—the fascinating but politically chaotic China of the 1920's. The story employs a rite-of-passage theme. Fu enters the story as a boy; as it concludes he has become a man. Although he is the central character, he is a very human figure and far from being an ideal hero. He is proud, innocent, and impulsive; his weaknesses are very characteristic of a young man his age and are balanced by his essential kindness and a desire to be helpful. Curiosity, for example, lures him to the fire at the foreign hospital, but his admiration for the foreign woman's courage overcomes his reluctance to assist a stranger.

Tang the coppersmith is the second most important character in the story. He becomes a father figure to young Fu, but like good fathers everywhere, he corrects as well as encourages and does not gloss over faults. The fact that Tang had known poverty and homelessness as a youth adds to the sympathetic bond between him and Fu, who still cherishes memories of country life, although he enjoys the many opportunities and amusements of Chungking.

The two more typical figures in *Young Fu of the Upper Yangtze* are Wang Scholar and Fu Be Be. Wang is the personification of a teacher and wise man, gentle, patient, dry-humored, and self-effacing. Although her character is more fully developed, Fu Be Be is also the familiar peasant mother: devout, superstitious, and self-sacrificing, acid-tongued yet protective of her child. She and the foreign woman are the most important females in the novel. There are no girls in this traditional society with whom Fu and his fellow apprentices would associate as friends.

Finally, both the Yangtze River and the city of Chungking, which is vividly described, serve as characters larger than life. One of the first hard lessons Fu learns is that in this great city there is constant danger, and human life is cheap. The river, described by one character as a dragon, not only enriches the city but also comes close periodically to destroying it. Young Fu must contend with the elements as well as demons of his own making, and this struggle makes the enmity of the hostile apprentice Den seem petty by comparison.

Context

The difficulties and rewards of coming of age, the development of understanding and trust between generations, and the meeting of East and West are major themes in Elizabeth Foreman Lewis' moving adventure tale *Young Fu of the Upper Yangtze*. In this her first novel, as well as those that followed, and her earlier short stories, Lewis drew upon her personal experiences as a young teacher in China. Sent by the Methodist Women's Mission Board to Shanghai in 1917, and later transferred to schools in Chungking and Nanking, Lewis acquired firsthand knowledge of the people and events that would become elements in young Fu's world. Originally conceived as a short story about a boy and his mother making a new life for themselves in Chungking, *Young Fu of the Upper Yangtze* became Lewis' most popular book, winning the Newbery Medal in 1933.

Although Elizabeth Lewis was forced by ill health to return to the United States, she never lost her love and appreciation of the Chinese people. This understanding and experience and the universal appeal of the characters has lent a certain timelessness to *Young Fu of the Upper Yangtze*, making it a classic children's book.

Comparisons have frequently been made of the writings of Lewis and Pearl Buck, because of their similar backgrounds; the comparison is particularly apt in regard to Buck's novel *The Good Earth* (1931), which preceded *Young Fu of the Upper Yangtze* by a year. There are a number of similarities; the obvious difference is that *The Good Earth* was written for an adult audience. Certainly the reading of Lewis' Chinese novels and short stories is an excellent prologue to the more complex and mature situations explored by Buck.

Lewis' skillful use of language, including Chinese words and expressions (translated in the glossary with a key to pronunciation), her fast-moving plots, and her clear vision and essential optimism have made her one of the best writers about early modern China. *Young Fu of the Upper Yangtze* can still, despite war and revolution, convey to the reader those special qualities that have allowed the Chinese people to survive the vicissitudes of fortune.

Dorothy-Bundy Potter

YOUTH

Author: Joseph Conrad (Józef Teodor Konrad Korzeniowski, 1857-1924)
Type of plot: Adventure tale
Time of plot: The late nineteenth century
Locale: Great Britain, the high seas, and the Far East
Principal themes: Coming-of-age and nature
First published: 1898, serial; 1902, book
Recommended ages: 15-18

A seaman recalls, years later, his youthful experience as second mate on an old cargo ship going from London to Bangkok. The voyage includes a series of calamities, and the crew finally abandons the burning vessel not far from its destination.

Principal characters:
>MARLOW, twenty years old, on his first voyage to the Far East and his first time as second mate
>JOHN BEARD, the captain, an experienced seaman, for whom the *Judea* is his first command
>MAHON, the first mate, who has been plagued by bad luck throughout his career

The Story

"Do or Die" is the motto on the faded coat of arms of the decrepit cargo ship *Judea*, whose crew attempts to take its coal from England to Bangkok. Heroism becomes foolhardiness, however, as the inevitability of failure nears, and by the time the flaming old vessel sinks, her motto has long since peeled off. For Captain John Beard, nearing the end of a long career, the voyage of the *Judea* is a landmark, his first command. Thus he is determined to succeed. The journey also is special for young Marlow, since it is his first to the Far East. The first mate, Mahon, who has spent years at sea being dogged by bad luck, is on one more voyage that he hopes will mark a positive turning point in his life.

From the start, however, the ship seems ill-fated. A North Sea gale batters the *Judea* on her way to get the cargo, and she is delayed in port for a month. The night before she is scheduled to depart, a steamer crashes into her, causing another long delay. Finally, the old barque leaves, but when a gale in the Atlantic Ocean causes the ship to take on water and her forward deck-house is swept overboard, Captain Beard returns to Falmouth for repairs. Another attempt for the East is aborted when the ship again leaks, but after a complete overhauling, the *Judea* embarks once more.

The trip into the tropics is uneventful, and the vessel finally reaches the Indian Ocean. Tranquillity is shattered, however, when spontaneous combustion starts the coal burning. Though the *Judea* is near Australia, Captain Beard will not stop. Determined to reach his destination, he tries to smother the fire, but smoke pours through imperceptible crevices, and wetting down the coal does not alleviate the problem. Eventually, a massive explosion turns the rusty barque into a smoldering wreck manned by injured men.

A steamer captain en route to Singapore agrees to tow the *Judea* to a port, where Captain Beard plans to extinguish the fire and proceed to Bangkok. To him, "Do or Die" is not simply a motto on a coat of arms. His hopes are dashed, however, when the fire becomes worse, fanned by the rapid towing. Mahon cuts the tow rope, but Beard refuses to abandon ship. Marlow, telling the story twenty-two years after the voyage, believes that the captain had become unbalanced, unable to cope with the prospective loss of his first—and surely last—command. The men nevertheless follow Beard's lead and attempt to salvage for the underwriters as much of the ship's gear as they can. When they abandon ship, one longboat would accommodate everyone, but Beard insists on three vessels in order to save more property. As a result, Marlow gets his first command, a fourteen-foot boat holding two other crewmen. When the boats reach Java, Beard, Mahon, and the others are asleep, spent by the experience. Young Marlow alone is awake, and he has beaten his captain to port by three hours. Overcome by youthful enthusiasm, he rejoices in his triumphant arrival in the Far East, only briefly recalling his "tussle" with the sea, and celebrating the romance and glamour of the moment, of "the good old time."

Themes and Meanings

"Youth" is a story of discovery, an initiation work whose hero voyages to a new place and confronts life-threatening hardships along the way. While the *Judea* is being repaired at Tyne, Marlow passes time reading *Sartor Resartus* (1833-1834) and *Ride to Khiva* (1876). He prefers the latter, Frederick Burnaby's narrative of a dangerous journey across Asia, to Thomas Carlyle's philosophical work. Like Burnaby, Marlow on his journey proves to himself that he can endure. Unlike Burnaby, however, Joseph Conrad's protagonist also has leadership qualities and succeeds when others fail. Yet withstanding rigors does not mean that young Marlow has completed his progress from youth to maturity, for he remains a romantic, converting a largely tawdry reality into heroic illusion. His epic journey on the *Judea* has matured him, but experiences alone do not complete this rite of passage; he also must place them into perspective.

Beard and Mahon have no such illusions. The skipper wants only to get his cargo to Bangkok. When this goal proves futile, he salvages what he can for the insurers. Young Marlow, unaffected by Beard's fate, focuses upon the wonders of the East and pride in his own achievements. His earlier reactions to the storms, fire, and explosion foreshadow this romanticism, for those dangers were to him only exhilarating challenges whose novelty he welcomed. Conrad calls attention to Marlow's youthfulness and the incompleteness of his progress toward adulthood by the title of the story and through the contrasting presence of the older Beard and Mahon. The narrative point of view is a third means by which Conrad highlights the theme. Marlow tells his story of the *Judea* to friends years after it occurred, and his ironic skepticism tempers his youthful romanticism. Yet the mature storyteller does not patronize or trivialize his former self; in fact, at the end he speaks wistfully of the glamour of the sea, "the good old time" when the sea "could whisper to you and roar at you and knock your breath out of you." The unnamed narrator who introduces Marlow closes the tale on a similarly nostalgic note about bygone youth with its strength, "romance of illusions," and unstinting optimism.

Context

Conrad wrote "Youth" at about the same time as he did *Heart of Darkness*, a more significant work, and both originally were published in *Blackwood's Magazine* in 1898-1899. Along with the "End of the Tether," they appeared in 1902 in a book entitled *Youth: A Narrative, and Two Other Stories*. In the preface to it, Conrad says that the title story "marks the first appearance in the world of the man Marlow, with whom my relations have grown very intimate in the course of years." Marlow also is in *Heart of Darkness* and in such other works as *Lord Jim* (1900) and *Chance* (1913). "Youth," therefore, is noteworthy as Conrad's first use of Marlow as his storyteller. Yet Marlow is more than a narrator, in this work and elsewhere, for he also is the author's alter ego. He is a sympathetic man who recalls his experiences honestly and forthrightly, not only reporting but also intuitively evaluating them. In "Youth," he tells a story in which he is a central figure; elsewhere, he is a peripheral player; in all instances, however, he is a self-revelatory narrator, not only the means by which the story is unfolded but also its central conscience.

To temper the personal revelations and provide objectivity, Conrad distances Marlow the narrator from the reader by creating an outer framework with a narrator who is unnamed and omniscient, but presumably the author. This narrator recounts the tale he heard from Marlow. Thus the reader is one step removed from Marlow the storyteller and two steps removed from young Marlow the hero. In "Youth," the framework is simple and brief (though Conrad recalls it to the reader throughout the story by occasional asides). In *Heart of Darkness* and elsewhere, it is more complex. Conrad's development and frequent use of this complex narrative point of view is a distinctive characteristic of his writing and one of his major contributions to twentieth century fiction. Another recurring trait in his work is the vital test of character. In this story, Conrad builds the theme not only around the young man's rite of passage but also around Captain Beard's initiation. Despite Beard's failure, this is one of the few Conrad works with a happy ending, though only a partial one.

In common with many of Conrad's works, "Youth" has a large autobiographical element. On September 19, 1881, Conrad was hired as second mate on an old, 425-ton barque, the *Palestine*, commanded by a Captain Beard, who was in his late fifties and for whom this was his first command. The first mate was named Mahon. Though Conrad in his story changed the name of the ship to *Judea*, he retained the men's names, and the events of the tale closely parallel the actual difficulties that the *Palestine* had on Conrad's own first voyage to the East. Only when he describes the conclusion of the trip does he depart significantly from the facts, and young

Marlow's enthusiasm also distorts the truth.

"Youth" is an excellent introduction to Conrad's later fiction, for aspects of the story's form, subject, and theme are present in more complex ways in *Heart of Darkness* and the novels. "Youth" also is of interest on its own merits as a memorable adventure and rite-of-passage narrative. Early readers hailed it as one of the world's best short stories; though it has since been overshadowed by other Conrad works, its merits are considerable, with some of its descriptive passages unmatched elsewhere. The story has special relevance for young adult readers, not only because of its central character and his formative experiences but also because Conrad provides the tempering perspective of adulthood on young Marlow's rite of passage.

Gerald H. Strauss

BIBLIOGRAPHY

General Works: Critical, Biographical, Historical

Avery, Gillian. *Childhood's Pattern: A Study of the Heroes and Heroines of Children's Fiction, 1770-1950.* London: Hodder & Stoughton, 1975. A social and literary examination of the images of childhood in such genres as moral tales, realistic stories, and school stories. Includes bibliography and index.

Baskin, Barbara H., and Karen H. Harris. *Notes from a Different Drummer: A Guide to Juvenile Fiction Portraying the Handicapped.* New York: R. R. Bowker, 1977. Includes an overview of books that portray the disabled as well as individual analyses of particular books. Includes indexes.

Bator, Robert, ed. *Signposts to Criticism of Children's Literature.* Chicago: American Library Association, 1983. An anthology of critical essays treating the major genres of children's and young adult literature as well as comments on writing by some well-known authors. Bibliography and notes.

Beetz, Kirk H., and Suzanne Niemeyer, eds. *Beacham's Guide to Literature for Young Adults.* 3 vols. Washington, D.C.: Beacham, 1989. A compilation of analytical essays on books written for young people, including biographical and bibliographical information. Arranged alphabetically by title.

Bingham, Jane. *Writers for Children: Critical Studies of Major Authors Since the Seventeenth Century.* New York: Charles Scribner's Sons, 1987. Critical, evaluative essays on eighty-four well-known European and North American writers. Includes bibliography.

Bingham, Jane, and Grace Scholt. *Fifteen Centuries of Children's Literature: An Annotated Chronology of British and American Works in Historical Context.* Westport, Conn.: Greenwood Press, 1980. A detailed discussion of society and attitudes toward children and works for six major time periods from the sixth century to 1945. Includes a bibliography and author and title indexes.

Blount, Margaret. *Animal Land: The Creatures of Children's Fiction.* New York: William Morrow, 1975. A discussion of the various literary treatments and symbolic uses of animal characters in children's literature. Includes bibliography and index.

Broderick, Dorothy M. *Image of the Black in Children's Fiction.* New York: R. R. Bowker, 1973. A social, cultural, and literary analysis of blacks in children's literature between 1827 and 1967. Includes bibliography and index.

Butler, Francelia. *Sharing Literature with Children: A Thematic Anthology.* New York: David McKay, 1977. Selections of various genres of children's literature and critical essays on each genre. Includes extensive bibliographies and index.

Butler, Francelia, and Richard Rotert, eds. *Reflections on Literature for Children.* Hamden, Conn.: Library Professional Publications, 1984. A collection of critical reviews, essays, and biographical pieces by and about children's authors. Includes notes and index.

—————————, eds. *Triumphs of the Spirit in Children's Literature.* Hamden, Conn.:

Library Professional Publications, 1986. A collection of essays that relate to the overall theme of personal, spiritual, and social survival in children's literature. Includes notes, index of authors, and index of titles.

Cameron, Eleanor. *The Green and Burning Tree: On the Writing and Enjoyment of Children's Books*. Boston: Little, Brown, 1969, reprinted 1985. Critical essays by a writer for children with a special emphasis on fantasy. Among authors discussed are E. Nesbit, Kenneth Grahame, Hugh Lofting, Lucy Boston, and Mark Twain. Includes bibliography and index.

Carpenter, Humphrey. *Secret Gardens: The Golden Ages of Children's Literature from "Alice in Wonderland" to "Winnie the Pooh."* Boston: Houghton Mifflin, 1985. A common theme of the rejection of adult values in favor of alternative worlds is brought forth in this collection of critical essays on authors such as Lewis Carroll, George Macdonald, Louisa May Alcott, and Kenneth Grahame. Includes bibliographical references and index.

Carpenter, Humphrey, and Mari Prichard, eds. *The Oxford Companion to Children's Literature*. London: Oxford University Press, 1984. Includes nearly two thousand entries on authors, genres, titles, and historical periods. Alphabetically arranged with cross-references.

Children's Literature: The Annual of the Modern Language Association Division on Children's Literature and the Children's Literature Association. Edited by Francelia Butler et al. Windham Center, Conn.: Children's Literature Foundation, 1972-   . An annual, multivolume collection of scholarly, critical essays and reviews relating to the literary aspects of children's literature. Includes index every five years.

Commire, Anne, ed. *Something About the Author: Facts and Pictures About Contemporary Authors for Young People*. Detroit: Gale Research, 1971-   . More than sixty volumes with periodic additions of biographical, critical, and bibliographical information about living children's and young adult authors.

Crouch, Marcus. *The Nesbit Tradition: The Children's Novel in England, 1945-1970*. London: Ernest Benn, 1972; Totowa, N.J.: Bowman and Littlefield, 1973. A scholarly discussion of the influence of E. Nesbit on British and American children's fiction of the mid-twentieth century. Includes bibliography and index.

Darton, F. J. Harvey. *Children's Books in England: Five Centuries of Social Life*. 3d rev. ed., edited by Brian Alderson. Cambridge, England: Cambridge University Press, 1982. A scholarly social and political history of children's literature in England from the Middle Ages through the early twentieth century. Hundreds of books are discussed. Includes bibliographies and index.

Egoff, Shelia, G. T. Stubbs, and L. F. Ashley, eds. *Only Connect: Readings on Children's Literature*. 2d ed. New York: Oxford University Press, 1980. A collection of scholarly essays on genres, themes, and particular works in children's literature. Includes bibliography and index.

Field, Elinor Whitney, ed. *Horn Book Reflections on Children's Books and Reading*. Boston: Horn Book, 1969. A selection of essays published in *Horn Book Maga-*

zine from 1949 to 1966 relating to various aspects of children's literature. Includes a bibliography.

Fryatt, Norma. R., ed. *A Horn Book Sampler on Children's Books and Reading.* Boston: Horn Book, 1959. A selection of essays published in *Horn Book Magazine* from 1924 to 1948, including criticism of particular works and genres as well as articles by children's authors. Includes bibliographical references.

Green, Roger Lancelyn. *Tellers of Tales: British Authors of Children's Books from 1800-1964.* Rev. ed. New York: F. Watts, 1965. A survey of authors and their works arranged chronologically and generically. Includes bibliographies and index as well as a chronological table of famous children's books.

Haviland, Virginia. *Children and Literature: Views and Reviews.* New York: Lothrop, Lee and Shepard, 1973. An anthology of classic essays on various aspects of children's literature, such as the classics, realistic fiction, and historical fiction. Includes index.

Hazard, Paul. *Books, Children, and Men.* Translated by Marguerite Mitchell. 5th ed. Boston: Horn Book, 1983. Intellectual essays, originally published in 1932, on the great children's books of the world by a distinguished French scholar. Includes bibliography of works cited.

Heins, Paul, ed. *Crosscurrents of Criticism: Horn Book Essays, 1968-1977.* Boston: Horn Book, 1977. A compilation of forty-five essays originally appearing in *Horn Book Magazine* grouped around topics such as fantasy, humor, internationalism, and the historical scene. Includes an index to titles and authors.

Higgins, James E. *Beyond Words: Mystical Fancy in Children's Literature.* New York: Teachers College Press, 1970. A discussion of the importance of fantasy in the development of the child with criticism of the works of such authors as George Macdonald, W. H. Hudson, J. R. R. Tolkien, and C. S. Lewis. Includes a bibliography.

Hoffman, Miriam, and Eva Samuels, eds. *Authors and Illustrators of Children's Books: Writings on Their Lives and Their Works.* New York: R. R. Bowker, 1972. Critical and biographical essays about fifty children's authors and illustrators arranged alphabetically by the subject's last name. Includes bibliography.

Horn Book Magazine. Edited by Anita Silver. Boston: Horn Book, 1924-   . Each issue includes critical articles as well as reviews of current books in children's literature. Published bimonthly with an annual index in December.

Hürlimann, Bettina. *Three Centuries of Children's Books in Europe.* Translated and edited by Brian W. Alderson. Cleveland: World Publishing, 1968. Detailed, critical analysis of writings through the 1950's. Includes bibliography and index.

Inglis, Fred. *The Promise of Happiness: Value and Meaning in Children's Fiction.* Cambridge, England: Cambridge University Press, 1981. Essays on the nature of popular culture as reflected in children's books. Includes bibliography and index.

Kingman, Lee, ed. *Newbery and Caldecott Medal Books: 1956-1965.* Boston: Horn Book, 1965.

_____, ed. *Newbery and Caldecott Medal Books: 1966-1975*. Boston: Horn Book, 1975.

_____, ed. *Newbery and Caldecott Medal Books: 1976-1985*. Boston: Horn Book, 1987. Each volume includes biographical sketches and texts of acceptance speeches of award winners as well as critical comments on trends in the awards. Includes indexes of authors and titles.

Kirkpatrick, D. L., ed. *Twentieth Century Children's Writers*. 2d ed. New York: St. Martin's Press, 1983. More than seven hundred brief critical and biographical essays. Includes bibliographies and a title index.

Lochhead, Marion. *The Renaissance of Wonder in Children's Literature*. Edinburgh: Canongate, 1977. Essays on the development of fantasy literature for children from the nineteenth century to C. S. Lewis and J. R. R. Tolkien. Includes bibliographies and index.

Lystad, Mary. *From Dr. Mather to Dr. Seuss: Two Hundred Years of American Books for Children*. Boston: G. K. Hall, 1980. A chronological discussion of children's books as a reflection of American societal and familial values. Includes bibliographies.

Meigs, Cornelia, et al., eds. *A Critical History of Children's Literature: A Survey of Children's Books in English*. Rev. ed. New York: Macmillan, 1969. A survey of children's literature arranged in four main parts from the beginnings to 1967. Includes evaluations of books and authors, as well as discussion of trends and bibliographies.

Miller, Bertha Mahoney, and Elinor Whitney Field, eds. *Newbery Medal Books: 1922-1955*. Boston: Horn Book, 1955. Acceptance speeches by the winning authors as well as biographical sketches and notes on the books. Includes indexes of authors and titles.

Rees, David. *Marble in the Water: Essays on Contemporary Writers of Fiction for Children and Young Adults*. Boston: Horn Book, 1980. Critical analyses of the works of eighteen British and American authors. Includes bibliographies and index.

_____. *Painted Desert, Green Shade: Essays on Contemporary Writers of Fiction for Children and Young Adults*. Boston: Horn Book, 1984. Retrospective criticism of thirteen British and American authors. Includes bibliographies and index.

Sale, Roger. *Fairy Tales and After: From Snow White to E. B. White*. Cambridge, Mass.: Harvard University Press, 1978. A highly personalized criticism of selected works of children's fantasy including essays on Lewis Carroll, Kenneth Grahame, Rudyard Kipling, L. Frank Baum, and E. B. White. Includes notes on sources and index.

Smith, Lillian H. *The Unreluctant Years: A Critical Approach to Children's Literature*. Chicago: American Library Association, 1953. Reprint. New York: Viking, 1967. Classic collection of critical essays on various genres such as fantasy and historical fiction as well as essays on individual works such as *Treasure Island* and *Men of Iron*. Includes bibliographies and index.

Thwaite, Mary F. *From Primer to Pleasure in Reading: An Introduction to the History of Children's Books in England from the Invention of Printing to 1914 with an Outline of Some Developments in Other Countries.* Boston: Horn Book, 1972. Chronological development of books from a historical perspective. Includes bibliography and index.

Townsend, John Rowe. *Written for Children: An Outline of English Language Children's Literature.* 2d rev. ed. Philadelphia: J. B. Lippincott, 1983. Readable account of the development of children's books in the United States, England, Canada, and Australia. Includes bibliography and index.

Ward, Martha E., and Dorothy Marquant, eds. *Authors of Books for Young People.* 2d ed. Metuchen, N.J.: Scarecrow Press, 1971. Supplement, 1979. Biographical and bibliographical information arranged alphabetically by author.

Wilkin, Binnie Tate. *Survival Themes in Fiction for Children and Young People.* Metuchen, N.J.: Scarecrow Press, 1978. Critical comments about books arranged by topics such as loneliness and fear. Includes general and historical overview, index, and bibliography.

Works by Author

Louisa May Alcott
Elbert, Sarah. *A Hunger for Home: Louisa May Alcott and "Little Women."* Philadelphia: Temple University Press, 1984.

Hollander, Anne. "Reflections on *Little Women.*" *Children's Literature* 9 (1981): 28-39.

Horn Book 44 (October, 1968). Special issue on Alcott.

MacDonald, Ruth K. *Louisa May Alcott.* Boston: Twayne, 1983.

Meigs, Cornelia L. *Louisa M. Alcott and the American Family Story.* New York: Henry Z. Walck, 1971.

Stern, Madeleine B. *Louisa May Alcott.* Norman: University of Oklahoma Press, 1950; London: Peter Nevill, 1952.

Thomas Bailey Aldrich
Beattie, Ann. "The Story of a Bad Boy." *Children's Literature* 5 (1976): 63-65.

Cosgrove, Mary S. "The Life and Times of Thomas Bailey Aldrich." *Horn Book* 42 (April, June, August, 1966): 223-232, 350-355, 467-473.

Geller, Evelyn. "Tom Sawyer, Tom Bailey, and the Bad-Boy Genre." *Wilson Library Bulletin* 50 (November, 1976): 245-250.

Samuels, Charles S. *Thomas Bailey Aldrich.* New York: Twayne, 1965.

Horatio Alger, Jr.
Hoyt, Edwin P. *Horatio's Boys: The Life and Works of Horatio Alger, Jr.* Radnor, Pa.: Chilton, 1974.

Tebbel, John W. *From Rags to Riches: Horatio Alger, Jr., and the American Dream.* New York: Macmillan, 1963.

James M. Barrie

Asquith, Cynthia. *Portrait of Barrie*. New York: E. P. Dutton, 1955.

Egan, Michael. "The Neverland of Id: Barrie, *Peter Pan* and Freud." *Children's Literature* 10 (1982): 37-55.

Green, Martin. "The Charm of Peter Pan." *Children's Literature* 9 (1981): 19-27.

Green, Roger Lancelyn. *J. M. Barrie*. New York: Walck, 1961. (A Walck Monograph)

L. Frank Baum

Beckwith, Osmond. "The Oddness of Oz." *Children's Literature* 5 (1976): 74-91.

Gardner, Martin, and Russell B. Nye. *The Wizard of Oz and Who He Was*. East Lansing: Michigan State University Press, 1957.

Greene, David L. "The Concept of Oz." *Children's Literature* 3 (1974): 173-176.

Hamilton, Margaret. "There's No Place Like Oz." *Children's Literature* 10 (1982): 153-155.

Hearn, Michael Patrick. *The Annotated Wizard of Oz*. New York: Clarkson N. Potter, 1973.

Mannix, Daniel P. "The Father of the Wizard of Oz." *American Heritage* 16 (December, 1964): 108-109.

Sale, Roger. "Baum's Magic Powder of Life." *Children's Literature* 8 (1980): 157-163.

Judy Blume

Garber, Stephen M. "Judy Blume: New Classicism for Kids." *English Journal* 73 (April, 1984): 56-59.

Weidt, Mary Ann. *Presenting Judy Blume*. Boston: Twayne, 1990.

Lucy Boston

Boston, Lucy M. "A Message from Green Knowe." *Horn Book* 39 (June, 1963): 259-264.

Rose, Jasper. *Lucy Boston*. New York: Walck, 1966. (A Walck Monograph)

Rosenthal, Lynne. "The Development of Consciousness in Lucy Boston's *The Children of Green Knowe*." *Children's Literature* 8 (1980): 53-67.

Stott, Jon C. "From Here to Eternity: Aspects of Pastoral in the Green Knowe Series." *Children's Literature* 11 (1983): 145-155.

Frances Hodgson Burnett

Burnett, Constance Buel. *Happily Ever After*. New York: Vanguard, 1965.

Keyser, Elizabeth Lennox. "Quite Contrary: Frances Hodgson Burnett's *The Secret Garden*." *Children's Literature* 11 (1983): 1-13.

Koppes, Phyllis Bixler. "Tradition and the Individual Talent of Frances Hodgson Burnett: A Generic Analysis of *Little Lord Fauntleroy*, *A Little Princess*, and *The Secret Garden*." *Children's Literature* 7 (1978): 191-207.

MacLeod, Anne Scott. "Ragged Dick and L. L. F.: A Curious Kinship." *Horn Book* 59 (October, 1983): 613-620.

Thwaite, Ann. *Waiting for the Party: The Life of Frances Hodgson Burnett 1849-1924*. New York: Charles Scribner's Sons, 1974.

White, Alison. "Tap-Roots into a Rose Garden." *Children's Literature* 1 (1972): 74-76.

Lewis Carroll

Ayers, Harry Morgan. *Carroll's Alice*. New York: Columbia University Press, 1936.

Gray, Donald J., ed. *Lewis Carroll's Alice in Wonderland*. New York: W. W. Norton, 1971.

Green, Roger Lancelyn. *Lewis Carroll*. London: Bodley Head, 1960; New York: Walck, 1962. (A Walck Monograph)

Jorgens, Jack J. "Alice Our Contemporary." *Children's Literature* 1 (1972): 152-161.

Kelly, Richard. *Lewis Carroll*. Boston: G. K. Hall, 1977.

Kutty, K. Narayan. "Nonsense as Reality." *Children's Literature* 5 (1976): 286-287.

Lennon, Florence Becker. *The Life of Lewis Carroll*. New rev. ed. New York: Collier, 1962; New York: Dover, 1972.

Reardon, Margaret. "A Present for Alice." *Horn Book* 38 (June, 1962): 243-247.

Beverly Cleary

Burns, Paul C., and Ruth Hines. "Beverly Cleary: Wonderful World of Humor." *Elementary English* 44 (November, 1967): 743-747, 752.

Cleary, Beverly. *A Girl from Yamhill: A Memoir*. New York: William Morrow, 1988.

Roggenbuck, Mary J. "Profile: Beverly Cleary—The Children's Force at Work." *Language Arts* 56 (January, 1979): 55-60.

Robert Cormier

Campbell, Patricia. *Presenting Robert Cormier*. New York: Twayne, 1985.

Clements, Bruce. "A Second Look: *The Chocolate War*." *Horn Book* 55 (April, 1979): 217-218.

Heins, Paul. Review. *Horn Book* 53 (August, 1977): 427-428.

Silvey, Anita. "An Interview with Robert Cormier." *Horn Book* 61 (March, May, 1985): 145-161, 289-296.

Charles Dickens

Donovan, Frank Robert. *Dickens and Youth*. New York: Dodd, Mead, 1968.

House, Arthur Humphry. *The Dickens World*. 2d ed. London: Oxford University Press, 1960.

Johnson, Edgar. *Charles Dickens: His Tragedy and Triumphs*. New York: Simon & Schuster, 1952.

Kotzin, Michael C. *Dickens and the Fairy Tale*. Bowling Green, Ohio: Bowling Green University Popular Press, 1972.

Miller, J. Hillis. *Charles Dickens: The World of His Novels*. Cambridge, Mass.: Harvard University Press, 1958.

Orwell, George. *Dickens, Dali, and Others: Studies in Popular Culture*. New York: Harcourt Brace Jovanovich, 1946.
Stone, Harry. "Dark Corners of the Mind: Dickens' Childhood Reading." *Horn Book* 39 (June, 1963): 306-321.

Louise Fitzhugh
Stern, Maggie. "A Second Look: *Harriet the Spy*." *Horn Book* 56 (August, 1980): 442-445.
Wolf, Virginia L. "*Harriet the Spy*: Milestone, Masterpiece?" *Children's Literature* 4 (1975): 120-126.

Alan Garner
Heins, Paul. "Off the Beaten Path." *Horn Book* 49 (December, 1973): 580-581.
McMahon, Patricia. "A Second Look: *Elidor*." *Horn Book* 56 (June, 1980): 328-331.
Philip, Neil. *A Fine Anger: A Critical Introduction to the Work of Alan Garner*. London: Collins, 1981.
Rees, David. "Alan Garner: Some Doubts." *Horn Book* 55 (June, 1979): 282-289.

Kenneth Grahame
Chalmers, Patricia R. *Kenneth Grahame: Life, Letters, and Unpublished Work*. London: Methuen, 1933; Port Washington, N.Y.: Kennikat Press, 1971.
Graham, Eleanor. *Kenneth Grahame*. New York: Walck, 1963. (A Walck Monograph)
Grahame, Kenneth. *First Whisper of the Wind in the Willows*. Philadelphia: J. B. Lippincott, 1944.
Green, Peter. *Kenneth Grahame: A Biography*. Cleveland: World Publishing, 1959.
Kuznets, Lois. "Toad Hall Revisited." *Children's Literature* 7 (1978): 115-128.
Poss, Geraldine D. "An Epic in Arcadia: The Pastoral World of *The Wind in the Willows*." *Children's Literature* 4 (1975): 80-90.

Rudyard Kipling
Amis, Kingsley. *Rudyard Kipling and His World*. New York: Charles Scribner's Sons, 1975.
Carrington, Charles E. *The Life of Rudyard Kipling*. Garden City, N.Y.: Doubleday, 1955.
Green, Roger Lancelyn. *Kipling and the Children*. London: Elek Books, 1965.
Haines, Helen E. "The Wisdom of Baloo: Kipling and Childhood." *Horn Book* 12 (May/June, 1936): 135-141.
Harrison, James. *Rudyard Kipling*. Boston: Twayne, 1982.
Havholm, Peter. "Kipling and Fantasy." *Children's Literature* 4 (1975): 91-105.
Sutcliff, Rosemary. *Rudyard Kipling*. New York: Walck, 1961. (A Walck Monograph)

Selma Lagerlöf
Berendsohn, Walter. *Selma Lagerlöf: Her Life and Work*. Translated and adapted by George F. Timpson, 1931. Reprint. Port Washington, N.Y.: Kennikat Press, 1968.
Edström, Vivi B. *Selma Lagerlöf*. Boston: Twayne, 1984.

Ursula K. Le Guin
Cameron, Eleanor. "High Fantasy: *A Wizard of Earthsea*." *Horn Book* 47 (April, 1971): 129-138.
Cunneen, Shelia. "Earthseans and Earthteens." *English Journal* 74 (February, 1985): 68-69.
De Bolt, Joe. *Ursula K. Le Guin: Voyage to Inner Lands and to Outer Space*. Port Washington, N.Y.: Kennikat Press, 1971.

C. S. Lewis
Como, James. "Mediating Illusions: Three Studies of Narnia." *Children's Literature* 10 (1982): 163-168.
Ford, Paul F. *Companion to Narnia*. New York: Harper & Row, 1980.
Gibb, Jocelyn, ed. *Light on C. S. Lewis*. New York: Harcourt Brace Jovanovich, 1965.
Green, Roger Lancelyn. *C. S. Lewis*. New York: Walck, 1963. (A Walck Monograph)
Hooper, Walter. *Past Watchful Dragons: The Narnian Chronicles of C. S. Lewis*. New York: Collier Books, 1971.
Wilson, A. N. *C. S. Lewis: A Biography*. New York: W. W. Norton, 1990.

George Macdonald
Douglass, Jane. "Dealings with the Fairies: An Appreciation of George Macdonald." *Horn Book* 37 (August, 1961): 327-335.
Reis, Richard H. *George Macdonald*. New York: Twayne, 1972.
Wolff, Robert L. *The Golden Key: A Study of the Fiction of George Macdonald*. New Haven, Conn.: Yale University Press, 1961.

E. Nesbit
Alexander, Lloyd. "A Second Look: *Five Children and It*." *Horn Book* 61 (May, 1985): 354-355.
Bell, Anthea. *E. Nesbit*. New York: Walck, 1964. (A Walck Monograph)
Bland, Edith Nesbit. *Long Ago When I Was Young*. London: Whiting & Wheaton, 1966; New York: Watts, 1966.
De Alonso, Joan Evans. "E. Nesbit's Well Hall, 1915-1921: A Memoir." *Children's Literature* 3 (1974): 147-159.
Horn Book 34 (October, 1958). Special issue on Nesbit.
Moore, Doris Langley-Levy. *E. Nesbit: A Biography*. London: Benn, 1933. Rev. with new material. Philadelphia: Chilton, 1966.

Streatfeild, Noel. *Magic and the Magician: E. Nesbit and Her Children's Books*. London: Benn, 1958.

Walbridge, Earle F. "E. Nesbit." *Horn Book* 29 (October, 1953): 335-341.

Howard Pyle

Abbott, Charles D. *Howard Pyle: A Chronicle*. New York: Harper & Bros., 1925.

Nesbitt, Elizabeth. *Howard Pyle*. New York: Walck, 1966. (A Walck Monograph)

Pitz, Henry C. *Howard Pyle: Writer, Illustrator, Founder of the Brandywine School*. New York: Clarkson N. Potter, 1975.

Marjorie Kinnan Rawlings

Bellman, Samuel I. *Marjorie Kinnan Rawlings*. New York: Twayne, 1974.

McDonnell, Christine. "A Second Look: *The Yearling*." *Horn Book* 53 (June, 1977): 344-345.

Robert Louis Stevenson

Blake, Kathleen. "The Sea-Dreams: *Peter Pan* and *Treasure Island*." *Children's Literature* 6 (1977): 165-181.

Butts, Dennis. *R. L. Stevenson*. New York: Walck, 1966. (A Walck Monograph)

Daiches, David. *Robert Louis Stevenson*. Norfolk, Conn.: New Directions, 1947.

——————. *Robert Louis Stevenson and His World*. London: Thames & Hudson, 1973.

Furnas, Joseph C. *Voyage to Windward: The Life of Robert Louis Stevenson*. New York: Sloane, 1951.

Heins, Paul. "A Centenary Look: *Treasure Island*." *Horn Book* 59 (April, 1983): 197-200.

Stern, Gladys Bronwyn. *Robert Louis Stevenson: The Man Who Wrote "Treasure Island": A Biography*. New York: Macmillan, 1954.

Noel Streatfeild

McDonnell, Christine. "A Second Look: *Ballet Shoes*." *Horn Book* 54 (April, 1978): 191-193.

Wilson, Barbara Ker. *Noel Streatfeild*. London: Bodley Head, 1961; New York: Walck, 1964. (A Walck Monograph)

J. R. R. Tolkien

Eiseley, Loren. "The Elvish Art of Enchantment: An Essay on J. R. R. Tolkien's *Tree and Leaf*, and on Mr. Tolkien's Other Distinguished Contributions to Imaginative Literature." *Horn Book* 41 (August, 1965): 364-367.

Helms, Randel. *Tolkien's World*. Boston: Houghton Mifflin, 1974.

Kocher, Paul H. *Master of Middle-Earth: The Fiction of J. R. R. Tolkien*. Boston: Houghton Mifflin, 1972.

Noel, Ruth S. *The Mythology of Middle-Earth*. Boston: Houghton Mifflin, 1978.
Tolkien, J. R. R. *Tree and Leaf.* Boston: Houghton Mifflin, 1965.

E. B. White
Cameron, Eleanor. "McLuhan, Youth, and Literature." *Horn Book* 48 (October, 1972): 572-579.
Elledge, Scott. *E. B. White: A Biography*. New York: W. W. Norton, 1984.
Griffith, John. "*Charlotte's Web*: A Lonely Fantasy of Love." *Children's Literature* 8 (1980): 111-117.
Neumeyer, Peter F. "The Creation of *Charlotte's Web*: From Drafts to Book." *Horn Book* 58 (October, 1982): 489-497; (December, 1982): 617-625.
Nodelman, Perry. "Text as Teacher: The Beginning of *Charlotte's Web*." *Children's Literature* 13 (1985): 109-127.
Sampson, Edward C. *E. B. White*. New York: Twayne, 1974.

Laura Ingalls Wilder
Bosmajian, Hamida. "Vastness and Contraction of Space in *Little House on the Prairie*." *Children's Literature* 11 (1983): 49-63.
Dalphin, Marcia. "Christmas in the Little House Books." *Horn Book* 29 (December, 1953): 431-435.
Jacobs, William Jay. "Frontier Faith Revisited: The Little House Books of Laura Ingalls Wilder." *Horn Book* 41 (October, 1965): 465-473.
Moore, Rosa Ann. "Laura Ingalls Wilder's Orange Notebooks and the Art of the Little House Books." *Children's Literature* 4 (1975): 105-119.
──────────. "The Little House Books: Rose Colored Classics." *Children's Literature* 7 (1978): 7-16.
Smith, Irene. "Laura Ingalls Wilder and the Little House Books." *Horn Book* 19 (September/October, 1943): 293-306.
Zochert, Daniel. *Laura: The Life of Laura Ingalls Wilder*. Chicago: Henry Regnery, 1976.

MASTERPLOTS II

JUVENILE
AND
YOUNG ADULT
FICTION
SERIES

TITLE INDEX

TITLE INDEX

Good-bye, My Lady (Street) II-550
Goodbye to the Purple Sage (Benedict) II-547
Governess, The (Fielding) II-557
Grande Alerte, La. *See* Flood Warning
"Great Mountains, The." *See* Red Pony, The
Green Dolphin County. *See* Green Dolphin Street
Green Dolphin Street (Goudge) II-561
Green Knowe books, The (Boston) II-565
Green Mansions (Hudson) II-570
Greenwitch. *See* Dark Is Rising sequence, The
Grey King, The. *See* Dark Is Rising sequence, The
Grosser-Tiger und Kompass-Berg. *See* Big Tiger and Christian
Gulliver's Travels (Swift) II-574
Guns of Bull Run, The (Altsheler) II-577

Half-Back, The (Barbour) II-580
Halfback Tough (Dygard) II-584
Hans Brinker (Dodge) II-588
Happy Endings Are All Alike (Scoppettone) II-591
Hardy Boys series, The (Dixon) II-595
Harpoon of the Hunter (Markoosie) II-599
Harriet the Spy (Fitzhugh) II-602
Harrow and Harvest. *See* Mantlemass series, The
Haunting of SafeKeep, The (Bunting) II-605
Hawkmistress! (Bradley) II-608
Heart of Aztlán (Anaya) II-612
Heidi (Spyri) II-616
Heidis Lehr und Wanderjahre. *See* Heidi
Helter-Skelter (Moyes) II-619
Hero Ain't Nothin' But a Sandwich, A (Childress) II-623
Hero and the Crown, The (McKinley) II-626
High King, The. *See* Prydain chronicles, The
His Own Where (Jordan) II-629
Hitty, Her First Hundred Years (Field) II-631
Hobbit, The (Tolkien) II-635
Home Before Dark (Bridgers) II-638
Hoops (Myers) II-641
Horatio Hornblower series, The (Forester) II-644
Horse and His Boy, The. *See* Chronicles of Narnia, The
Horse Without a Head, The (Berna) II-649
House at Pooh Corner, The (Milne) IV-1637
House in Norham Gardens, The (Lively) II-653
House Made of Dawn (Momaday) II-657
House of Sixty Fathers, The (De Jong) II-661
House of Stairs (Sleator) II-665
Hugo and Josephine (Gripe) II-668
Hugo och Josefin. *See* Hugo and Josephine
Hundred Million Francs, A. *See* Horse Without a Head, The
Hundred Penny Box, The (Mathis) II-672

I Am David (Holm) II-676
I Am the Cheese (Cormier) II-679

I Heard the Owl Call My Name (Craven) II-682
I, Juan de Pareja (Borton de Treviño) II-685
I Never Promised You a Rose Garden (Green) II-688
I Wear the Morning Star. *See* Ghost Horse cycle, The
If I Love You, Am I Trapped Forever? (Kerr) II-691
I'll Get There (Donovan) II-695
Im Westen nichts Neues. *See* All Quiet on the Western Front
In the Year of the Boar and Jackie Robinson (Lord) II-699
Incredible Journey, The (Burnford) II-703
Indian in the Cupboard, The (Banks) II-706
Innocent Wayfaring, The (Chute) II-709
Interstellar Pig (Sleator) II-712
Intruder, The (Townsend) II-715
Invisible Man (Ellison) II-719
Iron Lily, The. *See* Mantlemass series, The
Is That You, Miss Blue? (Kerr) II-723
Island of the Blue Dolphins (O'Dell) II-726
It's an Aardvark-Eat-Turtle World (Danziger) II-730
It's Like This, Cat (Neville) II-734

Jacob Have I Loved (Paterson) II-737
Jamie (Bennett, Jack) II-741
Jane Eyre (Brontë, C.) II-745
Jar of Dreams, A (Uchida) II-749
Jazz Country (Hentoff) II-752
John Diamond. *See* Footsteps
Johnny Tremain (Forbes) II-756
Journey to Topaz *and* Journey Home (Uchida) II-759
Judgment Day. *See* Studs Lonigan
Julie of the Wolves (George) II-764
Jungle Book, The (Kipling) II-767

Kestrel, The. *See* Westmark trilogy, The
Keys of Mantlemass, The. *See* Mantlemass series, The
Kidnapped (Stevenson) II-771
Kidnapping of Christina Lattimore, The (Nixon) II-774
Killer-of-Death (Baker) II-777
Kim (Kipling) II-781
King Matt the First (Korczak) II-784
King of the Golden River, The (Ruskin) II-788
King of the Wind (Henry) II-791
King Solomon's Mines (Haggard) II-796
Ki-Yu. *See* Panther
Król Marcius Pierwszy. *See* King Matt the First

Lad (Terhune) II-799
Language of Goldfish, The (Oneal) II-802
Lantern Bearers, The (Sutcliff) II-806

TITLE INDEX

TITLE INDEX

AUTHOR INDEX

ABBOTT, JACOB
Rollo series, The, III-1248
ACHEBE, CHINUA
Things Fall Apart, IV-1454
ADAMS, HARRIET STRATEMEYER.
See DIXON, FRANKLIN W.
ADAMS, RICHARD
Watership Down, IV-1582
AGEE, JAMES
Death in the Family, A, I-321
AIKEN, JOAN
Shadow Guests, The, IV-1315
Wolves of Willoughby Chase, The,
IV-1650
ALCOTT, LOUISA MAY
Little Men, II-857
Little Women, III-871
ALDRICH, THOMAS BAILEY
Story of a Bad Boy, The, IV-1376
ALEXANDER, LLOYD
Prydain chronicles, The, III-1180
Westmark trilogy, The, IV-1593
ALGER, HORATIO, JR.
Ragged Dick, III-1188
ALMEDINGEN, E. M.
Anna, I-45
ALTSHELER, JOSEPH ALEXANDER
Guns of Bull Run, The, II-577
ANAYA, RUDOLFO A.
Heart of Aztlán, II-612
ANGELL, JUDIE. *See* ARRICK, FRAN
ANGELO, VALENTI
Nino, III-1042
ANNIXTER, PAUL
Swiftwater, IV-1427
ANONYMOUS
Go Ask Alice, II-526
ARMSTRONG, RICHARD
Mutineers, The, III-999
ARMSTRONG, WILLIAM H.
Sounder, IV-1367
ARNOLD, ELLIOTT
Blood Brother, I-132
AROUET, FRANÇOIS MARIE.
See VOLTAIRE
ARRICK, FRAN
Steffie Can't Come Out to Play, IV-1370
ARTHUR, RUTH M.
Whistling Boy, The, IV-1627
ARUNDEL, HONOR
Family Failing, A, I-408

ASHLEY, BERNARD
Trouble with Donovan Croft, The, IV-1508
ASIMOV, ISAAC
Foundation trilogy, The, II-460
AVERY, GILLIAN
Warden's Niece, The, IV-1579

BABBITT, NATALIE
Tuck Everlasting, IV-1514
BAGNOLD, ENID
"National Velvet," III-1023
BAKER, BETTY
Killer-of-Death, II-777
Walk the World's Rim, IV-1572
BALDWIN, JAMES
Go Tell It on the Mountain, II-529
BANKS, LYNNE REID
Indian in the Cupboard, The, II-706
BARBOUR, RALPH HENRY
Half-Back, The, II-580
BARNE, KITTY
Musical Honors, III-996
Visitors from London, IV-1557
BARNE, MARION CATHERINE.
See BARNE, KITTY
BARRIE, SIR JAMES M.
Peter Pan, III-1122
BAUER, MARION DANE
On My Honor, III-1057
BAUM, L. FRANK
Wizard of Oz, The, IV-1646
BAWDEN, NINA
Carrie's War, I-194
Peppermint Pig, The, III-1115
BEATTY, JOHN, *and* PATRICIA BEATTY
Campion Towers, I-182
Royal Dirk, The, III-1255
BEATTY, PATRICIA
Behave Yourself, Bethany Brant, I-100
BELANEY, ARCHIBALD STANSFELD.
See GREY OWL
BELPRÉ, PURA
Santiago, III-1271
BENARY-ISBERT, MARGOT
Rowan Farm, III-1251
BENCHLEY, NATHANIEL
Only Earth and Sky Last Forever, III-1076
BENEDICT, REX
Goodbye to the Purple Sage, II-547
BENNETT, JACK
Jamie, II-741

SUBJECT INDEX

SUBJECT INDEX

SUBJECT INDEX

SUBJECT INDEX

Mrs. Frisby and the Rats of NIMH (O'Brien)
III-968
More Than Human (Sturgeon) III-978
Mouse and His Child, The (Hoban) III-982
Nordy Bank (Porter, S.) III-1045
Once and Future King, The (White, T. H.)
III-1063
Owl Service, The (Garner) III-1100
Peter Graves (du Bois) III-1119
Peter Pan (Barrie) III-1122
Phantom Tollbooth, The (Juster) III-1129
Pippi Longstocking (Lindgren) III-1144
Prydain chronicles, The (Alexander) III-1180
Pushcart War, The (Merrill) III-1185
Return of the Twelves, The (Clarke, P.)
III-1220
Ring of Endless Light, A (L'Engle) III-1227
Saturday, the Twelfth of October (Mazer, N.)
III-1281
Shadow Guests, The (Aiken) IV-1315
Summer Birds, The (Farmer) IV-1399
Swiftly Tilting Planet, A (L'Engle) IV-1424
Through the Looking-Glass (Carroll) IV-1465
Tom's Midnight Garden (Pearce) IV-1494
Tuck Everlasting (Babbitt) IV-1514
Winnie-the-Pooh (Milne) IV-1637

FOLKTALE
God Beneath the Sea, The (Garfield *and*
Blishen) II-533
Harpoon of the Hunter (Markoosie) II-599
King of the Golden River, The (Ruskin) II-788

FRIENDSHIP
About David (Pfeffer) I-1
Adam of the Road (Gray) I-7
Adventures of Huckleberry Finn, The (Twain)
I-10
Adventures of Pinocchio, The (Collodi) I-13
Adventures of Tom Sawyer, The (Twain) I-19
Angel Dust Blues (Strasser) I-38
Anne of Green Gables (Montgomery) I-49
Are You There, God? It's Me, Margaret
(Blume) I-61
Around the World in Eighty Days (Verne) I-65
Ballad of Benny Perhaps, The (Brinsmead)
I-80
Bambi (Salten) I-87
Bang the Drum Slowly (Harris) I-92
Big Tiger and Christian (Mühlenweg) I-116
Bilgewater (Gardam) I-119
Bless the Beasts and Children (Swarthout)
I-128
Blood Brother (Arnold) I-132
Borrowers, The (Norton) I-145
Bridge to Terabithia (Paterson) I-155
Bronze Bow, The (Speare) I-158

Call Me Charley (Jackson) I-173
Captains Courageous (Kipling) I-191
Cat Ate My Gymsuit, The (Danziger) I-202
Catcher in the Rye, The (Salinger) I-209
Charley Starts from Scratch (Jackson) I-173
Charlotte's Web (White, E. B.) I-220
Child of the Owl (Yep) I-227
Chocolate War, The (Cormier) I-233
Chosen, The (Potok) I-237
Chronicles of Narnia, The (Lewis, C. S.)
I-240
Circus Is Coming, The (Streatfeild) I-245
Color Purple, The (Walker) I-255
Come Alive at 505 (Brancato) I-258
Companions of Fortune (Guillot) I-264
Conquered, The (Mitchison) I-267
Constance (Clapp) I-278
Contender, The (Lipsyte) I-281
Court of the Stone Children, The (Cameron)
I-289
Cricket in Times Square, The (Selden) I-292
Dandelion Wine (Bradbury) I-295
Dark Behind the Curtain, The (Cross) I-298
David Copperfield (Dickens) I-307
Dear Mr. Henshaw (Cleary) I-318
Demian (Hesse) I-333
Dicey's Song (Voigt) I-337
Dragonwings (Yep) I-350
Dream-Time, The (Treece) I-354
Dreamsnake (McIntyre) I-357
Eagle of the Ninth, The (Sutcliff) I-371
Earthsea series, The (Le Guin) I-375
Emil and the Detectives (Kästner) I-383
Emperor's Winding Sheet, The (Walsh) I-387
Fat Girl, The (Sachs) I-415
Felita (Mohr) I-418
Fine White Dust, A (Rylant) I-424
Flood Warning (Berna) II-447
Folded Leaf, The (Maxwell) II-451
Forever (Blume) II-457
Fourth Form Friendship, A (Brazil) II-464
Freedom Road (Fast) II-467
Friedrich (Richter, H.) II-470
Friends, The (Guy) II-478
From the Mixed-up Files of Mrs. Basil E.
Frankweiler (Konigsburg) II-481
Garram the Hunter (Best) II-488
Gathering of Old Men, A (Gaines) II-494
Gentle Ben (Morey) II-501
Ginger Pye (Estes) II-512
Giver, The (Hall) II-523
Goodbye to the Purple Sage (Benedict) II-547
Governess, The (Fielding) II-557
Green Knowe books, The (Boston) II-565
Guns of Bull Run, The (Altsheler) II-577
Half-Back, The (Barbour) II-580
Halfback Tough (Dygard) II-584

SUBJECT INDEX

POLITICS AND LAW

POVERTY

SUBJECT INDEX

MASTERPLOTS II